REMARKABLE PRAISE FOR

KARIN SLAUGHTER

AND THE WILL TRENT SERIES

"It's Slaughter's prodigious gifts of characterization that make her stand out among thriller writers."
—*WASHINGTON POST*

"[*The Last Widow*] does what all great Slaughter books do: keeps you on the edge of your seat. It's a chilling whodunit for our times."
—*PARADE*

"A fearless writer. One of the boldest thriller writers working today."
—TESS GERRITSEN

"Her characters, plot, and pacing are unrivaled among thriller writers."
—MICHAEL CONNELLY

"Fiction doesn't get any better than this."
—JEFFERY DEAVER

"Enter the world of Karin Slaughter. Just be forewarned, there's no going back."
—LISA GARDNER

"If you're into mystery thrillers, then you're into Karin Slaughter."
—THESKIMM

THE LAST WIDOW

Also by Karin Slaughter

Blindsighted
Kisscut
A Faint Cold Fear
Indelible
Faithless
Triptych
Beyond Reach
Fractured
Undone
Broken
Fallen
Criminal
Unseen
Cop Town
Pretty Girls
The Kept Woman
The Good Daughter
Pieces of Her

EBOOK ORIGINALS
Cold, Cold Heart
Blonde Hair, Blue Eyes
Last Breath

NOVELLAS AND STORIES
Like a Charm (Editor)
Martin Misunderstood

Karin Slaughter

THE LAST WIDOW

A Novel

wm

WILLIAM MORROW

An Imprint of HarperCollins*Publishers*

Lyrics from:

"I'm on Fire" (written by Bruce Springsteen)
"Sara Smile" Hall & Oats (written by Daryl Hall, John Oates)
"Whatta Man" Salt-n-Pepa ft. En Vogue (written by Hurby "Luv Bug" Azor, Cheryl James with samples from the original song written by David Crawford and performed by Linda Lyndell)
"Love and Affection" (written by Joan Armatrading)
"Sure shot" Beastie Boys (written by Adam Keefe Horovitz, Adam Nathaniel Yauch, Jeremy Steig, Mario Caldato, Michael Louis Diamond, Wendell T. Fife)
"Two Doors Down" (written by Dolly Parton)
"Smalltown Boy" Bronski Beat (written by Steve Bronski, Jimmy Somerville, Larry Steinbachek)
"Because the Night" Patti Smith Group (written by Bruce Springsteen, Patti Smith)
"What I Am" Edie Brickell & New Bohemians (written by Edie Brickell, Kenny Withrow, John Houser, John Bush, John Aly)
"Give It Away" Red Hot Chili Peppers (written by Michael Balzary (Flea), John Frusciante, Anthony Kiedis, Chad Smith)

A hardcover edition of this book was published in 2019 by William Morrow, an imprint of HarperCollins Publishers.

FIRST WILLIAM MORROW PAPERBACK EDITION PUBLISHED 2020.

Library of Congress Cataloging-in-Publication Data has been applied for.

ISBN 978-0-06-285890-0

20 21 22 23 24 LSC 10 9 8 7 6 5 4 3 2 1

"We're doomed to repeat the past no matter what. That's what it is to be alive."

– Kurt Vonnegut

THE LAST WIDOW

PART ONE

Sunday, July 7, 2019

PROLOGUE

Michelle Spivey jogged through the back of the store, frantically scanning each aisle for her daughter, panicked thoughts circling her brain: *How did I lose sight of her I am a horrible mother my baby was kidnapped by a pedophile or a human trafficker should I flag store security or call the police or—*

Ashley.

Michelle stopped so abruptly that her shoe snicked against the floor. She took a sharp breath, trying to force her heart back into a normal rhythm. Her daughter was not being sold into slavery. She was at the make-up counter trying on samples.

The relief started to dissipate as the panic burned off.

Her eleven-year-old daughter.

At the make-up counter.

After they had told Ashley that she could not under any circumstances wear make-up until her twelfth birthday, and then it would only be blush and lip gloss, no matter what her friends were doing, end of story.

Michelle pressed her hand to her chest. She slowly walked up the aisle, giving herself time to transition into a reasoned and logical person.

Ashley's back was to Michelle as she examined lipstick shades. She twisted the tubes with an expert flick of her wrist because of course when she was with her friends, Ashley tried on all their make-up and they practiced on each other because that was what girls did.

Some girls, at least. Michelle had never felt that pull toward primping. She could still recall her own mother's screeching tone when Michelle had refused to shave her legs: *You'll never be able to wear pantyhose!*

Michelle's response: *Thank God!*

That was years ago. Her mother was long gone. Michelle was a grown woman with her own child and like every woman, she had vowed not to make her mother's mistakes.

Had she over-corrected?

Were her general tomboyish tendencies punishing her daughter? Was Ashley really old enough to wear make-up, but because Michelle had no interest in eyeliners and bronzers and whatever else it was that Ashley watched for endless hours on YouTube, she was depriving her daughter of a certain type of girl's passage into womanhood?

Michelle had done the research on juvenile milestones. Eleven was an important age, a so-called benchmark year, the point at which children had attained roughly 50 percent of the power. You had to start negotiating rather than simply ordering them around. Which was very well-reasoned in the abstract but in practice was terrifying.

"Oh!" Ashley saw her mother and frantically jammed the lipstick into the display. "I was—"

"It's all right." Michelle stroked back her daughter's long hair. So many bottles of shampoo in the shower, and conditioner, and soaps and moisturizers when Michelle's only beauty routine involved sweat-proof sunscreen.

"Sorry." Ashley wiped at the smear of lip gloss on her mouth.

"It's pretty," Michelle tried.

"Really?" Ashley beamed at her in a way that tugged every string of Michelle's heart. "Did you see this?" She meant the lip gloss display. "They have one that's tinted, so it's supposed to last longer. But this one has cherry flavoring, and Hailey says b—"

Silently, Michelle filled in the words, *boys like it more.*

The assorted Hemsworths on Ashley's bedroom walls had not gone unnoticed.

Michelle asked, "Which do you like most?"

"Well . . ." Ashley shrugged, but there was not much an eleven-year-old did not have an opinion on. "I guess the tinted type lasts longer, right?"

Michelle offered, "That makes sense."

Ashley was still weighing the two items. "The cherry kind of tastes like chemicals? Like, I always chew—I mean, if I wore it, I would probably chew it off because it would irritate me?"

Michelle nodded, biting back the polemic raging inside her: *You are beautiful, you are smart, you are so funny and talented and you should only do things that make you happy because that's what attracts the worthy boys who think that the happy, secure girls are the interesting ones.*

Instead, she told Ashley, "Pick the one you like and I'll give you an advance on your allowance."

"Mom!" She screamed so loudly that people looked up. The dancing that followed was more Tigger than Shakira. "Are you serious? You guys said—"

You guys. Michelle gave an inward groan. How to explain this sudden turnabout when they had agreed that Ashley would not wear make-up until she was twelve?

It's only lip gloss!

She'll be twelve in five months!

I know we agreed not until her actual birthday but you let her have that iPhone!

That would be the trick. Turn it around and make it about the iPhone, because Michelle had purely by fate been the one who'd died on that particular hill.

Michelle told her daughter, "I'll handle the boss. Just lip gloss, though. Nothing else. Pick the one that makes you happy."

And it did make her happy. So happy that Michelle felt herself smiling at the woman in the checkout line, who surely understood that the glittery tube of candy pink Sassafras Yo Ass! was not for the thirty-nine-year-old woman in running shorts with her sweaty hair scooped into a baseball cap.

"This—" Ashley was so gleeful she could barely speak. "This is so great, Mom. I love you so much, and I'll be responsible. So responsible."

Michelle's smile must have shown the early stages of rigor mortis as she started to load up their purchases into cloth bags.

The iPhone. She had to make it about the iPhone, because they had agreed about that, too, but then all of Ashley's friends had shown up at summer camp with one and the *No absolutely not* had turned into *I couldn't let her be the only kid without one* while Michelle was away at a conference.

Ashley happily scooped up the bags and headed for the exit. Her iPhone was already out. Her thumb slid across the screen as she alerted her friends to the lip gloss, likely predicting that in a week's time, she'd be sporting blue eyeshadow and doing that curve thing at the edges of her eyes that made girls look like cats.

Michelle felt herself start to catastrophize.

Ashley could get conjunctivitis or sties or blepharitis from sharing eye make-up. Herpes simplex virus or hep C from lip gloss and lip liner, not to mention she could scratch her cornea with a mascara wand. Didn't some lipsticks contain heavy metals and lead? Staph, strep, E. coli. What the hell had Michelle been thinking? She could be poisoning her own daughter. There were hundreds of thousands of proven studies about surface contaminants as opposed to the relative handfuls positing the indirect correlation between brain tumors and cell phones.

Up ahead, Ashley laughed. Her friends were texting back. She swung the bags wildly as she crossed the parking lot. She was eleven, not twelve, and twelve was still terribly young, wasn't it? Because make-up sent a signal. It telegraphed an interest in being interested in, which was a horribly non-feminist thing to say but this was the real world and her daughter was still a baby who knew nothing about rebuffing unwanted attention.

Michelle silently shook her head. Such a slippery slope. From lip gloss to MRSA to Phyllis Schlafly. She had to lock down her wild thoughts so that by the time she got home, she could present a reasoned explanation for buying Ashley make-up when they had made a solemn, parental vow not to.

As they had with the iPhone.

She reached into her purse to find her keys. It was dark outside. The overhead lights weren't enough, or maybe she needed her glasses because she was getting old—was already old enough to have a daughter who wanted to send signals to boys. She could be a grandmother in a few years' time. The thought made her stomach somersault into a vat of anxiety. Why hadn't she bought wine?

She glanced up to make sure Ashley hadn't bumped into a car or fallen off a cliff while she was texting.

Michelle felt her mouth drop open.

A van slid to a stop beside her daughter.

The side door rolled open.

A man jumped out.

Michelle gripped her keys. She bolted into a full-out run, cutting the distance between herself and her daughter.

She started to scream, but it was too late.

Ashley had run off, just like they had taught her to do.

Which was fine, because the man did not want Ashley.

He wanted Michelle.

ONE MONTH LATER

Sunday, August 4, 2019

1

Sunday, August 4, 1:37 p.m.

Sara Linton leaned back in her chair, mumbling a soft, "Yes, Mama." She wondered if there would ever come a point in time when she was too old to be taken over her mother's knee.

"Don't give me that placating tone." The miasma of Cathy's anger hung above the kitchen table as she angrily snapped a pile of green beans over a newspaper. "You're not like your sister. You don't flit around. There was Steve in high school, then Mason for reasons I still can't comprehend, then Jeffrey." She glanced up over her glasses. "If you've settled on Will, then settle on him."

Sara waited for her Aunt Bella to fill in a few missing men, but Bella just played with the string of pearls around her neck as she sipped her iced tea.

Cathy continued, "Your father and I have been married for nearly forty years."

Sara tried, "I never said—"

Bella made a sound somewhere between a cough and a cat sneezing.

Sara didn't heed the warning. "Mom, Will's divorce was just finalized. I'm still trying to get a handle on my new job. We're enjoying our lives. You should be happy for us."

Cathy snapped a bean like she was snapping a neck. "It was bad enough that you were seeing him while he was still married."

Sara took a deep breath and held it in her lungs.

She looked at the clock on the stove.

1:37 p.m.

It felt like midnight and she hadn't even had lunch yet.

She slowly exhaled, concentrating on the wonderful odors filling the kitchen. This was why she had given up her Sunday afternoon: Fried chicken cooling on the counter. Cherry cobbler baking in the oven. Butter melting into the pan of cornbread on the stove. Biscuits, field peas, black-eyed peas, sweet potato soufflé, chocolate cake, pecan pie and ice cream thick enough to break a spoon.

Six hours a day in the gym for the next week would not undo the damage she was about to do to her body, yet Sara's only fear was that she'd forget to take home any leftovers.

Cathy snapped another bean, pulling Sara out of her reverie.

Ice tinkled in Bella's glass.

Sara listened for the lawn mower in the backyard. For reasons she couldn't comprehend, Will had volunteered to serve as a weekend landscaper to her aunt. The thought of him accidentally overhearing any part of this conversation made her skin vibrate like a tuning fork.

"Sara." Cathy took an audible breath before picking up where she'd left off: "You're practically living with him now. His things are in your closet. His shaving stuff, all his toiletries, are in the bathroom."

"Oh, honey." Bella patted Sara's hand. "Never share a bathroom with a man."

Cathy shook her head. "This will kill your father."

Eddie wouldn't die, but he would not be happy in the same way that he was never happy with any of the men who wanted to date his daughters.

Which was the reason Sara was keeping their relationship to herself.

At least part of the reason.

She tried to gain the upper hand, "You know, Mother, you just admitted to snooping around my house. I have a right to privacy."

Bella tsked. "Oh, baby, it's so sweet that you really think that."

Sara tried again, "Will and I know what we're doing. We're not giddy teenagers passing notes in the hall. We like spending time together. That's all that matters."

Cathy grunted, but Sara was not stupid enough to mistake the ensuing silence for acquiescence.

Bella said, "Well, I'm the expert here. I've been married five times, and—"

"Six," Cathy interrupted.

"Sister, you know that was annulled. What I'm saying is, let the child figure out what she wants on her own."

"I'm not telling her what to do. I'm giving her advice. If she's not serious about Will, then she needs to move on and find a man she's serious about. She's too logical for casual relationships."

"'It's better to be without logic than without feeling.'"

"I would hardly consider Charlotte Brontë an expert on my daughter's emotional well-being."

Sara rubbed her temples, trying to stave off a headache. Her stomach grumbled but lunch wouldn't be served until two, which didn't matter because if she kept having this conversation, one or maybe all three of them were going to die in this kitchen.

Bella asked, "Sugar, did you see this story?"

Sara looked up.

"Don't you think she killed her wife because she's having an affair? I mean, one of them is having an affair, so the wife killed the affair-haver." She winked at Sara. "This was what the conservatives were worried about. Gay marriage has rendered pronouns immaterial."

Sara was having a hard time tracking until she realized that Bella was pointing to an article in the newspaper. Michelle Spivey had been abducted from a shopping center parking lot four weeks ago. She was a scientist with the Centers for Disease Control, which meant that the FBI had taken over the investigation. The photo in the paper was from Michelle's driver's license. It showed an attractive woman in her late thirties with a spark in her eye that even the crappy camera at the DMV had managed to capture.

Bella asked, "Have you been following the story?"

Sara shook her head. Unwanted tears welled into her eyes. Her husband had been killed five years ago. The only thing she could think of that would be worse than losing someone she loved was never knowing whether or not that person was truly gone.

Bella said, "I'm going with murder for hire. That's what usually turns out to be the case. The wife traded up for a newer model and had to get rid of the old one."

Sara should've dropped it because Cathy was clearly getting worked up. But, because Cathy was clearly getting worked up, Sara told Bella, "I dunno. Her daughter was there when it happened. She saw her mother being dragged into a van. It's probably naive to say this, but I don't think her other mother would do something like that to their child."

"Fred Tokars had his wife shot in front of his kids."

"That was for the life insurance, I think? Plus, wasn't his business shady, and there was some mob connection?"

"And he was a man. Don't women tend to kill with their hands?"

"For the love of God." Cathy finally broke. "Could we please not talk about murder on the Lord's day? And Sister, you of all people should not be discussing cheating spouses."

Bella rattled the ice in her empty glass. "Wouldn't a mojito be nice in this heat?"

Cathy clapped her hands together, finished with the green beans. She told Bella, "You're not helping."

"Oh, Sister, one should never look to Bella for help."

Sara waited for Cathy to turn her back before she wiped her eyes. Bella hadn't missed her sudden tears, which meant that as soon as Sara had left the kitchen, they would both be talking about the fact that she had been on the verge of crying because—why? Sara was at a loss to explain her weepiness. Lately, anything from a sad commercial to a love song on the radio could set her off.

She picked up the newspaper and pretended to read the story. There were no updates on Michelle's disappearance. A month was too long. Even her wife had stopped pleading for her safe return and was begging whoever had taken Michelle to please just let them know where they could find the body.

Sara sniffed. Her nose had started running. Instead of reaching for a paper napkin from the pile, she used the back of her hand.

She didn't know Michelle Spivey, but last year she had briefly met her wife, Theresa Lee, at an Emory Medical School alumni mixer. Lee was an orthopedist and professor at Emory. Michelle was an epidemiologist at the CDC. According to the article, the two were married in 2015, which likely meant they'd tied the knot as soon as they were legally able. They had been together for fifteen years before that. Sara assumed that after two decades, they'd figured out the two most common causes of divorce: the acceptable temperature setting for the thermostat and what level of criminal act it was to pretend you didn't know the dishwasher was ready to be emptied.

Then again, she was not the marriage expert in the room.

"Sara?" Cathy had her back to the counter, arms crossed. "I'm just going to be blunt."

Bella chuckled. "Give it a try."

"It's okay to move on," Cathy said. "Make a new life for yourself with Will. If you're truly happy, then be truly happy. Otherwise, what the hell are you waiting for?"

Sara carefully folded the newspaper. Her eyes returned to the clock.

1:43 p.m.

Bella said, "I did like Jeffrey, rest his soul. He had that swagger. But Will is so sweet. And he does love you, honey." She patted Sara's hand. "He really does."

Sara chewed her lip. Her Sunday afternoon was not going to turn into an impromptu therapy session. She didn't need to work out her feelings. She was caught in the reverse problem of every romantic comedy's first act: she had already fallen in love with Will, but she wasn't sure how to love him.

Will's social awkwardness she could deal with, but his inability to communicate had nearly been the end of them. Not just once or twice, but several times. Initially, Sara had persuaded herself he was trying to show his best side. That was normal. She had let six months pass before she'd worn her real pajamas to bed.

Then a year had gone by and he was still keeping things to himself. Stupid things that didn't matter, like not calling to tell her that he was going to have to work late, that his basketball game was running long, that his bike had broken down halfway into his ride, that he'd volunteered his weekend to help a friend move. He always looked shocked when she was mad at him for not communicating these things. She wasn't trying to keep track of him. She was trying to figure out what to order for dinner.

As annoying as those interactions were, there were other things that really mattered. Will didn't lie so much as find clever ways to not tell her the truth—whether it had to do with a dangerous work situation or some awful detail about his childhood or, worse, a recent atrocity committed by his nasty, narcissistic bitch of an ex-wife.

Logically, Sara understood the genesis of Will's behavior. He had spent his childhood in the foster care system, where, if he wasn't being neglected, he was being abused. His ex-wife had weaponized his emotions against him. He had never really been in a healthy relationship. There were some truly heinous skeletons lurking in his past. Maybe Will felt like he was protecting Sara. Maybe he felt like he was protecting himself. The point was that she had no fucking idea which one it was because he wouldn't acknowledge the problem existed.

"Sara, honey," Bella said. "I meant to tell you—the other day, I was thinking about when you lived here back when you were in school. Do you remember that, sugar?"

Sara smiled at the memory of her college years, but then the edges of her lips started to give when she caught the look that was exchanged between her aunt and mother.

A hammer was about to drop.

They had lured her here with the promise of fried chicken.

Bella said, "Baby, I'm gonna be honest. This old place is too much house for your sweet Aunt Bella to handle. What do you think of moving back in?"

Sara laughed, but then she saw that her aunt was serious.

Bella said, "Y'all could fix up the place, make it your own."

Sara felt her mouth moving, but she had no words.

"Honey." Bella held on to Sara's hand. "I always meant to leave it to you in my will, but my accountant says the tax situation would be better if I transferred it to you now through a trust. I've already put down a deposit on a condo downtown. You and Will can move in by Christmas. That foyer takes a twenty-foot tree, and there's plenty of room for—"

Sara experienced a momentary loss of hearing.

She had always loved the grand old Georgian, which was built just before the Great Depression. Six bedrooms, five bathrooms, a two-bedroom carriage house, a tricked-out garden shed, three acres of grounds in one of the state's most affluent zip codes. A ten-minute drive would take you downtown. A ten-minute stroll would have you at the center of the Emory University campus. The neighborhood was one of the last commissions Frederick Law Olmstead took before his death, and parks and trees blended beautifully into the Fernbank Forest.

It was an enticing offer until the numbers started scrolling through her head.

Bella hadn't replaced anything since the 1980s. Central heating and air. Plumbing. Electrical. Plaster repairs. New windows. New roof. New gutters. Wrangling with the Historical Society over minute architectural details. Not to mention the time they would lose because Will would want to do all the work himself and Sara's scant free evenings and long, lazy weekends would turn into arguments about paint colors and money.

Money.

That was the real obstacle. Sara had a lot more money than Will. The same had been true of her marriage. She would never forget the look on Jeffrey's face the first time he'd seen the balance in her trading account. Sara had actually heard the squeaking groan of his testicles retracting into his body. It had taken a hell of a lot of suction to get them back out again.

Bella was saying, "And of course I can help with any taxes, but—"

"Thank you." Sara tried to dive in. "That's very generous, but—"

"It could be a wedding present." Cathy smiled sweetly as she sat down at the table. "Wouldn't that be lovely?"

Sara shook her head, but not at her mother. What was wrong with her? Why was she worrying about Will's reaction? She had no idea how much money he had. He paid cash for everything. Whether this was because he didn't believe in credit cards or because his credit was screwed up was another conversation that they were not having.

"What was that?" Bella had her head tilted to the side. "Did y'all hear something? Like firecrackers? Or something?"

Cathy ignored her. "You and Will can make this your home. And your sister can take the apartment over the garage."

Sara saw the hammer make its final blow. Her mother wasn't merely trying to control Sara's life. She wanted to throw in Tessa for good measure.

Sara said, "I don't think Tess wants to live over another garage."

Bella asked, "Isn't she living in a mud hut now?"

"Sissy, hush." Cathy asked Sara, "Have you talked to Tessa about moving home?"

"Not really," Sara lied. Her baby sister's marriage was falling apart. She Skyped with her at least twice a day, even though Tessa was living in South Africa. "Mama, you have to let this go. This isn't the 1950s. I can pay my own bills. My retirement is taken care of. I don't need to be legally bound to a man. I can take care of myself."

Cathy's expression lowered the temperature in the room. "If that's what you think marriage is, then I have nothing else to say on the matter." She pushed herself up from the table and returned to the stove. "Tell Will to wash up for dinner."

Sara closed her eyes so that she wouldn't roll them.

She stood up and left the kitchen.

Her footsteps echoed through the cavernous living room as she skirted the periphery of the ancient Oriental rug. She stopped at the first set of French doors. She pressed her forehead against the glass. Will was happily pushing the lawn mower into the shed. The yard looked spectacular. He had even trimmed the boxwoods into neat rectangles. The edging showed a surgical precision.

What would he say to a 2.5 million-dollar fixer-upper?

Sara wasn't even sure she wanted such a huge responsibility. She had spent the first few years of her marriage remodeling her tiny craftsman bungalow with Jeffrey. Sara keenly recalled the physical exhaustion from stripping wallpaper and painting stair spindles, and the excruciating agony of knowing that she could just write a check and let someone else do it, but her husband was a stubborn, stubborn man.

Her husband.

That was the third rail her mother had been reaching for in the kitchen: Did Sara love Will the same way she had loved Jeffrey, and if she did, why wasn't she marrying him, and if she didn't, why was she wasting her time?

All good questions, but Sara found herself caught in a Scarlett O'Hara loop of promising herself that she would think about it tomorrow.

She shouldered open the door and was met by a wall of heat. Thick humidity made the air feel like it was sweating. Still, she reached up and took the band out of her hair. The added layer on the back of her neck was like a heated oven mitt. Except for the smell of fresh grass, she might as well be walking into a steam room. She trudged up the hill. Her sneakers slipped on some loose rocks. Bugs swarmed around her face. She swatted at them as she walked toward what Bella called the shed but was actually a converted barn with a bluestone floor and space for two horses and a carriage.

The door was open. Will stood in the middle of the room. His palms were pressed to the top of the workbench as he stared out the window. There was a stillness to him that made Sara wonder if she should interrupt. Something had been bothering him for the last two months. She could feel it edging into almost every part of their lives. She had asked him about it. She had given him space to think about it. She had tried to fuck it out of him. He kept insisting that he was fine, but then she'd catch him doing what he was doing now: staring out a window with a pained expression on his face.

Sara cleared her throat.

Will turned around. He'd changed shirts, but the heat had already plastered the material to his chest. Pieces of grass were stuck to his muscular legs. He was long and lean and the smile that he gave Sara momentarily made her forget every single problem she had with him.

He asked, "Is it time for lunch?"

She looked at her watch. "It's one forty-six. We have exactly fourteen minutes of calm before the storm."

His smile turned into a grin. "Have you seen the shed? I mean, really seen it?"

Sara thought it was pretty much a shed, but Will was clearly excited.

He pointed to a partitioned area in the corner. "There's a urinal over there. An actual, working urinal. How cool is that?"

"Awesome," she muttered in a non-awesome way.

"Look how sturdy these beams are." Will was six-four, tall enough to grab the beam and do a few pull-ups. "And look over here. This TV is old, but it still works. And there's a full refrigerator and microwave over here where I guess the horses used to live."

She felt her lips curve into a smile. He was such a city boy he didn't know that it was called a stall.

"And the couch is kind of musty, but it's really comfortable." He bounced onto the torn leather couch, pulling her down beside him. "It's great in here, right?"

Sara coughed at the swirling dust. She tried not to connect the stack of her uncle's old *Playboy*s to the creaking couch.

Will asked, "Can we move in? I'm only halfway kidding."

Sara bit her lip. She didn't want him to be kidding. She wanted him to tell her what he wanted.

"Look, a guitar." He picked up the instrument and adjusted the tension on the strings. A few strums later and he was making recognizable sounds. And then he turned it into a song.

Sara felt the quick thrill of surprise that always came with finding out something new about him.

Will hummed the opening lines of Bruce Springsteen's "I'm on Fire".

He stopped playing. "That's kind of gross, right? 'Hey little girl is your daddy home?'"

"How about 'Girl, You'll Be a Woman Soon'? Or 'Don't Stand So Close to Me'? Or the opening line to 'Sara Smile'?"

"Damn." He plucked at the guitar strings. "Hall and Oates, too?"

"Panic! At the Disco has a better version." Sara watched his long fingers work the strings. She loved his hands. "When did you learn to play?"

"High school. Self-taught." Will gave her a sheepish look. "Think of every stupid thing a sixteen-year-old boy would do to impress a sixteen-year-old girl and I know how to do it."

She laughed, because it wasn't hard to imagine. "Did you have a fade?"

"Duh." He kept strumming the guitar. "I did the Pee-wee Herman voice. I could flip a skateboard. Knew all the words to 'Thriller'. You should've seen me in my acid-washed jeans and Nember's Only jacket."

"Nember?"

"Dollar Store brand. I didn't say I was a millionaire." He looked up from the guitar, clearly enjoying her amusement. But then he nodded toward her head, asking, "What's going on up there?"

Sara felt her earlier weepiness return. Love overwhelmed her. He was so tuned into her feelings. She so desperately wanted him to accept that it was natural for her to be tuned into his.

Will put down the guitar. He reached up to her face, used his thumb to rub the worry out of her brow. "That's better."

Sara kissed him. Really kissed him. This part was always easy. She ran her fingers through his sweaty hair. Will kissed her neck, then lower. Sara arched into him. She closed her eyes and let his mouth and hands smooth away all of her doubts.

They only stopped because the couch gave a sudden, violent shudder.

Sara asked, "What the hell was that?"

Will didn't trot out the obvious joke about his ability to make the earth move. He looked under the couch. He stood up, checking the beams overhead, rapping his knuckles on the petrified wood. "Remember that earthquake in Alabama a few years back? That felt the same, but stronger."

Sara straightened her clothes. "The country club does fireworks displays. Maybe they're testing out a new show?"

"In broad daylight?" Will looked dubious. He found his phone on the workbench. "There aren't any alerts." He scrolled through his messages, then made a call. Then another. Then he tried a third number. Sara waited, expectant, but Will ended up shaking his head. He held up the phone so she could hear the recorded message saying that all circuits were busy.

She noted the time in the corner of the screen.

1:51 p.m.

She told Will, "Emory has an emergency siren. It goes off when there's a natural disast—"

Boom!

The earth gave another violent shake. Sara had to steady herself against the couch before she could follow Will into the backyard.

He was looking up at the sky. A plume of dark smoke curled up behind the tree line. Sara was intimately familiar with the Emory University campus.

Fifteen thousand students.

Six thousand faculty and staff members.

Two ground-shaking explosions.

"Let's go." Will jogged toward the car. He was a special agent with the Georgia Bureau of Investigation. Sara was a doctor. There was no need to have a discussion about what they should do.

"Sara!" Cathy called from the back door. "Did you hear that?"

"It's coming from Emory." Sara ran into the house to find her car keys. She felt her thoughts spinning into dread. The urban campus sprawled over six hundred acres. The Emory University Hospital. Egleston Children's Hospital. The Centers for Disease Control. The National Public Health Institute. The Yerkes National Primate Research Center. The Winship Cancer Institute. Government labs. Pathogens. Viruses. Terrorist attack? School shooter? Lone gunman?

"Could it be the bank?" Cathy asked. "There were those bank robbers who tried to blow up the jail."

Martin Novak. Sara knew there was an important meeting taking place downtown, but the prisoner was stashed in a safe house well outside of the city.

Bella said, "Whatever it is, it's not on the news yet." She had turned on the kitchen television. "I've got Buddy's old shotgun around here somewhere."

Sara found her key fob in her purse. "Stay inside." She grabbed her mother's hand, squeezed it tight. "Call Daddy and Tessa and let them know you're okay."

She put her hair up as she walked toward the door. She froze before she reached it.

They had all frozen in place.

The deep, mournful wail of the emergency siren filled the air.

2

Sunday, August 4, 1:33 p.m.

Will Trent took his hand off the lawn mower to wipe the sweat out of his eyes. The task was not without complications. First, he had to shake the sweat off of his hand. Next, he had to rub his fingers on the inside of his shirt to get the grit off. Only then could he squeegee the liquid from his eyebrows with the side of his fist. He used the momentary reprieve from near-blindness to check his watch.

1:33 p.m.

What kind of idiot mowed three hilly acres in the middle of an August afternoon? He guessed the kind of idiot who'd spent the morning in bed with his girlfriend. As sweet as that had been, he really wished he could go back in time and explain to Past Will how fucking miserable Future Will was going to be.

He turned the corner, angling the mower through a dip in the rough terrain. His foot caught in a gopher hole. Gnats snarled in front of his face. The sun felt like the lash from a belt on the back of his neck. The only reason he hadn't sweated his balls off was because a thick paste of dirt, clipped grass and sweat had glued them to his body.

Will glanced up at Bella's house as he made another pass. He could not get over how massive it was. Money practically dripped from the gables. There was actually a book on the design that Bella had loaned him. The stained glass in the stairwell was made by Louis Comfort Tiffany. The plaster moldings had been shaped by craftsmen shipped over from Italy. Inlaid oak floors. Coffered ceilings. An indoor fountain. A mahogany-paneled library filled with ancient tomes. Cedar lining in every closet. Real gold on the gaudy chandeliers. A toilet in the basement for the help that dated back to Jim Crow. There was even a man-sized safe behind a hidden panel in the kitchen pantry that was meant to hold the family silver.

Will felt like Jethro Bodine every time he came up the driveway.

He grunted, putting his shoulder into bulldozing through a clump of cat's claw that was bigger than an actual cat.

When Will had first met Sara, he'd figured out pretty quickly that she was well off. Not that she acted differently or spoke differently, but Will was a detective. He was a trained observer. Observation one: her apartment was the penthouse unit in a boutique building. Observation two: she drove a BMW. Three: she was a doctor, so his detective skills were not really needed to figure out that she had money in the bank.

Here's where it got tricky: Sara had told him that her father was a plumber. Which was true. What she'd failed to add was that Eddie Linton was also a real estate investor. And that he'd brought Sara into the family business. And that she had made a lot of money renting out houses and selling houses and her medical school loans had been paid off, plus she'd sold her pediatrician's practice in Grant County before moving to Atlanta, plus, she had money from her dead husband's life insurance policy and his pension, and as the widow of a police officer she was exempt from state taxes, so financially speaking, Sara was Uncle Phil to his way less cool Fresh Prince.

Which was actually okay.

Will was eighteen years old the first time someone put money in his pocket, and that was for bus fare to the homeless shelter because he'd aged out of the foster care system. He had qualified for a state scholarship to go to college. He had ended up working for the same state that had raised him. As a cop, he was used to being both the poorest guy in the room as well as the guy most likely to get shot in the face while doing his job.

So the real question was: Was Sara okay with it?

Will coughed out a clump of dirt that had launched like a Trident missile from the rear wheel of the lawn mower into his face. He spat on the ground. His stomach grumbled at the thought of lunch.

Bella's mansion was bothering him. What it represented. What it said about the disparity between him and Sara because the place Will had lived in while he'd attended college had been condemned because of asbestos, not listed on the National Registry of Historical Homes.

Sara's aunt was a whole other level of loaded—in more ways than one. Will guessed by the smell coming off her iced tea that she was a fan of day drinking. As far as he could tell, she had made her money by marrying up. And up. And up. Which wasn't his business until her incredible generosity had made it so.

Last week, Bella had given Will a trimmer that was worth at least two hundred bucks. The week before, she'd noticed him admiring one of her dead husband's record collections and foisted a boxful into Will's hands as he walked out the door.

Queen's original *A Night at the Opera*. Blondie's *Parallel Lines*. The 12-inch maxi single of John Lennon's "Imagine" with a pristine green apple on the label.

Will could mow this damn lawn for the next two thousand years and not even come close to repaying her.

He stopped to wipe his forehead with his arm. He ended up smearing sweat into sweat. He took a deep breath and inhaled a gnat.

1:37 p.m.

He shouldn't even be here.

At this very moment, there was a huge, big shot meeting happening downtown. These meetings had been happening for the last month, and bi-monthly before that. The GBI was coordinating with the Marshals Service, the ATF and the FBI on the transfer of a convicted bank robber. Martin Novak was currently residing in an undisclosed safe house as he awaited sentencing at the Russell Federal Building. The reason he wasn't biding his time in jail was because his fellow bank robbers had tried to blast a Novak-sized hole in the side of the building. The attempt had failed, but no one was taking any chances.

Novak wasn't a typical convict. He was a legit criminal mastermind who ran a team of highly trained bad guys. They killed indiscriminately. Civilians. Security guards. Cops. It didn't matter who was on the other end of the gun when they pulled the trigger. The team moved through the banks they targeted like the hands of a clock. Every indication was that Novak's group was not going to let their leader die in the bowels of a federal prison.

As a cop, Will despised these kinds of criminals—there was nothing worse, or more rare, than a really smart bad guy—but as a human being, he longed to be in on the action. Will had accepted a long time ago that the part of the job that appealed to him most was the hunt. He could never shoot an animal, but the thought of lying in wait, rifle trained on the center mass of a bad guy, trigger finger itching to remove their miserable souls from the world, was an incredible high.

Which fact he would never tell Sara. He had it on authority that her husband had been the same way, that Jeffrey Tolliver's love of the hunt was probably what had gotten him killed. Will's fight or flight was similarly stuck on fight. He didn't want Sara to be terrified every time he walked out the door.

He glanced up at the house again as he mowed the next row.

Rich, drunk aunts aside, he felt like things were going well with Sara. They had settled into a routine. They had learned to accept each other's faults, or at least to overlook the worst of them, as in two examples: a lack of desire to make the bed every morning like a responsible human being and a stubborn unwillingness to break the habit of throwing away a jar of mayonnaise even when there was enough in the bottom to make half a sandwich.

For Will's part, he was trying to be more open with Sara about what he was feeling. It was easier than he'd thought it would be. He just made a note on his calendar every Monday to tell her something that was bothering him.

One of his biggest fears had disappeared before a Monday confessional had rolled around. He'd been really worried when Sara had first started working with him at the Georgia Bureau of Investigation. Things had smoothed out, mostly because Sara had made them smooth. They each stayed in their own lane. Sara was a doctor and a medical examiner, the same job she'd had back in Grant County. Her husband had been chief of police, so she knew how to be with a cop. Like Will, Jeffrey Tolliver probably hadn't been in line for any promotions. Then again, what promotion would the man get when he was already at the top of the food chain?

Will pushed this out of his brain, because as dark as his thoughts were, letting them dip into that pool would be fairly treacherous.

At least Sara's mother seemed to be coming around. Cathy had spent half an hour last night telling him stories about the first few years of her marriage. Will had to think this was progress. The first time he'd met her, Cathy had basically spit nails in his direction. Maybe his Sisyphean battle against her drunk sister's lawn had persuaded her that he wasn't such a bad guy. Or maybe she could see how much Will loved her daughter. That had to count for something.

He stumbled as the mower jammed into another gopher hole. Will looked up, shocked to find that he was almost done. He checked the time.

1:44 p.m.

If he hurried, he could grab a few minutes in the shed to hose down, cool off, and wait for the dinner bell.

Will pushed through the last, long row of grass and practically jogged back to the shed. He left the mower cooling on the stone floor. He would've kicked the ancient machine but his legs were basically silly string.

He peeled off his shirt. He went to the sink and dunked his head under the ice-cold stream of water. He washed all the important areas with a bar of soap that had the texture of sandpaper. His clean shirt skidded across his wet skin as he put it on. He went to the workbench, pressed his palms down, spread his legs, and let everything air dry.

His cell phone showed a notification. Faith had texted him from the big shot meeting that Will was not invited to attend. She'd sent him a clown with a water gun pointing at its head. Then a knife. Then a hammer. Then another clown and, for some reason, a yam.

If she was trying to make him feel better, a yam wasn't going to pull him over the finish line.

Will looked out the window. He wasn't given to navel-gazing, but there was nothing to do but think as he stared at the expertly tended lawn.

Why wasn't he in that big shot meeting?

He couldn't begrudge Faith the opportunity. Or the nepotism. Amanda, their boss, had started out her career partnered with Faith's mother. They were best friends. Not that Faith was skating on her connections. She had worked her way up from a squad car to the homicide division at the Atlanta Police Department to special agent status at the Georgia Bureau of Investigation. She was a good cop. She deserved whatever promotion came her way.

It was what came next for Will that would be the real humiliation. Setting aside having to tell Sara that Faith had moved up while he treaded water, Will would have to break in a new partner. Or, more likely, a new partner would have to break in Will. He was not good with people. At least not with fellow cops. He was very good at talking to criminals. Most of Will's youth had been spent skirting the law. He knew how criminals thought—that you could lock them in a room and they would come up with sixteen different ways to break out, none of them involving just asking someone to unlock the door.

The point was that Will closed cases. He got good results. He was a crack shot. He didn't suck up all the air in the room. He didn't want a medal for doing his job.

He wanted to know why he wasn't asked to be in the meeting.

Will looked down at his phone again.

Nothing but yam.

He stared out the window. He sensed that he was being watched.

Sara cleared her throat.

Will felt his bad mood lift. He couldn't stop the stupid grin that came to his face every time he saw her. Her long, auburn hair was down. He loved it when her hair was down. "Is it time for lunch?"

Sara looked at her watch. "It's one forty-six. We have exactly fourteen minutes of calm before the storm."

He studied her face, which was beautiful, but there was a streak of something above her eyebrow that looked suspiciously like the smeared entrails of a dead bug.

She gave him a curious look.

"Have you seen the shed?" Will offered her the grand tour, but only as a ruse to get her onto the couch. He was exhausted from the mowing. He was starving. He was worried that Sara was only fine with a poor cop as long as that poor cop had ambitions.

He asked, "It's great in here, right?"

Sara coughed at the dust that huffed up from the couch. Still, she looped her leg over his. Her arm rested along his shoulders. Her fingers stroked the wet ends of his hair. He always felt a sudden calm when Sara was with him, like the only thing that mattered was the connection that tethered them together.

Will asked, "Can we move in? I'm only halfway kidding."

Sara's curious look turned guarded.

Will stopped breathing. The joke had landed wrong. Or maybe it wasn't a joke, because they had been dancing around this subject of moving in together for a while. He was basically living with Sara now, but she hadn't asked him to properly move in, and he couldn't figure out if that was a sign, and if it was a sign, was it a stop sign or a go sign or was it the kind of sign she was beating him over the head with, only he was missing it?

He desperately searched for a change in subject. "Look, a guitar."

Will fiddled with the strings. His teenage self had had the patience to learn exactly one song in its entirety. He started out slow, humming the tune so that he could remember the chords. And then he stopped, wondering why he'd ever thought "I'm on

Fire" was The Song that would persuade a girl to let him touch her breasts. "That's kind of gross, isn't it? 'Hey little girl is your daddy home?'"

"How about 'Girl, You'll Be a Woman Soon'? Or 'Don't Stand So Close to Me'? Or the opening line to 'Sara Smile'?"

He plucked at the guitar strings, hearing Daryl Hall singing in his head—

Baby hair with a woman's eyes . . .

"Damn," Will murmured. Why was every soft rock jam from his teenage years a Class A felony? "Hall and Oates, too?"

"Panic! At the Disco has a better version."

Will loved that she knew this. He'd initially been alarmed by the number of Dolly Parton CDs in her car. Then he'd seen her iTunes list, which featured everything from Adam Ant to Kraftwerk to Led Zeppelin, and known that they were going to be okay.

She was smiling at him, watching his fingers move along the cords. "When did you learn to play?"

"High school. Self-taught." He stroked her hair back so he could see her face. "Think of every stupid thing a sixteen-year-old boy would do to impress a sixteen-year-old girl and I know how to do it."

That, at least, got a laugh out of her. "Did you have a fade?"

"Duh." He listed all of his pathetic accomplishments, which had worked with exactly zero girls. "You should've seen me in my acid-washed jeans and Nember's Only jacket."

"Nember?"

"Dollar Store brand. I didn't say I was a millionaire." He couldn't ignore the dead bug anymore. He nodded toward the streak of bug guts above her eyebrow. "What's going on up there?"

Sara shook her head.

Will returned the guitar to the stand. He used his thumb to wipe away the bug. "That's better."

For some reason, she started kissing him. Really kissing him. He let his hands run down her waist. Sara moved closer. Kissed him deeper. She used her fingertips to press down his shoulders.

Then she pushed him down with her hands. Will was on his knees thinking he would never get tired of the taste of her when the ground started to shake.

Sara sat up. "What the hell was that?"

Will wiped his mouth. He couldn't joke about making the earth move for her because the earth had literally moved. He checked under the old couch to see if it was falling apart. He stood up and knocked at the beams, which was probably stupid because the whole shed could fall down on them.

He asked Sara, "Remember that earthquake in Alabama a few years back?" Will had been on a stakeout in north Georgia. The car had shimmied away from the curb. "That felt the same, but stronger."

Sara was buttoning her shorts. "There was a sound. The country club does fireworks displays. Maybe they're testing out a new show?"

"In broad daylight?" Will found his phone on the workbench. The screen gave the time.

1:49 p.m.

He told Sara, "There aren't any alerts." She worked at the GBI, too. She knew that the state had an emergency contact system that pinged all law enforcement phones in case of a terrorist attack.

Will considered where they were standing, what kind of cataclysmic event could be felt at these coordinates. He recalled attending a seminar given by an FBI agent who'd been at Ground Zero. Even over a decade later, the man could not find the words to describe the awesome kinetic energy dissipated into the ground when a skyscraper fell.

Like an off-the-scale earthquake.

The Atlanta airport was seven miles from downtown. More than a quarter of a million passengers flew in and out every day.

Will returned to his phone. He tried to check his messages and emails, but the wheel just spun on the screen. He called Faith but couldn't get through. He tried Amanda and got the same. He dialed the main office number at the GBI.

Nothing worked.

He held up the phone so Sara could hear the three tones, then the operator saying all circuits were busy. He dropped the phone onto the bench. It might as well be a brick.

Sara's expression was filled with anxiety. She said, "Emory has an emergency siren. It goes off when there's a natural disast—"

Boom.

Will almost lost his footing. He ran into the yard and looked up at the sky. A plume of dark smoke curled up behind the tree line.

Not fireworks.

Two explosions.

"Let's go." Will started running toward the driveway.

"Sara!" Cathy called from the back door. "Did you hear that?"

He watched Sara dart into the house. She was probably looking for her keys. He wanted her to stay inside but knew she wouldn't.

Will darted across the sloping front yard. The police would set up roadblocks. There would be nowhere to park a car and Will could probably run there faster. He thought about his gun locked in the glove box of Sara's BMW, but if the local cops needed him for anything, it would be crowd control.

Will's foot hit the road just as the wail of an emergency siren filled the air. Bella's house was on a straight stretch of Lullwater Road. There was a curve fifty yards ahead that followed the contours of the Druid Hills golf course. Will kept his arms tight to his body, legs pumping hard, as he closed the gap to the curve.

He was almost at the bend when he heard another sound. Not an explosion, but the weird *pop* that two automobiles make when they smack into each other. There was another *pop*. He gritted his teeth as he waited through the ensuing silence. A car horn started to whine along with the emergency siren.

It wasn't until Will had finally rounded the curve that he saw what had happened: two cars had marshmallowed a blue pickup truck between them.

A red Porsche Boxter S was at the front. Older model, naturally aspirated flat-six, a third radiator behind the opening in the lower front fascia. The trunk had popped open. The driver was slumped at the wheel, pressing the horn with his face.

A Ford F-150 truck was behind it. The doors must've crumpled on impact. One man was trying to climb out the open window. The other was leaning against the hood, blood dripping down his face.

A four-door, silver Chevy Malibu brought up the rear. Driver in front, two passengers in back, none of them moving.

The cop in Will immediately assigned blame. The Porsche had stopped too quickly. The truck and Malibu were following too closely, probably speeding. Whether or not the Porsche driver had antagonized the guy in the truck by tapping the brakes was a puzzle for the accident investigator to figure out.

Will looked past them to the roundabout at North Decatur Road. Parked vehicles filled the circle. A minivan. A box truck. Mercedes. BMW. Audi. They were all abandoned, doors hanging open. Drivers and passengers stood in the street looking up at the smoke curling into the blue sky.

Will's hard run downshifted to a jog, then he, too, came to a standstill.

Birds chirped in the trees. The smallest of breezes rustled the leaves. The smoke was coming from the Emory campus. Students, staff, two hospitals, the FBI headquarters, the CDC.

"Will."

He startled. Sara had pulled up alongside him. Her BMW X5 was a hybrid. The engine worked off a battery at low speeds.

She said, "I can triage them, but I need your help."

He had to clear his throat to bring himself back into the moment. "The driver in the Porsche looks bad."

Sara got out of the car. "Gas is leaking under the engine."

She ran to the Porsche. The driver was still collapsed over the steering wheel. The windows were up. So was the convertible top.

Sara tried the door to no avail. She banged her fist on the window. "Sir?" The horn kept blaring. She had to raise her voice. "Sir, we need to get you out of the car."

The smell of gasoline burned Will's eyes. There were any number of ways the electricity flowing to the horn could spark and ignite the fuel under the car.

Will told Sara, "Stand back."

He had a spring-loaded knife in his pocket that he'd used to cut ivy off Bella's trees. He gripped the handle with both hands and stabbed the four-inch blade into the soft convertible roof. The knife was partially serrated. He tried to saw into the material, but the canvas and insulation were too thick. Will pocketed the knife and used his fingers to pry open a gap wide enough to reach in and release the clamps so he could push the top out of the way.

He turned the key in the ignition.

The horn stopped.

Will unlocked the door. Sara took a few seconds before she started shaking her head. "His neck's broken. He wasn't wearing his seat belt, but it's weird."

"Weird how?"

"They weren't going fast enough for this kind of injury. Unless he had some kind of underlying medical condition. Even then—" She shook her head again. "It's not making sense."

Will looked at the skid marks on the road. They were short, indicating the Porsche had been going at a slower rate of speed. He rubbed his thumb on his shirt. The ignition key had been sticky with blood. So was the inside door handle, though there wasn't much blood anywhere else. Papers were scattered in the front seat.

"Ma'am?" The driver from the F-150 was standing behind the Porsche. He was a prototypical hillbilly, with long stringy hair and a ZZ Top beard, the kind of guy who drove down from the mountains every day to build decks and hang drywall. His fingers were pinching together pieces of his scalp. "Are you a nurse?"

"Doctor." Sara gently moved his hand so she could examine the cut. "Are you feeling dizzy or nauseous, Mister—"

"Merle. No, ma'am."

Will looked down at the asphalt. There was a trail of blood between the truck and the Porsche. So, Merle had checked on the driver, then he'd returned to his truck. There was nothing suspicious about his actions. Then again, Sara's intuition was generally reliable. If she thought something was off, then something was off.

So, what was Will missing?

He asked the passenger of the truck, "What happened?"

"Gas main exploded. We got the hell outta there." He was a redneck straight out of Lynyrd Skynyrd. Will could smell the cigarette smoke wafting off of him from ten feet away. The guy motioned toward the Malibu. "It's them people there you should be worried about. Guy in the back seat ain't lookin' so good."

Sara was already heading toward the sedan. Will followed, though she didn't need his help. Her suspicion had set off his internal alarm. He looked up and down the street. Some of the neighbors were standing in their doorways, but no one was approaching the scene. Smoke from the explosions had tinged the air with a charcoal odor.

"My friend needs help." The driver of the Chevy Malibu stumbled as he got out of the car. He was wearing a blue security uniform from the university. He opened the rear door. One of the passengers was slumped in the back seat. He was wearing the same blue uniform.

"She's a doctor," Merle provided.

The Chevy driver told Will, "Gas main exploded at one of the construction sites."

"Twice?" Will asked. "We heard two explosions."

"I dunno, man. Maybe something else blew. The entire site evaporated."

"What about casualties?"

He shook his head. "Contractors don't work on the weekends, but they're evacuating the entire campus just in case. All hell broke loose when the alarms went off."

Will didn't ask the Emory security guard why he wasn't helping evacuate the campus. He checked the horizon. The single pillar of smoke had taken on a strange, navy color.

"Sir?" Sara was kneeling at the open car door so she could talk to the man in the back seat. "Sir, are you okay?"

"His name's Dwight," the Chevy driver provided. "I'm Clinton."

"I'm Vince," the truck passenger offered.

Will raised his chin in acknowledgment. He could finally hear squad cars barreling down Oakdale Road, which ran parallel to Lullwater. A white air ambulance helicopter raced overhead. In the distance, fire engines bleated their horns. No one was using Bella's street. There must've been another accident at the Ponce de Leon end of Lullwater. There was no telling how many people had slammed on the brakes when the explosions started.

So, why did this particular car accident feel different?

"Dwight?" Sara pulled the man up to sitting. The windows were heavily tinted. Over the top of the door, Will could see Dwight's head loll to the side. The whites of his eyes showed like bone under his swollen eyelids. Blood dribbled from his nose. He hadn't been wearing a seat belt, either. He'd probably knocked himself out on the seat in front of him.

"We need to get him out of here." Clinton's tone had changed. He sounded scared now. "Get him to the hospital. Emory's closed. The emergency room. Everything's closed, man. What the fuck are we going to do?"

Will put a steadying hand on Clinton's shoulder. "Can you tell me exactly what happened?"

"I done told you!" The man's arms flew up, shirking Will's hand away. "Do you see that smoke, bubba? Shit's going down, is what's happening. And now this car wreck and none of us can get out of here. You think they're gonna send an ambulance for my pal? You think the cops are gonna arrest me for whacking into that stupid truck?"

"Clinton, it's nobody's fault," another voice said. The second passenger from the back seat. Mid-thirties, clean shaven. T-shirt and jeans. He had his hands clasped together on the roof.

Will could feel the danger radiating off this guy like heat from the sun.

What was he missing?

The man told Will, "I'm Hank."

Will gave him a cautious nod, but didn't offer his own name. It was weird that these guys were identifying themselves. It was weird that the Porsche driver's neck was broken. It was especially weird that Hank was so calm in the face of a fatal car accident where his friend was knocked out cold.

You weren't that calm unless you felt like you were completely in control.

Hank said, "We heard another explosion, then the guy in the red car just stopped." He snapped his fingers. "Then the truck hit the red car. Then we rear-ended the truck and—"

"Will?" Sara's tone had changed, too. She was holding out the key fob to her BMW. Will caught a slight tremble in her hand. She had worked in emergency medicine for years. She never got flustered.

What was he missing?

She told him, "I need you to get my medical bag out of the glove compartment of the car."

Merle offered, "I can get it."

Will took the fob. His fingers brushed against Sara's. He felt a jolt of panic as his brain processed her very specific request.

Sara kept her medical bag in the trunk because the glove box was too small. And also because that was where Will locked his gun when he wasn't wearing it.

She wasn't asking him to get her bag.

She was telling him to get his gun.

Will suddenly had too much spit in his mouth. Like darts on a board, his thoughts circled the bull's-eye. He'd heard the first car crash as he was heading toward the bend in the road. There was no bomb going off when it happened. Then there was another crash when the Malibu rear-ended the truck. The Porsche's horn had sounded at least five seconds later.

Five seconds was a long time.

In five seconds, you could stumble out of your truck, open the door to a Porsche and snap a man's neck. Which would explain the blood trail circling from the truck to the car.

Two Emory security guards who'd fled instead of doing their jobs. One guy dressed to blend in. Two guys dressed like the kind of handymen you saw all over Atlanta. They could've all been strangers, but they weren't.

This was what Will had been missing:

These men were part of a team.

A very good one, judging by their stealthy movements. Without Will realizing it, they had placed Will and Sara in the middle of a tactical triangle.

Clinton was behind them.

Hank was in front of them.

Standing at the apex between Will and his gun: Vince and Merle.

Dwight was knocked out cold, but Hank was limping around the rear of the car to stand near Sara.

Will rubbed his jaw as he silently probed for points of weakness.

There were none.

All of them were armed. Hank's weapon wasn't visible, but a guy like that was always strapped. The bulge at Vince's ankle was a concealed revolver. Clinton had a Glock on his belt as part of the security uniform. Merle's revolver was tucked into the small of his back. Will could see the outline of the grip when the man crossed his arms over his broad chest. He stood like a cop, feet planted wide apart, tailbone curved, because the weight of a thirty-pound service belt could break your spine.

They all stood the same way.

"Give us a hand, big guy." Clinton's feigned helplessness had evaporated. He gestured for Will to help him get Dwight out of the car. "Let's go."

"Wait," Sara tried. "He could have a spinal injury or—"

"Ma'am, excuse me." Merle didn't move her out of the way so much as stand there until Sara moved for him. Together, he and Clinton lifted Dwight out of the car. The guy was dead weight. His feet flopped against the asphalt until they finally flattened back like a duck's.

Will let his eyes slide toward Sara. She wasn't looking at him. She was taking in her surroundings, trying to figure out whether or not to run. Hank was standing beside her. Too close. Most of the front yards were more like football fields. If she took off, he would have a clear shot at her back.

So, Will would have to shoot him before that happened.

He told Sara, "I'll get your bag."

He didn't try to catch her eye. Instead, he stared at Hank in a way that let the man know if he touched a hair on Sara's head, Will would beat the skin off of his face.

There were thirty feet between Will and the BMW. Sara had parked it at an angle across the road to calm any oncoming traffic. Will walked just fast enough to keep his distance from Merle and Clinton, who dragged Dwight between them.

Will felt the heat leave his body. His heart slowed to a steady thump. Some people got calm when they were in control. Will had been out of control enough times in his life to find calm in chaos. His ears strained for sounds. He heard scuffs and grunts and sirens and horns. Nothing from Sara. No words, anyway. He felt her eyes on him, almost like a tractor beam trying to pull him back to her.

How the fuck had he let this happen?

Will looked down at his hand. There was a valet key hidden inside the fob. Will slid it out of the compartment. He took a cue from Faith, who always kept the longest key on her ring jutting out like a knife from between her fisted fingers. He thought about using it to rip open Hank's throat. The man wouldn't be so calm with his larynx dangling below his chin.

Motherfucker.

They weren't just going to take the BMW. That would've been an easy solve—all they'd needed to do was pull out their guns, jump in the car and make their escape. No conversation required. But they had kept talking. They had given their names, which was Interrogation 101: establish a rapport with the subject. They had given a bullshit story about a gas main explosion. They had a guy who was injured, one who was knocked out. They couldn't go to a hospital, but they needed medical help fast.

They were going to take Sara.

A very specific type of fury coiled every single muscle in Will's body. His nerves were electrified. His vision was crystal clear. His thoughts slid along the edge of a razor.

The folding knife in his pocket.

The key between his fingers.

The gun in the glove compartment.

Will couldn't reach into his pocket, press the button on the spring-loaded knife, and have it open in time to do anything but drop from his hand when he was shot.

The key was only good for close quarters combat, and Will didn't have a chance against two guys.

He had to get the gun.

Four armed cops or ex-cops. Maybe five if Dwight woke up. Will hadn't checked, but the guy should have a Glock on his belt, part of the security uniform. Part of the disguise.

Still a real gun.

Will could pretend to help Dwight into the car, then grab the Glock. Even close range, he would need to be fast. Clinton first because of the gun on his hip, then Merle because it would take longer for him to reach for the revolver tucked down the back of his pants.

The instructors at the range always said shoot to stop, but Sara's jeopardy changed the rules. Will was going to shoot to kill every single one of these fuckers.

He finally reached the BMW. Will opened the door, leaned into the passenger's seat. He slid the key into the glove box. He glanced up to locate Sara.

Will froze.

It felt like a literal thing—dry ice penetrating his bloodstream. Muscles cramping. Tendons splitting. He had a weird, unnatural quiver in his bones. All the angles he'd been trying to work evaporated because of one thing:

Fear.

Sara wasn't standing anymore. She was on her knees, but now she was facing Will. Her fingers were laced behind her head, the position a cop would put a suspect in so that he could search and cuff them.

Hank was standing behind her. Another woman was at his side. Separate from him, not with him. She had short, almost white hair. Her cheeks were sunken. She held up her unzipped khaki pants with both hands. Blood stained the inside seams, making a lurid, upside down V between her legs. She looked up at Will, her eyes begging him to make this stop.

Michelle Spivey.

The scientist had been abducted a month ago. She had worked at the CDC.

Not an explosion from a gas leak.

An attack.

"All right," Hank shouted at Will. "I need you to slowly get your head out of the car and put your hands up." He had taken a gun out of his pocket: PKO-45. The muzzle barely extended past his finger, which was placed above the trigger guard the way a cop would hold it. The extended magazine peeked out from the bottom of his fist. Tiny, but powerful. It was called a pocket cannon because it could blow the brain out of a woman's skull.

Sara's skull.

Because that's where the gun was pointing.

Will felt a physical illness rack his body. He did as he was told, his hands slowly going into the air. He looked at Sara now. Her bottom lip trembled. Her eyes filled with tears. Her fear was so palpable that he could feel it like a fist squeezing the blood out of his heart.

Merle jammed his revolver into Will's side. "We got no beef with you, big guy. Just need to borrow the doctor. You'll get her back eventually."

Will's eyes found the blood dripping down between Michelle's legs. He opened his mouth, but he couldn't draw air. Sweat streamed down the sides of his face. He looked down at the Smith and Wesson revolver that was prying apart his ribs. If he was shot in the gut, could he still grab one of the guns? Could he give Sara cover so that she could run?

From four armed men? Across open space?

Broken glass filled his throat, his chest, his lungs.

They were going to take Sara.

They were going to kill him.

There was nothing Will could do but watch it or make it happen faster.

Clinton loaded Dwight into the back of the BMW. Dwight was still out, slumped over to the side. His holster was empty. Vince was too far away for Will to take his gun. He had already slipped behind the wheel of Sara's car. The key fob was inside, so he was able to turn on the vehicle by pressing the button. The battery turned on, but not the engine.

Vince laughed. "Stealing a hybrid. We're owning the libs."

Will forced his shaking hands to still. He flooded out the fear with rage. This could not happen. He would not let them hurt Sara. He would eat every bullet in every gun if that's what it took to stop them.

"Careful, bro." Clinton's palm rested on the butt of his Glock.

"I'm a cop," Will said. "You're cops. This doesn't have to go sideways."

"We need a doctor," Hank called across the chasm between Will and Sara. "No offense, brother. Wrong place, right time. Let's go, lady. Get in the car."

Hank tried to pull Sara up, but she wrenched away. "No." Her voice was low, but she might as well have shouted the word. "I'm not going with you."

"Lady, that wasn't a gas main that exploded at the campus." Hank glanced up at Will. "We just blew up dozens, maybe hundreds of people. Do you think I give a shit about having your blood on my hands?"

Will could see the anguish on Sara's face. She was thinking about the hospitals, the sick patients, the children, the staff who had lost their lives.

Will did not care about any of them. All he cared about was Sara. These men were cold-blooded murderers. If they took her, she would be dead within a few hours. If she refused to go, she would be dead where she knelt on the ground.

"No," Sara repeated. She had already made the same calculations as Will. Tears ran down her face. She didn't sound scared anymore. She was clearly resigned to what was going to come next. "I won't go with you. I won't help you. You'll have to shoot me."

Will's eyes burned, but he would not look away from her.

He nodded his head.

He knew that she meant it.

He knew *why* she meant it.

"How about I kill her?" Hank pressed the gun against Michelle Spivey's head.

The woman didn't flinch. She didn't cry out. She said, "Do it. Go ahead, you spineless piece of shit."

Clinton laughed, though the woman sounded as resigned to her fate as Sara.

"You still think you're a good man." Michelle turned her head toward Hank. Her hands had clenched into fists as they held up her pants. "What's your father going to say when he hears about who you really are?"

Hank's calm composure started to slip. Michelle's words had hit their mark. She had spent a month with these men. She obviously knew their weak points.

"I heard you talking about your dad, how he's your hero, how you wanted to make him proud," Michelle said. "He's sick. He's going to die."

Hank's jaw clenched.

"His last breath, he's gonna know what kind of monster he helped bring into this world."

Clinton laughed again. "Damn, girl, the way you're talking makes me wonder how tight your daughter's pussy is."

There's always a moment right before bad things get worse.

Split second.

Blink of an eye.

Will had been in enough bad situations to recognize when it was coming. The air changed. You could feel it when you breathed in, like your lungs were getting more oxygen, or that percentage of your brain that was never used was suddenly awake and processing and preparing you for what was coming next.

This is what came next:

Hank's finger slid from the trigger guard down to the trigger.

But the gun wasn't pointing at Michelle Spivey when he pulled back. Neither was it pointing at Sara. Hank's arm had swung in an arc toward the man who had joked about raping an eleven-year-old girl.

Then—

Nothing.

Just a metallic *click-click-click*.

Here was the big problem with pocket cannons: pocket lint.

The gun had jammed.

Clinton screamed, "You son of a—"

Everything got slower.

Clinton jerked the Glock out of his holster.

Will felt the sweet relief of the Smith and Wesson revolver being excised from between his ribs as Merle reached out to stop him.

Will grabbed the revolver. It was almost easy, because that wasn't the gun Merle was worried about.

The Smith and Wesson didn't jam. The six-shot was one of the most reliable weapons on the market. As far as accuracy, that depended on the shooter and the range. Will was a good shooter. A three-year-old could kill a man at close quarters.

Which is exactly what Will did.

Merle dropped, opening up the space so Will had a clear line on Vince, who was reaching for his ankle holster when Will shot him. Wounded him. The fucker fell out of the car.

One dead. One wounded. That left Dwight, Hank, Clinton—

Will caught a blur out of the corner of his eye.

Clinton tackled him down to the pavement. Will lost the revolver. His head cracked against the sidewalk. Clinton didn't go for Will's face. You didn't kill a man by breaking his skull. You killed him by breaking open his organs.

Will's muscles clenched against the fists pile-driving into his belly. The breathless pain threatened to immobilize him. But this wasn't Will's first beat-down. He didn't use his hands to ward off the blows. He reached into his pocket. His fingers found the folding knife. He pressed the release. The blade flicked open.

Will slashed out blindly, opening a ribbon of flesh in the man's forehead.

"Jesus!" Clinton reared back. Blood filled his eyes. His hands went up into combat position.

Fuck combat. There was no such thing as a fair fight.

Will jammed the four-inch blade straight into the man's groin.

Clinton sucked air. His body seized. He rolled onto the pavement. Coughing. Spitting. Wheezing.

Will blinked his eyes, trying to clear the stars. Blood rolled down his throat.

He heard car doors slamming. The sound echoed like a kettledrum.

Did Sara call his name?

Will rolled to his side. He tried to stand. Vomit erupted into his mouth. Every part of his gut was on fire. He could only make it to his knees. He fell flat. He breathed into the pain coursing through his body. He tried again to get up to his knees.

That's when he saw a pair of work boots in front of him. The steel toes were spattered with blood. Will watched the boot swing back. He waited for the downswing, then bear-hugged the leg.

Drop and roll.

They both hit the ground like a sledgehammer.

But it wasn't Clinton.

It was Hank.

Will managed to pin him down. His fists windmilled into the man's face. He was going to punch Hank's fucking eyes to the back of his skull. He was going to kill him for putting a gun to Sara's head. He was going to murder every fucking one of them.

"Will!" someone screamed.

Sara's voice, but not her voice.

"Stop it!"

He looked up.

Not Sara.

Her mother.

Cathy Linton held a double-barreled shotgun in both of her hands. He could feel the heat from the muzzle. One of the triggers had already been pulled. The second was cocked and loaded.

Cathy stared up the road.

The BMW squealed around the curve. Will fell to the ground. His brain was still swimming. Vomit still burned his throat. He tried to count the heads in the car.

Four?

Five?

He looked behind him, expecting to find Sara's body. "Where—"

"She's gone." A sob came from Cathy's mouth. "Will, they took her."

3

Sunday, August 4, 1:33 p.m.

Faith Mitchell checked her watch as she pretended to study the diagram of the Russell Federal Building on the giant video monitor at the front of the classroom. The tedious asshole from the Marshals Service was running through the prison transport plan, which the previous asshole from the Marshals Service had run through an hour ago.

She looked around the room. Faith wasn't the only person having a hard time concentrating. The thirty people assembled from various branches of law enforcement were all wilting behind their desks. The city, in its wisdom, turned off the air conditioning in all government buildings over the weekends. In August. With windows that didn't open so that no one could jump out just for the pleasure of the wind in their face as they plummeted to their death.

Faith looked down at her briefing book. A drop of sweat rolled off the tip of her nose and smeared the words. She had already read through the book in its entirety. Twice. The asshole marshal was the fifth speaker in the last three hours. Faith wanted to pay attention. She really did. But if she heard another person call Martin Elias Novak a *high-value prisoner*, she was going to start screaming.

Her eyes rolled to the clock on the wall above the video monitor.

1:34 p.m.

Faith could've sworn the second hand was ticking backward.

"So, the chase car will go here." The marshal pointed to the rectangle at the end of the dotted line that was helpfully labeled *chase car*. "I want to remind you again that Martin Novak is an extremely high-value prisoner."

Faith tried not to snort. Even Amanda's composure was starting to slip. She was still sitting ramrod straight in her chair, seemingly alert, but Faith knew for a fact that she could sleep with her eyes open. Faith's mother was the same way. Both of them had come up in the Atlanta Police Department together. Both were extremely adaptable, like dinosaurs who'd evolved into using tools and forwarding memes that had stopped being memes two months ago.

Faith opened her laptop. Eight tabs were open in her browser, every one of them offering advice on how to make your life more efficient. Faith clicked them all closed. She was a single mother with a two-year-old at home and a twenty-year-old in college. Efficiency was not an attainable goal. Sleep wasn't an attainable goal. Eating an uninterrupted meal. Using the bathroom with the door closed. Reading a book without having to show the pictures to all the stuffed animals in the room. Breathing deeply. Walking in a straight line.

Thinking.

Faith desperately wanted her brain back, the pre-pregnancy brain that knew how to be a fully functioning adult. Had it been like this with her son? Faith was only fifteen years old when she'd given birth to Jeremy. She hadn't really been paying attention to what was happening to her mind so much as mourning the loss of Jeremy's father, whose parents had shipped him off to live with relatives up north so that a baby wouldn't ruin his bright future.

With her daughter Emma, Faith was aware of the not-so-subtle changes in her mental abilities. That she could multi-task, but she could barely single-task. That the feelings of anxiety and hypervigilance that came with being a cop were amplified to the nth degree. That she never really slept because her ears were always awake. That the sound of Emma crying could make her hands shake and her lips tremble and that sometimes Emma's nightlight would catch the tender strands of her delicate eyelashes and Faith's heart would be filled with so much love that she ended up sobbing alone in the hallway.

Sara had explained the science behind these mood changes. During the stages of pregnancy and breastfeeding and childhood, a woman's brain was flooded with hormones that altered the gray matter in the regions involved in social processes, heightening the mother's empathy and bonding them closely to their child.

Which was a damn good thing, because if another human being treated you the way a toddler did—threw food in your face, questioned your every move, unraveled all of the aluminum foil off the roll, yelled at the silverware, made you clean shit off their ass, peed in your bed, peed in your car, peed on you while you were cleaning up their pee, demanded that you repeat everything at least sixteen times and then screeched at you for talking too much—then you would probably kill them.

"Let's discuss the tactical quadrangle we've created on the west-bound streets," the marshal said.

Faith let her eyes take a really slow blink. She needed something outside of work and Emma. Her mother euphemistically called it a work/life balance, but it was really just Evelyn's polite way of saying that Faith needed to get laid.

Which Faith was not opposed to.

The problem was finding a man. Faith wasn't going to date a cop, because all you had to do was date one cop and every cop would think he could screw you. Tinder was a no-go. The guys who didn't look married looked like they should be chained to a bench outside of a courtroom. She'd tried Match.com but not one of the losers that she was even remotely attracted to could pass a background check. Which said more about the type of men Faith was attracted to than internet dating sites.

At this rate, the only way she was going to get laid was to crawl up a chicken's ass and wait.

"So," the marshal clapped his hands together once, loudly. Too loudly. "Let's review Martin Elias Novak's résumé. Sixty-one-year-old widower with one daughter, Gwendolyn. Wife died in childbirth. Novak served in the Army as an explosives expert. Not too expert—in '96, he blew off two fingers on his left hand. He was discharged, then took some odd jobs working security. In 2002, he was in Iraq with a private mercenary force. By 2004, we clocked him joining up with some fellow vets on a citizens border patrol in Arizona."

The marshal steepled together his fingers and slowly bowed his head. "Arizona was the last time we saw him. That was 2004. Novak went off the grid. No credit card activity. Closed his accounts. Canceled his utilities. Walked out on his lease. His pension and disability checks were returned as undeliverable. Novak was a ghost until 2016, when he popped up on our radar at a new job: robbing banks."

Faith noticed that he'd skipped over a big piece of the puzzle, the same way every single speaker had skipped over the glaring detail in all of the previous meetings.

Novak was an anti-government nut. Not just a guy who didn't want to pay taxes or be told what to do. Hell, no red-blooded American wanted those things. His time with the so-called citizens border patrol put him at a whole other level of dissent. For six months, Novak had kept company with a group of men who thought they understood the Constitution better than anybody else. Worse, they were willing to take up arms and do something about it.

Which meant that thanks to all of those bank robberies, someone, somewhere, had half a million bucks to aid the cause.

And no one in this room seemed to give a shit about it.

"All right." The marshal clapped his hands together again. Someone in the front row jumped at the sound. "Let's bring up Special Agent Aiden Van Zandt from the FBI to talk about the reason Novak is such a high-value prisoner."

Faith felt her eyes roll back in her head again.

"Thank you, Marshal." Agent Van Zandt looked more like a Humperdinck than a Westley. Faith didn't trust men who wore glasses. At least he didn't clap or offer a long preamble. Instead, Van Zandt turned toward the monitor, offering, "Let's go to the video. Novak is the first man through the door. You can see the two fingers of his left hand are missing."

The video started to play. Faith leaned forward in her seat. Finally, something new. She had read all of the police reports but hadn't seen any footage.

The screen showed the inside of a bank, full color.

Friday, March 24, 2017. 4:03 p.m.

Four tellers at the windows. At least a dozen customers standing in line. There would've been a steady stream all day. People cashing their checks before the weekend. No security glass or bars at the teller counter. A suburban branch. This was the Wells Fargo outside of Macon, where Novak's team had taken their last stand.

On the screen, things moved quickly. Faith almost missed Novak coming through the doors, though he was dressed in full tactical gear, all black, a ski mask covering his face. He held his AR-15 at his right side. A backpack was slung over his left shoulder. The pinky and ring finger were missing from his left hand.

The security guard entered the frame from Novak's right. Pete Guthrie, divorced father of two. The man was reaching toward his holster, but the AR swung up and Pete Guthrie was dead.

Someone in the classroom groaned, like they'd just watched a movie, not the end of a man's life.

The rest of Novak's team swarmed into the bank, quickly taking up position. Six guys, all dressed in the same black gear. All waving around AR-15s, which were as ubiquitous in Georgia as peaches. There was no sound with the video, but Faith could see open mouths as the customers screamed. Another person was shot, a seventy-two-year-old grandmother of six named Edatha Quintrell who, going by the witness statements, had not moved fast enough getting down on the ground.

"Military," someone needlessly said.

Needlessly, because these guys were clearly a tactical unit. Less than ten seconds through the door and they were already opening the teller drawers, tossing the hidden dye packs aside and shoving the money into white canvas bags.

Van Zandt said, "We scoured four previous months of footage trying to find someone casing the bank, but nothing stuck out." He pointed to Novak. "Look at the stopwatch in his hand. The closest precinct is twelve minutes away. The closest patrol is eight minutes out. He knows how much time they have down to the second. Everything was planned."

They hadn't planned on one of the customers being an off-duty police officer. Rasheed Dougall, a twenty-nine-year-old patrolman, had stopped by the bank on his way to the gym. He was wearing red basketball shorts and a black T-shirt. Faith's eyes had automatically found him in the bottom right corner. Belly flat to the ground. Hands not over his head, but at his side near his gym bag. She knew what was going to happen next. Rasheed pulled a Springfield micro pistol out of the bag and shot the guy closest to him in the belly.

Two taps, the way they were trained.

Rasheed rolled over and caught a second guy in the head. He was aiming for the third when a bullet from Novak blew off the bottom half of his face.

Novak seemed unfazed by the sudden carnage. He coldly looked at the stopwatch. His mouth moved. According to the statements, he was telling his men—

Let's go, boys, clean it up.

Four guys moved forward, two teams each shouldering one of their fallen accomplices as they dragged them toward the door.

Novak scooped up the white canvas bags of cash. Then he made his custom move: He reached into his backpack. He held up a pipe bomb over his head, making sure everyone saw it. The bomb wasn't meant to blow the vault. He was going to set it off once the car was out of range. But before he left, he was going to chain the doors shut so that no one could leave.

As violent criminal acts go, it was a solid plan. Small towns didn't have enough first responders to handle more than one disaster at a time. An explosion at the bank, casualties falling out of broken windows and doors, was the biggest disaster the locals would ever see.

On the screen, Novak slapped the bomb to the wall. Faith knew that it was held there by an adhesive sold at any home improvement store. Galvanized pipe. Nails. Thumb tacks. Wire. All of the components were untraceable or so common that they might as well be.

Novak turned toward the door. He started pulling the chain and lock out of his backpack. Then he unexpectedly collapsed face down on the ground.

Blood spread out from his body like a snow angel.

Some of the men in the classroom cheered.

A woman rushed into the frame. Dona Roberts. Her Colt 1911 was pointing at Novak's head. Her foot was on the man's tailbone to make sure he stayed down. She was a retired Navy cargo plane pilot who'd just happened to be at the bank to open an account for her daughter.

Damn if she wasn't wearing a strapless sundress and sandals.

The image paused.

Van Zandt said, "Novak took two in the back. Lost a kidney and his spleen, but your tax dollars patched him up. The phone to detonate the bomb was inside his backpack. According to our people, the first bad guy who was shot in the stomach could've survived with quick medical intervention. The bad guy with a hole in his head obviously died at the scene. No bodies were found dumped in a twenty-mile radius. No hospitals reported gunshot victims fitting the description. We have no idea who these accomplices are. Novak didn't crack under questioning."

He didn't crack because he wasn't the average bank robber. Most of those idiots got arrested before they could count their money. The FBI had basically been invented to stop people from robbing banks. Their solve rate was north of 75 percent. It was a stupid crime with a high chance of failure and a mandatory twenty-five-year sentence, and that was just for walking up to a teller and passing a note saying you would like to rob the bank, please. Waving a gun, making threats, shooting people—that was the rest of your life in Big Boy prison, assuming you didn't get a needle in your arm.

"So . . ." The marshal was back. He clapped together his hands. He was a real hand-clapper, this guy. "Let's talk about what happened in the video."

Faith checked her Apple Watch for messages, praying for a family emergency that would pull her out of this never-ending nightmare.

No luck.

She groaned at the time.

1:37 p.m.

She pulled up her texts. Will had no idea how lucky he was to be skipping this stupid meeting. She sent him a clown with a water gun to its head. Then a knife. Then a hammer. She was going to send him an avocado because they both despised avocados, but her finger slipped on the tiny screen and she accidentally sent him a yam.

"Let's look at this next chart." The marshal had pulled up another image, this one a flow chart detailing all the various agencies involved in the transport. Atlanta Police. Fulton County Police. Fulton County Sheriff's office. US Marshals Service. The FBI. The ATF. The who-the-fuck-cares because Faith had two hours of folding laundry ahead of her, six if her precious daughter insisted on helping.

She checked to see if Will had texted back. He hadn't. He was probably working on his car or doing push-ups or whatever else he did on the days he managed to get out of hideously long meetings.

He was probably still in bed with Sara.

Faith stared out the window. She let out a long sigh.

Will was a missed opportunity. She could see that now. Faith hadn't been particularly attracted to him when they'd first met, but Sara had Pygmalioned his ass. She'd dragged him to a real hair salon instead of the weird guy in the morgue who traded haircuts for sandwiches. She had talked him into getting his suits tailored so he'd gone from looking like the sale rack at a Big and Tall Warehouse to the mannequin in the window of a Hugo

Boss store. He was standing up straighter, more confident. Less awkward.

Then there was his sweet side.

He marked his calendar with a star on the days Sara got her hair done so he would remember to compliment her. He was constantly finding ways to say her name. He listened to her, respected her, thought she was smarter than he was, which was true, because she was a doctor, but what man admitted that? He was constantly regaling Faith with the ancient wisdoms that Sara had passed on to him:

Did you know that men can use lotion for dry skin, too?

Did you know that you're supposed to eat the lettuce and tomato on a hamburger?

Did you know that frozen orange juice has a lot of sugar?

Faith was diabetic. Of course she knew about sugar. The question was, how did Will not know? And wasn't it commonly understood that eating the lettuce and tomato meant you could order the fries? She knew Will had been raised feral, but Faith had lived with two teenage boys, first her older brother and then her son. She hadn't been able to leave a bottle of Jergens unmolested on the bathroom counter until she was in her thirties.

How the hell did Will not know about lotion?

"Thank you, Marshal." Major Maggie Grant had taken the floor.

Faith sat up in her seat, trying to look like a good student. Maggie was her spirit animal, a woman who had worked her way up the Atlanta Police Department food chain from crossing guard to Commander of Special Operations without turning into a testicle-gnarling bitch.

Maggie said, "I'll briefly run down the SWAT Bible on transport from the APD perspective. We're all following the Active Shooter Doctrine. No negotiation. Just pop and drop. From a tactical standpoint, we'll maintain a hollow square around the pris—the *high-value prisoner*—at all times."

Only Faith and Amanda laughed. There were exactly three women in the room. The rest were men who had probably not let a woman speak uninterrupted for this long since elementary school.

"Ma'am?" a hand shot up. So much for uninterrupted. "Concerning emergency egress for the prisoner—"

Faith looked at the clock.

1:44 p.m.

She opened Notes on her laptop and tried to trim down the grocery list she'd dictated to Siri this morning: *Eggs, bread, juice, peanut butter, diapers, no, Emma, no, for fuck sakes, Emma don't, oh Christ please stop, candy.*

Technology had finally caught up with her bad parenting.

Had she always been like this? By the time Jeremy was in the first grade, Faith was twenty-two years old and working out of a squad car. Her parenting skills fell somewhere between *Charlotte's Web* and *Lord of the Flies*. Jeremy still teased her about the note she'd once left in his lunch box: *The bread is stale. This is what happens when you don't close the bag.*

She had vowed to be a better mother to Emma, but what did that mean, exactly?

Not creating a Mount Vesuvius of unfolded laundry on the living room couch? Not letting carpet fuzz build up in the vacuum so that it smelled like burned rubber every time she turned it on? Not realizing until exactly three-twelve this morning that the reason the toy box smelled like rotten fruit roll-ups was because Emma had been hiding all of her fruit roll-ups in the bottom?

Toddlers were such fucking assholes.

"I'm Deputy Director Amanda Wagner with the GBI."

Faith jerked back to attention. She had gone into a fugue state from the heat and boredom. She said a silent prayer thanking Jesus, because Amanda was the last speaker.

She leaned on the desk in the front of the room and waited for everyone's undivided attention. "We've had six months to prepare for this transfer. Any failures to secure the prisoner are down to human error. You people in this room are the humans who could make that error. Put your hand down."

The guy in the front put his hand down.

Amanda looked at her watch. "It's five past two. We've got

the room until three. Take a ten-minute break, then come back and review your books. No papers are allowed to leave the room. No files on your laptops. If you have any questions, submit them in writing to your immediate supervisor." Amanda smiled at Faith, the only agent in the room that she was in charge of supervising. "Thank you, gentlemen."

The door opened. Faith could see the hallway. She weighed the consequences of pretending to go to the bathroom and slipping out the back door.

"Faith." Amanda was walking toward her. Trapping her. "Wait up a minute."

Faith closed her laptop. "Are we going to talk about why no one is mentioning the fact that our *high-value prisoner* thinks he's going to overthrow the deep state like Katniss from *The Hunger Games*?"

Amanda's brow furrowed. "I thought Katniss was the hero?"

"I have a problem with women in authority."

Amanda shook her head. "Look, Will needs his ego massaged."

Faith was momentarily without a response. The request was surprising on two levels. First, Will bristled at any kind of handholding and second, Amanda lived to crush egos.

Amanda said, "He's smarting over not being picked for this task force."

"Picked?" Faith had lost half a dozen Sundays to this tedium. "I thought this was a punishment for—" She wasn't stupid enough to make a list. "For punishing me."

Amanda kept shaking her head. "Faith, these men in the room—they're going to be in charge of everything one day. You need them to get used to your being part of the conversation. You know—network."

"Network?" Faith tried not to say the word as an explicative. Her motto had always been *Why go big when I can go home?*

Amanda said, "These are your prime earning years. Have you thought about the fact that you'll be eligible for Medicare by the time Emma's in college?"

Faith felt a stabbing pain in her chest.

"You can't stay in the field forever."

"And Will can?" Faith was perplexed. Amanda was like a mother to Will. If you were worried that your mother was going to run you down with her car. "Where is this coming from? Will's your favorite. Why are you holding him back?"

Instead of answering, Amanda flipped through the briefing book, pages and pages of single-spaced text.

Faith didn't need an explanation. "He's dyslexic. He's not illiterate. He's better with numbers than I am. He can read a briefing book. It just takes a little longer."

"How do you know he's dyslexic?"

"Because—" Faith didn't know how she knew. "Because I work with him. I pay attention. I'm a detective."

"But he's never told you. And he'll never tell anyone. Therefore, we can't offer him accommodations. Therefore, he'll never move up the food chain."

"Christ," Faith muttered. Just like that, she was closing down Will's future.

"Mandy." Maggie Grant walked into the room. She had a bottle of cold water for each of them. "Why on earth are you both still in here? It's cooler in the hallway."

Faith angrily twisted the cap off the bottle. She couldn't believe this Will bullshit. It wasn't Amanda's job to decide what he was capable of doing or not doing.

"How's your mother?" Maggie asked Faith.

"Good." Faith gathered up her stuff. She had to get out of here before she said something stupid.

"And Emma?"

"Very easy. No complaints." Faith stood from the chair. Her sweaty shirt peeled off her skin like a lemon rind. "I should—"

"Send them both my love." Maggie turned to Amanda, "How's your boy doing?"

She meant Will. All of Amanda's friends referred to him as her boy. The term reminded Faith of the first time you meet Michonne in the *Walking Dead*.

Amanda said, "He's getting by."

"I bet." Maggie told Faith, "You should've locked that down before Sara entered the picture."

Amanda guffawed. "She's not sweet enough for him."

"What the fuck does that mean?" Faith held up her hands to stop her own decapitation. "Sorry. I was up at three in the morning dragging a toy box into the front yard. The sky was awake, so I was awake."

Faith was saved bastardizing more lines from *Frozen* by a ringing cell phone.

Maggie said, "That's me." She walked over to the windows and answered the call.

Then Amanda's phone started to ring.

More rings echoed in the hallway. It sounded like every phone in the building was going off.

Faith checked her watch. She'd silenced the notifications before the meeting, but she turned them on again now. An alert had come in at 2:08 p.m. through the First Responder Notification System:

EXPLOSIONS AT EMORY UNIVERSITY. MASS CASUALTIES. THREE MALE WHITE SUSPECTS FLED IN SILVER CHEV MALIBU LP# XPR 932. HOSTAGE TAKEN. CONSIDERED ARMED AND DANGEROUS. PROCEED WITH CAUTION.

For a moment, Faith lacked the ability to comprehend the information. She felt a nervous sickness rattle her body, the same sensation she got when she saw an alert for a school shooting or a terrorist attack. And then she thought about the fact that Novak's team liked explosions. But a university wasn't their M.O. and Novak's safe house was well outside the city.

"Send all available agents," Amanda barked into her phone. "I need details. Descriptions. A casualty estimate. Have SOU coordinate with ATF on securing the campus. Let me know the second the governor calls out the National Guard."

"Amanda." Maggie's voice was tightly controlled. This was her city, her responsibility. "My bird will meet us on the roof."

"Let's go." Amanda motioned for Faith to come.

Faith grabbed her bag, the nervous sickness turning into a lump of concrete inside of her stomach as her mind started to process what had happened. An explosion at the university. A hostage taken. Mass casualties. Armed and dangerous.

They were all running by the time they reached the stairs. Maggie led them up, but the other officers from the meeting were pounding their way down in a furious rush because that's what cops did when something bad happened. They ran toward the bad thing.

"I'm giving the authorization . . ." Maggie yelled into her phone as she sprinted past the next landing, ". . . 9-7-2-2-4-alpha-delta. 10-39 every available. I want all birds in the air. Tell the commander I'm five minutes out."

"One of the bombers was wounded." Amanda was finally getting information. She glanced back at Faith as she climbed. Shock flashed across her face. "The hostage is Michelle Spivey."

Maggie muttered a curse, grabbing the railing to pull herself up the next flight. She listened into her phone a moment, then reported, "I've got two wounded, nothing about Spivey." She was breathing hard, but she didn't stop. "One perp was hit in the leg. Second in the shoulder. The driver was dressed in an Emory security uniform."

Faith felt the sweat on her body turn cold as she listened to the words echoing down the stairwell.

"A nurse recognized Spivey." Amanda was off the phone. She shouted to be heard over their footsteps scuffing the concrete treads. "There's conflicting information but—"

Maggie stopped on another landing. She held up her hand for quiet. "Okay, we've got an eye-witness from Dekalb PD saying that two bombs went off in the parking structure across from the hospital. The second detonation was timed to take out the first responders. We've got at least fifteen people trapped inside. Ten casualties on the ground."

Faith tasted bile in her mouth. She looked down at the ground. There were cigarette butts where someone had been smoking. She thought of her dress uniform hanging in the closet, the number of funerals she would be attending in the coming weeks, the number of times she would have to stoically stand at attention while families fell apart.

"There's more." Maggie started up the stairs again. Her footsteps were not as brisk. "Two security guards found murdered in the basement. Two Dekalb PD killed when the bombers made their escape. One more is in surgery. Fulton County sheriff's deputy. Doesn't look good for her."

Faith resumed the climb at a slower pace, feeling gut-punched by the news. She let herself think of her children. Her own mother who had done this job. She knew what it was like to wait for news, to not know whether your parent was dead or alive or hurting and all you could do was sit in front of the television and try to convince yourself that this wasn't the time they wouldn't come home.

Amanda stopped for a moment. She put her hand on Faith's shoulder. "Ev knows you're with me."

Faith made her legs keep moving, kept climbing up the stairs because that was all that she could do. It was all any of them could do.

Her mother was watching Emma. Jeremy was at a video game tournament with his friends. They all knew Faith was downtown at the meeting because she had complained loudly about it to anyone who would listen.

Two security guards murdered.

Two cops murdered.

A deputy who probably wouldn't wake up from surgery.

All of those patients in the hospital. Sick people—sick children, because there wasn't just one hospital at Emory, there was Egleston Children's Hospital a block down the street. How many times had Faith driven Emma to the emergency room in the middle of the night? The nurses were so kind. Every doctor so patient. There were parking structures scattered around the building. An explosion could easily send one collapsing onto the hospital.

And then what? How many buildings had been destroyed during the aftershocks on 9/11?

Finally, Maggie pushed open the door at the top of the stairs. Sunlight sliced into Faith's retinas, but her eyes were already filled with angry tears.

The second detonation was timed to take out the first responders.

She heard the distant chop of helicopter blades. The black UH-1 Huey was almost older than Faith. SWAT used it for fast roping and fire rescue. Men were already suited up in the back. Full tactical gear. AR-15s. More first responders. They would have to go room by room, structure by structure, and ensure there were no other bombs waiting for the signal to detonate.

The chopping got tighter as the aircraft drew closer.

Faith's thoughts kept a silent cadence between the slicing rotors—

Two-guards-two-families.

Two-cops-two-families.

One-deputy-one-family.

"Mandy." Maggie had to yell to be heard over the roar of the engines. There was something in her voice that made the air go taut, a knot being jerked into a string.

"It's Will, Mandy. They hurt your boy."

4

Sunday, August 4, 1:54 p.m.

Sara made a mental note of the Porsche driver's estimated time of death as she checked the F-150 driver's lacerated scalp.

"Gas main exploded. We got the hell outta there." The truck passenger pointed toward the silver Chevy Malibu. "It's them people there you should be worried about. Guy in the back seat ain't lookin' so good."

Sara was glad to hear Will keeping pace as she jogged toward the Chevy. There was something not adding up about this car accident. The rear-end impact from the truck didn't feel severe enough to break the driver's neck. A mystery for the Atlanta medical examiner to figure out. Eventually. There was no telling how long it would take to clear out the gas main explosion. It was sheer luck that the construction site was empty.

Still—

Broken neck. No other signs of trauma. No lacerations. No contusions.

Weird.

The Malibu driver told Will, "My friend needs help."

"She's a doctor," Merle said.

"Sir?" Sara knelt down to examine the unconscious man in the back seat of the Malibu. The passenger beside him watched her every move. Airway clear. Breathing normal. "Sir, are you okay?"

Sara heard names being tossed around behind her.

Dwight, Clinton, Vince, Merle.

"Dwight?" Sara tried. The back of the Malibu was dark, the windows tinted almost black. She pulled the unconscious man into the sunlight. His pupils were reactive. His vertebrae were aligned. His pulse was strong and steady. His skin felt sticky, but then it was August. Everyone's skin felt sticky.

"I'm Hank," the passenger beside him told Sara. "You're a doctor?"

Sara nodded, but that was all she could give him. This idiot had knocked himself unconscious because he hadn't bothered to put on a seat belt. The gas main explosion would have critical cases: burns, traumatic brain injuries, crush trauma, projectiles.

Hank opened the door and got out of the car.

Sara glanced up.

Then she stared.

Blood soaked the back of Hank's leg.

He turned around, leaning his arms on the roof of the car. His shirt slid up. There was a gun tucked into the front of his pants. Sara heard him say, "Clinton, it's nobody's fault."

Sara looked at her hands. The stickiness wasn't from sweat. It was from blood. She brushed her palm along Dwight's back. The familiar puckered hole in his left shoulder indicated the same type of injury she'd seen on the back of Hank's leg.

A gunshot wound.

The Porsche driver's broken neck. The short skid marks on the road. The blood trail leading to the truck. The names—would Will catch the fake names? Dwight Yoakam. Hank Williams. Merle Haggard. Vince Gill. Clint Black. They were all country music singers.

Sara took a deep breath and held in her panic.

She carefully searched the Malibu for a weapon.

Dwight's holster was empty. Nothing on the floorboards. She looked between the front seats and almost gasped.

A woman had wedged herself into the footwell. Petite with short, platinum blonde hair. Arms wrapped tightly around her legs. She hadn't moved or made a noise this entire time, but now she raised up her head and showed her face.

Sara's heart shuddered to a stop.

Michelle Spivey.

The missing woman's eyes were bloodshot with tears. Her cheeks were sunken. Her lips were chapped and bleeding. She spoke soundlessly, desperately—

Help.

Sara felt her own mouth open. She took a stuttered breath. She heard another word echoing in her head, the same word that came to every woman's mind when they were surrounded by aggressive, damaged men—

Rape.

"Will." Sara's hands trembled as she fumbled in her pocket for the key fob. "I need you to get my medical bag out of the glove compartment of the car."

Please. She silently begged. *Get your gun and stop this.*

Will grabbed the key. She felt the brush of his fingers. He didn't look at her. Why wouldn't he look at her?

Clinton said, "Give us a hand, big guy. Let's go."

"Wait." Sara tried to slow them down. "He could have a neck injury or—"

"Ma'am, excuse me." Merle's beard was long but his hair was buzz-cut. He had to be police or military. All of them were. They stood the same way, moved the same way, followed orders the same way.

Not that it mattered. They had already gained the upper hand.

Will had clearly made the same calculation. He was looking at Sara now. She could feel his eyes on her. Sara could not look back at him because she knew that she would fall apart.

He said, "I'll get your bag."

Hank had limped around the car. He stood beside Sara—not too close, but close enough. Sara could feel the threat of him like a chemical burning her skin.

Will gripped the key fob in his fist as he walked toward the BMW. He was angry, which was good. Unlike most men, fury cleared Will's mind. His muscles were tensed. She focused all of her strength, all of her hope, onto his broad shoulders.

"Vale." Hank was speaking to Vince. He wasn't using their code names anymore. The pretense was over. Either Sara or Will had given themselves away or Hank had figured out that the police sirens they were hearing in the distance would soon find their way down Bella's street.

Hank lifted his chin, indicating Vale should follow the rest of the team to the car.

"Out," Hank told Michelle, his voice low. He had a gun in his hand. It was small, but it was still a gun.

Michelle winced as she crawled over the center console. She held up her pants with one hand. The fly was unzipped. Blood dripped over her fist, ran down her legs.

Sara's heart turned to glass.

Michelle's bare feet slapped the asphalt. A bout of dizziness made her reach for the car to steady herself. She had open sores between the webbing of her toes. Needle tracks. They had drugged her. They had cut her. She was bleeding between her legs.

Rape.

"Don't scream," Hank said.

Before Sara could react, a blinding pain shot from her wrist to her arm and into her shoulder. She was forced onto her knees. The road bit into her skin. Hank twisted her arm again. Sara had her fingers laced behind her head by the time Will reached the BMW.

He leaned into the car.

He looked up.

His jaw tightened down so hard that she could see the outline of the bones.

Sara watched his eyes track—Hank pointing a gun at her head. Michelle holding up her bloody pants. Three armed men surrounding him. No way to save Sara even if he sacrificed himself in the process.

This final realization brought an expression to his face that Sara had never seen before:

Fear.

"You let—" Michelle's voice was hoarse. She was talking to Hank. "You l-let him rape me."

The words were a hammer to Sara's heart.

"You c-can't—" Michelle gulped. "You can't pretend it's n-not happening. I'm telling you now. You know what he—"

"All right!" Hank shouted over her. He told Will, "I need you to slowly get your head out of the car and put your hands up."

Sara could only watch as Will complied. His eyes kept darting around. His brain was furiously working, trying to find a way out of this.

There was no way out.

They were going to kill Will. They were going to make Sara fix them and then they were going to tear her apart.

"You let him do it," Michelle whispered. "You let him h-hurt me. You let him—"

"We need a doctor," Hank shouted at Will. "No offense, brother. Wrong place, right time. Let's go, lady. Get in the car."

Sara had been expecting this moment, but she did not realize until now what her response would be.

"No."

She didn't move.

Her knees were part of the asphalt.

She was as sentient as a mountain.

Sara had been raped in college. Viciously, brutally, savagely raped. She had been robbed of her ability to have children. Had her sense of self, her sense of safety, forever stolen. The experience had altered her in ways that she still, almost twenty years later, was discovering. She had vowed that she would never let that happen to her ever again.

Hank's grip tightened around her arm.

"No." Sara wrenched away from him. The fear had drained away. She would die before she let them take her. Sara had never been more certain of anything in her life. "I'm not going with you."

"Lady, that wasn't a gas main that exploded at the campus." Hank looked at Will. "We just blew up dozens, maybe hundreds of people. Do you think I give a shit about having your blood on my hands?"

His words nearly cut her in two. All of those sick and injured people. Students and children and staff who had devoted their lives to helping others.

"No," Sara repeated. She was openly crying. They were going to kill her eventually. All she could control was what happened between now and then.

"Get in the car."

"I won't go with you. I won't help you. You'll have to shoot me." She stared her resignation into Will. She needed him to understand why she was refusing to go.

Will's throat worked. Tears were in his eyes.

Slowly, finally, he nodded.

"How about I kill her?" Hank pointed the gun at Michelle.

"Do it." Michelle's voice was strong, devoid of her earlier stutter. "Go ahead, you spineless piece of shit." Her fist was clenched around the waist of her pants. Sara could see a bloody bandage, popped sutures, at her bikini line.

Had they operated on her?

"You still think you're a good man," Michelle told Hank. "What's your father going to say when he hears about who you really are? I heard you talking about your dad, how he's your hero, how you wanted to make him proud. He's sick. He's going to die. His last breath, he's gonna know what kind of monster he helped bring into this world."

Clinton laughed. "Damn, girl, the way you're talking makes me wonder how tight your daughter's pussy is."

There was a flurry of movement above Sara's head. Hank's arm swung around, pointing the gun at Clinton.

Click-click-click.

The gun had jammed.

"You son of a—" Clinton's Glock was out of his holster.

Hank dragged Michelle down to the ground as the gun fired. Sara closed her eyes. She stayed exactly where she was, sitting up on her knees, fingers laced behind her head, and waited for the bullet.

There wasn't one.

She heard two more gunshots in rapid succession.

Sara opened her eyes. Merle lay dead on the ground. Vince/Vale had been wounded. He fell out of the open door of the car. Blood flowered from the wound in his side.

Will had shot them. He was turning to do the same to Clinton when the man tackled him to the ground.

Sara pushed herself up to run.

She was flung back down.

Hank's arm wrapped around her neck. Chokehold. Her vision swam. She clawed at his skin. "Let me go!" she screamed, biting, scratching, kicking.

There was a dark blur out of the corner of her eye. The distinctive, long barrel of a Glock 22. Called a man-stopper because the .40 caliber ammo would stop a man dead in his tracks.

Hank had the gun pointed at the ground. His finger rested above the trigger guard, ready to fire if needed.

It wasn't needed.

Clinton was pounding his fists into Will's belly. Liver. Spleen. Pancreas. Kidneys. He was using his hands like a pile driver to break them apart.

"Stop him," Sara pleaded. "He's going to kill—"

Will's hand slashed out at Clinton's face. The folding knife. The four-inch blade was razor sharp. Blood ripped a line through the air.

Clinton reared back.

Will stabbed him in the groin.

Sara stood up, but Hank kept her from running. His arm was tight around her neck. He kept the Glock pointed downward, but his finger was stiff beside the trigger. The muscles in his forearm were like rope.

"Will—" His name got caught in Sara's throat.

He coughed up blood. He rolled to his side. He was clutching his belly, trying to stand up, looking for the revolver.

Hank told Sara, "You go with us, or I'll shoot him in the chest."

A sob bruised her throat. She reached out her hand as if she could help him.

Will's legs tensed as he tried to get up again. Vomit roiled from his mouth. Blood dripped from the back of his head. He got to his knees, but fell flat.

Sara cried out as if her own body had slammed into the ground.

"Doc?" Hank finally raised the gun, aiming it at Will.

Sara walked toward the BMW. She could barely stay upright. Her knees kept locking out. Will was still writhing on the ground. She looked up the street. Her mother was standing on the sidewalk. Cathy had a shotgun in her hands, an old double barrel that had been gathering dust above Bella's fireplace for the last fifty years.

Sara shook her head, pleading with Cathy not to interfere.

Hank dragged Michelle toward the BMW. He threw her at Vale to take care of. He was heading toward Will, his Glock at his side.

"You promised." Even as Sara said the words she understood the stupidity of trusting a mass murderer.

"Drive." Vale shoved Sara into the driver's seat. She could see out of the open passenger-side door. Will was on all fours. Vomit and blood dripped from his mouth. His eyes were closed. Sweat ran down his face.

"Fuck," Clinton muttered, climbing into the seat behind Sara. "Jesus fuck. Let's get out of here."

Sara watched helplessly as Hank swung back his leg. He was going to kick Will in the head.

"Will!" she screamed.

He grabbed the leg, dragging Hank down to the sidewalk. There was no struggle. Will straddled him. He started beating his face; quickly, methodically, furiously.

"Leave him!" Clinton yelled.

Vale strained to reach behind him, blindly feeling for the revolver that was stuck down the front of his pants. He was panicked from the gunshot wound in his side. Blood had soaked his shirt.

"I said fucking leave him!" Clinton pointed his Glock at Vale's head. "Now!"

"Jesus, Carter!" Vale hoisted himself into the passenger's seat of the car even as he said, "We can't leave Hurley."

Clinton. Hank. Vince.

Carter. Hurley. Vale.

"Drive!" The Glock banged against the side of Sara's skull. "Go!"

She put the engine in gear. She swung the car around. She saw Will in the side mirror. Merle was lying dead on the ground beside him. He was still straddling Hank or Hurley or whoever the hell the man was.

Kill him, too, Sara thought. *Beat the life out of him.*

The shotgun went off. Cathy had aimed for the tires but hit the rear panel instead.

"Fuck!" Vale screamed. "What the fuck, Carter!"

"Shut up!" Carter slammed his fist into Sara's seat. Blood dripped from the slash in his forehead. The handle of Will's knife was sticking out of his thigh. "Go right! Go right!"

Sara swerved right. Her heart was pounding so hard that she felt dizzy. Her stomach was clenched. She felt her bladder wanting to release. Vale was sitting beside her. Carter was directly behind her, his shoulder pressed against Michelle's. Dwight was passed out in the seat behind Vale, but there was no telling how long that would last. She had trapped herself with these monsters. Her only consolation was that Will was still alive.

"Fuck!" Vale rubbed his face with his hands. He was running out of adrenaline. His body was registering the shock of the gunshot wound. His breath came in sharp, panicked pants. "He got me in the chest, bro! I can't—I can't breathe!"

"Shut up, you fucking pussy!"

An Atlanta police cruiser was heading straight toward them, full lights and sirens. Sara prayed for it to stop. The car shook the BMW as it zoomed past.

"Go left!" Carter's voice was as sharp as the siren. "Here! Go left!"

She swerved onto Oakdale. Sara's eyes followed the cruiser as long as she could. The brake lights glowed red as it turned left onto Lullwater.

Toward Will.

"I can feel the air seeping out!" Vale sounded terrified. He could help set off bombs inside of a hospital but he was whining about a hole in his side. "Help me! What do I do?"

Sara said nothing. She was thinking about Will. Bruised ribs. Broken sternum. If the spleen had ruptured, he could be bleeding into his belly. Had she sacrificed herself only to leave him dying in the street? And now this man, this whining child, wanted her to help him?

"You're a doctor!" Vale whimpered. "Help me!"

Sara had never in her life felt so little empathy for another human being. She spoke through clenched teeth: "Seal the wound."

Vale lifted up his shirt, hand shaking as he reached to cover the hole.

"Put your finger inside," Sara told him, which was bullshit because his chest cavity was filling up with blood. Each time he breathed, he pushed more air into the pleural space, which pressed on the lung with the hole in it, causing the lung to collapse more quickly. Eventually, pressure would build up on the opposite lung and the heart and veins, causing them to collapse, too.

Her only concern was that it would take him too long to die.

"Jesus!" Vale screeched. The idiot had actually shoved his finger into the hole. The pain took away his breath. His eyes were so wide that the whites showed. Mercifully, he was in too much agony to complain.

Vale wasn't the one she should be worried about, anyway. Carter was angry, focused and prepared to do whatever it took to get them out of here. Sara was aware that at any moment, he could reach around the seat and grab her neck.

She looked at the time.

2:04 p.m.

The golden hour was already ticking down on Will's clock. Internal bleeding could be surgically repaired, but how quickly could they get him to a surgeon? He would need to be airlifted to a trauma center. Who would take him? Every cop in the vicinity would be responding to the explosion.

Two bombs detonated on campus. She couldn't think about that. Wouldn't think about that. All that mattered was Will.

"Pass them!" Carter yelled. "Get in the other lane!"

Sara hurtled into oncoming traffic. Tires screeched. Two cars smacked into each other. Vale screamed again. Sara pressed down on the gas. They were approaching Ponce de Leon.

"Blow the light!"

Sara put on her seat belt. She went through the light. Horns blared. The tires lifted off the ground as she struggled to keep the wheel straight.

Which—*why?*

Crash the car into a tree. Into a telephone pole. Into a house. Sara had the airbag in the steering wheel. Her seat belt. She didn't have a hole in her lung or a knife sticking out of her leg or a gunshot wound in her shoulder.

Michelle.

The woman was sitting in the middle of the back seat. On impact, she would fly through the windshield. She could break her neck. Broken metal and glass could rip open an artery. The car could run over her before she had a chance to scramble away.

Do it, Michelle had dared Hank, staring into the black hole of a gun. *Go ahead, you spineless piece of shit.*

Up ahead, there was a dog-leg turn in the road.

Sara would go straight. She would ram the car into the brick house just beyond the red light.

Will was okay. He understood why Sara had told them to shoot her. He knew that none of this was his fault.

Her shoulders relaxed. Her mind felt clear. The calmness inside of her body told her this was the right thing to do.

The turn was coming. Thirty yards. Twenty. Sara punched the gas. She held tight to the steering wheel. She tried again to find Michelle in the mirror.

The woman's eyes were wide. She was crying. Terrified.

At the last minute, Sara jerked the wheel right, then left, taking the dog-leg on two tires. The car bounced back to the ground. She went through two stop signs. She backed her foot off the gas. She tried to find Michelle again, but the woman had pulled up her legs and buried her head in her knees.

"F-fuck." Vale's nose whistled as he tried to draw air into his collapsing lungs. He had seen what Sara was going to do but been helpless to stop her.

"Slow down," Carter muttered, oblivious. "Jesus fuck, my nuts are on fire." He punched the back of Sara's seat. "You're the doctor. Tell me what to do."

Sara couldn't speak. Her throat was filled with cotton. Where was her earlier resolve? Why did she care what happened to Michelle? She had to start thinking about herself—how she was going to get out of this, whether it was by managing an escape or controlling her own death.

"Come on!" Carter jabbed the seat again. "Tell me what to do."

Sara reached up to the rearview mirror. Her hands were shaking so hard that she could barely find the right angle. The reflection showed Carter's injury. The knife handle was sticking out of his right inner thigh. Will had driven in the blade at an upward angle. The muscle was holding it in place.

Femoral artery. Femoral vein. Genitofemoral nerve.

Sara tried to clear her throat. Her tongue was thick in her mouth. She could taste bile. "The knife is pressing against a nerve. Pull it out."

Carter knew better. The blade could also be damming a nick in the artery. "How about I use it to cut open your face? Turn right, then left at the light."

Sara hooked a right at the stop sign. The light was green when she turned left onto Moreland Avenue. Little Five Points. There were only a few cars on the road. The parking lots in front of the shops and restaurants were sparsely packed. People had probably been directed to shelter in place. Or they were at home watching the news. Or the police had set up a tight perimeter around the hospital—so tight that the BMW had managed to get outside the boundary before they had time to implement the plan.

"Turn off that fucking noise," Carter said.

The seat belt chime. Sara had not noticed the dinging sound from the passenger's seat belt being left undone, but now it was all she could hear.

Vale didn't try to stop the noise. He closed his eyes. His lips were tensed. His finger was still inside of the hole. Every bump, every shift, must have felt like torture.

Sara scanned the road for potholes.

"Shut it off!" Carter yelled. "Help him, God dammit!"

Michelle reached through the split in the seats. She was moving slowly, painfully. The blood on her hands had dried to a burgundy film. She started to draw the belt over Vale's lap. Her hand hovered a few inches away from the buckle.

His gun was in the waist of his jeans.

Sara's body went rigid. She prayed for Michelle to pull the weapon and start shooting.

The buckle clicked. The chime stopped. Michelle sat back.

Sara let her gaze slip down to Vale's lap.

Her heart broke into a million pieces.

Michelle had strapped the revolver against his stomach.

Why?

"Bro?" Carter sounded nervous, uncertain. "Should I use my phone?"

Vale didn't answer. His teeth were chattering.

"Bro?" Carter kicked the back of his seat.

Vale screamed, "No!" His hand wrapped around the grab bar by the door. He hissed air through his teeth. "Orders," he said. "We can't—" He was cut off by a spasm of pain.

"Fuck." Carter wiped blood from his eyes. He told Sara, "Keep going straight. All the way to the interstate."

He was taking them to 285. They were going to skirt the perimeter of the city. The direction didn't seem arbitrary. If these men were really cops or military, then they would have a plan B—another getaway car, a rendezvous point, a safe house in which to lay low until the attention died down.

Sara tried to focus her thoughts on how to stop the car before they reached the interstate. The Atlanta police cruiser she had watched turn left onto Lullwater was her only source of hope.

If Will wasn't able to, Cathy would relay the details to the police officer. He would call command. Command would blast out an alert to every phone and computer in the tri-state area.

Three suspected domestic terrorists. Heavily armed. Two hostages.

The BMW was fully equipped. Satellite radio. GPS navigation. There was an SOS button above the rearview mirror. Sara had never pressed it before. She knew it was part of the system's telemetric roadside assistance, but did it send out a silent signal or would an actual human being's voice come through the speakers asking how to help?

"Dash?" Carter was trying to wake the man in the back seat.

Not Dwight.

Dash.

"Bro, come on." He reached over Michelle and patted the man's cheek, trying to rouse him. "Come on, bro. Wake up."

Dash's lips moved. He started to mumble. Sara adjusted the mirror again. She could see his eyes tracking back and forth under his eyelids.

She scanned ahead again, but not for potholes. There were more cars on the streets the farther away they got from Emory. Could she flash the headlights? Should she swerve erratically? Would either of those things endanger anyone who tried to help?

"Why isn't he waking up?" Carter was turning Dash's head side to side. "Vale, get that medical kit out of the glove box."

Vale didn't move, but Sara saw the key was still in the lock.

The gun.

"Dash!" Carter yelled, slapping at his face. "God dammit."

"He needs a hospital." Sara pried her eyes away from the key. "All I have in my bag is Band-Aids and disinfectant."

"Fuck!" Carter punched his fist into the back of her seat. "Dash, come on, bro."

Sara cleared her throat again. She pressed her palm to her chest. Her heartbeats clicked as fast as a stopwatch.

Think-think-think-think.

She told Carter, "He's been out almost fifteen minutes. He's probably in a coma." Another lie. His brain was clearly trying to reboot itself. "We should leave him near a fire station so they can help him."

"Shit. This is Dash we're talking about. We ain't leaving him nowhere." Carter reached over Michelle again.

"No!" the woman screamed. She scrambled out of his way, pushing herself over the seat and into the cargo area. Her shoulders were pressed to the glass. Arms spread. She looked at Sara with a wild panic in her eyes.

Sara stared back at her in the mirror. She let her eyes dart to Michelle's right.

Her medical bag was in the storage bin.

Scalpels. Needles. Sedatives.

Michelle broke contact. She crumpled in on herself. Legs drawn up to her chest. Head on her knees.

"What's wrong with him?" Carter snapped his fingers in front of Dash's face.

The man's eyelids had slit open, but he wasn't responding.

"Dash? Come on, bro. Wake up."

Sara looked at the clock.

2:08 p.m.

Cathy would take care of Will. Make sure that he was taken to the hospital. Question the doctors. Be there when he woke up from surgery. She would advocate for him the same way she had for Jeffrey.

Wouldn't she?

"Doctor?"

Sara looked into the mirror. Michelle was talking to her.

"Help him," Michelle said. "Dash isn't—he's bad, but not like—"

"Shut your fucking mouth," Carter warned. The only thing keeping him from jumping over the seat was the knife in his leg.

Look on your right, Sara silently begged the woman. *Open the black bag.*

Michelle stared at Sara's reflection. She shook her head once. She knew about the bag. She wasn't going to do anything.

Sara's heart sank. She was completely alone.

"Hey." Carter slapped Dash again, hard enough for the *smack* to fill the car. "Bitch, tell me what to do."

Sara had to swallow past her grief. "He needs a stimulus."

Carter slapped him again. "I'm fucking stimulating him."

"Stick your finger in the bullet hole in his shoulder."

"Yeah, that's working out great for him."

Sara studied Vale with a cold eye. His wheezing had turned sporadic. His lips were tinged blue. His nostrils collapsed and expanded as he desperately tried to bring air into his deflating lungs.

"Hey," Carter said. "I think he's waking up."

Dash's eyelids began to flutter. A rumble came from deep inside his throat. He raised his hands, the right higher than the left, fingers spread, like a marionette doll.

"What's he doing?" Carter was alarmed.

Sara kept her silence. She tried to find Michelle again, but the woman had returned to her cowered position.

Carter demanded, "What's wrong with him?"

Dash's eyes had opened. The rumble in his throat turned into a murmur. He blinked once. Twice. Slowly, he took in the passengers around him. Michelle. Carter. Vale. He looked at Sara, confused.

"Who fhee?" His words slurred. "She. Who if—"

"We p-picked up a doctor," Carter stammered. He was clearly scared, which meant that Dash was important. "We lost Hurley and Morgan."

"What—" Dash tried. "Wha—"

"We took a doctor." Carter didn't answer the implied question. "I got a fucking knife in my crotch. Vale's not sounding so good."

Dash blinked again. He was still disoriented, but coming around.

Sara lied, "His pupils are fixed. He's probably bleeding into his skull. An aneurysm or—"

"Fuck." Carter wiped sweat off his face. He scanned the side of the road.

Dash cleared his throat. "What happened?" He looked at Sara. "Who is she?"

"I told you—" Carter gave up. He asked Sara, "What's wrong with him?"

"Post-traumatic amnesia." She tried to think of a way to scare him into dropping Dash by the side of the road. "It's a sign of a deep brain injury. We need to leave him at a hospital."

"Fuck-fuck-fuck."

Dash's hand went up to his face. He touched his cheek with his fingers. He squeezed his eyes shut. He would be feeling nauseous, disoriented. But he was coming back into himself. She could tell by the controlled movements. The way his eyes were focusing on fixed points.

"Dammit." Carter was looking out the front windshield. "Don't even think about waving this guy down."

There was a lone squad car coming from the opposite direction. Sara held her breath, waiting for the cop to recognize the BMW from a system-wide alert.

Dash reached clumsily between the seats and rested his hand on her arm. "Stay cool, miss."

His voice was soft, but his authority was clear. Vale was the whiner. Carter was the hothead. Dash was the man they all obeyed.

Sara watched the cruiser disappear in the side mirror. No brake lights. He wasn't slowing down. There was a license-plate scanner mounted to the front and rear of his car. The system would've pinged her plate.

Which meant that the BMW was not in the system.

"Carter." Dash winced as he leaned back. He looked older now that he was awake. Fine lines wrinkled from his eyes. "That bullet still in my shoulder?"

"Yeah," Carter said. "Blood ain't flowing as much."

"Well, that could be a good thing or a bad thing." He carefully enunciated each word. He wasn't 100 percent, but he was trying to make them think that he was. "Isn't that right, Doctor?"

Sara did not answer. The shoulder was mostly bone and cartilage. The bullet would've been white-hot going in, cauterizing the tissue.

Bad for Sara. Good for Dash.

He groaned as he crossed his leg over his knee. "Carter, use my shoelace to strap the knife to your leg. You don't want it to do any more damage. Paracord snake knot lanyard."

Carter started unlacing the boot.

Dash said, "Doctor, we need medical attention. All of us."

"I'm a pediatrician," Sara said, which was technically true. She was also a board-certified medical examiner and crime scene investigator. "I'm not a surgeon. These are serious medical issues."

"They are in-geed." Dash was losing control of his words again. His eyes were watering. The sunlight was too much stimulus. He was clearly concussed. Sara had no idea how badly. Every brain reacted to trauma in its own way.

Dash cleared his throat. He rubbed his fingers into his eyes. "Carter, has it occurred to you that we're in a stolen, traceable vehicle with a GPS system?"

Carter was focused on tying the lanyard. "We didn't have a lot of options. We had to get out of there. Right, Vale?"

Vale mumbled a non-answer. His index finger was still deep in the hole in his side. His other hand gripped the grab bar. Sara studied the revolver trapped underneath the seat belt. Carter's hands were busy tying down the knife. Dash's reflexes were compromised. She could—

"Miss." Dash put his hand on Sara's shoulder. He said, "Follow that van, please."

A white van was turning into a strip club off of Moreland. The sign outside showed a scantily clad woman beside the words Club Shady Lady. Work trucks filled the parking spaces. The white van braked, then took a right turn behind the building. There was a Lay's Potato Chip logo on the side.

Dash said, "Ah, that's lucky. Keep following."

Sara drove slowly into the narrow alley. She took another turn. The building was on the right, a thick stand of trees on the left. There was no way she could reach over, unlock the glove box and retrieve Will's gun without being shot. She could open the door, roll out. Carter couldn't chase her with the knife in his leg. Vale was too terrified to move. Dash was in no condition to pursue her.

Would Michelle help? Or would she just wait for the bad things to happen?

The white van was parked beside the service entrance. The delivery man got out. He gave them no more than a glance as he opened the van doors and started pulling out boxes.

"Stop here," Dash ordered.

Sara put the gear in park. The music from the strip club was so loud that she could feel it in her chest.

She looked at the glove box again.

"Vale," Dash said. "I wonder if you can fetch me whatever is in that glove compartment our friend seems so interested in."

Sara looked out the window at the trees. She could hear the lock click open. Vale's gasp of shock when he saw Will's service weapon.

Dash took it from him, saying, "Thank you, sir."

Sara closed her eyes. She thought about the BMW's safety features. The doors locked automatically when the speedometer hit fifteen miles per hour. The handle required two pulls to open. Could she do it fast enough to escape?

Dash seemed to realize something. "Where are Hurley and Monroe?"

"Dead," Carter answered. "We had to leave them. Fucking guy came out of nowhere. It was like punching a sack of rocks."

Sara looked at him in the mirror. His head was down. He was still tying the knot.

Dash asked Sara, "What's going on with our friend in the front seat?"

"I don't have the correct diagnostic equipment," she said, implying it was necessary. "My best guess is his lung is collapsing."

Dash asked, "Pardon me again, but can't you put in something hollow, bring air back into the lungs that way?"

Sara didn't know if he was testing her. Saran Wrap would've probably helped make a seal around the wound, and she had an IV needle in her medical bag that could deflate the tension.

She decided to answer the question with a question: "Would you put a hollow tube in a flat tire to re-inflate it?"

Vale sucked in a shallow breath of air. He was trying to follow along. He still had his finger uselessly sticking into the hole in his side. She wanted to tell him to stick it in farther. If the shock didn't kill him, the infection would.

"We should get to know each other," Dash said. "What should I call you?"

"Sara." She watched the driver of the white van. He was doing his job, stacking boxes onto a dolly, checking the order on his tablet.

"Last name?"

Sara hesitated. He wasn't asking to be sociable. He could look her up online. Sara was listed on the GBI's website as a special agent attached to the medical examiner's office. There was a big difference between kidnapping a pediatrician and kidnapping a government agent.

"Earnshaw," she said, giving them her mother's maiden name.

Dash nodded. She could tell he knew she was lying. "You got any children?"

"Two."

"All right, Dr. Sara Earnshaw. I know you don't wanna be here, but lend us your chauffeur services for a little bit longer and we'll get you back to that husband and kids of yours."

Sara bit her lip. She nodded. She could tell he was lying, too.

Dash opened the car door. The thumping bass of the club music shook her eardrums.

He held up his hand to block the sunlight. He called behind him, "Michelle, I'll need you to join me."

Michelle robotically picked her way over the back seat. She flinched away from Carter. She avoided Sara's questioning look. Her pants were still hanging open when she jumped out of the car. The gravel must've been sharp on her bare feet, but she gave no reaction.

What had they done to break her so irrevocably?

"Let's go." Dash indicated that Michelle should walk toward the van. He'd tucked his hand into the opening between his shirt buttons, fashioning a sort of sling. The bullet had missed his humerus. There was muscle damage that would make it hurt when he moved, but he could still move.

Carter mumbled, "What's he doing?"

Sara knew what he was doing, even as she silently prayed that it would not happen.

The delivery man came out of the building. His dolly was empty. He had his back to them as he closed the service door. Dash reached into his holster and pulled out Will's gun. The delivery man turned around, and that was the last movement his body voluntarily made.

Dash shot him twice in the face.

Sara watched the closed door at the rear of the building. No one came out. They hadn't heard the gunshots over the music. Or they'd heard them, but this was the type of neighborhood where gunfire was not unusual.

Carter said, "If you tell him what happened back there, I'll make sure you regret it."

Sara looked into the mirror. "That you abandoned Hurley? Or that your *bro* Hurley tried to kill you?"

Carter's eyes slid toward the front. He silently watched Dash and Michelle load the dead delivery man's body into the van.

Carter said, "I figure it'll take less than ten minutes for me to fuck that bad attitude out of your mouth."

Sara felt her throat constrict. She looked at her fingers wrapped tightly around the steering wheel. She had transferred blood from Dash's shoulder wound onto the leather. Merle's blood had to be mixed in there, too; Sara had touched his head wound at the crash site. Carter's leg had probably bled in the back seat of her car. Vale had provided his own DNA in the front.

She told Carter, "Enjoy that burning sensation you're feeling in your balls." She locked eyes with him in the mirror. "Once that knife is out, that's the last time you'll feel your scrotum."

Vale gave a sharp wheeze as he inhaled. "Sh . . . shut up . . ." He pointed his revolver at Sara. His hand was steady. "Walk a-around . . . the front. The front . . . of the c-car."

Sara reached for the door handle. She saw the time on her watch.

2:17 p.m.

She didn't pull the handle.

Her Apple Watch.

The back door opened. Carter slid out of the car, careful not to bump the knife. He clicked the door shut. He stood outside the car, waiting.

Sara's mind raced through the options as she slowly pulled twice on the handle. The watch had both cellular and GPS. She could make a phone call, but the speaker would play the caller's voice. Sending a text was too cumbersome. There was a Walkie-Talkie app, but she would have to tap the icon, scroll to the right person, and hold the yellow button long enough to send a message through.

She got out of the car. She moved slowly, trying to buy herself some time.

"Go around the front of the car and help Vale." Carter showed her the Glock, as if she'd forgotten about it. "Don't fuck around or I'll put a bullet in your head."

Sara tried to stall. "You should leave him. He's going to die anyway."

"We don't leave men behind."

"Does Hurley know that?"

He punched her in the stomach. The pain was an explosion inside of her body. Sara doubled over. Dropped to her knees. Her head started to swim. She couldn't breathe.

"Get up, bitch."

Sara pressed her forehead to the ground. Saliva dripped from her mouth. Her hands had automatically gone to her stomach. The muscles spasmed. She blinked open her eyes. The watch screen was glowing. She tapped the Walkie-Talkie button. Faith was the first name on her list. She held the yellow circle down and said, "Carter, do you—do you really think the cops aren't going to spot a white potato chip van on 285?"

"Not your problem."

Gravel crunched under tires. The van had pulled up.

Sara raised her head. The world tilted sideways. She could barely make it to her feet. The pain in her belly forced her to walk doubled over. She tried not to think about Will experiencing the same agony, but worse. She had to steady herself on the car as she made her way around to the other side.

Vale had already opened the door. His lips looked bruised. His eyelids drooped. He was decompensating faster than she had hoped.

"Gimme," Carter said, grabbing the revolver away from Vale.

Sara had no choice but to help the injured man from the car. Vale's arm went around her shoulder. His other arm was still looped around his chest, his finger jammed inside the gunshot wound.

"Hurry up." Carter waved the gun to get her moving.

Vale tried to push himself up with his legs. He was muscular, much heavier than he looked. Sara took a step away when he was expecting her to step forward. Instinctively, she tried to keep him from falling, but she could not move quickly enough.

Vale landed on his back. What little breath he had left was knocked out of him. He gasped for air. His eyes were wild.

Sara went to her knees. She didn't give a shit about Vale. She didn't want to be punched again. She pretended to examine him—looking at his pupils, pressing her ear to his heart. His shirt was raised. Blood dribbled in a steady stream from the gunshot wound. Bright red, not venal blood but arterial. The bullet had entered through the axilla, where all the nerves and arteries were bundled.

Dash was out of the van. He helped Vale sit up. He told Sara, "A hand with my friend, if you don't mind?"

There was something weirdly commanding about his polite, calm tone. He wasn't helplessly panicked like Vale or blinded by anger like Carter. Dash struck Sara as the type of person who could wield his moods like a sword. She didn't want to ever find herself on the sharp end.

Along with Dash, Sara used her shoulder to raise Vale to standing. They got him to the van. He was able to crawl on his own into the back.

Sara felt Dash's hand on her shoulder.

"Let's take that off, please, ma'am."

He had noticed the watch.

Sara turned the face down as she undid the strap. Instead of handing it to Dash, she threw it into the woods.

"Thank you," he said, as if this was exactly what he'd wanted to happen. He motioned for Michelle. He didn't have to give her instruction. She silently helped move the delivery man out of the van and into the BMW.

Why was she so compliant?

"Gonna fuck you up," Carter whispered to Sara. He edged into the van on his ass, dragging his stiff leg across the floor.

The driver's side door shut. Michelle put on her seat belt. She turned on the ignition. She put both hands on the wheel. She stared straight ahead, waiting to be told what to do next.

Why?

"I just need another coupla three seconds." Dash had managed to open the fuel door to the BMW. He pulled an emergency road flare out of his pocket. He struck the top, which was like a giant match head. Burning white sparks shot out like a sparkler.

He told Sara, "You might want to hurry."

Sara got into the back of the van. The last thing she saw before she closed the sliding door was Dash jamming the burning flare into the mouth of the gas tank.

He jumped into the front seat. "Go."

Michelle hit the gas. The van lurched. They took a sharp turn around the building.

Gasoline burned, but only the fumes could cause an explosion. Dash had timed it right. They were fifty yards away when the shock of the blast reached the van.

If the police found the BMW, all the forensics would be burned away.

The blood on the steering wheel. The blood on the seats. The delivery man's body.

All gone.

"Shit," Carter muttered. "Shit-shit-shit." The knife had shifted despite his best efforts. He was cupping his groin. He glanced over at Sara, a helpless look in his eyes.

She looked away.

Dash called, "We good, brothers?"

"Yeah," Vale mumbled.

"Hell, yeah," Carter said, though his voice was hoarse.

Sara listened to the steady drone of the wheels on the road. She reached into her empty pocket. She used her thumb to methodically clean beneath her fingernails.

She had scratched Vale's back when he fell down, gouging out rows of his skin.

At the site of the car accident, she had touched Merle's head wound and rubbed her fingers clean on her shorts. She had run her palm across Dash's wounded shoulder. She had transferred Hurley's blood from the back seat of the Malibu. She would put her hand in the pool of blood seeping out of Carter's leg when they eventually dragged her out of the van.

Sara knew the statistics. They were taking her to a second location. Statistically, her chances of survival had been cut to roughly 12 percent.

She was not going to end up like Michelle Spivey—alive, but not alive.

Whatever it took, she was going to make these men kill her. Her only job between now and then was to take a piece of them down with her.

Sara wanted her family to have closure. She wanted Will to get vengeance.

Her own sweat was on her shorts by virtue of the fact that she was wearing them. Vale's skin cells were in the pocket. Merle's blood would transfer from her hand. Dash's blood. Eventually Carter's.

Their DNA would conclusively link all four men to Sara when her body was found.

5

Sunday, August 4, 2:01 p.m.

"Where are they taking her?" Will grabbed Hank by the shirt and gave him a violent shake. "Tell me where, God dammit!"

Hank stared up from the bloody pulp of his face. His teeth were broken. His nose was bent to the side. His jaw was crooked.

Will scooped up the revolver from the sidewalk. He cocked the hammer. He took aim.

"Don't shoot him!" Cathy screamed.

Will felt the same jolt of recognition. Sara's voice, but not her voice.

"She's gone!" Cathy gripped the shotgun with both hands, shaking with grief. "You let them steal my daughter!"

His eyes started to water. He had to squint against the sunlight.

"You did this!" Cathy stared straight at him. Straight into him. "My son-in-law would've never let this happen."

Will felt her words harder than any blow he'd ever taken. He uncocked the hammer on the gun. He wiped his mouth with the back of his hand. He forced the part of his brain that understood Cathy was right to shut down.

A siren whooped. An Atlanta police cruiser screeched to a stop ten yards away.

Will tossed the revolver onto the sidewalk. His hands went into the air. He told Cathy, "Put down the—"

"Put it down!" the cop screamed. He rested his gun on the open door of his cruiser. "Now!"

Slowly, Cathy placed the shotgun at her feet.

She raised her hands.

"I'm GBI." Will worked to keep his tone even. "This is one of the bombers. He had a team. They abducted a wo—"

"Where's your ID?"

"I don't have my wallet. My badge number is 398. A woman was—" Will had to stop. Vomit had rushed up his throat. He spit it out. "A woman was abducted. Silver BMW. License plate—" Will couldn't remember the number. His brain felt like a balloon that was trying to float away. "BMW X5 hybrid. There are four more men. Three."

Fuck.

Will had to close his eyes to stop the world from spinning. Three men? Four? Merle's dead body was between him and the cop. Hank had been beaten senseless.

Will said, "Three men. Call it in. BMW X5. A wo— two women abducted."

"The radios are jammed." The cop hesitated. He wanted to believe Will. "Phones are down. I can't—"

Will didn't have time for this shit.

He picked up Hank and threw him against the hood of the cruiser. He wrenched together Hank's wrists and pinned them together with one hand. He kicked out his legs. He patted down the man's pockets. Android phone. Folded money. Some coins. Driver's license and an insurance card.

Will matched the photo on the license to Hank's face. He watched the tiny letters of the name jump like fleas across the white background. He handed over both to the cop. "I don't have my glasses."

"Hurley," the cop read. "Robert Jacob Hurley."

"Hurley." Will saw the bullet hole in the back of his leg. He wanted to jam a pencil into it. "He's going to bleed out. We have to get him to the hospital."

Will grabbed Hurley up by the collar. He stumbled, the road tilted like a funhouse.

The cop tried, "Are you—"

"Let's go." Will shoved Hurley into the back of the cruiser and slammed the door so hard that the car rocked.

Will braced his hands on the roof. He closed his eyes, trying to regain his equilibrium. He was suddenly aware of all of the pain in his body. The skin on his knuckles was broken open. Rivulets of blood were streaming down his neck. There were no words to describe what was going on inside his belly. Every single organ felt like it was strapped tight with a thousand rubber bands. His ribs had turned into straight razors.

Will walked around the car. The front door was at the wrong end of a telescope. He blinked his eyes. He fumbled for the handle.

The minute he was inside, the car lurched forward.

Will didn't look at Cathy as they pulled away.

She called his name.

Will.

Sara's voice, but not her voice.

The cop said, "I'm getting something." He had his phone to his ear. "It's ringing."

"A woman was—" Will felt his stomach clench. He leaned over and threw up into the floorboard. The splatter went everywhere. He had to wipe it off of his face. "Sorry."

The cop rolled down the front windows.

Will's eyes started to close. He could feel his body wanting to give up. He told the cop, "Silver BMW. Michelle Spivey was with them."

"Mi—" the cop's mouth dropped open.

"They were a team. Cops. Military."

"Shit. Phone stopped ringing." the cop hung up and dialed again. The cruiser cut into the empty lane. Coasted through Emory Village. There were people on the sidewalk running toward the hospital. Druid Hills was filled with doctors and medical support staff and people from the CDC. They were all doing what Will and Sara had tried to do—reach the site of the disaster as quickly as possible.

Will's vision fought him as he tried to look at his watch. It took all of his focus to make the numbers sharpen.

2:06 p.m.

"Thank fuck," the cop mumbled. "This is 3-2-9-9-4."

Will felt the anvil lift off of his chest. The call had finally gone through.

"I need the commander. I've got one of the bombing suspects in custody. I have details on—"

"S-shilver BMW X5." Will heard his words slur. "Three sush-pects. They abducted two wahh—" He couldn't get the information to come out. His head didn't want to stay upright. "Amanda Wagner. You need to fah . . . tell . . . tell her they took Sara. Tell her . . .". He had to close his eyes against the sunlight. "Tell her I fucked up."

Will's eyelids peeled open like wet cotton. Thumb tacks were drilling into his pupils. Tears leaked out as he struggled to maintain consciousness. There wasn't a moment of disorientation or forgetfulness. He remembered exactly what had happened and knew exactly where he was.

He swung his legs over the side of the hospital gurney. He nearly fell to the floor.

"Steady." Nate, the cop from the cruiser, was still with him. "You passed out. You're in the ER."

Will strained to hear him over the loud noises. "Did they find Sara?"

"Not yet."

"The car?" Will pressed. "They can't find the car?"

"There's a full-on manhunt. They'll find her."

Will didn't just want them to find her. He wanted—needed—them to find her alive.

The cop said, "Maybe you should lay down, buddy."

Will rubbed his eyes to clear them. The fluorescent lights were like sewing needles. He realized that he was sitting on one of dozens of gurneys that were parked on each side of the hallway. Patients were bleeding, moaning, crying. Debris covered their faces in gray dust. The atmosphere was eerily calm. No one was shouting. Nurses and doctors walked briskly back and forth with tablets tucked under their arms. The hospital staff were prepared for this. The real panic would be out in the streets.

Will asked Nate, "How many people are dead?"

"There's no official count. Maybe as few as twenty, maybe as many as fifty."

Will's brain couldn't comprehend the number. He had heard the bombs go off. He had run to help the survivors. He had been mentally prepared to do whatever it took to save as many people as possible.

Now, his only concern was Sara.

Nate said, "They're clearing each building in teams. Looking for more—"

Will slid off the bed. He waited for the nausea and dizziness to return. Neither made a repeat appearance, but his head throbbed with each beat of his heart.

He closed his eyes, tried to breathe. "What about the BMW?"

"It's in the system, but the system—"

"What time is it?"

"Two thirty-eight."

Which meant that Sara had been gone for over half an hour. Will's head dropped to his chest. His stomach was still grinding inside of his belly. His hands were bleeding from punching Hurley while Sara was taken right out from under him.

My son-in-law would've never let this happen.

Her son-in-law.

Sara's husband.

The chief of their town.

Would not have let this happen.

"Hey," Nate said. "You want some water or something?"

Will rubbed his jaw with his fingers. He could still smell Sara on his hands.

"Will!" Faith was running down the hallway. Amanda walked behind her. She was talking into a satellite phone.

Will's throat felt so raw that he could barely get out the question. "Did you find Sara?"

"The entire state is looking for her." Faith pressed her hand to his forehead the same way she did when she was worried that Emma had a fever. "Are you okay? What happened?"

"I let them steal her."

Faith put her hand back to his head.

"We stopped to help them." Will bullet-pointed the details of the car accident. "They drove up The By Way. That's the last I saw of her. I don't—" He stopped to cough. It felt like another punch to his gut. "I don't know why she went with them."

Amanda asked, "Why are you slumped over like a hobo?"

Before he could answer, she raised his shirt. Red and purple splotches showed the broken blood vessels under his skin.

"Jesus Christ," Faith whispered.

Amanda told Nate, "You're dismissed, Officer. Report to your squad. Faith, go find a doctor. Tell them he could be bleeding internally."

Will tried, "I'm not—

"Shut up, Wilbur." Amanda made him sit down on the gurney. "I'm not going to play that game where I order you to go home and you wander off like a wrecking ball. I'll keep you with me. You'll hear everything I hear. But you have to do exactly as I say."

Will nodded his agreement, but only as a way to make her talk.

"First, you need to take this. It's aspirin. It'll help with the headache."

Will stared at the round tablet in her palm. He hated drugs.

Amanda broke the tablet in half. "This is the last time I compromise. You're either playing by my rules or you're not."

He tossed the pill into his mouth and dry swallowed.

And then he waited.

Amanda said, "Michelle Spivey was admitted through the ER this morning. Her appendix had burst. She was immediately sent to surgery. Robert Jacob Hurley identified her as his wife, Veronica Hurley. He showed Admitting his group insurance card. He's divorced from his wife, but she's still on his SHBP."

"The state healthplan," Will said. "So, Hurley's a cop."

"He served on the GHP until eighteen months ago. Shot an unarmed man during a traffic stop."

"Hurley," Will said. The connection to Georgia Highway Patrol made the name familiar. Will had followed the story the way every cop followed that kind of story, hoping like Christ that the shoot was legit because the alternative was first-degree murder.

He said, "Hurley was cleared."

"Correct. But he couldn't right himself. He dropped off the force six months later. Pills and alcohol. His wife left him."

"Who was with him? Who planted the bombs?"

"Unsubs." Unknown subjects. "The FBI is using facial recognition on the CCTV footage. One of them left fingerprints, but they're not in the NGI."

The FBI's Next Generation Identification system. If the Unsub had ever been in law enforcement, military, or cleared a background check for a job or licensing, his details would've been stored in the searchable database alongside the criminals.

"Why did they have Spivey?" Will asked. "They deliberately bombed the hospital. They took Sara by chance."

He heard Hurley's words—*wrong place, right time.*

He asked Amanda, "Where are they going? What do they want? Why did they blow up—"

"Doctor?" Amanda was waving her hand toward a man in scrubs. "Over here."

"A nurse is the best you're going to get." The man lifted Will's shirt and started jamming his fingers into his belly. "Any of this hurt more than you think it should?"

Will's jaw had clamped tight at the first touch. He shook his head.

The nurse pressed his stethoscope around, listening, moving it along, listening. When he was finished, he spoke to Amanda instead of Will. "All the MRIs are backed up. We can do a CT to check for internal bleeding."

Will asked, "How long does it take?"

"Five minutes if you can walk down the stairs on your own."

"He can walk." Amanda helped Will off the gurney. The top of her head came up to his armpit. He leaned into her more than he should've. His stomach muscles burned like cordite. Still, he asked, "Why did they bomb the hospital?"

"To get away," Amanda said. "They need Michelle. For what, we have no idea. We have to operate on the assumption that the bombing was a diversion. They could've done a hell of a lot more damage, garnered a lot more dead and wounded, in any number of other locations. The *what* can't be our focus. We need to get to the bottom of the *why*."

Will squeezed his eyes shut. He couldn't break down anything she was telling him. His brain was packed with glass beads. "Sara. I couldn't—I didn't—"

"We're going to find her."

Faith met them on the stairs. She darted ahead of them and walked backward, giving Amanda updates. "They found a broken flip phone on a side street. ATF thinks it was used to trigger the bombs. We're taking it to our lab for fingerprinting. First look says they're the same as the ones we found from the Unsub."

Will winced as his foot slipped on the stair. His ribs had turned into knives. He said, "The GPS. Sara's BMW has—"

"It's all in motion," Amanda said. "We're relaying information as quickly as we can."

"Through here." The nurse was waiting at the bottom of the stairs. He held open the door.

Will didn't move.

There was something else they weren't telling him. He could sense the tension between Amanda and Faith. One of them was a consummate liar. The other was the same—except when it came to Will.

He asked Faith, "Is she dead?"

"No," Amanda said. "Absolutely not. If we knew something, we would tell you."

He kept his eyes on Faith.

She said, "I promise I would tell you if we knew where she was."

Will chose to believe her, but only because he had to.

"On your right," the nurse said.

Amanda steered Will down the hallway and into a room. A table was in the middle of a giant metal ring. He put his hand to the back of his head. His fingers found the sharp edge of a staple holding together his scalp.

When had that happened?

Amanda said, "We'll be out here."

The door closed.

Will was helped onto the table by a technician. She disappeared inside a little booth and told him what to do, that he needed to lie still, hold his breath, let it go. Then the table was moving back and forth through the circle and Will had to squeeze his eyes shut because the metal ring turned into a quarter spinning on its edge.

He didn't think about Sara. He thought about his wife.

Ex-wife.

Angie had disappeared on him. Constantly. Repeatedly. She had grown up in state care, too. That's where Will had met her. He was eight years old. He was in love the way you can love something that's the only thing you have to hold on to.

Angie could never settle in one place for long. Will had never blamed her for leaving. He had always had a knot in his stomach while he waited for her to return. Not because he missed her, but because when Angie was away from him, she did bad things. She hurt people. Maliciously. Unnecessarily. Will had always felt a sick sense of responsibility every time he woke up to find her things gone from his house, like she was a rabid dog he couldn't keep chained up in the yard.

It was different with Sara.

Losing her—letting someone *steal* her—felt like he was dying. Like there was a part of him that Sara had breathed life into, and without her, that part would wither away to nothing.

Will didn't know how to be alone anymore.

"All right." The scan was finally over. The technician helped him off the table. Will rubbed his eyes. He was seeing double again.

The technician asked, "Do you need to sit down?"

"No."

"Any nausea or dizziness?"

"I'm fine. Thank you." Will stepped outside so that the next patient could be rolled in. She was a nurse still dressed in scrubs. Blood streaked her face. She was covered in concrete dust, mumbling for someone to call her husband.

Will found Amanda in the room across the hall. The lights were off, which was a godsend. The blazing pain in his eyes melted into a slow burn.

The nurse from before lifted his chin at Will. "Those crunches paid off, my man."

"This is your lower abdomen." The radiologist was pointing to a screen of blobs that Will guessed were his organs. "I don't see any bleeding. Most of the bruising is in the surface. He's right about the crunches. Your abdominal muscle created a corset around the organs. But here, you have a micro-tear in the periosteum." He traced around a rib that looked like it was still in one piece. "That's a tissue-thin membrane that surrounds the bone. You need to ice it three times a day. Take Advil or get something stronger if you need it. We'll put you on a pulmonary plan to keep your lungs healthy. Moderate activity is okay but nothing strenuous." He looked up at Will. "You got lucky, but you need to take it easy."

Faith held up her phone. "Amanda, the video just came through."

Will didn't ask what video. They were clearly doing things without him.

"Let's go somewhere else." Amanda took them to the stairway opposite the one they'd come down.

She pointed to the treads. "Sit."

Will sat because he needed to.

Amanda pulled a wrapped piece of gum out of her purse. He heard a snap, then she waved it under his nose.

Will reared back like a horse. His heart slammed against his spine. His brain broke open. Everything got sharper. He could see the grout in the joints between the concrete blocks.

Amanda showed him the packet he'd mistaken for gum. "Ammonium ampoules."

"Fuck," Will panicked. "Did you drug me?"

"Stop being a baby. It's smelling salts. I woke you up because I need you to pay attention to this."

Will's nose was running. She handed him a tissue as she sat beside him.

Faith stood on the other side of the railing. She held out her phone so they could all watch a video.

Will saw a parking lot. The footage was in black and white, but sharp. A woman was walking with her daughter toward a Subaru.

Dark hair, slim build. Will recognized her from the stories on the news a month ago, not from the woman he'd seen today.

Michelle Spivey.

Her daughter was walking ahead of her. Looking at her phone. Swinging the shopping bags. Michelle was searching her purse for her keys when a dark, unmarked van pulled up beside her daughter. The driver's face wasn't visible through the windshield. The side door slid open. A man jumped out. The daughter ran.

The man reached for Michelle.

Faith paused the video and zoomed in on the man's face.

"That's him," Will said. The driver of the Chevy Malibu. "Clinton. That's what they called him, but I'm sure that's not his name."

Faith mumbled under her breath.

"Who is he?"

"He's not in the system." Amanda motioned for Faith to close the video. "We're working the case. This is another piece of the puzzle."

Will shook his head. She had made a mistake using the smelling salts. He wasn't half out of it anymore. "You're lying to me."

Her satellite phone rang. She stuck her finger in the air for silence, answering, "Yes?"

Will held his breath, waiting.

Amanda shook her head.

Nothing.

She walked out into the hallway, letting the door close behind her.

Will didn't look at Faith when he said, "You know his name, don't you?"

Faith took a sharp breath. "Adam Humphrey Carter. He's been in and out of prison for grand larceny, B-and-E, domestic violence, making terroristic threats."

"And rape," Will guessed.

Faith took another breath. "And rape."

The word stayed balanced on the edge of the cliff between them.

The door opened.

"Faith." Amanda waved her over, whispered something into her ear.

Faith headed up the stairs. The hand she put on Will's shoulder as she ran past did nothing to reassure him.

"The elevators are too slow," Amanda said. "Can you manage six flights?"

Will gripped the railing and pulled himself up. "You said you'd tell me everything."

"I said you would hear everything I hear. Do you want to be with me when I talk to Hurley or not?" She didn't wait. She started up the stairs. Her spiked heels stabbed into the treads. She rounded the corner without looking to see if he was following.

Will trudged up after her. His brain kept throwing up images—Sara standing in the doorway of the shed. Sara running ahead of him to the Chevy. The panicked expression on her face when she'd handed him the key fob. She had known something was wrong before he did. She had called it back at the Porsche. Will should've dragged her to the BMW and taken her home.

He looked at his watch.

3:06 p.m.

Sara had been missing for over an hour. She could be crossing the Alabama state line right now. She could be tied down in the woods while Adam Humphrey Carter ripped her in two.

His stomach clenched. He was going to be sick again.

You let them steal my daughter.

"Hold up." Amanda had stopped on the fourth-floor landing. "Take a minute."

"I don't need a minute."

"Then maybe you should try this in heels." She took off her shoe and rubbed her foot. "I need to catch my breath."

Will stared down at the stairs. He tried to clear away all the dark thoughts. He looked at his watch again. "It's 3:07. Sara's been gone for—"

"Thank you, Captain Kangaroo. I know how to tell time." She shoved her foot back into the shoe. Instead of continuing the climb, she unzipped her purse and started digging around inside.

Will said, "That man, Carter. He's a rapist."

"Among other things."

"He has Sara."

"I'm aware of that."

"He could be hurting her."

"He could be running for his life."

"You're not being completely honest with me."

"Wilbur, I've never been completely anything."

Will didn't have the strength to keep chasing his own tail. He leaned against the wall. He wrapped his hands around the railing. He looked down at his sneakers. They were stained green from mowing the grass. Red streaks of dirt and blood wrapped around his calves. He could still feel the cold stone floor of the shed against his knees. He closed his eyes. He tried to summon up the memory of that blissful moment before everything went wrong, but all he could feel was guilt gnawing a hole in his chest.

He told Amanda, "She was driving the car."

She looked up from her purse.

"When they left, Sara was driving. They didn't have to knock her out or—" He shook his head. "She told them to kill her. She wasn't going to go with them. But she went with them. She drove them away."

He looked down. Amanda had wrapped her hand around his. Her skin felt cool. Her fingers were tiny. He always forgot how small she was.

"I haven't—" Will was an idiot to confess anything to her,

but he was desperate for absolution. "I haven't felt scared like that since I was a kid."

Amanda rubbed his wrist with her thumb.

"I keep thinking of all these things I could've done, but maybe—" He tried to stop himself, but he couldn't. "Maybe I did the wrong thing because I was scared."

Amanda squeezed his hand. "That's the problem with loving someone, Will. They make you weak."

He had no words.

She patted his arm, signaling that sharing time was over. "Pull up your panties. We've got work to do."

She bounded up ahead of him.

Will followed more slowly. He tried to wrap his brain around what Amanda had said. He couldn't tell whether she'd meant it as a condemnation or an explanation.

Not completely one or the other.

He took a deep breath at the top of the next landing. The stabbing pain in his rib had turned into a dull ache. Will became aware of minor improvements as he moved his body, like that his head had stopped throbbing and the rolling lava in his gut was starting to smother itself out. He told himself it was good that his vision was no longer wonky. That the balloon of his brain had re-tethered itself to his skull.

He used the relief to plot ahead, past the interview with Hurley. He was certain the man wouldn't give them anything. Will needed to go home to get his car. He would try to find Nate for a lift. Will had a police scanner in his hall closet. He would take it with him and look in the places that no one else was looking. Will had grown up in the middle of downtown. He knew the bad streets, the dilapidated housing, where criminals laid low.

The door opened to the sixth floor. Will followed Amanda down another long hallway. Two cops at each end. One across from the elevator. Two more guarded a closed sliding glass door.

Amanda showed them all her ID.

The glass door slid open.

Will looked down at the threshold, the metal rails recessed into the tiles. He took as deep a breath as he could. He couldn't make himself forget that Sara had been abducted by a convicted rapist, but he could make himself appear calm enough to do whatever Amanda needed him to do in order to get information out of Hurley.

He stepped into the hospital room.

Hurley was handcuffed to the bed. There was a sink and toilet out in the open, a flimsy curtain for privacy. Sunlight filtered through the open blinds. The fluorescent lights were off. The glowing monitor announced Hurley's steady heartbeat.

He was asleep. Or at least pretending to be. Sutures Frankensteined his face. His broken nose had been straightened, but his jaw hung crookedly from his face.

His heartbeat was steady, like a lazy pendulum swinging back and forth.

Amanda cracked open another ammonium ampoule and shoved it under his nose.

Hurley jerked awake, eyes wide, nostrils flaring.

The heart monitor sounded like a fire alarm.

Will looked at the door, expecting a nurse to come running in.

No one came.

The cops hadn't even turned around.

Amanda had her ID out. "I'm Deputy Director Amanda Wagner with the GBI. You've met Agent Trent."

Hurley looked at the ID, then back at Amanda.

She said, "I'm not going to read you your rights because this isn't a formal interview. You've been given morphine, so nothing you say can be used in court." She waited, but Hurley didn't respond. "The doctors have stabilized you. Your jaw is dislocated. You'll be taken to surgery as soon as the more critical patients have been helped. For now, we have some questions about the two women who were abducted."

Hurley blinked. Waited. He was making a point of ignoring Will. Which suited Will, because if the man looked at him wrong, he wasn't sure he could keep his shit together.

"Are you thirsty?" Amanda pushed aside the curtain around the sink and toilet. She unwrapped a plastic cup, turned on the faucet.

Will leaned against the wall. He shoved his hands into his pockets.

"You were a cop." Amanda filled the cup with water. "You know the charges. You've murdered or participated in the murder of dozens of civilians. You aided and abetted the abductions of two women. You were part of a conspiracy to use a weapon of mass destruction. Not to mention healthcare fraud." She turned around, walked to the bed with the full cup of water. "These are federal charges, Hurley. Even if by some miracle a jury deadlocks on the death penalty, you're never going to breathe free air ever again."

Hurley reached for the cup. The handcuff clanged against the rails.

Amanda paused long enough to let him know that she was in charge. She held the cup to his mouth. She pressed the tips of her fingers below his jaw to help his lips make a seal.

He made an audible gulp with each swallow, draining the cup.

She asked, "More?"

He didn't respond. He leaned back in the pillow. He closed his eyes.

"I need those women home safe, Hurley." Amanda found a tissue in her purse. She wiped out the cup before tossing it into the trashcan. "This is the only time in this entire process that you'll have any bargaining power."

Will stared at the cup.

What had she given him?

"On average, it takes fifteen years for the federal government to administer the death penalty." Amanda dragged over a chair and sat by the bed. She crossed her legs. She brushed lint off her skirt. She looked at her watch. "It's a bit ironic, but did you know that Timothy McVeigh was caught on a traffic violation?"

The Oklahoma City Bomber. McVeigh had set off a truck bomb outside of the Murrah Federal Building, murdering almost two hundred people, injuring almost one thousand more.

Amanda said, "McVeigh was sentenced to death. He had four years at Florence ADMAX before he petitioned the courts to bring forward his execution date."

Hurley licked his lips. Something had changed. Her words—or maybe what she'd tricked him into drinking—were chiseling away at his calm.

Amanda said, "Ted Kaczynski, Terry Nichols, Dzhokhar Tsarnaev, Zacarias Moussaoui, Eric Rudolph." She paused in her list of domestic terrorists serving out their multiple life sentences on what was called Bomber's Row. "Robert Hurley could be added to those names. Do you know what it's like inside an ADX?"

She was asking Will, not Hurley.

He knew, but he said, "What's it like?"

"Inmates are confined to their cells for twenty-three hours a day. If they're allowed out, it's only for an hour, and then it's at the pleasure of the guards. Do you think the guards are kind to people who blow up people?"

"No," Will said.

"No," Amanda agreed. "But your cell has everything you need to survive. The toilet is your sink and your water fountain. There's black-and-white TV if you want to watch educational classes or religious programming. They bring you your food. The window is four inches wide. Do you think you can see much of the sky through four inches, Will?"

"No," he repeated.

"You shower in isolation. You eat in isolation. If you're lucky enough to get yard time, it's not really a yard. They have a pit, like an empty swimming pool. You can pace it off in ten steps, thirty if you walk in a circle. It's fifteen feet deep. You can see the sky, but you can't write home about it. They stopped giving inmates pencils because they kept using them to rip open their own throats."

Hurley's eyes were open. He stared up at the ceiling.

Amanda looked down at her watch again.

Will checked the time for himself.

3:18 p.m.

"Hurley," Amanda said. "I don't care about your other charges. I care about returning those two women to safety. So this is what I'm offering."

She waited.

Hurley waited.

Will felt his stomach tighten.

"You'll die in prison. I can't do anything about that. But I can keep your identity out of the news. I can give you a new name, a new rap sheet. The marshals oversee plenty of prison inmates in witness protection. You'll be in gen pop, maximum security, but you won't be caged like an animal while you slowly lose your mind." She paused. "All you have to do right now is tell me where to find those women."

Hurley sniffed. He turned his head to look out the window. Blue skies. Sun on his face. His heart had returned to its slow, lazy beat. He was calm because he felt like he was in control, the same way he'd been back at the car accident.

At least until Michelle Spivey had opened her mouth and started talking about Hurley's father.

He's your hero . . . you wanted to make him proud.

Will said, "Your father's sick, right? That's what Michelle said—that he was going to die."

Hurley's head had swiveled around. His eyes burned with fury.

This was the way into him. Hurley didn't care about the people he'd murdered. Whatever cause had driven him to commit an act of terrorism was not going to be compromised in a few minutes. Every man had a weak spot. For a lot of men on the wrong side of the law, that weak spot centered around their father.

"Was your old man a cop?" Will asked. "Is that why you joined patrol?"

Hurley glared at him. The monitor started throwing off quick beats as his heart rate increased.

"I bet he was proud when you joined up. Took the oath, the same as he did. His. Son." Will said the words individually, the way he had heard so many old timers on the force talk about their kids. Not as individuals, but as extensions of themselves. "I bet he's not going to be so proud when he hears that you helped a convicted rapist abduct another woman."

The silence between the beeps shortened.

Will said, "I remember what it was like when my father died. I was with him in the hospital when he drew his last breath."

Amanda said nothing. She knew that the first time Will had seen his father's face was when he'd identified the man's dead body.

Will said, "I'd never held my dad's hand before. Maybe when I was a little kid and I needed help crossing the road. But never as a man. He was just so—so vulnerable, you know? And I felt vulnerable, too. That's what it's like when you love somebody. You feel weak. You want to take away their pain. You'll do anything you can to keep them safe."

A tear slid from the corner of Hurley's eye.

Will said, "Toward the end, Dad's hands and feet were cold. I pulled on his socks for him. I rubbed his skin. Nothing could warm him. That's what the body does. It diverts all of the heat to the brain and the organs. They can feel you holding their hand, but they can't hold you back."

Amanda had vacated the chair. Will sat down. He pulled it closer to Hurley. He fought the revulsion as he held the man's hand.

This was for Sara.

This was how they found her.

He said, "You can't erase what you did, Hurley, but you can try to make up for it." Will felt Hurley's fingers clench around his own. "Save those two women. Don't let them get hurt. Give your dad something that makes him proud of you again."

Hurley gulped.

"Tell us how to find the women," Will said, trying not to beg. "It's not too late to protect them from what you know is coming. Let your dad's last thoughts be that his son was a good man who did some bad things. Not a bad man who couldn't do good."

Hurley's eyes were closed again. Tears soaked the pillow.

"It's all right." Will looked down at their hands. Hurley was squeezing so tight that the broken skin on Will's knuckles was bleeding again. "Just tell us how to save them. Be the man your father knows you can be."

Hurley stuttered in a deep breath. His tears ran unabated. He looked not at Will, but at Amanda. His mouth moved. There was a clicking in his jaw.

"Guh—" Hurley's face creased with exertion. He couldn't use his lips to form the word. "Guh—"

"Gilmer? Gwinnett? Gordon?" Amanda gave up on naming counties and searched her purse. "I have something you can write on."

"Nuh—" Hurley shook off Will's hand, frustrated. "Fuh—" he tried again.

Will leaned forward, straining to hear.

"Fuh—" He grabbed the rails of the bed, gave them a violent shake. "Fuck off."

6

Sunday, August 4, 2:13 p.m.

Faith's tailbone rattled against the plastic seat in the rear section of the helicopter. Her sense of helplessness was becoming more overwhelming with each passing second. Will was down there somewhere—probably feeling just as hopeless, while she was trapped inside an overloaded washing machine. The sun baked the metal skin of the Huey. To her left were six very large men wearing SWAT uniforms and carrying AR-15s. Their legs were spread wide. Their arms were the size of tree trunks. Their expressions were hard. They were angry, ready to do battle.

But for now, they were stuck in a holding pattern. The air ambulances had priority over the hospital's landing pad. The interior of the Huey had taken on the stench of prolonged agony. They were ready to spring out of the cramped space the moment they touched down. The pilot's silence in the chunky headphones was excruciating. Still, Faith's ears strained against the static. Only Maggie and Amanda had taken theirs off, choosing to keep their conversation private by shouting into each other's ears. Amanda looked furious, which was understandable unless you knew Amanda. She never looked furious. She was usually the calm in the middle of the storm.

There was a lot to be angry about.

Will was in the emergency room. There was no word on Sara.

No idea who had taken her, why they had set off bombs, what they were going to do next.

Fifteen confirmed dead. Thirty-eight wounded. Cops murdered. Security guards murdered. A sheriff's deputy who had died on the operating table.

"They've cleared fifty percent of the campus buildings." Maggie was back on the headphones. Her voice echoed as if she was using a tin can. "The first bomb was on the fifth level of the Lowergate East parking deck. It brought down the roof. The second bomb was bigger, the rainmaker. Sub-level one, strapped to a major support column. Strategically planted to take the whole thing down."

"This wasn't an escalation," Amanda yelled. "This was an opportunity."

Maggie pointed to the headphones. The line was not secure.

The pilot said, "We're clear for landing."

The helicopter made a sharp dip before hurtling toward the campus. Faith's stomach dropped—not from the sudden loss of altitude, but from the sight of the cratered parking deck.

Smoke fogged the air. Faith counted six fire trucks battling separate blazes. Broken glass and chunks of concrete littered the ground. Cars had been blown out of the deck, scattered onto the street, shot like missiles into the adjacent buildings. The sky bridge across Clifton Road had a van on top of it, wheels up like a dying cockroach. She saw shoes, papers, metal bent like paperclips. It reminded Faith of when her son was little and he'd steal items from her desk to play with his toys.

"The Porsche driver." Maggie had gotten another update on her phone. "He's a doctor from the children's hospital. They think his neck was broken after the crash. They wouldn't want to leave any witnesses. Wrong place, wrong time."

Faith thought about the randomness of the car accident. The poor man had probably been thinking about slipping into bed when the truck rear-ended him.

"The students are being bussed out." Amanda pointed down at the line of kids with backpacks and suitcases. There were white tents for triaging patients. Uniformed law enforcement swarmed over the broken concrete. Firemen and civilians were moving away debris, passing buckets from one person to the next.

Maggie told Amanda, "Press conference is in fifteen minutes. Do you want to be in on it?"

"No, but I'll draft some language." Amanda took out her notepad and started writing.

Faith tried to orient herself as the helicopter approached the landing pad. They were directly above what was called the Clifton Corridor. The bombed-out parking deck was on the opposite side of the road from the hospital. Behind the three clinic buildings and the Winship Cancer Institute. A block away from Egleston Children's Hospital. Even farther from the student dormitories and libraries on the other side of Clifton.

Of all the places the terrorists could've detonated the bombs, the parking deck was the one that offered the least awful outcome. They had killed some people, but they could've killed a hell of a lot more.

This wasn't an escalation.

The helicopter touched down with a bone-jarring bump.

"Go-go-go!" the SWAT leader yelled.

They moved quickly so that the Huey could make space for the next air ambulance. Faith jumped out with the help of a hospital orderly. They jogged into the building. The roof access door was already open. A patient was strapped to a gurney, waiting for the next chopper to arrive. The SWAT team disappeared down the stairs, rifles clutched in their hands.

Faith's eyes were watering so badly that she could barely see. She coughed. The air was thick enough to eat. She didn't want to know what she was breathing. She squinted her eyes onto the back of Amanda's navy blue suit jacket and followed her down the stairs.

The air had cleared by the next floor. They kept going down. Faith used the tail of her shirt to wipe the grime out of her eyes. Maggie was already on her satellite phone. It was the same as before. She rapid-fired information over her shoulder as she bolted downward. "The man that Will shot at the car accident. They scanned his fingerprints. He's not in the system." She listened again before continuing. "Robert Hurley's Android phone is a wash. He only called one number, a burner phone. We're trying to track it down."

They all stepped aside so two orderlies could run past.

Amanda said, "My people can get a warrant faster. Let us do the paperwork."

"Good," Maggie propelled herself down the next flight. "I'll reach out to Murphy. I can't make any promises."

"Neither can I." Amanda sounded furious again. Her breathing was audible. Her high heels stabbed into the stairs.

Faith checked her watch.

2:17 p.m.

The bombings would be on the news by now. Evelyn would assume that Faith was responding with Amanda. Then, she would call Jeremy and tell him that she'd talked to Faith and everything was okay. Then, she would break the iPad rule with Emma and pretend like it was a treat rather than a distraction. She had been a cop for thirty years. She knew how to lie to her family.

Faith rounded the landing. She took the last few steps two at a time. They had reached the second floor. An Atlanta police sergeant was holding open the door. He told Maggie, "The doctor couldn't wait. He said to find him when you're here."

"Find him." Maggie rolled her hand. "Walk and talk."

The sergeant skipped to catch up, saying, "They left the bullet in Hurley's leg. Safer that way. His jaw needs to be wired shut, but there are a lot of criticals ahead of him. The sixth floor was cleared. We've got him covered. Nobody's taking a piss. Excuse me, ma'am."

"We all piss, Sergeant." Maggie asked, "Is Hurley awake?"

"In and out, ma'am. He refused pain meds once they moved him up from the ER."

"He doesn't want to slip up and say something." Amanda turned to the officer, "See that his jaw stays a low priority. I need him to talk. Keep him alone in the room. Make sure he can see out the window." She added, "Don't give him any water."

The sergeant looked at Maggie. She nodded her okay, then turned back to Amanda.

"Take this." Amanda ripped a page out of her notebook. "Tell the press it's the official statement from the GBI. I need you to read it out *exactly* as written."

"Understood." Maggie traded the paper for her satellite phone. "Find one of my people if you need me. Good luck."

Amanda headed down the hallway, calling to Faith, "We need to go up a flight. I want to talk to the nurse."

Lydia Ortiz. Faith knew about the woman from the debrief they'd gotten in the helicopter. Ortiz had recognized Michelle Spivey in the surgical recovery area. She'd called security but before they could arrive, all hell had broken loose.

"This way." Amanda passed the elevator. There was a closer set of stairs, but crime scene investigators were scouring it for clues.

Robert Jacob Hurley had dragged Michelle Spivey out of the recovery area on the third floor. He had met his two accomplices outside the second-floor landing. As they were going down to the ground floor, two cops were coming up. The officers were responding to Lydia Ortiz's SOS. Both were shot in the head. Another officer, a sheriff's deputy, was waiting for them when they exited the building. She was shot in the chest when they made their escape to the silver Chevy Malibu. She had gone down firing, hitting Hurley in the leg and his accomplice in the shoulder before Hurley turned around and shot her in the face.

Faith opened the door. She told Amanda, "They detonated the bombs in the parking deck while they were driving away."

"Correct."

"It's like Novak," Faith said. "He always set off bombs as a distraction, not as a means to an end."

"Good girl. You've been hammering around that nail all day."

Amanda sprinted up the stairs. They ended up in the third-floor recovery room. Rows of gurneys were screened off by hospital curtains. There was a nurse's station, an ice machine, a clearly marked bathroom. The space was empty except for a cop and three crime scene techs. The bed in the second bay was cordoned off with yellow tape. Blood dripped across the floor, heading in the direction of the second set of stairs.

Amanda showed her ID to the officer by the door while Faith signed them into the crime scene log.

The cop said, "Dr. Lawrence is on his way up. He did two tours in Iraq. No-bullshit kind of guy."

"Are you the police?" A woman had appeared behind the nurse's station. She was crying, clearly distraught. "I couldn't stop it. I tried to—"

"You're Lydia Ortiz?" Amanda asked.

The woman cupped her hands to her face. All she could do was nod. She probably had friends in the parking deck. She had come face to face with a mass murderer and a woman who had been abducted right in front of her eleven-year-old daughter.

Faith said, "Take your time." She found her notebook in her bag. She flipped past a bunch of empty pages. She twisted her pen open.

Amanda asked, "What are the symptoms of appendicitis?"

"Uh—" Ortiz hadn't been expecting the question. "Nausea, vomiting, spiked fever, constipation."

"Does it hurt?" Amanda asked. She was trying to center the woman with the familiar.

"Yes, the pain is off the charts. Here." She put her hand to her right lower abdomen. "Breathing, moving, coughing—it feels like you're being stabbed."

"How long before it ruptures?"

She shook her head, but said, "Twenty-four to seventy-two hours from onset of symptoms. And it doesn't rupture like a balloon. It's more like a tear. The bacteria leaks into your bloodstream, where it leads to sepsis."

Faith could've looked this up on WebMD, but she wrote it down in her notebook anyway.

"Now," Amanda said. "Take me through when you first saw Michelle. They brought her into recovery. Was she on a gurney?"

"Yes." Ortiz took a tissue from her pocket. She blew her nose. "She was in bay two. One of the porters brought her husband—he said to call him Hurley—from the waiting room. I introduced myself to him. I ran down the usual post-op care."

"Did he ask any questions?"

"No. He barely listened. He kept asking for the scripts."

"Scripts?"

"Prescriptions. Antibiotics. Generic. You can get them for free at Walmart. I got the feeling that he wanted them so they could leave."

"What was her medical prognosis?"

"I'm not supposed to tell you because of patient's rights, but fuck it. She needed to be admitted. The husband refused. She signed herself out AMA—against medical advice. The doctor was loading her up with antibiotics. She's going to need follow-up care. Sepsis isn't a joke."

"Would she have died without the surgery?"

"Yes. She could die anyway. Hurley didn't seem interested in managing her care."

Faith stared at her notepad. Ortiz didn't know about the car accident, that Hurley had a team and that the team had abducted a doctor. Faith wrote down a question for later: *Hurley needed Michelle alive—for what?*

Amanda asked, "When did you recognize the patient as Michelle Spivey?"

"I didn't. Not at first. It was the husband who set me off. There was something about him. He felt squirrely. We get abusers sometimes, where the husband won't leave the wife alone. He's afraid she'll ask for help."

"Did she show any signs of abuse?"

"She looked malnourished. I gave her some warm blankets, but then I realized she didn't have socks. So I put socks on her feet. That's when I saw the track marks."

Faith looked up from her notebook.

Ortiz said, "That's when it happened. I was putting on her socks. I looked up at her face, and from a different angle, something clicked. Her hair's been cut and bleached blonde, but I recognized her. And that's when she looked at me—right in the eye. She mouthed the word 'Help.'"

Faith wanted to make sure she got this right. "She asked you for help?"

"Not audibly. But you can read the word on somebody's lips,

right?" Ortiz walked over to the bed. "I was here. She was sitting up."

"Did the husband see her mouth the word?"

"No. I mean—I don't know for sure. I went back to the nurse's station. I said I was going to get her some Vaseline. Her lips were really chapped. I gave the emergency code to Daniel, the porter. He was real cool about it, just slipped out the door, but the husband had picked up on something. When I turned around, he was making her put on her pants. She couldn't get them zipped. The sutures broke. She was bleeding. She started to cry. He wouldn't let her put on her shirt. He gave her his jacket. He pulled her into the stairs. That's the last I saw of them. I heard gunfire downstairs. We got the alarm to shelter in place. Then a few minutes later, the bombs went off." She shook her head. "They're saying Hurley had a group of men with him, that they shot a bunch of people."

Amanda didn't offer to fill in the blanks. She walked around the gurney. She looked down at the floor. "Is this her shirt?"

Ortiz nodded.

Amanda bent down. She used a pencil to move the shirt. Cotton, short-sleeved, button-up front, white with red vertical stripes. "Homespun."

Faith knelt beside her. The seams looked handstitched. The cloth could've been from a sack of flour.

"Thank you, Ms. Ortiz." Amanda stood up. She told Faith, "Meet me in the hall."

Faith used her phone to photograph the shirt. She zoomed in on the seams. The buttons were all the same color, but they were mismatched. Michelle Spivey had worked at the CDC. She was a marathoner, a mother of an almost teenager. She didn't strike Faith as the type of woman who would make her own clothes.

"I'm sorry," Ortiz said. "I should've—I don't know. I should've stopped him."

"He would've killed you." Faith found one of her business cards. "Call me if you think of anything else, okay?"

Back in the stairwell, Amanda was ending a call on the satellite phone. She told Faith, "Sara's mother is claiming that her daughter went with the kidnappers in order to protect Will."

Faith could very easily see that happening, but putting it in a police report could mean a lot of bad things for a law enforcement career, especially if the press got hold of it.

Amanda said, "I asked her to take a cooling-off period before she signs her statement. I'm not sure she was listening. She came across as a raving bitch."

Faith felt a new knot in her stomach. She would be a raving bitch, too, if someone abducted one of her children.

She asked Amanda, "Who wears homespun?"

"Not a woman who makes $130,000 a year."

Faith skipped over the astounding salary and tried to talk out what she knew. "So, Hurley kidnaps Michelle Spivey. He makes her wear homespun. He takes her to the hospital to get her appendix out instead of dumping her on the side of the road. He calls up his buddies to bring some bombs so they can escape?" She couldn't put together any of this. "Why?"

Amanda looked over the railing. "Dr. Lawrence?"

"Guilty." A short, stocky man came into view. He was wearing pinstriped pajama pants and dress shoes. His scrub shirt was spattered with blood. Smeared black eyeliner rimmed his eyes. He looked like he'd rolled out of bed after a night of raving and run to the hospital the second he'd heard the siren.

Lawrence didn't make apologies for his appearance. "I can hold off wiring his jaw shut as long as you want. He deserves to suffer."

"What about my man downstairs?"

"I popped a staple in his scalp. He's disoriented, concussed. He took a hell of a beating to his lower belly. He's probably got a cracked rib or two. He needs a CT to rule out bleeding."

Amanda asked, "What can you give him to get him back on his feet right now?"

Lawrence thought for a moment. "This'll have my ass in front of the medical board, but a tab of Percocet 10 should do the trick. Tell him to take half if you want to keep him awake."

"What if I need him more than awake?"

Lawrence scratched his prickly beard. "An ammonium inhaler might—"

"Poppers?" Faith felt the word explode out of her mouth. "You can't be serious."

"It's not a popper. It's a nasal irritant. It'll make him take a really deep breath and put a lot of oxygen in his body." He told Amanda, "We've got some downstairs. Give him a hit when he needs his game face on."

Faith shook her head. She didn't trust any of this.

Lawrence was already leaving. "Find Conrad downstairs if you want the meds."

"He won't take medication," Faith told Amanda. Will treated headaches with root beer and strained muscles with more exercise.

Amanda said, "I have a hunch that Robert Hurley didn't abduct Michelle Spivey. I think a man named Adam Humphrey Carter took her. He spent six years upstate for sexual assault. And I think he's with Sara right now."

Faith put her hand to her mouth. Georgia distinguished the crime of rape from sexual assault. The latter meant that the assailant had supervisory or custodial authority over the victim; a teacher or a daycare worker or—

"Carter was a Newnan County police officer," Amanda confirmed. "He pulled over a twenty-two-year-old woman, dragged her into the woods, raped and battered her, then left her for dead."

"Where did—" Faith struggled to get out a question. "You didn't pull Carter's name out of a hat. Why do you think he's involved?"

"There are things I can't tell you right now. It's a hunch, but it's a well-informed hunch." Amanda gave Faith a moment. "I've asked a friend to send the video of Spivey's abduction to your private email."

"Wait, there's video?" Faith had been following the story over the last month. She'd thought it was just another horrible, random kidnapping. "The news said there were no suspects."

Amanda didn't explain the deception. "These are the pieces

we need to focus on putting together right now: Is Carter the man in the Spivey abduction video? If Carter is the abductor, can Will identify him as one of the men who took Sara?"

The idea that Carter could have Sara made Faith feel sick. "And then?"

"Then they can't argue that Michelle is being trafficked. You heard about the track marks. They could say that Carter finished with Michelle, then sold her on to Hurley. A transaction, not an alliance."

The more she talked, the less clear things got. "Who's 'they' who're going to argue that? And why does it matter what the motivation is?" Faith felt her watch tapping her wrist. The haptic feedback was signaling that she had an alert. She glanced down, saying, "I guess cell service is—"

Sara Linton tried to reach you, but you were unavailable.

"Fuck." Faith scrolled through the Walkie-Talkie options. "Sara—"

Talk With Sara.

Open Walkie-Talkie.

"Fuck."

"Faith," Amanda said. "For godsakes. Sara what?"

"She tried to Walkie me at 2:17. That was twenty-one minutes ago." Sara could be on her way to Tennessee, the Carolinas, Alabama, Florida. "Fuck."

"What did she say?"

"It doesn't work like that." Faith started to explain that the app worked on the FaceTime platform, but then she remembered her audience. "It's like a real walkie-talkie. It doesn't record or store the message. You have to listen to it when it comes in."

Amanda's lips snapped into a tight line. She exhaled sharply, then said, "They found the BMW ten minutes ago."

Faith's jaw dropped.

"There was an explosion. The gas tank was set on fire. There's a body in the back seat. They can't tell if it's male or female. The car has to cool down before they can go in."

Faith reached behind her to find the wall. She needed something solid to keep her anchored. Sara wasn't only Will's girlfriend. She was Faith's friend. Maybe even her best friend.

"You can't tell Will any of this." Amanda started down the stairs. "He can't help us if he's in mourning."

Faith dragged behind her. She felt punch-drunk. Will had a right to know what was happening. Faith was his partner. Her job was to be honest with him. Or at least as honest as she could be.

Amanda pulled open another door. They were in the ER. She stopped the first worker she could find. "I need Conrad."

Will was slouched on a gurney at the end of the hall. Faith ran toward him, calling, "Will."

He blinked long and slow. "Did you find Sara?"

"No. The entire state is looking for her." Faith told herself it was useless to tell him about the burned-out BMW until they knew who was inside. She gently pushed up his head so she could see his face. "Are you okay?"

His chin dropped back to his chest. "I let them steal her."

She tried to make him look up, but he shook away her hand.

"It-it fast." He said. "The shed. It— the street. But, before a-an explosion. And then the cars. They took her."

Amanda had no patience for his rambling. "Why are you slumped over like a hobo?" She tried to force him to lie down. Her hand lifted his shirt.

"Jesus Christ," Faith said. His skin looked like a bunch of jumbled Rorschach ink blots.

Amanda gave Faith a sharp look, telling her to pull herself together. "Faith, go find a doctor. Tell them he could be bleeding internally."

Faith walked down the hallway. She used the back of her hand to wipe her eyes. Grit scratched at her skin. It killed her to see Will this way. She turned around and watched Amanda holding out a pill for Will to take. He shook his head. She broke it in half and Will tossed it into his mouth.

"You need me again?" A male nurse stood with his hands gripped around his stethoscope. His name tag read CONRAD. He said, "Your boss is a bitch."

"Tell her that while you're helping my partner." Faith pushed open the bathroom door. She went into the first stall, sat down, and put her head in her hands. She didn't cry. She just sat there until she no longer had the desire to curl into a ball.

Adam Humphrey Carter.

Why did Amanda have the man's name in her mouth? The abduction video was being sent to Faith's private email to keep it out of official channels. Amanda called it a hunch, but she had to be working on a theory. Was this what she had been screaming into Maggie's ear while they waited for the helicopter to land? It would explain why she'd been so visibly furious.

Not an escalation. An opportunity.

Faith checked her watch for notifications.

2:42 p.m.

Nothing.

She flushed the toilet. She washed her face. She looked at her wan reflection in the mirror.

She had to stop scanning the forest and look at the individual trees. Amanda said they needed to definitively connect Carter and Hurley as part of a team. If Will could identify them both from the accident site, then the connection would be proven. That was all Faith was going to worry about for now. Once the connection was made, she would move on to the next tree. It was the only way she was going to make it through the forest.

She pushed open the door. Down the hall, Amanda was struggling to help Will navigate the stairs. He was almost one hundred pounds heavier than she was, at least a foot taller. The sight would've been comical if it wasn't so tragic.

Faith skirted around them, stepping backward down the stairs in front of Will in case he fell. His words slurred as he asked about Hurley, the GPS on Sara's car.

"It's all in motion," Amanda soothed. "We're relaying information as quickly as we can."

"Through here." Conrad stood at the open door.

Amanda tried to lead Will into the tunnel, but Will's docility had finally run out.

He looked at Faith. "Is she dead?"

Her mouth opened, but Amanda spoke first.

"No. Absolutely not. If we knew something, we would tell you."

Faith forced herself to look him in the eye. She told him the only truth she could muster. "I promise I would tell you if we knew where she was."

He nodded, and she let them walk ahead of her so she wouldn't give anything else away.

She looked down at her watch. She took out her cell phone. They were underground. There were no bars on either device. She would need to go upstairs or try to find the Wi-Fi login.

"Faith." Amanda was alone in the hall, riffling through her purse. She held out her pill case. "I can't find my reading glasses. Locate the oval, blue pills. I need two."

"Are you—" Faith was going to ask if Amanda was sick, but she saw the tiny words on the blue tablet.

XANAX 1.0

"Put them in here." Amanda uncapped a small plastic bottle. Faith dropped the pills in. Amanda started twisting the top like a pepper grinder. She saw Faith's expression and said, "You can unclench your asshole. It's not for Will. I need to loosen up Hurley, and before you lecture me, call your mother and ask her about her famous Blabbermouth pills."

Faith chewed at the tip of her tongue. She hated when Amanda told her terrible things about her mother.

Amanda dropped the container in her suit jacket pocket. "Human rights are women's rights. This is how we level the playing field."

"Ma'am?" A man had appeared in the hallway. "I'm Dr. Schooner, the radiologist. He fell asleep on the table, so we thought we'd give him some time before the next patient comes down."

He motioned them into a dark room filled with glowing screens. Conrad was in the chair with his arms crossed. There were signs taped to the walls. What to do if someone had an allergic reaction. The numbers for poison control. The Wi-Fi password.

Faith started tapping the network info into her phone as Dr. Schooner explained Will's results.

"His brain shows no anomalies." He pointed to the monitor

in the middle. "No swelling. No bleeding. No fractures to the skull, though the bone is bruised. He needs to rest somewhere, eyes closed, lights off, no stimulus. Should be better in a week, but full recovery is closer to three months."

"We'll make sure he gets rest," Amanda said.

Faith went into the hall to give herself some deniable culpability. She tried to think about what Sara would want her to do right now. She would be worried about Will. She would want Faith to knock him out and drag him home and make him sleep in a dark room so that he could recover.

But he would eventually wake up. And he would never forgive Faith.

Faith checked her email. The video hadn't come through.

She opened the browser on her phone. She logged into the GBI's secure site. She pulled up Adam Humphrey Carter's rap sheet. Another knot twisted into her stomach. Not just a rapist, but a car thief, a burglar, a batterer. Like Robert Hurley, a woman had taken out a restraining order against him. His sheet was littered with domestic violence charges because these kinds of men always had domestic violence charges. The hatred of women was as much of an indicator of future criminal behavior as animal torture and bed wetting.

Violence never worked in the service of women.

Faith scrolled to the end of Carter's file. He had two Failure to Appear warrants, one for grand theft and another for assaulting a man during a bar fight. Both dated back two years. Which didn't make sense. FTAs were issued by judges when criminals didn't show up for trial. Carter had made bail on two very serious charges. The bondsman who secured the bail would have placed a bounty on his head upwards of $100,000.

So why hadn't Carter been rounded up?

A notification slid down the screen.

Anon4AnonA@gmail.com had sent her a file.

She went back in the room and told Amanda, "The video just came through."

"Let's go somewhere else."

Will and Faith followed her to the opposite end of the tunnel.

Another door.

Another stairwell.

Amanda made Will sit down on the stairs. Before Faith knew what was happening, she'd popped an ammonium ampoule and stuck it under Will's nose.

"Fuck!" Will reared like a horse, arms flailing. "Did you drug me?"

"Stop being a baby. It's smelling salts."

Faith watched the download circle until the video opened.

She leaned over the railing so that Will and Amanda could see the screen.

Watching the abduction of Michelle Spivey was not as shocking as it should have been. Between work and *Dateline*, Faith had seen countless black-and-white images of women being snatched under the watchful lens of a security camera. The thing that pulled at her heart was Ashley Spivey-Lee, Michelle's little daughter who was blissfully texting into her phone when a van pulled up a few feet away from her.

The little girl ran.

Michelle reached into her purse, her mouth opened in a scream.

Faith paused the video when a man jumped out of the van. She zoomed in on the abductor's face. She had recognized the scumbag from his mugshot. She prayed like hell that Will would not.

He said, "That's him. Clinton. That's what they called him, but that's not his name."

"Fuck," Faith muttered.

"He's not in the system." Amanda gestured at Faith to play along.

"You're lying to me," Will said. He wasn't guessing. Faith was only good at hiding the truth when she felt there was a good reason to hide it.

Amanda's phone rang.

She held the receiver to her ear and waited.

They all waited—Will for news of Sara. Faith for whether or not the charred body in the back of Sara's car had been identified.

Amanda shook her head, then disappeared into the tunnel. There was a finality to the click from the door closing.

In the silence, Faith could hear her own heart beating in her ears.

Will said, "You know his name, don't you?"

She told him the man's name. She gave him the rundown of his sheet. At least part of it.

Will wasn't stupid. He knew that she was leaving something out.

He said, "And rape."

Faith had to swallow before she could speak. "And rape."

The door opened. Amanda called her over. She put her mouth near Faith's ear. "Charred remains are a male delivery driver. His van was found abandoned at the Bullard Road exit off I-16."

Florida. Alabama. South Carolina.

Amanda whispered, "They're going to read you in upstairs. Give them hell. Don't take anything they say at face value. There's always an ulterior motive."

Faith didn't ask questions she knew would not be answered in front of Will. She squeezed his shoulder as she made her way up the stairs, around another landing, then to the first floor of another building.

The Winship Cancer Institute. Faith recognized the entrance. Air whistled past her head. The windows had been shattered on the east side. The air conditioning was being sucked out. She heard heavy equipment beeping, diesel engines revving. The air was like breathing sand. Her eyes immediately started to water. Her nose was running so bad that she had to search her bag for a tissue.

"Mitchell."

The FBI agent from the Martin Novak meeting waved to her from the end of the hall. The sweaty classroom seemed like a lifetime ago. Both of them were worse for the wear. Gonc was the strait-laced G-man. The bridge of his glasses was held together with white surgical tape. His face was caked gray with dust. Blood streaked his previously white shirt. The sleeve was ripped open. Blood seeped from the arm.

"We're down here." He bypassed the elevator, then took a left beyond the stairs. The overhead lights were off. Faith had never been in this part of the building. "I gotta say, I'm surprised Amanda sent you."

"What was your name again?"

"Aiden Van Zandt. Call me Van. It's easier." He used his sleeve to wipe his face. "Look, you can spare the lecture. Our CI has been solid for the last three years."

Faith didn't ask who his confidential informant was. Never get in the way of a talker.

Van said, "We've been able to flip or lock up some high-value targets because of the information he's provided us."

Faith kept her expression neutral.

"I know how your boss feels about this whole operation, but keep in mind, she was the one using us." He glanced at Faith. "And we were ready. We had it all lined up." He wiped his face again. He was just smearing dirt around.

Faith had tissues in her bag, but fuck this guy.

He said, "We can still slot in another agent. They don't know what he looks like, just that he's a guy who's had some problems."

Faith felt a lightbulb flickering on over her head, not completely on, but getting there. Was this why Will wasn't in the Novak meetings? Amanda was keeping him out of the mix because she wanted him to go undercover in a joint operation with the FBI.

Faith tried to frame a question she could climb out of. "When was Will supposed to get involved?"

"We were discussing dates, but it was going to be a matter of days. The online chatter about the group has been huge lately. There's some kind of statement they're planning to make. And trust me, these guys don't make little statements."

Group?

Faith's mouth went dry. Michelle's abduction and the attack were bigger than the five men at the car accident. There was an organization behind this, a cell that was working on an even bigger act of destruction.

She quoted Amanda, "The bombs weren't an escalation."

"No, they were about getting Spivey's medical emergency dealt with and making sure they all got the hell out of here so they could live to fight another day." He added, "Classic diversion tactic for these people. The crime is never about the explosion."

She tested the waters. "And Novak?"

"Careful," he warned. "Through here."

Van held open the door for her. The conference room had a large table with about twenty chairs around it. A very elegant blonde woman stood up from one of the side chairs and walked over with her hand out. She was about Amanda's age, but taller and thinner and beautiful in a way that was disconcerting if you were not.

"I'm Executive Assistant Director Kate Murphy from Intelligence." The woman had a firm handshake. "Has Aiden brought you up to speed?"

Faith felt waylaid by the title. The executive assistant part didn't make her a secretary. This woman was three rungs down from the director of the FBI. She would've been stationed out of DC, in charge of overseeing the intelligence-gathering services of every field office in the country.

Faith's bladder felt weak. She wanted to think Amanda had given her this task out of trust, but sending a flunky to meet a high-level director was basically a big fuck you in the face.

"Agent Mitchell?" the woman asked.

Faith tightened her resolve. She didn't work for the FBI. She worked for Amanda, and Amanda had told Faith to give them hell. "My boss is tired of your bullshit. She wants information."

Murphy exchanged a look with Van.

Don't take anything they say at face value. There's always an ulterior motive.

"Well?" Faith asked.

Murphy hesitated. Then she reached into her briefcase. She pulled out a folder and slapped it open on the table.

Adam Humphrey Carter.

This was why Carter had two warrants on his head but no one had picked him up. The FBI had turned him into a confidential informant.

Faith said, "Your CI has abducted two women. One of them is an agent with the GBI."

"And the other is an infectious disease specialist with the CDC." Murphy opened a second file. A color photograph was clipped to a stack of official-looking documents.

Michelle Spivey was standing in what looked like a Third World country. Water flooded around her boots. A green Army tent was in the distance. She was in combat fatigues. There were captain's bars on the collar. Faith always forgot that the CDC was attached to the uniformed services through the Marines. The agency had started out quarantining ships to keep diseases out of ports and evolved into a world-wide response unit for public health.

Murphy said, "This is Dr. Spivey in Puerto Rico after Maria hit."

So, not a Third World country, just an abandoned US territory.

Faith asked, "What was she doing there?"

"Monitoring and preparing for cholera and the associated pandemics you see with these types of natural disasters." Murphy pulled out two chairs and sat down. "Spivey is an Epidemic Intelligence Officer attached as a rapid responder through the emergency ops center."

Faith sank into the chair. She took out her notebook. EIOs were field investigators deployed into hot zones. They could work on anything from tying a lettuce farm to a salmonella outbreak or trying to stop the spread of Ebola.

Faith said, "The news is making Spivey out to be a scientist who spends all day with her eyes stuck to a microscope."

"She *is* a scientist. But she's also a licensed MD with a master's in public health and a Ph.D. in diseases and vaccinology."

"Vaccines?" Faith asked.

"Her recent focus has been the resurgence of pertussis, or whooping cough, in the United States. But she's worked on other classified projects. Her clearance is 0-6. Top Secret."

Faith looked down at her empty notepad. "How does Carter enter the picture?"

Murphy nodded toward Van.

He said, "The locals assumed Spivey was the victim of a kidnap and rape. Carter's image was pretty clean in the CCTV. They kept the video from the media and ran it through RISC."

The Repository for Individuals of Special Concern.

He said, "When we signed him up, I entered Carter's biometrics into the database in case he showed up somewhere else."

Faith said, "You mean in case he kidnapped and raped another woman, like he did back when he was a police officer?"

Van let her sarcasm slide. "Carter was feeding us solid intel from the IPA."

Faith nodded, though she had no idea what the IPA was, other than an abbreviation for India Pale Ale. Traffickers didn't tend to name their organizations. They were part of mobs—Russian, Yakuza, Sinaloa. Hurley and Carter were white, so that ruled out street gangs like the Latin Kings and the Black Disciples. That left the Hell's Angels, the Hammerskins or whatever else the neo-Nazi club-of-the-month was calling itself—all of which Carter would've come into contact with during one of his many incarcerations.

Faith asked, "Did you recruit Carter out of prison?"

Murphy hesitated again. Faith couldn't tell if it was a manipulation or true reticence.

The woman said, "He came to us through a separate, unrelated investigation."

Faith doubted it was unrelated. This woman oozed bullshit.

Van said, "What we can tell you is, in the beginning, it was clear Carter wasn't a true believer. He joined the IPA for the joy of being a violent shithead. Picking bar fights. Knocking heads at political rallies. A few months ago, I had to jerk his leash. It seemed like he was turning into a good solider. Cut his hair. Shaved off his beard. Stopped drinking, which was a giant neon warning. He went radio silent after that. That's when the chatter started on our channels telling us something big was in the works. The next time I saw Carter was in the video snatching Spivey."

Faith said, "The IPA directed him to kidnap her."

"Not necessarily," Murphy countered. "The Bureau isn't convinced that the IPA is involved in the abduction. Carter is a bad actor with a lifetime of crimes under his belt."

The lightbulb over Faith's head turned into a solar flare.

Kate Murphy was the "they" Amanda was referring to when she had talked about removing the sex-trafficking angle from the equation. If the FBI was running a joint operation with the GBI, the FBI would be in charge of setting the parameters. If Amanda didn't play by their rules, then it would no longer be a joint operation.

So it was up to Faith to convince the FBI that they were wrong. Michelle hadn't been abducted for sex. She had been abducted for something far more sinister.

Faith told Murphy, "My partner already identified Adam Humphrey Carter as the man who abducted Michelle Spivey. He recognized Carter's face because Carter was one of the men who took Sara Linton."

Murphy's eyebrow raised, but that was all she gave.

Faith said, "Carter was part of the team that brought Michelle Spivey to the hospital. She was going to die without surgery. They risked everything to keep her alive. You don't open yourself up to that kind of exposure if you're trafficking a woman for sex. She gets sick, you cut her up and cram her into a suitcase, or you dump her in a field and drive away. You can always grab another woman off the street—assuming you've got a kink for forty-year-old lesbian mothers."

Without thinking, Faith had leaned forward the same way she would during an interrogation, cutting off Murphy's personal space to let her know who was in charge.

She went with her body's instinct. "Either Michelle Spivey's got a golden pussy, or she's integral to whatever the IPA wants to do next. That's what the chatter is about. They're planning a large-scale attack, and they need Michelle, a doctor from the CDC, to do it."

Murphy sat back in her chair. She looked at Faith as if she'd just seen her for the first time. "Everything you've said is conjecture. Show me the concrete pieces that link them all together. Give me the evidence to present to a judge so I can get warrants."

Faith so badly wanted to roll her eyes. "You're the FBI. Break down some doors. Carter gives you all the probable cause you need."

Van took over. "There are no doors to break down. The IPA is nomadic. They live in tents in the middle of nowhere. We find one camp and they've bugged out to the next. They have people on the inside. Our inside, your inside, every inside you can imagine. And no offense, but your boss hasn't been a lot of help."

Murphy said, "Georgia and New York are the only two states in the country whose constitutions do not explicitly subordinate all military groups to civil authority. But in all honestly, every state has been looking the other way on these private militia and paramilitary groups."

Paramilitary groups.

Faith felt her body break out in a cold sweat.

This was the nail Faith had been hammering around all day.

Martin Elias Novak, their *high-value prisoner*, had spent time with a so-called civilian border patrol in Arizona. These were men who felt like the federal government wasn't doing enough to secure the southern border, so they set out with rifles and shotguns to do the job themselves. From what Faith could tell, most of the men were just looking for a reason to camp out, get away from their wives, and pretend they were more important than their actual lives as accountants or used car salesmen would indicate. The more dangerous factions were steeped in the theories of the Posse Comitatus, who believed that the government should be violently overthrown and returned to white Christian men.

Apparently, they lacked access to photographs of the majority of the United States Congress, the president, the cabinet, and most of the judges packed onto state and federal courts.

Murphy provided, "There are around three hundred paramilitary groups active in the US right now. This isn't a regional issue. Every state has its share. So long as they keep their heads down, there's no reason to poke the bear. We don't want another Waco or Ruby Ridge."

She wasn't wrong to worry. Both sieges had not only been public relations disasters for the FBI, they had reportedly inspired countless acts of violence, from the bombing of the Murrah

Federal Building and the Boston Marathon to perhaps even the Columbine High School Massacre.

Then again, the FBI had mishandled tip-offs about the Parkland Shooter, Larry Nassar, the Pulse Night Club Shooter, the Texas Terrorist Attack and countless red flags around Russia's involvement in various misdeeds. Not to mention one of their own informants had just helped a bunch of his buddies set off two bombs at a major urban hospital.

Van seemed to read her mind. "These multi-pronged investigations take money and patience. We're hoping this latest display will shake more resources out of DC. Novak robbed all of those banks for a reason. They're sitting on a ton of cash. The chatter points to something big happening."

"Novak is not necessarily connected to any of it." Murphy kept tempering Van's words. You didn't climb that high in the FBI without being a political animal. "The IPA cannot at this time be definitively linked to anyone but Carter. Yes, we have chatter, but it's called chatter for a reason. It could be nothing. We don't leap to conclusions in the Bureau. We build solid cases based upon actionable evidence. Your partner was supposed to go undercover and gather that evidence, but that's impossible now that they know what he looks like."

Faith felt a question niggling in the back of her mind. "Why is an agent from the GBI going undercover if this is an FBI investigation?"

Murphy's eyebrow went up. She was either surprised or impressed.

Van said, "We can't get the resources. The current climate at the Bureau dictates that white Christian males can't be terrorists."

"Aiden." Murphy's voice was a warning.

He held up his hands in a shrug. "My grandmother and great grandmother walked out of a Nazi death camp. I tend to take these things a bit more seriously."

Murphy stood up. "In the hall, please."

Faith didn't wait for the door to close behind them. Nor did she try to eavesdrop on the dressing down. She started paging through the files.

The Invisible Patriot Army.

Black-and-white photos showed groups of young white men dressed in tactical gear. Some of them were marching in procession. Others were practicing drills in a boot-camp course with climbing walls and razor wire. Every last one of them was armed with some kind of weapon. Most had two or three. Their belts were strapped with holsters and knife sheaths. AR-15s were slung over their shoulders.

She found the photo of Michelle Spivey in Puerto Rico. The woman had devoted her life to saving people, vaccinating children, stopping pandemics in the most inhospitable parts of the world.

There was another photo pinned to the documents. A selfie showed Michelle with her wife and daughter. The eleven-year-old was ebullient. A Christmas tree was behind them. Newly opened presents were strewn across the couch. The Michelle in the photo had roughly six more months before life as she knew it was over.

Which begged the question—

What did a well-funded, well-trained paramilitary organization want with a woman who specialized in the spread of infectious diseases?

7

Sunday, August 4, 2:26 p.m.

Sara closed her eyes against the darkness. She could feel the vibrations of the road shaking through her body. They were in the back of a box truck now, the sort of thing you rented to move an apartment. Michelle and Sara were handcuffed to rails on opposite sides. Both of them were gagged so they couldn't communicate with each other or call for help. As if their voices would carry over the truck's diesel engine and the rumble of endless roads they traveled down.

What this meant in the immediate was that Sara's Walkie message to Faith about the white van was useless. Two men had met them at a closed gas station off of 285. They were muscle-bound and young, sporting the sort of square-jawed looks that you saw on Army recruitment posters. One drove off in the white van. The other followed him in a nondescript car.

Sara didn't have to be told that they were going to abandon the van as far away from their true destination as possible. Nor did she have to be told it was a very bad sign that neither man had bothered to conceal his face.

Sara knew too much, and what she didn't know, she was quickly figuring out.

Dash never raised his voice, but the effect of his words was like a general on the battlefield. Sara had overheard him relaying softly worded instructions into a burner phone as she was being led to the truck. She'd caught some names—Wilkins, Peterson, O'Leary—before Dash had broken the phone in two and tossed it into the woods. Every man that Sara had laid eyes on so far had the bearing of a soldier. Shoulders back. Eyes forward. Hands clenched. They were organized into a command structure. They had committed an act of domestic terrorism against a hospital.

Militia. Freemen. Weathermen. Guerillas. Eco-terrorists. Antifa.

The groups went by different names, but they were all aligned by the same purpose: using violence to bend the rest of America to their will.

Did it matter?

Sara's world had shrunk to the four walls in which she was trapped. She had no idea how much time had passed since the gas station, but she'd been captive long enough for her thoughts to keep spinning in the same cramped circle.

She worried about Will. She worried that Cathy would not take care of him. She worried about the pain in her wrists from the handcuffs. The sweltering heat depleting fluid from her body. The darkness making her lose track of direction and time. She worried about Will.

Only occasionally did she drop the barrier that kept her thoughts so tightly wound and worry about herself.

Sara knew what was coming next.

Michelle Spivey had been raped and drugged into submission. Even if Carter was waylaid by his injury, there would be others like him, comrades in arms.

There were numbers to the organization.

In the squalid heat of the truck, arms handcuffed above her head, Sara tried to resign herself to the inevitable.

She had survived it once before.

Hadn't she?

Back in college, Sara had been lucky in her rape.

It felt strange to frame it that way, but Sara was not considering the physical violation. That act had been the most devastating moment of her life until the death of her husband.

The luck came after.

She was a young, educated white woman. She came from a solidly middle-class family. She had at that point in her life only had one sexual partner, her boyfriend from high school. She was more likely to dress in sweatpants than a miniskirt. She seldom wore make-up. She didn't really drink. She had tried pot once in high school, only to prove to her sister that she could. Most of Sara's life had been spent with her head in a textbook or her butt in a desk chair.

In other words, there wasn't a lot of material for the defense lawyer to use in his quest to turn the blame on to Sara.

The attack had happened inside a women's toilet stall at Grady Hospital. Sara had been handcuffed. Vaginally raped. Stabbed in the side with a serrated hunting knife. She had yelled "no" once before her mouth was duct-taped shut. There was no argument to be made for consent. She couldn't recall many of the details before or after—that was the nature of trauma—but she could to this day clearly summon the face of the man who had raped her.

The crystal blue eyes.

The long, stringy hair.

The rough beard that smelled of cigarettes and fried food.

The clamminess of his pale skin when he thrust against her.

And still, Sara was lucky that her attacker had been found guilty of rape. That he wasn't offered a plea deal on a lesser charge. That she was given the opportunity to have her voice heard in court. That the judge wasn't lenient in his sentencing. That there were other women her attacker had raped, so there was not just one lone woman accusing him but several.

Which mattered so much more than it should.

After the trial, Sara was very lucky that her parents had forced her to move back home. She'd already dropped out of her hard-won neo-natal surgical fellowship. Fallen behind on her bills. Stopped going outside. Stopped eating. Stopped breathing the same, sleeping the same, seeing the world the same as she had before.

Because nothing was the same as before.

When Sara had left for college, she had vowed that she would never live in Grant County again, but she'd found herself grateful for the familiarity. She knew almost everyone in town. Her mother and sister were there to hold her when she was wracked by uncontrollable sobbing. Her father slept on the floor of her bedroom until Sara felt safe enough to be on her own.

But, she never truly felt safe the way she had before.

She did eventually feel better. She'd managed to gather the remaining pieces of herself and put them back together. She'd started to date again. She'd gotten married. She'd lied to her husband about why she couldn't have children. Even after Sara had told Jeffrey the truth, they had never really talked about it. He was a police officer, but he couldn't bring himself to say the word rape. On the rare occasion it came up, they both referred to it as *what happened at Grady.*

The truck's tires hit a rut in the road.

Sara felt her body lift into the air, then slam down. A sharp pain jarred her tailbone. Her wrist jerked against the handcuffs. Her shoulders ached.

She waited, teeth clenched, until the ride smoothed out again.

Sara took in a deep breath. Her lungs strained against the wet, stagnant air. She squeezed her eyes closed and tried to circle her thoughts back into the previous loop: Will needed medical attention. Cathy would not take care of him. Sara's wrists ached from the handcuffs. She was dehydrated from the heat. She had no idea how much time had passed or where she was.

Will.

Cathy would advocate for him. She would force him to stay in the hospital. She would put cool cloths on his head because she knew that Sara loved him.

Didn't she?

Sara had only ever bickered with her mother about Will. She had never told Cathy that she was deeply, irrevocably in love with him. This was what Sara should've said in the kitchen: She still got butterflies when Will walked through the door. She left lipstick hearts on the bathroom mirror for him to find. She had intrinsically trusted Will from the moment she'd met him—so much that Sara had told him what happened at Grady even before they had started a relationship.

His childhood had been steeped in abuse. He hadn't tried to soothe Sara or fix her or soften the language around what had happened because he couldn't live with the truth. Will understood at a basic level why a random noise could still terrify her. Why she never went for a run past dusk, even with the dogs. That, without explanation, she was going to circle a parking lot twenty times to get a spot closest to the door. That sometimes, she wouldn't flush the toilet at night because she was afraid the noise would drown out the sound of an intruder.

That was what Sara would tell her mother if she ever got away—

Will understood why she still thought of herself lucky.

The truck started to slow. Sara waited, straining to hear other cars or people or anything that would indicate their location.

The gears stripped. The engine rumbled. Sara lurched against the wall as the truck backed up. The brakes squealed, then the truck stopped again.

There were male voices outside. She heard a low murmur and guessed this was Dash. Then there was shouting. Feet kicking up gravel. She assumed that an unpaved road meant that they were in a remote area. They hadn't paused for a light or a stop sign in a while. The air had gotten cooler. Perhaps they were at a higher altitude. Sara had not heard another car around them for quite some time.

The door rolled up. She closed her eyes against the light.

Sunlight. Still daytime.

She looked for Michelle. The woman was sitting opposite Sara. Her hands were cuffed above her head. The gag in her mouth had slipped out, but she hadn't said one word this entire time.

"Dr. Earnshaw." Dash's arm was in a proper sling. The white edge of a bandage jutted above the collar of his fresh T-shirt. Someone had already taken the bullet out of his shoulder. There was a man with a rifle standing beside him.

He told Sara, "Or should I call you, *local doctor*?" He waited for Sara to ask for clarification. She would not give him the satisfaction. "That's what they're calling you on the radio. A *local doctor* was taken hostage when she ran to the hospital to offer help."

Sara tried to swallow, but her mouth was too dry. She didn't know what emotion he was expecting—relief that they were looking for her? Gratitude to be told the information? She already knew that they were looking for her. She would stab out her own eyes before she showed this man any appreciation.

She said, "Maybe they're holding back my name because they don't want you to threaten my family the way Carter did with Michelle's eleven-year-old daughter."

He shook his head. "I'm sure he was only fooling around."

"His exact words were—" Sara had to clear the rasp from her throat before she could continue. "'The way you're talking makes me wonder how tight your daughter's pussy is.'"

Dash looked off to the side. "That's jarring language coming from a woman."

"Try hearing it with a loaded gun pointed at your head."

Dash nodded to someone in the parking lot. "Let's get her out of the truck and into the air conditioning. I think the heat's gone to her head."

A large, hairy man climbed into the back of the truck. His belt had an eight-inch hunting knife sheathed on one side and a holstered gun on the other. He fished out a set of keys from his pocket and uncuffed Sara from the rail.

She rubbed her sore wrists. Her mind threw up options. She could punch him in the groin. Try to get his knife or gun.

And then?

"Dr. Earnshaw?" Dash said, his tone indicating she had a choice, the armed men around her making it clear that she did not.

Sara stood up on shaky legs. She used her hand to shield her eyes from the sun. Her inner Girl Scout guessed it was mid-afternoon, between three and four o'clock. Her watch had read 2:17 behind the strip club. An hour or two on the road. They could be anywhere.

Dash offered a hand to help her down.

Sara refused. She took in her surroundings as she climbed from the truck. They were parked in front of a one-story motel with a long porch lining the front of the rooms. Rustic-looking, like a fishing lodge. Sara couldn't tell if the business was closed or just vacant. There were no other cars in the lot. The area was definitely rural. Mountainous. Trees were everywhere. She couldn't hear traffic from the road. Across the street, she saw a skeezy-looking bar. The sign outside had a cartoon rabbit holding a mug of beer.

Peter Cottontail's.

"This way, please." Dash gestured toward one of the hotel rooms.

The door was already open. Cool air pushed against the heat. Michelle Spivey was behind Sara as she walked inside. Plastic table and chairs. TV on the wall. A chest of drawers for clothes. A mini-fridge. A nightstand between two queen beds. Vale was lying on the bed by the wall, Carter was sitting up on the one by the window. Particles of dust floated in the sunlight. The smell of Pine-Sol was pervasive.

Vale's head turned. He looked at Sara, desperate. His chest shook. He had developed a dry, hacking cough.

Behind her, the truck rumbled to life. The gravel spun as it pulled away.

Sara watched it leave. Nondescript, white, like all the other trucks on the roads and highways.

"Doctor?" Dash waited for her to move aside before he shut the door.

He had kept three men with him. Two were armed and cut from the same mold as the others. One was dressed more casually in an untucked, long-sleeved dress shirt with the sleeves rolled up. A pair of cargo shorts hung loose from his slim hips. His hair was longer than the others. His beard was growing out. He carried a large backpack over his shoulder. There was a Red Cross emblem on the front above an American flag.

An Army field medical kit.

Sara looked for Michelle. She'd gone to the far corner of the room and sat down on the floor. Her arms circled her knees. Her head was down again.

Was this how Carter had trained her to sit or was it merely self-preservation?

"Dr. Earnshaw." Dash handed Sara a bottle of water. He nodded for the two men to station themselves outside. The third one, the casual one, rested his backpack on the plastic table. "My friend Beau here would be happy to assist you."

Sara couldn't find her voice. The monotony of the truck had beaten down her terror, but now it was revving up again. She was inside a seedy motel. Trapped with these men who reeked of testosterone. Michelle had been right to cower in the corner.

Beau started unzipping the field kit. His fingers traced down items, removing gear to start an IV drip. There was a bag of saline in the rear compartment. He had enough equipment to perform minor surgery.

Sara watched his hands move. Quickly. Efficiently. Despite the casual wear, he clearly knew what he was doing. More importantly, he would know what Sara was doing. She had lost her opportunity to either kill Vale and Carter or to let them die through neglect.

"Damn, dude," Carter said. "Hook me up with that. My sac is on fire."

Beau ignored the request. He had already inserted the catheter in Vale's arm. He secured it with tape. He opened the drip. The man had clearly done this thousands of times before. Sara assumed he'd been the one to take the bullet out of Dash's shoulder.

"Bro," Carter tried. "Come on."

Beau said, "Most critical first."

"I'm fucking critical. I got a knife half an inch from my junk."

Beau glanced at Carter's injury. "You strapped it down too tight, bro. You don't fix a vagina by making the hole bigger."

Dash chuckled, but said, "Let's keep the locker room talk at bay around the ladies."

He found the remote and turned on the television.

Sara gawked at the footage. A news helicopter was flying over the bomb site. Hot tears burned her eyes. The campus and hospital grounds were barely recognizable. She had spent seven years of her life training there, helping people, learning how to be a good doctor.

"Nice." Dash turned up the volume. A woman was standing at a podium dressed in an Atlanta police uniform. The banner said the news conference had been pre-recorded.

". . . all agencies searching for the kidnapped woman . . ."

"That's you," Dash said. "Local doctor."

Sara tuned him out, listening to the officer. "I can confirm there were two devices timed approximately—"

Dash muted the volume.

Sara's eyes searched the scroll at the bottom. *Eighteen confirmed dead. Forty-one wounded. Two Dekalb Co. police officers, one Fulton Co. sheriff's deputy and two security guards among murdered.*

"What a handsome devil," Dash said.

The police had released CCTV footage from the hospital. The images showed several different angles on Dash, but even Sara, who had spent the last few hours with him, did not recognize Dash as the man on the screen. He had been vigilant about keeping his hat pulled down and his head low. Carter had not been as careful, but he'd gotten lucky. The close-up of his face had pixelated. A third set of images showed Hurley dragging Michelle down the stairs.

Dash mumbled, "Rest your soul, brother."

Sara kept herself still. Dash still thought that Hurley was dead. Carter and Vale had doubled down on their lie about what had really happened after the car accident. You didn't hide information from the boss unless you knew the boss was going to be pissed off if he knew the truth. They weren't feeling guilty for abandoning one of their *brothers*. They were worried that Dash would punish them for leaving a witness.

Which begged the question: How could Sara use this information against them?

"Dr. Earnshaw?" Beau had a stethoscope waiting for her.

Sara pulled her eyes away from the television. The scroll at the bottom of the set was what had her attention.

Two ATL firemen and three ATL police officers injured. Two

Dekalb Co. police officers, one Fulton Co. sheriff's deputy and two security guards among murdered.

They were being very specific in the description. Will's rank was special agent. Should Sara take it as a good sign that he was not on the injured list?

Beau said, "I don't have a Pleur-Evac."

Sara drank from the water bottle. She tried to pull herself back into the moment. In medical school, they had drilled into her that taking the oath to practice meant that you treated whoever needed your help. You put politics and personal beliefs aside. You fixed the body, not the patient.

Sara worked to summon that young, eager student who had fervently believed this was possible.

She handed the water bottle to Dash. "I need three of these. Duct tape. Tubing. I have to create a water seal, so cork would be better. The other two bottles will regulate the pressure and collect the blood from his chest. If you have a drill, the bit needs to be slightly smaller in circumference to the tubes."

Dash opened the door and relayed the request to one of the men.

Sara caught Michelle's eye. The woman worked at the CDC. At the very least, she had a veterinary degree if not a medical degree.

"Steady," Beau told Vale, using a pair of scissors to cut away his shirt. Vale's chest was heaving. He was in a full-on panic as Sara approached the bed. Dry coughs shook his body.

Sara snapped on a pair of nitrile gloves. Clipped the stethoscope around her neck. She found a pair of safety goggles and a surgical mask.

She told Beau, "If you have it, two mgs of Versed, then one mg every five minutes as needed."

"That won't depress his breathing?"

"It might, but I can't have him moving around."

"I'll keep some adrenaline on hand." Beau went back to the medical kit. In addition to Versed he had packets of pre-loaded syringes. She recognized the distinctive 10 inside an open burgundy square. Five individual doses of ten milligrams of morphine.

Sara could use them to knock out the men in the room.

She could use them all on herself.

"Versed on board." Beau injected the drug into the IV port.

Sara tore herself away from the promise of the morphine. She knelt on the floor beside Vale.

Beside *the body*.

More of Beau's handiwork was evident. The gunshot wound had been patched with a Halo Chest Seal, an occlusive bandage that was basically a sticky version of Saran Wrap. This was good, but the Russell Chest Seal she'd seen in the kit would've been better.

Beau knew some things, but he didn't know everything.

Sara palpated the patient's ribs, feeling the pointed shards of displaced fractures. Counting down from his nipple, the bullet had entered between the seventh and eighth rib. His skin was taut. The pleural cavity had filled with air. She used her stethoscope. Breath sounds were absent on the right side. The thorax was hyperresonant. The jugular vein showed distention.

Vale coughed, wincing at the pain.

She looked up at Beau. He was monitoring Vale's blood pressure. The adrenaline syringe was nearby just in case.

Sara listened to the chest again, moving the stethoscope around. She checked bowel sounds. She pressed into the abdomen. None of this was necessary. She wanted time to study the hem of Beau's untucked shirt. The edge below the last button showed a crescent-shaped tear.

Not just a tear. A repetitive use mark, the sort of thing she used to identify John Does in the morgue. Carpenters tended to have little notches worn in their front teeth from holding nails in their mouths. Warehouse workers had extremely well-developed calves, no matter the width of their waists. UPS drivers had callouses on their ring fingers because that was where they were trained to keep their key rings when they got out of their trucks.

And bartenders oftentimes used the tails of their shirts to open bottles.

This wasn't a random motel or fishing lodge. They had stopped here for Beau. He most likely worked at the bar across the street.

Sara finished the fake part of the exam. She told Beau, "Tension pneumothorax."

He nodded once, but she could tell he understood that this wasn't the only issue. The symptoms of the collapsed lung presented the most visible sign of injury, but there was a bullet inside this man's chest. Judging by the cracked ribs, the projectile had ricocheted around before settling. The heart was always the primary concern with a chest wound, but in truth, every area of the chest was a concern. Nerves, arteries, veins, lungs, thorax.

Sara was not a cardiothoracic surgeon. She could make him more comfortable, but he would need someone far more skilled and with very precise equipment to repair the damage inside his body.

Beau must have known this. Still, he offered Sara an IV catheter from the transfusion pack.

Sara found the midpoint of the clavicle. Beau swabbed the area clean. She inserted the catheter perpendicular to the skin, just under the clavicle.

The hiss of air coming out of the hollow needle was like a balloon being deflated.

Vale's chest rose with a deep breath. He gasped. His eyes opened. He blinked.

Every man in the room seemed to breathe easier alongside him.

Carter said, "Okay now, fix me."

Sara looked to Beau for his input. She had to remind herself that he was not her nurse. He was a bad man. He was of his own volition using his skills to patch up other bad men.

Sara came clean with Dash: "I can keep Vale comfortable, but his surgical needs are beyond my capabilities."

Dash rubbed his jaw with his fingers.

Sara had to look away. Will did the same thing when he was upset.

Beau said, "She's giving it to you straight. If you're not going to take him to a hospital, the chest tube will delay the inevitable."

Dash asked, "He's going to die?"

"Jesus Christ!" Carter's tone was somewhere between pleading and belligerent. "Why are you wasting time on him when my scrotum could be fucking dying?"

Dash kept rubbing his jaw, considering. "All right. Get the knife out of his leg."

Beau returned to the medical kit.

Sara struggled against her revulsion. Treating Vale was one thing. The man was terrified, floating in and out of consciousness. But every time Carter opened his mouth—whether it was to threaten to rape Michelle's daughter or to tell Sara he was going to fuck the bad attitude out of her mouth—she was reminded of how much she wanted him to die.

Beau had already started cutting away Carter's jeans. He went up and over, exposing the man's naked lower half.

Carter sneered at Sara. He didn't speak, but she knew what he was thinking.

She ignored him.

Will made him look like a Ken doll.

Beau asked, "What's the plan?"

Sara said, "You're going to have to knock him out if you want me to do this."

"I can take the edge off." Beau drew Versed into a fresh syringe. He hadn't bothered to run a saline line. He jabbed the needle into Carter's arm so hard the plastic tube popped against the skin.

So, Beau wasn't a Carter fan, either.

He started lining up supplies on the top of the mini-fridge by the bed. Clamps, scalpels, gauze, forceps.

"Get thish . . . bith . . ." The drug hit Carter in slow motion. His chin dropped to his chest. His mouth gaped open. His eyes were slitted as he tried to follow what they were doing.

Sara changed out her gloves. Mentally, she worked to separate Carter the abhorrent human being from the patient with a knife in his leg. She studied the insertion point of the blade. Summoned her anatomy mnemonic for the femoral triangle. NAVEL. Starting laterally: nerve, artery, vein, empty space—the femoral canal—and lymphatic.

Beau cut the shoelace lanyard away from the knife. His fingertip held it in place.

They could both see the handle pulsing.

The blade had shifted, or maybe Carter had been lucky this whole time, because there was clearly a hole in his femoral artery. The pulse was from his heart pushing out oxygenated blood. The effect was like a high-pressure hose. The only thing keeping Carter from bleeding out was the side of the blade plugging the hole.

She told Beau, "I'm not a vascular surgeon."

"Understood."

"I can cut down while you hold the knife steady. I'll try to clamp the bleed. We don't have any suction. I'll be feeling around blind."

"Understood," he handed her the scalpel.

They were doing this.

Sara felt unusually shaken by the prospect of cutting into this man. Surgery was not a time for introspection; it was a moment for pure arrogance. If she couldn't move quickly enough, if there was too much blood to isolate the bleed, then Carter would be dead in less than a minute. Vale was already as good as dead. With both men gone, they wouldn't need her—or worse, they would find another use.

Beau said, "Doctor?"

She held breath in her lungs, then slowly pushed it out. "This has to be fast. I need you to pack the wound with gauze as I go. Can you hold open the forceps?"

Beau nodded, but said, "We need a third set of hands."

Sara could feel the heat of Michelle staring at her back. She probably hadn't operated on a person in years, if ever, but she could hold a knife steady.

Dash indicated his sling. "I'm down half a set."

"Fuhch—" The word jumbled out of Carter's mouth. "She ain't touching—"

He meant Michelle.

Dash said, "It appears that you don't have a choice."

Sara wasn't sure whether he was talking to Carter or Michelle, but it didn't matter in the end. Slowly, Michelle stood. Her head was still down. Her eyes stayed on the floor.

It wasn't until the last second that Sara saw her hands clench.

What happened next was clearly planned—maybe Michelle had been thinking about it at the car accident or when she'd walked into this dingy motel room or maybe her actions were something she'd practiced in her mind for the last four weeks. The *when* didn't matter. The *what* was spectacular.

Michelle waited until she was close to the bed, then pushed off from the balls of her feet. She launched herself into the air. She straddled Carter. She ripped the knife out of his leg and started stabbing him.

Slap-slap-slap.

The blade made the same sound over and over again as it punctured the skin.

There were no wasted movements. The attack was the visual realization of a deep understanding of human anatomy.

The jugular. The windpipe. The axillary arteries. The heart. The lungs. Michelle gave out a primal scream and drove the final blow into the man's liver.

Then she collapsed.

Beau had injected her with the rest of the Versed.

The vestiges of Michelle's primal screams echoed around the room. No one could move. Vale's staggered breathing served as an audible pulse to the blood squirting from Carter's carotid.

Slowly, Sara took off her streaked safety glasses. Ropes of blood had slashed across her face and hair.

At some point, the door had flung open. The two sentries stood motionless, weapons drawn.

Dash's arm was out. He said, "Let's keep it calm, boys. We need her alive."

The men stayed where they were. They didn't seem to know what to do.

Sara wiped her face. She wiped blood from her forehead. Every item in the room shadowed the slashing of the knife, from the beds to the TV to the ceiling.

Even in death, Carter was a nuisance. He hung on for twenty

seconds or more. Gurgles came from the back of his throat. Red bubbles popped on his blue lips. He stared blindly down at the knife sticking out of his belly. Urine soaked his pants. His hands and fingers twitched. A line of blood dripped from his open mouth. The spray of blood coming from his carotid dwindled into a leak, like a lawn sprinkler that had suddenly lost pressure. His last breath was taken with visible terror.

He had known what was coming every single second that preceded his death.

Sara put her hand to her chest. Her heart was like a trapped bird.

She was elated by his suffering.

"Well." Dash went into the bathroom. He came out wiping his face with a hand towel. He had a second towel for Sara. She caught it mid-air. He looked down at Michelle. She had collapsed across Carter's legs.

Sara had expected Dash's preternatural calm to finally break, but he only said, "I wonder why she did that?"

Sara put her face in the clean towel and shook her head.

"Gentlemen. Let's clear the room."

She could hear them lift Michelle from the bed.

Dash said, "Put her next door. Make sure she's handcuffed. We don't want any more sudden acts of mayhem."

Mayhem?

Sara wiped her face. Michelle's arms flopped to the side as she was carried out. Her eyes were closed. There was something like peace in her expression.

"Dr. Earnshaw?" Dash asked. "Can you enlighten me?"

Sara studied his face for guile. Did he really not know that Carter had raped Michelle?

She said, "He—"

She felt Vale's hand on her shoulder. The sudden violence had pierced the fog of the muscle relaxer. His eyes were opened, filled with fear.

Dash waited another moment, then asked, "Dr. Earnshaw?"

Sara shook off Vale's hand. "He raped her. Repeatedly. He threatened to rape me."

Dash's jaw tightened. His expression began to change. Sara watched the slow transformation from amicable to enraged.

He looked at Vale, not Sara, and asked, "Is this true?"

Vale shook his head wildly.

"Soldier, is this true?"

Vale kept shaking his head.

Dash turned away from him. He rubbed his jaw with his fingers.

Then he turned around and shot Vale twice in the chest.

Sara jumped. She had been close enough to feel the heat of the bullets whizzing past her face.

Dash returned the gun to his holster. He told Sara, "I hope, Doctor, you don't think that we are the sort of animals who use rape as a weapon of war."

Sara said nothing. They had bombed a hospital and kidnapped two women. Pretending to hold themselves above the pettiness of rape was laughable.

Beau grabbed the handle of Will's folding knife and pulled it out of Carter's belly. He wiped the blade with cotton gauze. He folded the knife and stuck it into his own pocket. Then he started to pack up the medical kit. He put the used items in a pile on the table. He took out a card to start an inventory.

Or to make sure Sara hadn't taken anything.

Dash patted Vale's pockets. He found some cash, but nothing else. He did the same pat-down on Carter. This time, he found a cell phone. Not a flip phone, but an iPhone.

The screen was cracked.

"Unfortunate." Dash went to the door. He asked the sentry, "Do you have a cell phone?"

"No, sir. None of us do. Your orders were to leave anything identifiable at the Camp."

The Camp?

"Thank you." Dash closed the door. He sat on the bed beside Carter. He tried one-handed to press Carter's finger to the home button on the phone.

Beau said, "Won't work when they're dead. You need a capacitance signal in your skin to activate the ring. Gotta have a heartbeat to make that happen."

"Is that so?" Dash held up the phone. He stared at it as if he could divine a way into the contents. "We don't want to be using any of your devices, do we?"

"No, sir, we don't." Beau's tone implied he was taking a position.

So maybe he wasn't as aligned with the group as the others. A former recruit? A hired gun? A medic who charged by the injury?

Dash tossed Carter's phone onto the bedside table. He rubbed his jaw again. He turned to Sara.

"Doctor, if I could have your attention?" He pointed to the front and back of the room. "I've got your exits blocked. I can handcuff you to the bed, or you can believe me."

Sara swallowed so hard that her throat made a sound. "I believe you."

Dash left, but the tension did not leave with him.

Beau was clearly angry. He yanked on the zips to his field kit. He collected the trash into a pile—the bloody gauze, the scissors, even the water bottles. He used an alcohol swab to wipe down the field medical kit. Sara bit her lip so that she would not smile. Carter's blood would be embedded in the seams, the teeth of the zippers. Beau's sentimental attachment would put him in the middle of a double homicide.

Sara looked at the television. She read the scroll at the bottom of the screen.

. . . two Dekalb Co. police officers, one Fulton Co. sheriff's deputy and two security guards among murdered . . . Official Statement: "GBI will put on active duty ATL agents to assist local and state law enforcement . . ."

Sara's heart flipped inside her chest. Her eyes followed the text before it disappeared from the screen.

. . . will put on active duty ATL agents to assist local and state law enforcement . . .

She kept her eyes on the television as the program went into a commercial break. Sara tried to do a reality check. Amanda would've been responsible for writing the official statement. Was Sara reading too much into the stilted language? Was she so desperate for news that she was making crazy leaps?

Will put on active duty. ATL. Agents assisting local and state law enforcement.

Tears welled into Sara's eyes. She wanted so badly to believe that Amanda had written the statement specifically for her, because what the statement could be saying filled her with relief.

Will was classified as active duty.

ATL was the common abbreviation for Atlanta, but it was also police slang for *Attempt to Locate.*

Will was all right. He was looking for Sara. Local and state law enforcement was looking for her.

Beau said, "Dash is suspicious."

Sara wiped away her tears.

He said, "The news hasn't mentioned Michelle. They just keep saying local doctor missing."

Sara tried to get her shit together. She knew GBI protocol was to withhold names. "You say *missing* like I walked out of the house and got lost. I was abducted. Michelle was abducted. We've both been kidnapped. We are being held against our will and forced to do things we do not want to do."

His jaw tightened down. "It's making him suspicious, is all I'm saying."

"Your friends set off two bombs on a university campus. Eighteen people are dead, almost fifty more are wounded. Three cops were murdered. Two security guards. That field kit and your training tell me you're ex-military, but you're helping a group of mass murderers. That's all I'm saying."

Beau angrily shoved trash into a plastic bag.

Sara's eyes tracked the news scroll. She wanted to see the information again, the confirmation that Will was okay. He had survived. He was looking for her.

The time was in the right-hand corner.

4:52 p.m.

Just over two and a half hours since Sara had sent Faith that useless message.

Three hours since she'd had her mouth pressed to Will's in the shed.

Beau said, "Don't be stupid in here, okay? Dash is fine until he ain't fine, and you don't wanna ever see that happen."

Sara kept her eyes on the TV. The scroll was repeating.

Official Statement: "GBI will put on active duty ATL agents to assist local and state law enforcement . . ."

Beau finally left, slamming the door closed behind him.

Sara stood up. She walked to the window at the front of the room. The curtains were drawn. She could see the large shadow of the sentry outside.

She listened, holding her breath so that she could make out any sound. She picked up the low tones of Dash talking to Beau. They were close, but not too close.

Sara got down on her knees, keeping herself low.

She lifted Carter's iPhone from the nightstand.

Beau was right that the fingerprint ID required a capacitance signal. The human body was basically an electrical capacitator. Positively charged protons and negatively charged neurons created conductivity; a battery of sorts. This was why you got a shock when you dragged wool socks across the carpet, then touched another person. The low current of electricity in the body was also what activated the fingerprint reader on older iPhones.

When you died, that charge dissipated, but not as rapidly as Beau thought. It took about two hours before the skin desiccated. That was the real reason that Carter's finger could not unlock the phone:

He was dehydrated.

Unlike Vale, Carter had not been given an IV bag of saline. The heat and trauma had caused him to sweat for hours. Dehydration had flattened out the ridges of his fingerprints. The reader was detecting a capacitance signal, but it wasn't recognizing the fingerprint.

Sara lifted Carter's right hand.

A sudden revulsion sent a shudder through her body.

Sara put the man's index finger in her mouth.

She gagged, but she kept her lips closed tight, trying to generate enough saliva to rehydrate the skin.

Hepatitis B. Hepatitis C. HIV.

There was no telling what diseases the man carried.

Sara held the finger in her mouth, sucking to move the saliva around. Her eyes went from the door to the clock on the television, then back again. She did this until a full minute had passed.

Her hands shook as she pressed Carter's finger to the home button.

The screen was cracked. He could've programmed his thumb or a different finger into the reader. The door could open and Dash would see what she was doing and shoot her twice in the chest the same as he had with Vale.

None of that happened.

The screen unlocked.

Sara didn't have time to celebrate. She tapped the telephone icon. No luck. The crack in the screen radiated up from the bottom. The glass wasn't recognizing her touch. She touched the text icon. The keyboard slid up. The cracked glass made most of the letters unusable. Through fits and starts, she was able to enter Will's phone number.

Sara never texted him words. She sent him sound files or emojis to save him the trouble of reading.

She pressed the microphone icon. She opened her mouth to speak, but only a sob came out.

Will—

She sent the sound file anyway. Her heart pounded like a metronome until the blue status bar indicated it had been sent.

She pressed the microphone again. She opened her mouth, but to say what?

The name of the bar across the street. Beau. Dash. Carter. Vale. The box truck. The fact that they were a group. That they were organized. That she loved Will. That she ached for him. That she knew he was looking for her.

Sara started to speak, but the doorknob turned.

Dash opened the door. His back was to her.

He was still talking to Beau. "Well, son, I'm sure we can make that happen."

Sara clicked the phone off. She had tossed it onto the nightstand by the time Dash turned around.

Sara stood up. She smoothed down her shorts. She had been so eager to transfer Carter's DNA onto them, but now she was almost soaked in his blood. "You said you would return me to my family after I helped you."

"In fact, that's exactly what I told you." He watched the television. They were showing aerial video of the decimated parking garage. "What does your husband do?"

Sara realized the truth might be something that could work to her advantage. "I'm a widow. My husband was a cop. He died in the line of duty."

"I'm very sorry for your loss. The streets are a dangerous place these days." Dash stared at her, still full of suspicion. "Tell me, Miss Pediatrician, do you have a familiarity with measles?"

Sara felt her head shaking, but only to bide time while she tried to see around his question. She answered, "Yes."

"Good. We happen to have ourselves a bit of a problem with measles at our Camp. An outbreak, you'd call it. If you're amenable, there are some very sick children who could use your help."

Measles?

Was that why they had taken Michelle Spivey? They thought they needed an infectious disease expert to control a measles outbreak?

"Dr. Earnshaw?" Dash prompted.

Sara said, "You're framing this as a choice."

"We all have choices, Doctor. Sometimes, there are good options and sometimes, there are bad ones. But there's no such thing as *not* having a choice."

"I need to go to the bathroom."

"Will an empty bladder assist you in your decision-making?"

Sara didn't answer, nor did she dare to leave without his permission.

Dash drew out his response. He picked up Carter's phone. He dropped it onto the floor. He crushed it with his heel. He leaned down. He used his fingers to probe the pieces. Found the SIM card and the battery. The former contained all of the stored information from the phone. The latter kept the signal transmitting the phone's location.

Sara pressed together her lips. She had seen the text go through. The little blue bar at the bottom had swooped across the screen. The metadata would include the time and location.

Wouldn't it?

Dash pocketed the phone components. He told Sara, "You know this entire room will be cleaned by tomorrow morning. The bodies will be removed. You won't even know we were here."

Sara understood that he wasn't bluffing. Beau was too thorough. He had even counted out the layers of gauze for his inventory card.

"Well, Dr. Pediatrician. I need an answer." Dash adjusted the sling around his shoulder. "Can I count on you to help heal our sick little ones?"

She said, "If I leave with you, I'll never see my family again."

"Everything is negotiable."

"What Carter did to Michelle—"

"Is not going to happen to you."

There was nothing but folly in taking this monster at his word.

Still, Sara told him, "All right."

He nodded toward the bathroom, permission granted.

She clenched together her fists as she walked past him. She shut the door. She turned on the faucet and washed Carter from her mouth. She dried her face on another towel.

This is what she told herself: The text had gone through. The signal would be traced. The motel would be located. Carter and Vale's bodies would be found. Beau would be interrogated.

Dash called, "Doctor, I'm going to step outside for a moment."

Sara listened to the door open in the other room. There was no telltale *click* as it closed. Dash was waiting to see what she would do. Sara looked around the bathroom. The narrow window mounted above the shower stall showed the tip of a rifle pointed at the sky.

Sara pulled down her shorts. She sat on the toilet. She had to force the muscles to relax. Her bladder was painfully full. The sound echoed against the tiled walls.

She finally heard the *click* of the door closing.

Will had told her a long time ago that the calmest suspect was always the most guilty. They appeared relaxed because they thought they were in control. They had outwitted everyone. There was no way they were going to get caught.

Dash was a perfect example of this arrogant calm. The way he talked to Sara—treating her with respect, framing his commands as requests, trying to appear amenable and logical—all of these were tools he was employing to control her.

Maybe he had tried and failed to do the same thing with Michelle. So he had turned her over to Carter. Which meant that Dash had known exactly what Carter was doing to the woman. Vale had clearly participated, but he just as clearly was going to die anyway. Shooting him in the chest for the crime of rape made Dash look like an honorable commander.

Sara would respect this veneer of honor as long as it kept her safe.

Dash had no idea that Will was looking for her.

He did not know that Sara was lucky.

8

Sunday, August 4, 4:26 p.m.

Will slouched in the front seat of Amanda's Lexus as she drove him to Sara's apartment. His headache had returned, but not with its previous ferocity. The sunlight wasn't so hard on his eyes anymore. Then again, it was late afternoon, so the sunlight wasn't as hard on anyone's eyes.

He told himself that Sara was still alive. That she was safe. Will had stabbed Carter in the groin. He had shot another man in the chest. The third had been unconscious the whole time. None of them would be walking around with their heads up anytime soon. Without Hurley, they might decide to go their separate ways.

Or they might regroup and get stronger.

Amanda stopped at a light. She put on the blinker. She asked Will, "Do you have any questions?"

Will stared up at the glowing red light. He considered everything that she had told him so far. There was only one question. "Your gut says that Carter took Michelle by order of this group, the Invisible Patriot Army. We've got proof that they murdered a bunch of cops. They blew up a parking deck. They kidnapped a GBI agent. Even if you take Martin Novak's possible involvement out of the equation, they're still terrorists. Why isn't the FBI balls to the walls going after them?"

Amanda gave a heavy sigh. Her hands were tight on the steering wheel. Instead of answering his question, she said, "Ruby Ridge. A US marshal was murdered. Randy Weaver's wife and son were killed. The standoff lasted eleven days. Weaver was acquitted. The family was awarded three million dollars in a wrongful death case. The FBI was publicly eviscerated."

The light turned green. Amanda took the turn.

"Twelve months later, there was the siege at Waco." She took another turn onto the road to Sara's apartment. "Four agents murdered, six wounded. Eighty-six Branch Davidians killed, many of them women and children. The entire nation watched the compound burn. No one blamed the child molester leading the cult. The FBI was torn apart. Janet Reno never fully recovered."

"Amanda—"

"The Bundy standoff. The Occupation of the Malheur National Wildlife Refuge. Armed militias tried to seize federal land and when the smoke cleared, most of them were acquitted by juries of their peers. Two anti-government arsonists received presidential pardons." Amanda slowed the car to turn into Sara's building. "Most of the agents at the FBI are hard-working patriots who believe in our country. But then there are some who are blinded by politics, and others by ideology. They're either terrified to make a decision because of the political fallout or, worse, they agree with the groups they're supposed to be locking up."

Will said, "Send me in undercover. We don't need the FBI. These are state charges on state land. I'll get the evidence to—"

"Will."

"You said yourself that the IPA is planning something big. All the signs point to it. That agent—Van—he said it to Faith in the meeting. The chatter—"

"No reporters. That's good." Amanda looked for a parking space. "I asked Sara's family to keep their mouths closed. I didn't take her mother for discreet, but perhaps Sara's father persuaded her that we actually know what we're doing."

Will didn't think Sara's mother was persuadable. "Amanda—"

"If this stretches out, you need to impress upon them both how important it is that we keep Sara's name out of the public domain. It's bad enough the IPA has Michelle. If they realize they have a medical examiner, a special agent with the GBI—"

"I want to go undercover. I'll take the risk."

She had pulled into a parking space by the front door. She turned to Will. "You will not. I won't repeat myself. The subject is closed."

They had seen Will's face. Carter and the man who'd identified himself as Vince were still out there. The minute they recognized Will, they would kill him.

He looked at his watch.

4:28 p.m.

He asked, "How long are you going to hold back the fact that we've captured Hurley? You could make it seem like he's talking to us, use him as bait to lure them out."

"That's APD's call."

Maggie Grant was running point on the bombing investigation. She was also one of Amanda's oldest friends. There was no way they weren't coordinating.

He asked, "Do you really think Hurley's going to rat out his team?"

"I think he needs a few more hours to consider his limited options. We only get one chance to flip him. That can't happen if his face is on the cover of the *New York Times*. He'll turn into a martyr for the cause. These men thrive on notoriety." She told Will, "I have it on authority that Carter's mugshot is going to be leaked. Not that blurred image from the hospital CCTV. His actual mugshot. He's searchable in the felon database. The reporters will do the rest of the work."

Will rubbed his jaw. His fingers felt stiff. They were cut and bruised from being repeatedly punched into Hurley's face.

Amanda said, "We are doing everything we can. And I promise you, Sara is doing everything she can to get back to you."

Will wasn't sure there was anything that Sara *could* do. They had no idea where she was, or even in which direction she was heading. Her Apple Watch had been found in the woods near the burned-out BMW. The Walkie-Talkie message to Faith had disappeared seconds after it was recorded.

Why hadn't Sara tried to reach Will? Had she remembered that his phone was in the shed? Or did she blame him, too?

My son-in-law would've never let this happen.

Cathy's voice sounded so much like Sara's. When Will replayed the words in his head, it felt like the indictment was coming from both of them.

"Go change, Wilbur." Amanda patted his leg. "Shower off. Take care of the dogs. I'll grab us some food from Mary Mac's. Shouldn't take more than twenty minutes. Then we'll head to Panthersville."

GBI headquarters. The body of the man who'd called himself Merle was in the morgue. Sara's BMW was being scoured by arson investigators. The white potato chip van was being evaluated by the forensic team. The bomb squad was preparing a briefing on the explosive devices. The Hostage Rescue Team was on standby. Hurley had a twenty-four-hour babysitter in case he decided to talk. A group of agents was generating a profile on Adam Humphrey Carter—past known associates, prison cellmates, family ties, possible connections with underworld groups and gangs.

They would all submit their findings to Amanda. It would be good intelligence, but probably not actionable intelligence.

Will craved action.

He opened the car door. His legs ached when he stood up. He was still wearing the grass-stained shorts and sweaty T-shirt from before. His feet dragged as he walked into the building. He could've gone to his own house, his tiny two-bedroom house that felt weirdly smaller without Sara. Most of his clothes were at her apartment. His shaving kit. His toothbrush. His dog.

His life.

Will bypassed the stairs and punched the button for the elevator. His belly pain had simmered into a low boil. His headache was worse under the artificial light. He leaned against the wall as he waited for the doors to open. He was completely depleted. His heart ached in his chest. He shouldn't be stopping for something as mundane as a shower and taking out the dogs, but what other options did he have?

He looked at his watch.

4:31 p.m.

The elevator doors opened. He got on. He pressed the button for Sara's floor. He leaned back. He closed his eyes.

This morning, Sara had kissed him in the elevator. Really kissed him. He could still feel her hands on his shoulders. She'd stroked the nape of his neck and whispered into his ear—*You look so sexy with your hair longer.* Which was how he'd ended up being a jackass who paid sixty dollars for a haircut when the cool guy in the morgue would do it for the price of a sandwich.

The elevator dinged. Will opened his eyes. He looked at his watch.

4:32 p.m.

His shoes dragged across the carpet in the hallway. Will's keys were in Sara's purse. She kept a spare on the ledge. Will was reaching up to find it when the door opened.

Eddie Linton looked up at Will. Sara's father. His eyes were bloodshot. His face was ashen. "Did you find her?"

Will shook his head as he lowered his hand. He felt like a thief caught in the act. "I'm sorry, sir."

Eddie left the door open as he walked back into the apartment.

Sara's dogs rushed at Will. The greyhounds looked worried. Their routine had been broken. Sara was supposed to be here. Betty, the Chihuahua Will had accidentally adopted, pranced around his feet until he picked her up. Her head went to his chest. Her tongue and tail wagged in opposite directions.

Will tried to soothe all of the animals while he watched Sara's mother move around the kitchen. The apartment was modern, with an open floor plan that combined the living room, dining room and kitchen. Cathy was opening and closing kitchen cabinets. She found a glass. She poured tea from a pitcher. She sat down at the island. There were bowls of uneaten food in front of her.

She looked at Will, then looked away.

Eddie said, "All the news stations are repeating the same thing every thirty minutes. Nobody knows anything." His eyes were focused on the muted television in the living room. Words ran in the banner along the bottom. "Sir Verb-A-Lot just wants to gallop in on his cartoon horse and stirrup trouble."

Will stared at the TV, head tilted to the side. The reporter was actually Jake Tapper.

"We found your phone when we closed up the shed." Eddie pointed to Will's phone charging on the other end of the island. "And, uh, Tess is flying over. She'll be here Tuesday morning. It's a fifteen-hour flight, but she's got to get to the airport, and . . ." His voice trailed off. "We haven't told anybody but Tess that Sara was kid— was taken. We're doing exactly what the police said, keeping her name out of it so they can't go on their computers and find out who she is. We don't want to jeopardize the investigation. We just want her home." He rubbed his stomach. "Do you think they'll demand a ransom?"

Cathy stiffened.

Eddie changed the subject, asking Will, "Are you hungry?"

Will's jaw was so tight that he could only shake his head. Betty licked his neck. He put her down on the floor. Her toenails clicked across the hardwood as she joined the greyhounds on their dog bed.

"Come eat." Eddie waved toward the vacant stool beside Cathy.

She jumped up like the seat had caught on fire. She went into the kitchen. She started opening and closing the cabinets again. Will didn't know if she was looking for something or just relishing the slamming of cabinet doors.

He sank down onto the bar stool, the one Sara always sat in. He tilted up his phone, but only to see the wallpaper. The screen showed Sara with the dogs, a greyhound on each side, Betty in her lap. Smiling for Will.

4:38 p.m.

Cathy slammed the cabinet door so hard that the glasses clinked.

Will cleared his throat. He tried, "Are you—"

Cathy cut him off with a furious look. She bent down and rummaged through the lower cabinets. She slapped an empty storage bowl on the counter. Then another. She was looking for lids. Will knew she wouldn't find ones that fit. Sara said that lids were the unicorns of the storage world.

"I should—" Will tried to get up from the stool. A stabbing pain in his ribs almost doubled him over. "I came to take a shower. And to change. For work. I have clothes here. All my—"

"Stuff," Cathy finished. "Your stuff is here. Your dog is here. He lives here, Eddie. Did you know that?"

The words had rushed out like an accusation.

Eddie sat down beside Will. He clasped his hands on the counter. "No, I did not know that."

Will chewed at the side of his tongue. Why hadn't Sara told her father that they were together?

"You can't—" Cathy put her fist to her mouth. Her earlier anger had only intensified. "Sara is my oldest daughter. My first born. You have no idea—no idea—what she's been through."

Will said nothing, but he did know what Sara had been through. He was basically living with her. He shared her bed. Loved her more than any woman he had ever known. He spent every free moment he had with her.

All of which she had apparently not shared with her parents.

"She is not a fighter!" Cathy was talking to Eddie, screaming at him. "You think that she is, but she's not! She's my baby. We should've never let her leave home. Nothing good has ever come of it. Nothing!"

"Cath." Eddie shook his head, clearly pained by her recriminations. "Not now."

"It's too late!" she yelled. "She was swallowed up again by this horrible place. This horrible city. With this—"

Will waited to hear what he was, the *this* in Sara's life.

Not her husband. Not Cathy's son-in-law. Not someone Sara had talked to her father about.

"I . . . uh . . ." Will cleared his throat. He had to get out of this room.

He managed to slide off the stool without the pain stopping him. The dogs scrambled up from their bed. They thought they were going out. Will pushed past them as he walked toward the hallway. He had five yards before turning the corner, but his feet were encased in concrete.

There wasn't a part of this apartment that didn't conjure a memory of Sara. The couch where she sprawled across him like a cat while they watched TV. The dining room table where he'd met her friends from the hospital. Will had never been to a dinner party before. He'd been nervous because he knew that he was bad with people, but Will had done okay because Sara had made it okay. That's what she did for him. She made everything okay.

He turned around.

He looked at Sara's parents. Cathy's arms were crossed. She was staring angrily at the floor. Only Eddie would look him in the eye. He was waiting for Will to say something, to justify his existence in this space that belonged to their beloved, oldest child.

Will didn't want to say anything, but words started coming out of his mouth.

"She listens to Dolly Parton when she's sad."

Cathy kept her gaze on the floor.

Eddie's brows zigged in confusion.

Will said, "She doesn't listen to Dolly with me." He added, "At least, not like—"

When your son-in-law cheated on her, or when he got himself murdered because his ego was more important than his wife.

Will said, "We've been riding our bikes on the Silver Comet trail. Did she tell you?"

Eddie hesitated, then said, "She showed us the thing, the satellite stuff."

"GPS," Cathy mumbled. She wiped her eyes with her fist, but still would not look at Will.

He told them, "She made me get my hair cut different. And change my suits. I had to get rid of a lot of them." He shook his head, because that sounded bad. "I mean, not like she forced me to, but she does this thing where she says, 'I bet you'd look good in a shorter jacket,' and before I know it, I'm at the mall spending money."

Eddie gave a reluctant smile, as if he was familiar with the tactic.

"She beats my ass at tennis," Will told them. "Seriously. She will not let me win. But I'm better at basketball. And I don't get colds, which is good, because she gets angry when you're sick. Not patients, but people she knows. Cares about. She says it's not true, but it is."

Eddie was no longer smiling, but he looked like he was waiting for more.

Will said, "We're re-watching *Buffy* together. And we both like the same movies. And pizza. And she makes me eat vegetables. But I stopped eating ice cream before bed because the sugar was keeping me up, which I didn't know about. And—"

There was too much saliva in his mouth. He had to stop to swallow.

"I'm good for her, too. That's what I'm saying that maybe you don't know. Hadn't realized. I'm really good for your daughter."

Eddie was still waiting.

"I make her laugh. Not all the time, but she laughs at my jokes. And she cleans the house, but I do the bathrooms. And she washes the laundry and I fold it. And I do the ironing. She says she's bad at it, but I know she doesn't like to do it."

Will laughed, because he'd just figured that out. "She smiles when she kisses me. And—"

He couldn't get into the details with her parents. That Sara sometimes drew tiny hearts on his calendar. That once she had spent a wonderful amount of time using her mouth to suck a heart-shaped hickey onto his stomach.

Will said, "We eat lunch together at work every Tuesday. She's really good at her job. We talk about things. Cases. And I know—I know she was raped."

Cathy's lips parted in surprise.

She was looking at him now.

Will swallowed again. "She told me a while ago. Before we were dating. That she was raped. And then later, she told me the details—that he stabbed her, that she testified at the trial. What it was like to move back home. Everything she had to give up. I know that you helped her get through it. All of you. I know she was grateful, that she was lucky."

Will gripped his hands together like he was begging them to understand.

"She told me she was raped because she trusts me. I grew up with kids who were—who were raped. More than raped."

Christ, all he was saying was rape.

"I know it's different because Sara was in college, but it's not really that different, no matter what age it happens. Right? Abuse is always with you. It's in the DNA of your shadow. You turn around, and it's never *not* there. All you can do is learn to live with it."

He walked toward Cathy. He needed to know she was listening.

"Sara told me that she would die before she was raped again. That's why, when we were in the street today, when she was on her knees with a gun pointed at her head, she told the man to shoot her. She had two choices, and she was ready to die rather than go with them. Rather than risk being raped again. And I believed her. The guy with the gun believed her."

Will had to sit down. He leaned across the counter. His hands were still gripped together because he was begging for an answer.

"Why did she go?" he asked Cathy. "That's what I can't understand. Why did she go with them?"

Tears ran down Cathy's cheeks. She closed her eyes. Shook her head.

"Please tell me," Will pleaded. "She looked right at me when she told him to shoot her. She wanted me to know why she had made the choice." He waited, then said, "Sara didn't want me to live with the guilt, but now you're saying that—that I should." Will would've gotten on his knees right now if it made Cathy give him an answer. "Please tell me why you blame me. Tell me what I did wrong."

Cathy's lips trembled. She turned her back to him. She rolled off a paper towel and wiped her tears. She blew her nose.

Will thought she wasn't going to answer him, but she said, "I don't blame you."

You let them steal her.

"It's not your fault."

My son-in-law would've never let this happen.

Cathy turned around. She folded the paper towel and dabbed at her eyes. "They grabbed her. The two men. They lifted her up and carried her to the car. She tried to fight them. She couldn't."

Will shook his head, disbelieving. "They were both injured. Sara is strong. I know you don't think she's a fighter, but she could've fought them off."

"She tried to. They overpowered her."

"But she was driving the car."

"She didn't have a choice." Cathy wiped her eyes again. "She lost her nerve. I've known my daughter a hell of a lot longer than you, Will Trent. It's easy to say you're willing to die in the moment, but that moment passed. I watched it happen. They carried Sara to the car. They handcuffed her to the steering wheel. They put a gun to her head and made her drive. You can question it all you want, but that's what happened. That's what I'll put in my sworn statement."

He tried, "But—"

Cathy's hard look dared him to contradict her.

Eddie said, "It's been a long day, son." He walked around the counter. He wrapped his arms around his wife. He told Will, "Go take your shower."

Will was glad to get away from them. So many times, he had stood exactly where Eddie now stood and held Sara.

Betty followed him down the long hallway. Will was too sore to bend down and pick her up again. She ran ahead and jumped onto the bed. Will lingered at the door. The sheets were still tangled from their bodies. He could smell Sara on everything. She didn't use perfume, but there was something magical about the soap she used. It didn't smell the same on anything except her body.

In the bathroom, Will didn't know what to do with his dirty clothes. There was something permanent about putting them in the laundry basket on top of Sara's things. A promise that she would be there to wash them and he would be there to fold them.

Will left his clothes on the floor and got into the shower.

The hot water was the first relief his body had felt in hours.

He let the spray dig into his muscles, tried to keep it away from the staple in his scalp. His hair still had pieces of grass in it. The foam from the shampoo was gray from his sweat. He looked down at the drain. Sticks and twigs from Bella's yard danced on top of the holes, trying to wash down.

Will thought about the two men picking Sara up and carrying her to the car. One had a knife in his leg. The other had a hole in his side.

He got out of the shower. He wiped the fog off the mirror. He carefully combed his hair. He brushed his teeth. He rubbed the rough stubble on his face. Will usually shaved in the morning, then again when he got home from work. Sara liked his face smooth.

He left the razor on the counter and went into the closet. Will dressed in the gray suit and blue shirt that Sara had picked out for him. He took his Sig Sauer P365 out of the gun safe. The pistol was a Christmas gift from Sara. His service Glock would either be found by the arson investigators who processed Sara's BMW or by a cop who took it off a bad guy.

Or maybe Will would get it back and find whoever was holding Sara and shoot him in the head.

He braced himself before making his way up the hallway. Sara's parents had moved to the couch. The same couch where Sara and Will watched TV.

Eddie said, "We'll keep an eye on your dog."

"Thank you." Will grabbed his phone off the counter.

4:56 p.m.

Amanda would be waiting downstairs. Will thought about packing some clothes. He couldn't sleep here tonight. But that would mean returning to the bedroom, then going up the hall again, which meant he'd have to say goodbye to Sara's parents again. Which meant he would be tempted again to ask Cathy why she was lying.

He told Sara's parents, "I'll let you know if I hear anything."

Will didn't wait for their answer. He carefully closed the door behind him. In the hall, he pressed the button for the elevator.

His phone vibrated with a message.

He cursed, assuming it was Amanda, but the number was one he didn't recognize. Will opened the text. A sound file had been sent at 4:54 p.m. The length of the recording was 0.01, less than a second.

Will stopped breathing.

Sara was the only person who texted him sound files.

He swallowed so hard his throat hurt. His hand was shaking. He had to tap the arrow twice to get the recording to play. The sound was faint, like someone clearing their throat.

He maxed out the volume.

He pressed the speaker to his ear.

"Wi—"

Sara.

The Lexus was sweating heat by the time Amanda exited off the split-lane state highway. Sara's voice text had served as a beacon. All they knew back in Atlanta was that the cell tower that had pinged her text was located in North Georgia. Amanda had started driving toward the downtown connector while the phone company worked on triangulating the signal. Ten minutes later, they were told to go northeast, so Amanda had jumped onto I-85. There was a long, unbearable stretch of silence, then suddenly, the cell phone's last known location was pinpointed to a radius of less than twenty feet. Amanda had forked onto Lanier Parkway by the time the Rabun County sheriff's department had raided the King Fisher Camping Lodge.

Two deceased males. No witnesses. No suspects.

"There it is," Amanda said, steering a hard turn into the motel parking lot.

Gravel spit up from her tires. She had trimmed the nearly two-hour journey by half an hour. Every minute had felt like a year off Will's life. No Sara. No Michelle. No license plates to follow up on. No witnesses. No suspects. No one to talk to who could tell them a damn thing.

Amanda slotted the Lexus into a space between the motel office and the GBI's Crime Scene Unit bus.

Will reached for the door handle.

Amanda put a hand on his arm. "Careful what you say."

She nodded toward the cops milling on the wide porch that skirted the front of the motel. Rabun County sheriff's deputies. The Georgia Highway Patrol. The City of Clayton Police Department.

Will asked, "You don't trust them?"

"This is a small town. I don't trust the people they'll talk to at church or over fried chicken at the diner." She let go of his arm. "There's Zevon."

Zevon Lowell, the GBI agent from the Appalachian Regional Drug Enforcement Office, approached the car with two cups of coffee in his hands.

Amanda took one of the cups as she got out of the car. "Run it down for me."

"Nothing new to report, boss. Charlie's processing the room as fast as he can. He's got a crew coming up from Atlanta."

Will stared at the motel room in the center of the building. The door was open. A sheet of plastic kept the air conditioning inside. Bright work lights beamed onto the porch, leaked around the curtain in the window. Charlie Reed would be on his hands and knees combing the carpet for evidence. He was the best crime scene investigator in the state. He worked closely with Sara. He would do everything in his power to help find her.

"Motel's been vacant for over a year." Zevon took his notepad out of his pocket and flipped it open. "Owner was a guy named Hugo Hunt Hopkins. Real estate attorney from Atlanta. He died without a will. It's been caught up in probate while his two kids battle it out."

"Are they local?"

"One lives in Michigan, the other is in California. There's a caretaker in and out, makes sure the roof's not leaking, pipes aren't freezing." He shifted around so that Amanda's eyes were out of the sun. "Look over my shoulder."

Across the street from the motel, Will saw a metal building clapboarded in wood to give it the appearance of a hunting lodge. The parking lot was empty. The sign showed a rabbit holding a mug of beer.

"Peter Cottontail's," Amanda said. "This isn't a dry county. Why is it closed?"

"It's a social club. Keeps its own hours. The building's held by a shell corporation. Been that way for eight years. The guy we believe runs the place is Beau Ragnersen. He's also the motel caretaker. He makes his money down in Macon."

"Ah." Amanda pursed her lips. Something had rung a bell, but she didn't stop to explain. "Go direct that choir practice for me." *Choir practice* was slang for a bunch of gossiping police officers. She told Will, "Let's go."

He followed her toward the motel room. Part of the parking lot was taped off. The gravel showed tracks where a box truck had backed into the space. The wheels had stopped six feet from the porch. The tires had lost traction in the gravel, but Charlie had already set plaster casts in the best impressions.

Will stared at the spot where the truck would've parked. The gravel looked disturbed where someone's feet might have been, but maybe that was wishful thinking. He wanted to believe that Sara had jumped down under her own steam. That she wasn't carried in kicking and screaming. That she wasn't knocked out, tied up, drugged into oblivion.

"Here." Amanda found two pairs of shoe protectors in Charlie's duffel bag outside the door. She pulled aside the plastic sheet. She took a moment to collect herself before going in.

Will instinctively ducked his head down as he followed her. The ceiling was low. The room felt claustrophobic. Brown shag carpet. Beige walls. Looking around, he understood Amanda's need to steel herself. Will had been to hundreds of crime scenes. He had seen worse, but he had never *felt* worse.

Blood painted the room in dark, violent streaks—across the two beds, the mini-fridge, the nightstand, the television, the chest of drawers, the ceiling, the ugly carpet. The source seemed to be the dead man sitting up in the bed by the window. His head was bent down, but not in the guise of peacefulness. His torso was ripped open like an animal had torn its way out of his chest.

Will swallowed down acid. The man was naked from the waist down. His penis was black with blood.

"This is the phone Sara used to text Will."

Will pulled his gaze away from the dead man on the bed.

Charlie Reed was dressed in a white Tyvek suit. He was holding an evidence bag that contained the remnants of a shattered cell phone. He told Amanda, "The IMEI number matches what the wireless company has on file. We're getting a warrant for the user's name."

"Good," Amanda said. "Don't waste your time telling me you're not a medical expert. How did these men die?"

Charlie pointed to the bed by the wall. "This one received medical treatment prior to death. The bullet wound in his side was patched with a chest seal. An IV was run into his right arm. A needle was used to draw the tension out of what was probably a pneumothorax."

"Sara," Amanda guessed.

"I'm assuming," Charlie said. "I'm praying, actually."

Will didn't care about prayers. "That's the guy who called himself Vince. He was the passenger of the F-150. I shot him in Sara's BMW."

Amanda did not respond.

Charlie offered, "Someone shot him again, twice, in this room. One of the bullets penetrated the mattress. The other round is still in his chest. We're going to rush ballistics and see if anything comes up on the gun."

Amanda asked, "And the second man?"

"Without being a doctor—" Charlie caught her look. "I think we can assume he was stabbed to death. Look at the handprint on the headboard."

Now that he was pointing at it, Will could make out the bloody outline of four slender fingers and a thumb wrapping around the wooden edge.

Charlie said, "My guess is that the attacker was either a woman or a very small man."

Will looked at his own hand, as if holding Sara's hand for so long had made him an expert on the bloody impression her fingers would leave. Could she kill a man like that? Straddle him, stab into his neck and chest so many times that the skin started to pulp?

He fucking hoped so.

Amanda snapped her fingers for Will's attention. She was waiting.

He walked around the bed. He squatted down on the floor. He looked up. The taste of the man's name filling his mouth was sickening. "Adam Humphrey Carter."

Charlie said, "That tracks with the wound in his upper thigh. The femoral artery was nicked. His pants were cut off. I'm assuming a procedure was started to remove the knife. Then—"

"The *then* doesn't matter." Will drilled his words into Amanda. "There were five guys at the car accident. The one called Merle is already at the morgue. Vince is dead. Carter is dead. The fourth guy, Dwight, was knocked out the entire time. Hurley is the only man left who can identify my face, and he's cuffed to a hospital bed under armed guard."

She pressed her lips together. "Anything else, Charlie?"

Charlie looked uncomfortable to be caught between them. "I think someone was taken into the adjacent room. The bedspread shows blood transfer, not active bleeding. Also, you probably didn't smell it when you walked in, but I caught a whiff of rubbing alcohol when I opened the door. Someone tried to remove any trace of their fingerprints from the scene. The table has been wiped down, so he or she must've been confined mostly to this area by the window. I'll need to luminol the entire motel to make sure we're not missing anything. But if we find a fingerprint in blood, that puts the person here when the murders took place."

Amanda asked, "What about blood typing? Are we sure that no one else was bleeding?"

"I can't say with absolute certainty, but it seems probable that the majority of the blood came from Carter. Latent fingerprints are going to give us the quickest snapshot. Sara's are on file. So are Michelle Spivey's. I need the laptop from the other bus to start running comparisons. Half of my equipment is being repaired. The only reason I started without the team is because of Sara. I wanted to see if something jumped out at me."

"Nothing jumped out?"

He shook his head, but said, "There are some bloody shoeprints on the bathroom floor. Looks like a man's size seven, maybe a woman's nine, which would match Sara." He motioned for them to follow him. He stood outside the cramped bathroom. "The toilet's not flushed, but the seat is down. It's weird. These guys don't strike me as the type who sit down to take a piss."

Weird.

Will ducked his head under the door frame and looked around. The first thing he smelled was urine. The first thing he saw was bloody footprints pacing out almost every part of the laminate floor. The walls were clad in the same laminate. The drop-ceiling hung half a foot lower than the ceiling in the room, probably to hide a roof leak. Plastic sink with a cabinet base. Blood in the basin where someone had washed their hands. Toilet crammed against the shower/tub combination. Grab bar bolted to the wall through a piece of plywood.

He felt Sara in here the same way he'd felt her outside in the parking lot.

Amanda asked, "Did you check above the ceiling?"

Charlie said, "All I found were spider webs and rat droppings. There's no access to the room next door. It's a decorating choice, I guess?"

Amanda said, "Will, finish up here and meet me outside. We need to regroup."

Will did not immediately follow her. He couldn't shake the sense that he was missing something. He took one last look around the tiny bathroom. He ducked his head under the door frame, but then—

Maybe it was the grab bar or maybe it was because he'd just said the word rape eighty times to Sara's parents, but Will looked up at the ceiling.

Sara had been attacked in a public restroom. The rapist had crawled through the drop-ceiling in the adjacent men's room and jumped down into her stall. Before Sara could manage more than a gasped *no*, the attacker had handcuffed her to the grab bars on either side of the toilet.

Will asked Charlie, "Where's your black light?"

"It's on the other bus. Why?"

"Did Sara show you that trick?"

Charlie grinned. He went to his duffel bag outside the door. He returned with two colored Sharpies and a roll of clear tape. Then he took out his cell phone.

Will said, "You have to layer it," even though Charlie knew what he was doing. He knew because of Sara. Her nerdiness ran deep. The only thing she loved more than helping people was regaling them with the magic of science.

Charlie stuck a clear piece of tape over the light on his phone. He used the Sharpie to color a blue circle over the light. He fixed the ink with another piece of tape. Then he colored a purple circle over the blue one and fixed that with more tape.

Will turned off the lights. He closed the door. The curtains were already pulled. The room was dark.

Charlie tapped the flashlight app on his phone. The blood slashing around the room started to glow, because that was the point of a black light: the ultraviolet wave turned bodily fluids luminescent.

Fluids like urine.

Will said, "Point it up at the bathroom ceiling."

Charlie stood outside the door. He shined the light upward.

Will blinked at the glowing greenish-yellow letters that Sara had written on the drop-ceiling. Four tiles across, three tiles deep, all but one had either a single word or a number.

Charlie read, "Beau. Bar. Dash. Thinks. Hurley's. Dead. Spivey. Me. OK. 4. Now."

Will heard the words, but at the moment, he didn't care. All he could see was the crude little heart that Sara had drawn for him in the corner.

PART TWO

Monday, August 5, 2019

9

Monday, August 5, 5:45 a.m.

Sara was pulled awake by her own sweat dripping into her eyes. She squinted at her watch, but found only her bare wrist. She turned to see if Will was in bed, but there was no Will and there was no bed. Sara had fallen asleep with her back wedged into the corner.

The Camp.

At least Sara assumed she was in the Camp. Last night, a black van had picked them up at the motel. Sara was loaded into the back, blindfolded and gagged, handcuffed to Michelle. The woman was unconscious through most of the journey. Even after she'd finally stirred from her drugged stupor, Michelle had not uttered a word. The only noise out of her mouth was a grief-filled cry when the door to the van had opened and she'd realized where they were.

But where was that, exactly?

Sara pushed herself up against the corner. Her legs were stiff. Sweat rolled off her body. Her clothes were so filthy they scratched her skin. She had only seen the rustic, one-room cabin by lamplight. Twelve paces wide. Twelve paces deep. Ceiling pitched higher than she could reach. No windows. A tin roof. Rough-hewn walls and floor. Surrounded by trees.

The bucket by the door served as a toilet. Another bucket in the opposite corner held water and a ladle. There was a straw mattress on a crude wooden frame. The makeshift box spring was a long length of rope tied into a series of knots, forming a net. Sara had chosen to sleep in the corner nearest the backswing of the door. She wanted as much time as possible to prepare if a stranger came in.

She tried the doorknob. The padlock bumped against the frame. She paced the room. The walls were unpainted wood. There was no insulation between the studs. No electricity, but sunlight streaked through the gaps in the boards. She peered between the slats. Green leaves, dark tree trunks. The sound of water burbling. A stream, maybe, or a river that she could follow downstream if she found the chance.

She walked to the other side of the room. Same view of dense forest. She pressed her hand against the board. The nails were rusting. If she pushed hard enough, she might be able to force off the bottom slats and crawl out.

A key slid into the padlock.

Sara stepped back, fists clenched.

Dash smiled at her. His arm was still in a sling, but he had changed into jeans and a button-down shirt. "Good morning, Dr. Earnshaw. I thought you might enjoy taking your breakfast with us after you meet your patients."

The idea of food made her stomach turn, but she would need to keep up her strength in case the opportunity presented itself to run.

Dash said, "I can handcuff you again, but I think you've already figured out how remote we are from civilization."

Sara had figured no such thing, but she nodded.

"Good girl." He stepped aside so she could go ahead of him.

Sara tried not to let the *girl* grate, as if she was a child or a horse. One of the sentries from the motel stood outside the door. AR-15, black tactical gear.

Sara stepped down onto a log that served as a stair. She tried to orient herself. The forest was thick, but there was a cleared path beyond the cabin. She squinted at the sun peeking over the horizon. Five thirty or six in the morning. They were in the foothills of the Appalachian mountain chain, though that didn't narrow things down. If she assumed the motel had been in the western part of Georgia, they could be in Tennessee or Alabama. Or she could be completely wrong, and they were in the North Georgia Mountains near the Carolinas.

Sara started down the cleared path. She picked her way over a fallen tree. She could feel Dash reaching out to help her. She moved away from him, away from his feigned chivalry.

He said, "I think you'll be pleasantly surprised by what you find here."

Sara bit her lip. Unless she found a car at the end of this path that was going to drive her home, there was nothing pleasant about her surroundings. "I am a hostage. I am here against my will."

"You had a choice." His tone had an overly familiar teasing element. He was trying to establish an easiness between them, as if the gun on his hip and his armed sentry didn't give him all of the power.

Sara pushed a branch away from her face. Her skin was furred with grime, blood and sweat. She had furtively washed herself with tepid water from the bucket, but had no choice but to put back on her dirty clothes. The shorts were rigid with blood. Her shirt reeked of her own body odor. Her bra and underwear had turned into sandpaper. There was no shortage of forensic evidence on her now. She wondered if there was something she should do—cut herself on a bramble, leave a blood trail, mark the path in some way so that Charlie Reed or Will would know that she had been here.

Will.

At the motel, Sara had drawn the heart on the ceiling first. She had been taking a risk leaving the message, but the most important thing she wanted to convey was that she knew that he was looking for her.

Will put on active duty. ATL.

"Daddy!" a little girl screamed with excitement. "Daddy!"

Sara watched a child running across a clearing. She guessed by the girl's wriggling movements that she was around five, possibly six years old. Her fine motor skill hadn't yet gotten the hang of running at speed. She fell, but quickly pushed herself up again, giggling. The child was wearing a plain white dress that swept down to the ground. The collar was buttoned to her neck. The sleeves stopped just below her elbows. Her blonde hair was down to her waist. Sara did not feel so much like she was stepping back in time as walking onto the set of a Laura Ingalls Wilder adaptation.

She glanced around the clearing, which was roughly the size of a basketball court. There were eight more one-room cabins tucked into the trees. These were larger than her nighttime cell, with windows and Dutch doors, stone chimneys. They felt permanent, but impermanent at the same time. Women sat in chairs peeling corn and snapping beans. Some were sweeping the dirt patches in front of their cabins. Others were cooking in large pots or boiling laundry over open fires. All of them had long hair piled onto the tops of their heads. No highlights or color in sight. No make-up. They wore simple, white, long-sleeved dresses with high collars. No jewelry except for gold wedding bands.

No faces that were not white.

"Sweetpea!" Dash scooped up the little girl with his good arm. He held her on his hip as he walked ahead of Sara. "Where is my kiss?"

The girl pecked him on the cheek like a bird.

"Daddy!" another little girl screamed. Then another. In all, five more girls ran toward Dash and threw their arms around his waist. Their ages ranged from the five-year-old in his arms to a teen who couldn't be more than fifteen. They wore the same long, white dresses. The younger girls kept their hair down, but the fifteen-year-old wore hers in a bun like the older women. She gave Sara a wary glance as she wrapped her arms around Dash's waist.

Six children in total, all calling him father. Two were clearly twins, but the rest either belonged to different women or to a single mother who had been pregnant or nursing for sixteen of the last twenty years of her life.

"Sir?" a young, clean-cut man called from the other side of the clearing. The juxtaposition was jarring. Like the sentry, he was dressed in all black, a rifle over his shoulder. Unlike the sentry, he was barely out of his teens. He could've been a Boy Scout or a school shooter. He told Dash, "The team is back from the mission, brother."

Mission?

"All right, my little ladies." Dash extricated himself from his children. They all dutifully lined up to give him a kiss on the cheek. The older girl was the only one who didn't seem happy about it. She gave Sara another wary glance. It was hard to tell whether she was being protective of her father or just embarrassed the way teenage girls were always embarrassed.

Dash told Sara, "Dr. Earnshaw, please excuse me. My wife will be with you momentarily."

Her eyes followed him as he walked up a steep hill. In the light of day, she thought Dash was older than she'd initially guessed, probably mid-forties. He had one of those baby-faces that made his age hard to pin down. Actually, everything about him was hard to pin down. His relentless pleasantness made him inscrutable. Of all human emotions, anger was the fastest and most direct way to communicate emotion. Sara did not want to be on the receiving end of Dash's true feelings if he ever exploded.

"I'm hungry!" one of the little girls announced. There was much giggling as the children trundled off like kittens, falling over themselves, tripping, pushing and pawing—except for the oldest one, who offered another wary glance as she stomped off toward the cooking area.

Sara tried to catch her eye, but the teenager was having none of it. She watched the little girls instead. They were spinning in circles, trying to make themselves dizzy. They made Sara think of her niece, which made her think of her sister, which made her consider the dominoes that had probably started to fall since she'd last seen her mother standing in the street holding Bella's shotgun. Tessa would be flying in from South Africa. Eddie would've immediately driven up from Grant County. Bella would be too high-strung to host them at her house. They would all end up at Sara's apartment, which meant that Will would become displaced.

Sara felt her earlier weepiness return.

Her parents would overwhelm him. He would worry about saying the wrong thing, which would make him say even more wrong things, then Cathy would snap at him and Eddie would try to smooth it over with a bad pun, but Will didn't understand puns because dyslexia was a language-processing disorder, so instead of smiling or even laughing to break the tension, Will would tilt his head to the side and give that puzzled look, which would make her father wonder what was wrong with him, and Sara's only hope was that Tessa's flights wouldn't take more than twenty-four hours because her sister was the only person on earth who could rescue Will from their parents.

Sara blinked away tears. She tried to fill her brain with practical information. Will would come for her. She knew that as a fact. He would need to know what he was dealing with in order to work out a plan.

She scanned the woods. Sara hadn't noticed before, but there were at least six armed men sitting in deer stands up in the trees. What were they guarding? Surely not Sara. Were they trying to keep people out or hold them in? Inside the clearing, Sara counted eight adult women and thirteen children from the ages of three to fifteen. There were eight cabins and a long, low bunkhouse that sat at twelve o'clock. Dash had disappeared over the top of the hill. She assumed there were more cabins, more men, women and children, and likely even more guards.

Why?

Her attention was pulled away from the question by a child screeching in delight. They were playing hide-and-seek. Dash's youngest girl covered her eyes and started counting. The rest of the girls scattered off into the forest or down cleared paths. Five meandering lanes spoked off the clearing. The tree canopy was thick, shadowing the cabins. A helicopter or plane might fly overhead without noticing the Camp. Sara wondered if the buildings were part of a former homesteader settlement. The area looked untouched. Many of the trees had thick trunks, indicating old growth.

Based on her time in the van, Sara made the educated guess that she was still in Georgia. Eddie Linton had dragged his family on many camping trips into the mountains, but that didn't help narrow down her location. If anything, it expanded Sara's sense of isolation. The Chattahoochee National Forest was comprised of almost 800,000 acres and spanned eighteen counties. Two thousand miles of roads and trails. Ten wilderness areas. Springer Mountain in Blue Ridge was the starting point for the 2,200-mile Appalachian Trail, which ended at the tip of the country in Maine.

Coyotes and foxes roamed the area. Venomous snakes hid under rocks and alongside the water. Black bears moved higher into the range during the summer months, foraging for fruits and berries.

Sara watched two children picking apples from a tree.

"I'm Gwen." The woman who walked up to Sara was probably in her early thirties, but she looked worn past her years. Her face was drawn. There was no color in her skin. Even her eyes had taken on a depleted dullness. "I've been told you're a doctor."

"Sara." Sara offered her hand.

Gwen looked confused, as if she'd forgotten how to meet another person. She reached out tentatively. Like Sara, she was sweating. Her palms were calloused from work.

Sara asked, "You've had a measles outbreak?"

"Yes." She wiped her hands on her apron as she started to walk. She was leading Sara toward the long bunkhouse in the distance. As they got closer, Sara could see that solar panels were on the roof. There was an outdoor shower, a sink basin.

Gwen said, "The outbreak started six weeks ago. We tried to quarantine, but it kept getting worse."

Sara was not surprised. Measles was one of the most contagious diseases known to man, carried on sneezes, coughs, breaths. Simply being in a room for up to two hours after an infected person had left still put you at risk of catching the disease. Which was why it was critically important to vaccinate as many healthy children as possible.

Sara asked, "How many were infected?"

Gwen's eyes brimmed with tears. "Two adults. Nineteen children. Eleven are still quarantined. We lost—we lost two of our little angels."

Sara tried to tamp down her anger. Two children dead by a disease that had been successfully eradicated from the United States almost two decades ago. "You're sure it's measles and not German measles?"

"Yes, ma'am. I'm a nurse. I know the difference between rubeola and rubella."

Sara pressed together her lips so that she would not explode.

Gwen had not missed her reaction. She said, "We're a closed community."

"One of those infected adults brought in measles from somewhere." Sara told herself to stop, but she couldn't. "Your husband and his men were in Atlanta yesterday. They murdered dozens of people, police officers among them, and set off two bombs." Sara watched the woman's face. Gwen did not register surprise or even shame, so Sara drilled down into the medical implications. "There are thousands of international visitors in the city every day. Any one of your people could've brought back whooping cough, mumps, rotavirus, pneumococcal disease, Hib."

Gwen's chin tucked to her chest. She wiped her hands on her apron again.

Sara asked, "Where is Michelle?"

"I understand the appendix ruptured before they could remove it. I gave her 400 mgs Moxifloxacin PO and re-sutured the incision."

Sara let out a long breath. The bloody surgical bandage on Michelle's lower abdomen finally made sense. "She needs five days of that, minimum. Push fluids. Keep her on clear liquids and bed rest."

"I will."

"Why did they bring her here? What was she supposed to do?"

Gwen kept her head down. She held out her arm, indicating the bunkhouse. "This way."

Sara walked ahead of her. She wasn't finished needling this woman for information. "Clearly, you know quarantine protocols. You can provide supportive care. You obviously have access to antibiotics. Why did they abduct Michelle?"

Gwen stared at her feet as if she needed to concentrate on her steps. She was stooped, cowered just as much as Michelle. Her hands went to her apron again. She kept wringing them into the cloth.

In the distance, Sara heard children laughing—not the ones from the clearing, but to the northeast, in the direction Dash had taken moments ago. She assumed that the second part of the Camp was where they were keeping the uninfected. Questions filled Sara's mind—*How many people were here on the mountain? Why did they take Michelle to Atlanta when there were dozens of hospitals that were closer? Why did they set off those bombs? Why was it so important to keep Michelle alive? What did they really want from Sara?*

"Here." Gwen had stopped at the sink outside the bunkhouse.

Sara washed her hands with lye soap. The water was hot. She scrubbed at her arms, around her neck and face.

Gwen said, "We could give you clean clothes."

"No thank you." Sara was not going to dress like a Victorian toddler. "How many adults here are vaccinated?"

Gwen saw through her query. "We have twelve unvaccinated men, two women."

"And the others?"

"They're staying at the main Camp."

Sara had been right about the uninfected part of the compound. She thought about Dash letting his children kiss him on the face before heading up the path. If any of them were infected, he could carry the virus to the other side.

Gwen said, "My girl, Adriel. She's still in quarantine."

"You have seven children?" Sara was struck incredulous. The woman was barely into her thirties. No wonder she looked so depleted.

Gwen only offered, "God is good."

Sara took a towel from the pile over the sink to dry her hands. The material was linen, not terrycloth. There were no tags. The seam looked hand-sewn. Was the Camp some type of religious cult? Those types of organizations didn't tend to blow things up. They drank poison or picketed funerals.

Sara asked, "Does your religion forbid vaccination?"

Gwen shook her head. "You have two children?"

Sara had to catch herself before she responded. "Yes, two girls."

A thin smile tightened Gwen's mouth. "Dash told me that your husband died in the line of duty. It seems like lately, the world is filled with widows."

Sara wasn't going to bond with this woman. "Do Vale and Carter have wives who live up here, too?"

The smile turned into an angry, straight line. "They were not among us. They were mercenaries."

"Mercenaries fight in wars."

"We *are* at war." She handed Sara a surgical mask. "We must use whatever resources we have available. Cyrus was a pagan, but he restored the world to order."

Sara had spent a lifetime listening to her mother's Bible stories. "King Cyrus also encouraged tolerance and compassion. Can you say the same about your husband?"

"We will blow the trumpet from the mountain," Gwen said. "'I form the light and bring darkness. I make peace and deliver evil.' So saith the Lord."

Sara tied the surgical mask behind her head so that the woman could not read her expression. She wasn't against religion so much as the people who sought to use it as a weapon. One of the things that had drawn Sara to medicine was the immutability of facts. The atomic number for helium would always be two. The triple point of water was indisputably the basis of the definition for the kelvin. You didn't need faith to believe either of these things. You just needed math.

She walked up the stairs. The door made a sucking sound when she opened it. The scent of disinfectant stung her eyes. The bunkhouse was long and narrow, cooled with two portable air conditioning units that hummed softly in the corners. A large medicine cabinet was stocked with rubbing alcohol, swabs, hypodermics and Ziploc bags filled with various colored pills. IV fluid was stored in overflowing coolers.

Three women were tending to the patients, rubbing them down with cold cloths. Their demeanor seemed to change as Gwen walked over to the medicine cabinet, her feet heavy across the wooden floor. Their hands moved faster. They quickly moved to the next patient. Furtive glances were exchanged. Sara reminded herself to pay attention to these subtle shifts. These women were afraid of Gwen, which meant that Gwen had given them good reason.

Sara's gaze went around the room as Gwen laid equipment on a rolling cart. She counted twenty cots. Only eleven were occupied. White sheets draped over small bodies, pale faces blending in with white pillowcases. Every part of Sara keyed into their suffering. Coughing, sneezing, shaking, crying. The worst were the ones who were not moving at all. She was enveloped by sadness.

"We have these—" Gwen indicated the cart, which held gloves, a stethoscope, an otoscope for looking at the ear canal and tympanic membrane, and an ophthalmoscope for examining the retina and eye.

A child in the corner was racked by a sudden fit of coughing. One of the women ran to her, holding a bucket under her mouth. Another little girl started to quietly sob. This set off the rest of the children. They were all so miserable, so sick, so desperate for help.

Sara wiped away tears with the back of her hand, asking Gwen, "Tell me where to start."

"Benjamin." Gwen led her over to a young boy lying beneath a window. The glass had been covered with a white sheet to keep the heat at bay.

There was a chair beside him. Sara held his hand as she sat down. The child was shivering, though his skin was hot. His face showed the telltale rash that would eventually cover his entire body. The lesions were starting to coalesce. With every cough, his cheeks turned a brighter red.

"I'm Dr. Earnshaw," Sara told the child. "I'm going to try to help you, okay?"

His eyelids would barely open. His cough echoed inside of his chest. Normally, Sara would explain everything she did and why, but this boy was too sick to follow along. All she could do was give him the peace of a quick examination so that he could return to his broken sleep.

She found a chart by his bed. Eight years old, BP 85/60, temp 100°. The prodrome started with fever, malaise, anorexia and the three Cs: cough, coryza and conjunctivitis. The cough was on full display. The child could not stop. His nose was running so badly that the mucus had chapped his upper lip. His eyes looked as if someone had poured bleach into them. According to the record, his temperature had not dropped below 100° since three this morning.

Measles was a virus, not a bacterial infection that could be treated with antibiotics. All they could do was give him Tylenol, IV fluids and tepid sponge baths to keep him comfortable. Then they would need to pray he didn't go blind or deaf, develop encephalitis or, in seven to ten years, show signs of acute SSPE, a degenerative disease that led to coma and death.

Gwen said, "Benjamin is our most recent case. The spots showed up two days ago."

That tracked with the rash. He had probably been exposed fourteen days ago, which meant that the quarantine could potentially stop the outbreak in its tracks. Slim consolation for the parents who had already lost their children or might have them returned with irreparable damage.

Gwen said, "His cough worsened overnight."

Sara bit her tongue so she would not lash out at Gwen again. She had a hard time believing a woman who had gone to nursing school would risk her children's lives over repeatedly disproven pseudoscience and the word of a former *Playboy* model. If anyone wanted a real-life documentation of the vital necessity of vaccines, they should look to the life of Helen Keller.

Sara slipped her hands into a pair of gloves. "Benjamin, I'm going to examine you now. I'll be as fast as I can. Will you open your mouth for me?"

He struggled to keep his mouth open as he coughed.

Sara used the light from the otoscope to see inside. The Koplik's spots were on the soft palate and oropharynx. The light reflected off the pearly centers. She told Gwen, "We need to get his fever down."

"I can have them bring in ice."

"Get as much as you can," Sara told her. "Acute encephalitis has a fatality rate of fifteen percent. Lasting neurologic damage occurs in twenty-five percent of cases."

Gwen nodded, but she was a nurse. She knew this already. "Our two angels were taken by seizures."

Sara did not know whether to rage or cry.

"Gwen?" one of the women called. She was standing over another cot, another deathly ill child.

Sara brought the chair so she could sit by the girl's bed. Three, maybe four years old, blonde hair fanned out on a thin pillow. Skin as pale as the moon. The sheet was soaked through with sweat. Her breathing was labored, punctuated by an unproductive cough. The child's rash had taken on a coppery hue, so she was well into a week of the disease. Sara changed into a fresh pair of gloves. She pressed open the girl's eyelids. Gwen passed her the ophthalmoscope. Sara's chest filled with dread. The conjunctiva was red and swollen. The edge of the cornea had become infected. She listened to the girl's lungs. Both had an achingly familiar crackle.

If the double pneumonia didn't kill her, then she would probably be blind for the rest of her life.

Gwen said, "This is my Adriel."

Sara struggled against an overwhelming helplessness. "We need lab tests to see if the pneumonia is bacterial or viral."

"We have Zithromax."

Sara took off one of her gloves. She pressed her hand to Adriel's head. She was roasting with fever. The antibiotic could wreck the girl's intestinal tract, but they had to take the chance. "Give it to her."

Gwen started to speak, then stopped. She changed her mind again. "If you give me a list, I can try to get whatever you think would help."

What would help was an air ambulance to take these children to civilization.

Gwen found a notepad and pencil beside one of the beds. "We can get bulk from the pharmacy. Tell me what you need. We can dose it ourselves."

Sara looked at the sharp pencil end resting on the first line of the page. She tried to gather her thoughts. "Ten tubes of Tobrex ointment, ten of the drops. Ten of Vigamox. We don't know if these eye infections and earaches are going to spread." Sara changed her gloves. She watched Gwen's pencil move down the page, the quantity, a dash, then the name of the medication. "Five Digoxin, five Seroquel, twenty or more tubes of hydrocortisone cream for the rashes. Ten erythromycin, five Lamisil cream for the fungal infections . . . are you getting this?"

Gwen nodded. "Ten erythromycin, five Lamisil."

Sara kept dictating until the page was filled. They weren't going to the local pharmacy for these supplies, which meant that they needed someone on the outside to bring them in. "I'm assuming you don't want my license or DEA number?"

"No." Gwen checked the list, tapping each word with her pencil. "I don't—I'm not sure. This is a lot."

"There are a lot of sick children," Sara said. "Whoever's going to the pharmacy, tell them it's listed in order of importance. Anything is better than nothing."

Gwen tore the page from the pad. She passed the list to one of the women, who silently left the bunkhouse.

Sara hooked the stethoscope into her ears. She turned to the girl in the next cot, whose name was Martha. The rash in the corners of her mouth was cracked with candida. The child beside her, Jenny, had pneumonia. Sara moved to the next patient, then the next. Their ages ranged from four to twelve. All but Benjamin were girls. Six had pneumonia. Adriel's conjunctivitis had spread to another child. Two were showing ear infections that could be cultured and diagnosed in any pediatrician's office. Sara could only advise warm compresses in the slim hope that they would keep their hearing.

There was no telling how much time had passed when she

finished with the last little girl, a dark-haired, blue-eyed four-year-old named Sally who'd coughed so hard that she'd developed a bleed in her right eye. Sara made a second round with the sickest children. All she could do was hold their hands, stroke their hair, give them the impression that as a doctor, she could magically restore their health. They would be playing soon, drawing with their crayons, running around in the fields, spinning like tops until they were so dizzy that they fell down.

The weight of her lies felt like a rock pressing the breath out of Sara's chest.

She peeled off her gloves as she walked down the steps to the bunkhouse. The heat sweltered around her. She washed her hands at the sink. The water was so hot she could feel the skin burning. Sara was numb to the pain. There was a tremble she could not get out of her body. One, maybe two more of those children were going to die. They needed to be in a hospital right now. They needed nurses and doctors and lab results and machinery and modern life to pull them back into the living.

Gwen walked down the steps, her hands wringing in her apron again. "Dash sent the list to our supplier. We should have it this afternoon around—"

Sara walked away. She didn't know where she was going, only that she could not go far. The armed men tightened the periphery as she walked across the clearing. Two jumped down from their deer stands. Two more appeared out of the trees. They had knives on their belts, guns in their holsters, rifles gripped between their meaty hands. Without exception, they were young, some of them no more than teenagers. All of them were white.

Sara ignored them. She pretended that they were nothing in her life because at this moment, they did not matter. She listened for the burbling sound of water that told her the stream was nearby. She followed one of the meandering paths. The burbling turned into a rush. The stream was actually a river. Sara fell to her knees at the water's edge. Rocks had created a waterfall. She put her hands into the rush of ice-cold water. She dunked her head underneath. She needed something to shock herself out of this nightmare.

There was no shock that was strong enough. She sat on her knees, hands in her lap, hair hanging down in thick, wet strands. Sara felt useless. There was nothing she was going to be able to do for these children. Had Michelle felt the same way? She had been here for a month. She had watched two children die, tracked the infection spreading around the Camp. She had known what was coming and been unable to stop it.

Sara couldn't stop it, either.

Her hands went to her face. Tears streamed from her eyes. She could not stop crying. Her body shook from grief. She was doubled over by it, unable to stop. Sara gave in to every emotion—not just her fears for these children, but for her own loss. Years ago, she had come to terms with her inability to have a child, but she found herself hating Gwen, hating every woman in this Camp who had left their child, their gift, so vulnerable.

A twig snapped behind her.

Sara jumped up, fists raised.

Dash said, "Thank you for your help, Doctor. I know it's difficult."

She wanted to spit in his face. "Who are you people? What are you doing up here?"

"We are families who've decided to live off the land."

"Those children are sick. Some of them—"

"That's why you're here, Doctor. The Lord was kind enough to send us a pediatrician."

"He should've sent you oxygen tents, IV antibiotics, respirators—"

"We'll get you everything you put on the list," Dash said. "Gwen has told me she is confident in your abilities."

"I'm not!" Sara realized she was shouting. She didn't care. "If you believe in miracles, then pray for one. Your daughter is gravely ill. All of those children are in critical danger. I understand having a religious objection to vaccines, but you don't. You clearly don't object to modern medicine. You took Michelle to the hospital. You could help your children, but instead you're letting them suffer for—for what?"

Dash steepled together his hands, but not in prayer. He was

giving her time to collect herself. As if it was possible to recover from the tragedy she had been dragged into.

Finally, he said, "You seem to have some questions for me."

Sara didn't believe she'd get an honest answer, but she asked, "What's the point of this place?"

"Ah," he said, as if she was speaking a different language that only he could decipher. "You want to know how we got here, yes?"

Sara shrugged, because he was going to say what he was going to say.

"We've been on the mountain for over a decade. Our way of life is simple. We take care of our own. The family units remain whole. We respect the land. We don't take more than we need and we give back when we can. Our blood is in this soil."

Dash paused, as if he expected Sara to key into the familiar white nationalist chant of blood and soil.

When Sara did not oblige, Dash said, "We were led here by Gwen's father, a righteous believer in the Constitution and American sovereignty."

Sara kept waiting.

"Our leader has been taken away from us, but we'll continue the mission without him." Dash explained, "That's the beauty of the system. We don't need a leader so much as believers in the world that we're trying to return to. A world of law and order, where people know their place and understand where they belong in the system. Every wheel needs a cog if it's going to turn properly. Our beliefs guide us in this crusade, not any particular leader. When one man falls, another man stands up to replace him."

"And the leader always happens to be a man?"

He smiled. "That's the natural order of things. Men lead. Women follow."

Sara ignored the reductive bullshit. "Are you part of some religious group, or—"

"There are some true believers among us. I can't count myself among those, much to my wife's chagrin. Most of us are pragmatists. That's our religion. We are all Americans. That unites us."

"Michelle is an American, too."

"Michelle is a lesbian who gave birth to a mixed-race mongrel child."

Sara was momentarily stunned. It wasn't so much what he'd said about Michelle's daughter, it was the way the mask had slipped from his face. His expression was angry, ugly. This was the true Dash, the one who set off explosives and murdered indiscriminately.

Just as quickly, the mask slid back up.

Dash adjusted the sling around his neck. He smiled. He told Sara, "Dr. Earnshaw, you're clearly a good woman. I respect that you chose to come here to help us with our children." He gave her a wink, as if to let her know that he was in on the joke. "As I said yesterday, as soon as our little ones are tended to, you'll be free to go."

She held on to his vile words about Michelle's daughter. That was who he really was, not the overly mannered caricature he showed the world. "You're a terrorist. I watched you shoot a man in cold blood. I'm supposed to take you at your word?"

His composure held fast. "Vale was executed for war crimes. We are soldiers, not animals. We operate under the Geneva Convention."

War.

The word kept coming up, first from Gwen and now from Dash. "Who are you fighting against?"

"We are not fighting *against*, Dr. Earnshaw. We are fighting *for*." His smile was smug, but then men like Dash were always smug in the knowledge that the rest of the world was wrong and they alone knew the truth. "I know you missed breakfast because you were with your patients. Lunch is being put on the tables. I hope you'll join us."

The thought of sitting with him, having a normal meal, was more revolting than the idea of putting food in her mouth, but she had to keep herself strong. Sara could not give into despair. She would not end up beaten down like Michelle.

"This way, please." He indicated the path, waiting.

Sara walked through the woods toward the clearing. Her hands were still shaking. Her stomach was filled with bile. Her clothes were disgusting. Everything about her felt disgusting. She combed her fingers through her wet hair. Steam rose from her scalp. The sun was high above the ridgeline. She was momentarily blinded by a flash of light. The sun had hit a pane of glass. She stumbled on a rock.

She righted herself before Dash could.

Sara kept walking, her head pointed straight, her eyes looking to the side.

There was a greenhouse just beyond the trees.

She had missed the glass enclosure on her way to the stream. The roof was peaked in the center. Skylights vented heat. The building was narrow, roughly the size of a mobile home. The roof and walls were glass, but a tent had been erected inside the structure. The material was reflective, the color of aluminum foil.

Electrical cords ran outside to a wooden shed. She saw a towable generator with a muffler. More solar panels. Her ears picked up a soft hum of machinery behind the glass walls. Inside the tent. Metal scraping metal. Items being moved around. The occasional murmur of a voice.

Sara heard the industrious sound of people working long after she had lost sight of the building.

The Camp.

Women and sick children. Boys playing GI Joe. A compound hidden amongst the trees. A glass greenhouse with a reflective thermal tent that would prevent a helicopter or plane with a heat-seeking camera from peering inside.

When Sara had questioned Gwen about her husband, she had quoted Isiah—

I form the light and bring darkness. I make peace and bring evil.

Fifteen people had been murdered at Emory. One of their own team had been killed during their escape. Dash had murdered a delivery man and one of his mercenaries right in front of Sara's eyes.

What other evil was he planning to bring?

10

Monday, August 5, 6:10 a.m.

Will sat across from Amanda's desk at the GBI's Panthersville Road headquarters. The clock on the wall said it was ten after six in the morning. He watched her read through the overnight reports. Autopsies on the man Will had shot at the car accident and the two men found dead at the motel. Forensic results from the abandoned potato chip van, Sara's BMW, the motel room.

Beau. Bar. Dash. Thinks. Hurley's. Dead. Spivey. Me. OK. 4. Now.

Will gripped his hands together. The knuckles were swollen and bruised. His headache was tapping on the back of his eyeballs like a ball-peen hammer. His thoughts had turned into Velcro, sticking to inconvenient parts of his brain. The pain in his belly had spread into his kidneys. He was sitting on the edge of his seat because it hurt too much to lean back.

He told Amanda, "Sara wrote that she was okay *for now*. The voice text was sent at four fifty-four yesterday. That's basically thirteen hours ago—sixteen hours since she was taken."

Amanda glanced at him over her reading glasses.

He said, "Whatever you're reading in those pages, it won't change the fact that three men from the car accident are dead and a fourth is in custody. No one knows what I look like, or that I was even there. Put me undercover. The IPA is four men down. They need somebody with skills for whatever they're planning next. I need to be in there so we can figure out how to stop them."

Amanda was silent for a moment longer, giving him the impression that she might be considering his request. "The FBI's confidential informant was your way into the IPA. Unfortunately, he's currently in a refrigerator drawer."

Adam Humphrey Carter couldn't be the only way in. "I know you, Amanda. You wouldn't send me in with someone else's CI. You've got another guy on the inside who can vouch for me."

She didn't disagree with him. "Are you forgetting that there were five men at the car accident? You can't be sure that Dwight didn't see you."

"He was unconscious the entire time."

"What about Michelle?"

Will couldn't answer that. He didn't know what would happen if Michelle Spivey recognized him. She was defiant one second, then terrified the next.

"Wilbur—"

"What about Sara's message?" he asked. "The first word she wrote on the ceiling was *Beau*. Sara's second word was *bar*. Maybe she overheard Beau talking to Dwight. Or they went to the bar. I know that you—"

"Here's what I know." Amanda threw one of the stapled reports at him. "Charlie's findings at the motel."

Will stared at the pages. His head was hurting too much to try to decipher the words. He wasn't going to use a ruler to pin down each letter like a first grader, especially not in front of Amanda.

He settled on a belligerent, "So?"

She snatched the report out of his hands. "Michelle Spivey stabbed Carter to death. Her fingerprints were on the headboard. The evidence suggests that she jumped on him, straddled his legs, braced her right hand by his shoulder, then stabbed him seventeen times in the neck, chest and belly."

Will tried to frame the killing frenzy into a positive. "She's fighting back. She could be an ally."

"She's dangerous and unpredictable, and I can't risk her nutting up around you. At worst, she could stab you to death. At best, she could tell her captors exactly how she knows you."

Will shrugged, because he had already decided that the next time it came down to Sara's life or his, he was going to make the decision for both of them.

Amanda thumbed through the pages of another report. "The man you killed at the car accident. He called himself Merle. He's been identified as Sebastian James Monroe. Ex-Army Corps of Engineers. Dishonorable discharge for domestic violence. He's kept his nose clean since then, but obviously, he's been up to something."

Will didn't ask her how she'd come across the information. The Pentagon didn't usually volunteer details without a warrant and ten miles of paperwork. "Domestic violence. Does that include rape?"

"It does not."

He couldn't tell if she was lying. "What about Vince? The guy I shot in the chest."

"Oliver Reginald Vale. Also ex-Army, but he has no overlaps with Monroe that we can find. Honorable discharge five years ago. No rap sheet. And going by the fact that these men chose country-western pseudonyms corresponding with the first letters of their names, we can assume that Dwight is the Dash from Sara's bathroom ceiling message. Obviously a nickname."

"Dash," Will repeated. The name stirred up a boiling fury. Will couldn't remember a damn thing about the man beyond his average height, weight and coloring. All of his attention had been on the conscious men. He'd thought Hurley was in charge.

He told Amanda, "Sara's message said that Dash thinks Hurley is dead."

"And we plan to keep it that way."

She was missing the point, probably on purpose. Sara had told them that what Dash thought about Hurley was what mattered. Which meant that their focus right now should be on identifying Dash. If they didn't know who he was, then they wouldn't know how to find him, and if they couldn't find Dash, then they would likely never find Sara.

So, this is what they had to do: Track down the social security numbers for Hurley, Carter, Vale and Monroe. Run credit reports that listed addresses, cell phones, credit cards, vehicle registrations. Talk to their neighbors about their comings and goings. Mine the phone numbers they had called, the stores or restaurants they had frequented. Look for overlaps. Methodically put together known associates until Dash's real name, or an identifying feature, told them who he was.

Or Will could fuck his stupid brain and ask Amanda the obvious question. "Are Dash's fingerprints in the military database?"

"They are not in any searchable database. We have the blood from Dash's shoulder wound in the back seat of the Chevy Malibu, but that will take another twenty-four hours to process. And you know as well as I that if Dash's fingerprints don't come up in the databases, then it's highly unlikely his DNA profile will lead us to his front door. At best, it will give us confirmation after the fact."

Will rubbed his jaw with his fingers. He felt the rough stubble of his beard. He hadn't shaved this morning. He was wearing the same gray suit from the day before. He had sat on his couch all night listening to Sara's text message, trying to hear something in her voice that told him she was okay.

All he kept coming back to was this:

At 4:54, Sara had sent him a message.

What had happened at 4:55?

He said, "Dash is at the top of the IPA."

"Correct," Amanda said. "Carter, in his capacity as an informant, told the FBI that Dash is the shot-caller for the group. He didn't start the IPA, it's been around for ten years or more, but under Dash's leadership, he's managed to bring focus and organization to the group. The FBI deigned to share this information with me just this morning. The description they have for Dash is about as good as yours—which is to say, nothing. And the Emory CCTV video was as useless as the both of you. Dash knew exactly where the cameras were. He wore a hat and kept his head down. The man is incredibly adept at avoiding identification. You could say that Dash puts the *invisible* in the Invisible Patriot Army."

Will gripped his hands together and rested them on her desk. "Amanda, I am begging you. Put me undercover. I will find Dash. I will serve him up to you on a platter."

Amanda scooped up another report. She read, "'Comparison weapon is a registered Glock 19 Gen5 with reversed magazine catch and slide stop lever for a left-handed shooter. The NIST algorithm using the CMC method produced a probability rating of—'"

"It's my gun," Will said.

"Your Glock was used to kill Vale in the motel room."

Will tried to shrug again, but the twinge in his rib stopped him.

"You discharged your weapon twice at the car accident. You killed a suspect. You shot a second one as he was fleeing. You beat the hell out of a third. Technically, you should be suspended with pay pending an internal investigation."

"Suspend me," Will said. He had a plan. Sebastian James Monroe. Oliver Reginald Vale. Adam Humphrey Carter. Robert Jacob Hurley. He would circle their lives like a coyote going in for the kill.

"Stay in your seat, Wilbur." Amanda looked past Will into the hallway. "What've you got?"

Faith dropped a pile of sealed evidence bags onto Amanda's desk. She looked at Will, then did a double take.

"Faith?" Amanda was waiting.

Faith rested her hand on Will's shoulder. She told Amanda, "This is everything Ragnersen had in his pockets. They're going through his truck. Zevon already found a sawed-off shotgun under the seat."

Will rubbed his jaw. The name Ragnersen drew a blank, but Zevon Lowell was the GBI agent who had met them at the motel last night. He asked Amanda, "What's going on?"

"An investigation. What did you think was going on?" Amanda pushed around the bags on her desk. A man's leather wallet. An iPhone. A set of car keys. A folding knife.

"Wait." Will moved the knife around inside of the bag so he could get a better look. "This is mine. I stabbed Carter with it. The last time I saw it, it was sticking out of his crotch."

Amanda said, “I imagine that’s the four-inch blade that was repeatedly stabbed into Carter’s chest and torso.”

Will could not stop staring at the knife. He forced his thoughts to sharpen on this one piece of evidence. Will had stabbed Carter with this knife. Michelle had used it to stab Carter. Someone had removed the knife from Carter’s dead body, which meant that the someone who had the knife had been at the motel last night.

A man’s leather wallet. Keychain with a GMC Denali logo. An iPhone in a black rubber case.

Will had to swallow before he could speak. “Where did you get this?”

Amanda motioned for Faith to shut the door. She sat back in her chair. She took off her glasses. She folded her arms across her chest.

She told Will, “The knife was found on Beau Ragnersen.”

Beau. Bar.

“He’s an ex-Army medic attached to Special Forces. The Green Berets. The file on him is too tight for me to break open. We’ve sent the paperwork up the chain to the Pentagon, but it’ll be at least a month before we hear anything. All my contact can give me is that Ragnersen saw heavy action in Iraq and Afghanistan. He was awarded a Purple Heart and took shrapnel in his back.”

Will recalled Zevon’s cryptic conversation with Amanda last night. The special agent worked with the drug squad. He hadn’t gathered all of that background information on Beau Ragnersen in the two hours it had taken Amanda to drive up to Rabun County.

Will quoted Zevon: “‘He makes his money down in Macon.’”

Faith sat down beside Will. She gave him a worried look. “Ragnersen runs black tar heroin.”

“Jesus.” Will couldn’t hide his shock. Black tar heroin was usually cut with black shoe polish or sometimes even dirt. Georgia’s distinctive red clay gave it a brownish color. You didn’t use it unless you were desperate or had a death wish.

Amanda said, “When I was in uniform, I saw a lot of vets coming home from Nam chasing the dragon. Shooting it up calcifies your veins. Distilling it into nose drops can cause you to choke to death on your own blood. Suppositories lead to internal bleeding. There's no easy way out of it that doesn't take you through the morgue."

Will rubbed his jaw. This was why he hated drugs. As a kid, he'd seen too many adults do too many unspeakably terrible things in search of a fix.

Amanda said, "The Mexicans have a stranglehold on the H flowing into the suburbs. Black tar is mostly used by minorities. In Macon, this means African Americans. The price point is on par with crack in the mid-1980s. Ragnersen isn't a big dog in the trade. He's established a niche market."

Faith had her notebook out. She said, "Beau's serious bank comes from pills, but not what you're thinking. Antibiotics, insulin, statins—legitimate medications that people need but can't afford. There's a huge black market for it in Macon. Lots of uninsured people with chronic medical conditions. Macon PD picked him up twice with pills in his glove box. Unmarked Ziplocs. They assumed opiates. May of 2017, the lab result came back with Metformin and Beau's record was cleared. The second time, February 2018, it was something called gabapentin. It's used to treat a lot of things, but mostly nerve pain. The judge kicked him with time served."

Amanda took over. "Macon PD suspects that Ragnersen is also an on-call medic—courtesy of his Army training, I would assume. He mostly works with the local gangs. If you get shot and don't want the police asking questions at the hospital, he's your man."

Faith said, "Okay, I've got a wild hair on this one."

Amanda waited.

"The Wells Fargo bank where Martin Novak was apprehended was just outside of Macon. One of Novak's guys was shot in the belly. We were told in the meeting yesterday that there was no way the guy could've survived the gunshot wound without medical intervention." She waited for Amanda to pick up on her train of thought, but when she didn't, Faith asked her directly. "Do you think Beau Ragnersen got the bullet out?"

Amanda passed an autopsy report to Faith. "Sebastian James Monroe, aka Merle, the man who was killed by Will at the car accident, showed extensive abdominal scarring from a previous gunshot wound, likely received within the last two years. The report says he was patched up by someone with medical knowledge—a veterinarian or a surgical nurse."

"Or a former special forces medic." Faith snapped her fingers. "Jackpot. That puts Monroe at the Wells Fargo, which ties him to Novak. This is proof that Novak is connected to the IPA. You've got to tell the FBI. They can rain hellfire down on this thing."

"Everything you've told me is either speculation or wishful thinking," Amanda said. "The FBI has already been informed of your theory. They remain unconvinced."

Faith tossed the report onto the pile. "Of course they do."

"I want to make this very clear to both of you," Amanda said. "Our focus is on finding Sara and Michelle Spivey. That's it. The larger conspiracy pieces are not in our purview. The marshals have custody of Martin Novak. It is not the job of the GBI to tie Novak to the IPA. The FBI is investigating the bombing. It is not the job of the GBI to tie the IPA to the bombing. We are working an abduction and kidnapping case."

Faith said, "So, we hammer everything *but* the nail?"

"Listen to me." Amanda tapped her desk for attention. "Why do I have to keep reminding you of Waco and Ruby Ridge? The FBI has dealt with these paramilitary, white nationalist organizations far longer than we have."

"Yeah, they've made them too white to fail."

"Faith." Amanda was clearly trying to hold in her temper. "We need to take a page from the history books. Do you want the GBI to turn Dash and the IPA into a group of martyrs that inspire the next generation of domestic terrorists, or do you want us to slowly, methodically work the case and bring about a solid conviction?"

Will didn't give a shit about building a case. He was going to find Dash because that was how he would find Sara. "Where is Beau? Is he here?"

Faith waited for Amanda to nod her permission. "He's cooling off downstairs." She told Amanda, "On the plus side, we've arrested him for assaulting an agent. Beau wasn't happy about being yanked out of bed in the middle of the night. He punched Zevon hard enough to break his nose."

The middle of the night.

The phrase woke up Will's brain. Beau hadn't been arrested on a whim. Amanda had brought him in while Will was sitting on his couch waiting for the alarm to go off so he could do his fucking job and find Sara.

Amanda asked, "Wilbur, do you have something to say?"

He had a lot to say, but he settled on, "I want to talk to him."

"I'm sure you do."

Inside one of the evidence bags, Beau's cell phone screen flashed with a notification. Faith turned her head to read, "It's an email—gmail account with random letters and numbers. The subject line is ASAP, but that's all I can see with the screen locked."

Amanda stood up from her desk. She took her jacket off the back of the chair and slipped it on. "Faith, bring his phone."

Will opened the door. He kept his hand tight on the knob, fighting against the spin in his eyeballs. Amanda walked ahead of him, BlackBerry out, thumbs moving across the keys. Will's vision turned rickety as he followed her down the hall, which had rolled out like a giraffe's tongue. The fluorescent lights were strobing. Or he was having a stroke.

"You look like shit," Faith hissed. "Either go home or ask Amanda for the other half of that pill."

Will gritted his teeth, but that only made his headache worse. The lights were the problem. Someone had turned them up too high.

"You can barely walk straight." Faith was no longer using her inside voice. "If you want to help Sara, then you need to look like a human being. Take the fucking pill."

Will kept his fingers to the wall as he walked. She was worried about him. She always yelled when she was worried. He should probably acknowledge that in some way. "I'm fine."

"Sure you are, dumbass." Faith used her teeth to rip open the evidence bag. Beau's iPhone X dropped into her hand. It was the bigger kind that didn't have a home button. Will guessed the black tar heroin and pill trade was pretty lucrative.

Amanda opened the door to the stairs. "Faith, I need you to do another meeting for me this afternoon."

Faith muttered under her breath as she trundled down the stairs behind Amanda. She was examining Beau's phone. The screen was still locked. The case was black rubber with a corrugated grip. She peeled away the corners to see if there was anything hidden between the phone and the case.

Nothing.

The door opened below them. Two agents stood at the bottom of the stairs. They waited until Amanda was down before going up. Each one lifted his chin at Will, he guessed as a sort of recognition for what he was going through. Sara was the only reason they even saw him. Will had never felt a sense of camaraderie with anyone in this building aside from Faith and Charlie. Then Sara had started working here and after fifteen years, Will suddenly belonged.

Amanda was already halfway down the hall. Will had to lengthen his stride to catch up. She opened the door to the viewing room, but didn't go in. She nodded for Faith to continue down the hall.

She told Will, "The FBI took Hurley into custody. They're moving him out of state. We won't get another bite at him. The bombing is a federal investigation. So long as the FBI keeps insisting there's no connection to the IPA, we've got Dash all to ourselves."

"We need to run social security numbers and—"

"It's being handled, Will. We've been on it since last night." Her eyes narrowed. "Are you up for this?"

He went into the viewing room. The lights were off. His headache instantly backed off a notch. He stood in front of the two-way mirror with his hands in his pockets. He stared at the man he assumed was Beau Ragnersen. The former soldier was slumped over the table with his cuffed hands gripped together. A chain ran through a metal ring on the table. Two plastic chairs were across from him. His head was down. Sweat rolled down his face. He had been arrested at least twice before, but that was Macon PD. A man who had cornered the market on desperate sick people knew the difference between wrangling with the locals and coming up against the full force of the state.

Faith opened the door. She said, "Hey, asshole."

Beau looked up.

Faith showed him his iPhone. The facial recognition software scanned Beau's features and unlocked the screen.

"Fuck!" Beau's wrists jerked against the chains. The table was bolted down. All he could do was kick a chair into the wall.

On the other side of the glass, Will heard a muffled *thunk*. The walls inside the interrogation room were paneled in thick acoustic board so that the microphones could catch every sniff, cough or mumbled confession.

Faith was smirking when she came into the viewing room. She told Amanda, "The ASAP email to Beau's phone says, 'Meet at regular spot 4pm today', then there's a long list of medications with quantities. '10-Tobrex. 10-Vigamox. 5-Digoxin. 5-Seroquel. 20-Hydrocortisone cream. 10-Erythromycin. 5-Lamisil. 5-Phenytoin. 10-Dilantin. 10-Zovirax. 10—'"

"Wait a minute." Amanda was looking over Faith's shoulder. "Hydrocortisone. Erythromycin. Lamisil. Phenytoin. What do the first letters of each word spell?"

"Oh fuck, are you kidding me?" Faith was practically shouting. "Look farther down the list—Lidocaine. Ibuprofen. Neosporin. Taxol. Ofloxacin. NebuPent."

"Clever girl!" Amanda pumped a triumphant fist into the air.

Faith swooped up her hand for a high five. Will offered a lame slap. He had no idea why they were celebrating a list of medications.

"Will!" Faith showed him the phone. "There's a message embedded in the list. Ignore the other words. Look at these two sections here. The first letters of each medication—they spell out a code: 'H-E-L-P, then L-I-N-T-O-N.'"

Will shook his head, hearing what she was saying but not understanding.

Amanda said, "Sara dictated this list. She sent us another message. 'Help Linton.'"

Help Linton.

The words had a weird echo in his ears. Will braced his hand against the wall. He stopped breathing, stopped thinking, stopped processing anything but the fact that Sara was reaching out to him again.

Help.

"Here." Faith zoomed in the list, like that would make it better. She pointed at the letters. "H-E-L—"

Will nodded so she would stop. He could see the numbers, but the words got tangled. This was the important part: at 6:49 this morning, Sara was alive and okay enough to send a coded message.

"We know Sara met Beau," Amanda told Faith. "She must've put it together that he would be the one who filled the shopping list."

"Band-Aids. Gatorade." Faith kept reading. "Boudreaux's Butt Paste. That's for diaper rash, but you can use it for chapped skin, burns, scrapes. Most of this looks like the kind of stuff you need for kids. Amoxicillin, Cefuroxime, liquid acetaminophen. I've got gallons of this stuff in my medicine cabinet."

"Aspirin," Amanda read. "You wouldn't give that to a child because of Reye's syndrome."

Faith said, "We need a doctor to look at this list and tell us if there's anything that we're missing."

"Go," Amanda said, but Faith was already out the door.

"The subject line said ASAP." Will told Amanda. "Beau has to meet them in person to give them the drugs. I want to be there. We can figure out a cover story."

"It won't be Dash who meets Ragnersen. The man in charge doesn't run errands. He'll send a flunky."

"A flunky can—" Will put his hand on the wall to steady himself. "A flunky can take me to them. Lead me to them. I can find a way in. All I need is one guy who—"

"Keep babbling while I send this email." Amanda was on her BlackBerry again. Her thumbs were a blur as she typed.

Will looked away. The bright screen had shot tiny swords into his eyes. His brain had turned back into a balloon. He could feel it bumping against his skull. He breathed in as much as he could, then out as much as his ribs would let him. He forced away the same dread that had niggled at him all night.

Sara had sent the coded message at 6:49 this morning.

What had happened at 6:50?

Amanda asked, "Do you need to sit down?"

Will shook his head. The motion made the dizziness worse. He was missing things, not making the right connections. He silently replayed Amanda's excited conversation with Faith until his thoughts cleared enough to pose a question.

He said, "You told Faith, 'We know Sara met Beau.' What proof do you have of that? All Sara wrote on the ceiling was *Beau* and *Bar*. That doesn't mean that she met him. She could've overheard his name. Or Dash or one of his men could've—"

Amanda held up her finger for silence. She finished her email. She dropped the BlackBerry into her pocket, then looked up at him. "At the motel last night, Charlie found a partial fingerprint on the inside lip of the plastic table by the door. It came back as a match to Beau Ragnersen."

Will remembered another detail Zevon had relayed to Amanda. "Beau is the caretaker at the motel. His prints are probably all over the place."

"Ragnersen's fingerprint was pressed into Carter's blood. Charlie says that based on the composition of the print, the blood was fresh when Ragnersen touched it. That puts him at the scene at the time of the stabbing. That's how we got the search warrant for Ragnersen's house. The print is clear proof that he was in the room where a murder took place. We served a no-knock warrant at three this morning."

At three this morning, Will was sitting on his couch replaying Sara's phone message like a desperate teenager. He felt his jaw clench in anger—not at Amanda; he might as well be mad at a snake for slithering. He should've never gone home in the first place.

He asked, "Why didn't you tell me this last night?"

"Because you needed, still need to, rest. Alone, without sound, in the dark. You are severely concussed. You killed one man and shot another. You've lost the woman you were too stupid to marry as soon as your divorce was finalized, and I can either stay here and change your diaper or we can both go into that room and force Beau Ragnersen to take you undercover so you can persuade Dash's flunky to take you into the IPA."

Will glared at her. Then he realized what she had just told him.

He looked through the glass mirror. Beau's hands were still gripped together on the table. His beard was long, but his hair was military tight. He was wiry and muscled in an MMA way. He sold black tar heroin to desperate junkies and took cash for patching up criminals. Right now, he was the only chance Will had to get Sara back.

He asked, "Do you have the other half of that aspirin?"

She reached into her coat pocket. Her pill case was silver with a pink rose enameled into the top. "I've got more in my purse. You'll have to ask if you need them. Aspirin can tear up your stomach."

Will dry-swallowed the pill. He didn't let Amanda leave the room first. He didn't hold open the door for her. He walked into the hall. He headed down to the interrogation room. The bright lights cut into his pupils. His eyes started to water. He opened the door.

Beau didn't look up this time. He stared down at his hands. There was a wiriness about him. Spring-loaded, like Will's stolen knife. His heel tapped against the floor. He was either a junkie who needed a fix or he had realized that life as he knew it was over. Actually, he was probably both. You didn't wear long sleeves in August unless you were trying to hide the scars on your arms.

Will clenched his stomach muscles so he could pick up the chair Beau had kicked across the floor. He gently placed it in front of the table. He gripped the back with his hands and waited.

"Good morning, Captain Ragnersen." Amanda breezed into the room and took the second chair. "I'm Deputy Director Amanda Wagner with the GBI. This is Special Agent Will Trent."

Beau finally looked at Will, sizing him up. Will straightened his fingers on the chair, drawing attention to the cuts and bruises. He wanted this guy to know that he was not above beating the shit out of somebody.

Amanda said, "Captain Ragnersen, you've already been read your rights. I want to remind you that anything you say in this room is being recorded. You should also know that lying to an agent with the Georgia Bureau of Investigation is a crime punishable by up to five years in prison. Do you understand me?"

Beau's eyes were still on Will. He clearly didn't like another man hovering over him. He lifted his chin up in a defiant nod to Amanda.

"For the record, the prisoner nodded his understanding," Amanda said. "Captain Ragnersen, you are currently under arrest for assaulting Special Agent Zevon Lowell, but a few more charges have been added to the list since we last spoke to you."

Beau pulled his gaze away from Will. He looked Amanda up and down, his mouth twisted inside the pelt of his beard. He clearly didn't like a woman being in charge, which to Will, was the beauty of having a woman in charge.

Amanda said, "Based on the search of your vehicle, we've added to your arrest warrant that you illegally altered the barrel of a weapon designed to be shot from the shoulder, which is a violation of Georgia Code Title 16. Further, the barrel was sawed off to seventeen and three-quarter inches, which is a quarter inch less than allowable under the National Firearms Act of 1934. That's a Class 4 felony with a two- to twenty-year sentence. If you are proven to have possessed that weapon while you were involved in or abetting the commission of other felonies—kidnapping, murder, rape, robbery—that bumps your possession of the illegal weapon to a Class 2 felony with a twenty-year to life sentence. And that's before we start layering in your Macon side business in black tar heroin and pharmaceuticals."

Beau's mouth kept working, but he said nothing.

Amanda sat back in her chair, arms crossed. She had been facing down bad guys longer than this man had been alive. Ragnersen thought his silence was keeping him in control when he was actually following the same script as every stupid perp before him.

Amanda said, "I'm glad you're choosing to remain silent for now, Captain Ragnersen. I need you to listen to me very carefully because, when I'm finished, you're going to have an important decision to make. I think, actually, that you're going to be begging me to accept whatever help you can offer."

She had given Hurley roughly the same speech in the hospital, but Ragnersen was no Robert Hurley.

He said, "What if I ask for a lawyer?"

"That's certainly your right."

"Damn straight it is." The chain clicked against the edge of the table as Beau slowly leaned back in the chair. He sniffed the way perps sniff when they can't be bothered to tell you to go fuck yourself.

But he didn't ask for a lawyer.

He told Amanda, "Make your gorilla sit down."

Will waited for Amanda to nod. The aspirin hadn't kicked in yet. He had to tighten every muscle in his body to leverage himself into the chair without wincing.

Beau asked Will, "What do you bench, bro?"

Will kept his expression neutral, like he hadn't been asked a douche question.

Amanda said, "Tell us about Dash."

One of Beau's shoulders went up in a defiant shrug. "We do business sometimes."

"Which of your businesses? Pharmaceuticals? Emergency surgery? Black tar heroin?"

"Tar is the negro's drug. I don't sell that shit to white people."

"We all have standards."

"Damn straight I do." Beau leaned forward. "I'm helping people, lady. The government has failed us. Left sick people to die in the street. Abandoned our soldiers. Closed our factories. Stolen food from our mouths. Somebody's gotta step up."

Amanda ignored the speech the same way she'd ignored the racism. "The 2019 GMC Yukon Denali you drive starts at $71,000 for the base model. That's some pretty high stepping for a good Samaritan."

"Shit." Beau shrugged her off again. "What do you want from me, bitch? You'd have my ass in jail right now if you were finished with me. What's the trade?"

"You'll know when the time comes," Amanda promised. "First, let's establish whether or not you're worth this conversation. Captain Ragnersen, please describe for me the events that took place with Dash yesterday between the hours of four and five p.m. at the King Fisher Camping Lodge."

Beau went silent. He was clearly trying to craft an answer that would be his quickest way out of this room. The man wasn't stupid, but being trapped had narrowed his focus to the point of a pin. Otherwise, he would've worried more over the question, which assumed that both he and Dash had been at the motel yesterday during the same time period that Sara had sent the text to Will.

"Okay," Beau said. "The truth, all right? I got there after the shit went down. Dudes were both dead. Blood was everywhere. The blonde, I don't know her name. She was in the room next door. There was another lady with red hair sitting on the floor."

Will bit the inside of his cheek so hard that the skin broke open.

Amanda asked, "List for me everyone who was there."

"Dash, couple'a three of his guys. I don't know names. Two were at the door, one was around the back. Guarding these two women, all right? Only one of them went fucking psycho with a knife. The other dude on the bed, he was already shot in the chest. He was dead when I got there. Dash wanted me to clean that shit up, but I said no fucking way. Do it yourself. I was in that room less than sixty seconds before my ass was back in my truck. Drove it across the street, had myself a beer, tried to forget what I'd seen."

"You wiped down the table in the motel room," Amanda said.

Beau hesitated. "That wasn't me. Musta been one of the women."

Amanda raised an eyebrow, but she seemed content to let him play out the story.

"Look, I'm telling you the truth," Beau nervously rubbed at his wrists under the handcuffs. "Dash said they'd leave. I went to the bar. It's right across the street. I wasn't waiting around, all right? None of my business. Next thing I know, it's dark and I'm hearing sirens. I look out the window and there's cops crawling all over the place. I jumped in my truck and went home. Got nothing to do with me." His shoulder gave an eat-shit shrug. "That's all I know."

Will flexed his hands under the table. Even with his brain on fire, he could spot the gaping holes, like—*How did Dash get into the motel room in the first place? The lock on the door wasn't broken. Beau claimed to have been in the room for less than a minute. How did he know that Vale was shot in the chest without examining him? How did he know that Michelle was in another room? How did he know that Dash had placed another guard at the rear of the property?*

And, most importantly—*How did this fucker end up with Will's knife in his pocket?*

Amanda said, "Tell me about the hostages. How many were there?"

"Two women. I already told you." Beau shrugged again. The only thing that kept Will from driving a spike into the man's shoulder was the knowledge that Beau was on tape admitting that he knew both Sara and Michelle Spivey were being held hostage.

Amanda asked, "How were they acting?"

"Normal," Beau said. "I mean, the redhead, she was trying to help. Dash told me she was a doctor." He seemed to spot an opportunity. "Which is why they didn't need me. They already had a doctor."

Then why were you there, asshole?

Amanda asked, "Did Dash tell you the doctor's name?"

He pretended to think. "Earnest? Early?"

Earnshaw.

Amanda asked, "And the other hostage?"

"Fake blonde, small tits, older. She was quiet, like, dead quiet. Never said a word, but—" His mouth snapped closed. His tongue went into his cheek. He had realized another mistake. "They were taking her out of the room when I went in. I saw them go next door. That's how I knew she was in the other room."

Amanda said, "They must've broken the lock."

"The doors were unlocked. All of them."

"That seems very irresponsible for a caretaker to leave all of the doors open." Amanda paused. "I spoke to Mr. Hopkins' daughters in Michigan and California. They told me that the estate pays you to watch the property for them. Is that why you were at the motel, to check on the property?"

Beau had the wisdom to understand he was already deep into the hole and needed to stop digging.

"Let me sum up your statement." Amanda looked at her watch as she spoke. "You were at the motel, but not for any particular reason. None of the doors were locked, so Dash and his men didn't need to break in. In the sixty or so seconds that you were in the motel room, you saw two dead men on the beds—one stabbed, one shot in the chest. Two women were being held hostage, one of whom you were told was a doctor, the other you saw being taken into an adjacent room. There were two members of the IPA guarding the front door, another you could magically see guarding the back. For some reason, you grabbed the under-edge of the table, leaving your fingerprint in fresh blood. Then, you turned on your heel and left the room, got into your truck, drove across the street, closed the blinds and poured yourself a beer." She looked up from her watch. "That description alone took thirty-eight seconds. Are you sure you only spent sixty seconds in the room?"

Beau licked his lips. He homed in on the fingerprint under the table. "I don't remember what I touched. I was freaked out. I told you they were already dead. I had to get out of there. I don't know what I touched. There could be more prints."

"That's understandable," Amanda allowed. "Is my forensic team going to identify Adam Humphrey Carter's blood in the zippers of the medical field kit we found hidden behind your bedroom bookcase?"

Beau's tongue froze mid-lick.

"One of the Halo Chest Seals is missing, but, coincidentally, Vale had one stuck over the hole in his chest. He was shot three times, by the way. Once before he was at the motel, and two killshots while he lay on the bed." Amanda leaned forward again. "It's very hard to get blood off of metal, Captain Ragnersen. You wouldn't think so, but it's true. The teeth of a zipper, for instance. The handle of a folding knife, for another. It has a spring inside, gears, a button to flick it open, crevices where microscopic flecks of blood can dry."

Beau's sweat had a chemical odor. Will could smell it from three feet away.

Amanda said, "Captain Ragnersen, do you remember me telling you at the beginning of our conversation that lying to the GBI is a crime? And that you'd be looking at a life sentence if you were found to abet felonies such as kidnapping and murder while in possession of a sawed-off shotgun?"

"It was in my truck."

"Which was parked in a wildlife management area of the Chattahoochee Forest, where it's illegal to keep a loaded firearm uncased inside your vehicle."

Desperation turned him hostile. "You're a fucking bitch. You know that?"

"I know that you met Adam Humphrey Carter while he was still in uniform for the Georgia Highway Patrol."

Beau's jaw almost hit the table.

Will looked down at his hands so that his own surprise was less evident. His shock wasn't over the information that Amanda had clearly withheld, it was from the last clue clicking into place.

Last night at the motel, Special Agent Zevon Lowell had known a hell of a lot about Beau Ragnersen—that he was the caretaker at the motel, that he ran the social club across the street, that the ownership of both businesses was tied up one way or another. You didn't gather all of those facts in two hours, just like Amanda had not uncovered the connection between Beau Ragnersen and Adam Humphrey Carter this morning. Digging through that kind of paperwork took a hell of a lot of time. You had to make phone calls, talk to people who worked the cases, figure out exactly how the details fit together.

Which meant that Beau had been on Amanda's radar for a while.

Which also meant that Will was right. There was no way Amanda would trust the FBI's confidential informant to take Will undercover into the IPA. She had her own man. A man who was currently sweating out every ounce of water inside of his body.

Amanda said, "Captain Ragnersen, according to your storied rap sheet, Carter arrested you in 2012 on a packet of Oxy he found in your glove box during a traffic stop. Unfortunately, the case fell apart when the evidence disappeared. Carter didn't log it in properly, which seems like a very hard mistake for a seasoned officer to make. Though I will say that falsifying evidence is a nice beginning to a friendship."

Will looked up. He wanted to see Beau's face when he realized there was a bazooka pointing at his chest.

Amanda said, "Carter's basically hired muscle. Over the years, you've used him to help collect debts and knock over pharmacy supply houses. Carter also referred you to some friends who might require your skills. One of those men he introduced you to was Dash. You've been helping him and the IPA ever since."

Beau's jaw was clamped down like a bear trap.

Will could feel the man's desperation—*what else had she figured out?*

Amanda asked, "How well do you know Dash?"

He started shaking his head. "I don't know him. I met him in person maybe three times before yesterday. That's over, like, five years. Dash is a good customer. He emails me a list, one of his dudes shows up with a bag of cash. He doesn't ask for weird shit, just antibiotics and statins and normal stuff. Sometimes I patch somebody up for him at the motel. Young guys doing stupid things—a knife fight gets out of hand or some dumbass shoots himself in the foot. That's it."

"It's always at the motel?"

"Yeah, or we meet near Flowery Branch off 985."

"Dash meets you there?"

"I told you, he sends one of his guys with the cash. Another guy serves as backup, but I've never seen him get out of the van. I don't meet the same guy every time. I can't give you any names. We don't fucking introduce ourselves. I sit on the bleachers. Dude swings by with the cash. We trade out our bags—pills for the money—then he hoofs it and I wait around a couple beats before I go. Just like in the movies."

"Dash called you directly yesterday," Amanda said, which had to be a calculated guess.

"He was in a jam," Beau confirmed. "I hadn't heard from him

in months. Listen to what I'm saying. Dash was Carter's guy, all right? And I always had to cut Carter in because he's a thieving, conniving dick. I was never his friend. Not in any way. I'm glad he's dead. He was a sick motherfucker. Everybody knows what he was sent up for. What he did to that woman. I've got a sister. A mother. I could never hurt a woman like that."

"I'm not implying that you would, Captain Ragnersen. As a matter of fact, I know exactly what kind of man you are because I've been following you."

Beau was too shocked to form a response.

Amanda said, "I have a tracking device on your truck. I've got another one on your Harley. I even put one on your fishing boat. I've listened to your mother cry about your drug addiction at her Nar-Anon meetings in the basement of her church. I've bought gum at the 7-Eleven where your sister works and talked to your ex-wife at the daycare center off Route Eight. I know *who* you are, *what* you are, *where* you are, at all times."

He looked scared, but he tried, "You don't know shit about me."

"I know the pain from the shrapnel you picked up in Kandahar made you chase the dragon at the end of Oxy Road. That the scars you're hiding under those long sleeves are from black tar heroin. I know what's in your kit, that you use a brown shoelace from a tactical boot to tie off. I know where you go to shoot up, who you do it with, who you sell to, what gangs you triage and perform surgery for, who runs your pills, who owes you money, who you owe, and I know that right now at this moment, Captain, I've got my foot so far up your ass that you can taste my nail polish in the back of your throat."

Beau's nostrils flared. He was panicked, trying to see a way out of this. There was no way out. Every shot had hit the target. His mother. His sister. His ex. His business. His addiction. He was desperate enough to beg, "What do you want from me?"

Amanda smiled. She sat back in her chair. She brushed lint from her jacket sleeve. "Thank you, Captain Ragnersen. I thought you'd never ask."

11

Monday, August 5, 4:30 p.m.

Sara paced her cabin cell. Twelve wide, twelve deep. As she adjusted her stride, she realized that the room was not exactly square. She got on her knees, went hand over hand, measuring out the space. Then she lost count in the middle and had to start over again. Then she put her head in her hands and tried not to scream because she was going mad with boredom in this gray prison.

At least four hours had passed since Dash had escorted her back to the cabin. The sun coming through the slats in the walls worked as a sundial across the floor. Sara squeezed her eyes closed to keep her thoughts from wandering. She summoned up the memory of the greenhouse. The building hadn't appeared overnight. The forest had already grown in around it. This was what the sentries in the deer stands and the armed men blending into the woods were guarding.

Why?

Sara tried to consider the logistics that went into erecting that kind of structure in such an isolated location. There had to be an access road nearby, a way for heavy trucks to move in the components. The iron frame would've been brought up in pieces that were assembled on site. Transporting the thick, large panes of glass would've taken special equipment. Lifting it into place.

Securing it to the frame. The generator was the size of a large playhouse, heavy enough to require a trailer. They weren't plugging in lamps and hand tools. The electrical draw had to be around 15kW, enough to power a small home.

Someone had put a hell of a lot of thought into the functionality of the design. The glass and thermal tent were overkill, inasmuch as Sara understood their purposes. The thermal imaging cameras mounted in most police helicopters detected infrared radiation, or heat signatures, in the 7–14 micron wavelength. This meant that the energy wavelength would not transmit through glass. From above, the greenhouse would be virtually invisible. The thermal tent provided roughly the same benefit, blocking the waves from being detected. Which led Sara to believe the tent wasn't meant to obscure the goings-on from above, but to block prying eyes on the ground.

She had to get inside of that tent.

How the hell was she going to do that when she couldn't even get out of this cabin?

She looked up at the ceiling, dragging herself out of despondency. Her fingers got caught in her filthy hair. The humidity had tightened the curls into a clown wig. Her skin felt raw from the lye soap she'd used to clean herself. She wanted body lotion—the good kind she got at the mall. Her La Mer lip balm that cost more than a full tank of gas. That slinky black dress that Will loved because he knew it meant that he was going to get laid. A comb. Shampoo. Nice soap. Fresh underwear. A clean bra. A hamburger. French fries. Books.

God, she wanted her books.

Sara leaned over, pressing her forehead to the bare floor. Her entire adult life had been spent wishing that she had more time, but not this kind of time. This endless, tedious, nothingness of wasted time.

She had managed to sleep, but only fitfully. Her thoughts kept bouncing around to different topics, different books and songs and stupid lists. She had tried to name all of the sorting houses from Harry Potter, recited some passages from *Goodnight Moon* that she recalled from her pediatric days, listed all of the elements in the periodic table from hydrogen to lawrencium then back again, tried to count the seconds into minutes by scratching a mark on the wall, but then she kept forgetting her place and finally gave up because what was the point? They were going to leave her locked inside of this tomb until they needed her again.

"For what?" Sara asked herself in the gray light. The women in the bunkhouse were doing everything they could to make the children comfortable. Sara was not needed until the medications arrived.

If the medications arrived.

Could Sara allow herself the hope that Beau would be the one who filled the shopping list? He would surely be in custody by now. Back in the motel bathroom, his name was the first word that Sara had written on the ceiling. Was she stupid to think that the list she'd dictated to Gwen would somehow fall into Will's hands? Was she stupider still to think that he would be able to figure out the code?

Faith would spot the letters. Amanda. Charlie. Will had people around him who could help.

"Help." Sara kept her voice at no more than a whisper.

She was mindful of the sentry outside her cell. For the most part, he sat on the stair with his rifle on his lap. The two-inch gap under the door gave her a sliced view of his left shoulder. Sometimes, he would stand, stretch and walk from one side of the cabin to the other. Occasionally, he would check the perimeter. She could hear his feet shuffling, his sniffles and coughs and frequent bouts of intestinal distress that took place mercifully downwind.

Sara made herself stand up from the dirty floor. She felt lightheaded. She pressed her palm to her growling stomach. She hadn't eaten much lunch. The vegetables and venison had looked delicious, but the food wasn't the problem.

Watching Dash play the good father to his doting girls was nauseating. He was clearly putting on a show. Sara had seen the real Dash down by the river when his formal, gentlemanly mask had slipped away. He had spoken about Michelle's daughter as if her heritage made her less than human. Less than American.

Jeffrey had been murdered by a gang of Neo-Nazi skinheads. Hearing Dash regurgitate their racist ideology had made Sara look at the man's children through a different lens. Their blonde hair, sparkling blue eyes and white dresses that made them look like they belonged on top of a wedding cake now felt more Stepford than Laura Ingalls Wilder.

She blinked in the darkness.

Who wrote that book—*The Stepford Wives*? The original movie starred . . . the woman who played Mrs. Robinson's daughter in *The Graduate*, and wasn't she in *Butch Cassidy and the Sundance Kid*, too?

The names had disappeared from Sara's memory. Her brain was melting. She needed to eat. She needed to figure out a way into that greenhouse. She needed to get the hell out of this stifling box.

She turned and paced back the way she'd come. The heel of her sneaker caught on the sheet trailing behind her. Sara mumbled a curse. The material had torn. The hem was stained from the floor.

She had been forced to change out of her dirty clothes. She'd improvised with the sheet from the bed. There was a way to tie a toga that didn't make you look like an idiot, but the skill was beyond her reach. After endless, frustrating minutes, Sara had ended up wrapping the sheet once around her body, then tying a giant, rabbit-eared knot over her right shoulder. She looked like Joan of Arc, but older and sweatier and bored out of her ever-loving mind.

"Fuck." She had reached the wall. Again. Sara pressed her hands against the boards. Outside, the sentry sniffed. He was clearly not feeling well. His cough was tight in his chest.

She hoped he died of pneumonia.

Sara turned and paced a diagonal line. Then she zigzagged, which brought some novelty to the exercise. Then she exercised. Lunges, squats, deep knee bends. She thought about the gym in her apartment building. The treadmill. The elliptical machine. She didn't miss her phone or her computer or television. She missed air conditioning. She missed having things to do. She missed Will.

Frankly, she didn't just miss him.

Sara longed for Will the same way she had longed for him during the first year of their relationship. Not that it could've been called a relationship during those early months. Angie, Will's wife, was still in the picture. Sara was still mourning Jeffrey. They had met in the ER at Grady Hospital. Will had looked at Sara the way a man looks at a woman. She hadn't realized until that moment how much she had craved that look. His desire had drawn her in, but in truth, Sara had fallen in love with Will because of his hand.

To be completely accurate, it was his left hand.

They were both standing in one of Grady's long, subterranean hallways. Sara was enduring one of Will's maddening, prolonged silences. She had been about to walk away, but then he had grabbed her hand.

His left. Her right.

His fingers had laced through hers. Sara had felt like every nerve in her body was suddenly awake. Will had traced his thumb along the inside of her palm, caressing the lines and indentations, then pressing gently into the pulse at her wrist. Sara had closed her eyes, trying not to purr like a cat, thinking about nothing but what his mouth would feel like against her own. There was a jagged scar above his lips, a faint, pink line that followed the ridge up to his nose.

Sara had spent hours wondering what that scar would feel like if she kissed him. *When* she kissed him, because she had eventually realized that she was going to have to make the first move. Will wouldn't pick up on a signal if it reached down and cupped his balls.

She had seduced him in her apartment. He'd barely had time to walk through the front door. Sara had unbuttoned the cuff to his long-sleeved shirt and licked the scar that traced up his arm. Will's breath had caught. She'd had to remind him to exhale. His mouth had felt perfect against hers. His body, his hands, his tongue. Sara had wanted him so badly, had anticipated that moment so many times, that she'd started to come the second he was inside of her.

She stopped pacing the cabin floor. She looked up at the ceiling. The sun was baking the tin roof. Sweat poured from her skin. She was torturing herself.

She kept going.

That first time, they hadn't even made it to the bed. The second time was slower, but somehow more exciting. For all of his missed signals, Will was exceptionally good in bed. He knew exactly what to do and when to do it. Rough sex. Sensual sex. Dirty sex. Kinky sex. Hate sex. Love sex. Make-up sex. Missionary. Mutual masturbation. Oral.

"Shit," Sara whispered into the dark, not because of Will but because from out of nowhere, she heard a song lyric pinging around inside her head—

My man gives good lovin' that's why I call him Killer, He's not a wham-bam-thank-you-ma'am, he's a thriller . . .

Sara groaned.

What was the name of the song?

She shook her head. Sweat flung onto her bare shoulder. Two women rappers. 1990s. One of them had the side of her head shaved.

He's got the right potion . . . Baby, rub it down and make it smooth like lotion . . .

Sara covered her ears, trying to trap the melody. Tessa had sung it to her over the phone. Sara was telling her about Will, then suddenly her sister was rapping about *mac shit* and—

From seven to seven he's got me open like Seven-Eleven . . .

Sara started laughing. She couldn't stop. She doubled over. Tears came into her eyes. There was something hilarious about a toga-wearing white woman being held hostage on a militia compound trying to remember rap lyrics about a man who knew how to fuck.

"Oh, Christ." Sara stood up straight. She wiped her eyes. She tried to think of a different song to get the first one out of her head. The one about the waitress working at a . . . was it a motel bar? Hotel bar?

Sara shook her head again, longing for a reset. Will got so annoyed when she could only remember fragments of songs. She would wake him up at night asking him to finish the lines, name the band, the album, the year. Now, she was awash in fragments—

With a lover I could really move, really move. 'Cause you can't, you won't, you don't stop. They're laughin' and drinkin' and having a party. Run away turn away run away turn away run away. Take my hand as the sun descends. Choke me in the shallow water before I get too deep. Give it away give it away give it away now.

"Salt-N-Pepa!" Sara yelled the group's name so loudly that it echoed off the ceiling. "Whatta Man" was the song that Tessa had rapped over the phone.

Sara gripped together her hands and looked at the ceiling. "Thank you," she said, though she was certain this wasn't what her mother had in mind when she told Sara that she needed to pray more.

Two voices came from the other side of the door. Sara recognized Dash's distinctive tenor, but couldn't make out his words. The sentry was probably telling him that Sara had started screaming for seasonings.

Ain't nobody perfect, as Salt-N-Pepa would say.

The padlock clicked open. Dash opened the door. Sara held up her hand to shield the bright light. The sun was just over the peak. She had judged the time wrong, which meant that it had taken less than three hours of isolation to make her go insane.

Dash raised his eyebrows at her sheet dress, but he kept his opinion to himself. "Dr. Earnshaw. I wondered if you'd like to join us for afternoon prayers." He winked at her. "Participation is optional."

Sara would've bellowed "Ave Maria" at the top of her lungs if it got her out of this cramped room. She stepped down onto the log. The sentry gave her a curious look. His eyelids were droopy. Air whistled through his clogged nostrils. He was definitely coming down with something. Sara didn't ask him if he was vaccinated. She wanted him to worry.

"Doctor." Dash indicated a second path that she hadn't seen before. "We study by the river."

Sara picked her way down the path. His word choice was

strangely formal, as if he'd learned to speak by listening to phonographs of Franklin Roosevelt's Fireside Chats. In different circumstances, she would wonder if English was his first language.

Sara felt a tug at the hem of her dress. She'd managed to snag herself in a thicket of catbrier.

"Allow me." Dash reached down to help.

Sara tore the material away from the thorny weed. She casually turned her head to the left, trying to locate the greenhouse. The sun was at a different angle. There would be no telltale flare off the glass.

She asked Dash, "What's his name? The guy outside of my door."

"Lance."

"Lance?" Sara laughed. *Lance* was the name of a guy who tied balloon animals in the park, not a militiaman with an AR-15.

Dash said, "I'm assuming that's not your only question?"

He seemed to want her to talk, so she talked. "Did they find more bodies?"

Dash didn't answer.

"At Emory." Sara turned to look at him. "The last I saw on the news, there were eighteen dead, fifty wounded."

"Deaths were up to twenty-one as of a few minutes ago. I'll have to get back to you on the unfortunate survivors." He didn't seem bothered by the numbers. Nor did he seem bothered that he'd given Sara proof that he was in contact with the outside world.

There had to be a phone or tablet in the Camp with internet access.

Dash said, "My apologies, miss. I almost forgot. I brought you something."

Sara turned around again. He was pulling an apple out of his sling. Sara didn't take it. She was starving, but she was suspicious.

"I'm not the snake, though you could certainly make a case for being Eve in that attire." He took a small bite near the stem to prove it wasn't tainted. "By my estimation, you haven't eaten a meal in twenty hours."

More time had passed than that. Sara took the apple. Instead of continuing down the path, she stood in place, taking as big a bite as she could. Taste flooded her mouth. This was not the irradiated produce from her local grocery store. Sara had forgotten what a real apple was supposed to taste like.

Dash said, "We can get you some cheese if you like. I assume you aren't eating our meals because you're a vegetarian."

Sara had no idea why he'd made this assumption, but she said, "Cheese would be good. Beans, lentils, peas. Anything you can muster."

"I'll tell Gwen to pass it on to the kitchen. Your requested medical supplies should arrive soon." Dash was watching her carefully. "I sent one of my men to pick them up. He should be back in a few hours."

Sara nodded, wondering if that meant they were a few hours away from Atlanta or a few hours away from the motel. She told Dash, "I meant what I said before. Those children need a hospital."

"It won't be your concern for much longer." He indicated the path ahead. "Please."

Sara finished the apple as she walked. She considered his words. Was Dash referring to his false promise of letting her leave, or was there a clock ticking down on what he had planned next? Sara furiously scanned the woods around her for the greenhouse. The *next* was connected in some way to what they were hiding underneath the tent. There was another path parallel to the one she was on. If Sara managed to sneak out of her cabin, she could go to the greenhouse. Lance would probably fall asleep at some point. Sara looked for markers she could follow in the dark. She was so intent on strategizing that she didn't notice what was twenty feet in front of her.

Michelle Spivey was walking up the path. Instead of continuing straight toward Sara, she took a fork to Sara's left.

Toward the general direction of the greenhouse.

Sara slowed her pace. Her eyes followed Michelle. The woman must have known that Sara was there, but she didn't look up from the ground. She was limping. Her skin was pale, almost ghost-like. She was wearing the same homespun dress as the rest of the women. Her hand was pressed to her lower abdomen. She was clearly in a lot of pain. There was a sentry behind her, a young man with a rifle. He was floating his hand along the tops of an elderberry bush. He was barely giving Michelle any of his attention. There was no need to. Even from ten yards away, Sara could tell that Michelle was very sick.

She told Dash, “She should be resting. She’s septic. The bacteria in her blood is going to kill her.”

“She’ll rest when she’s finished.”

Sara didn’t ask what Michelle was expected to finish. What she knew was that the infectious disease specialist had not been abducted and dragged into the mountains to stop a measles outbreak. Michelle was here to do whatever they were doing in the greenhouse. Her contribution was so invaluable that Dash had risked taking her to the hospital to save her life.

Which meant that Michelle was close to completing whatever project she had started. Otherwise, they would’ve kept her in bed and given her time to recover.

It won’t be your concern for much longer.

“Daddy?” The fifteen year-old with the wary eye was standing with her hands on her hips. “Mama says hurry.”

Dash chuckled. “She’s old enough to start nagging me.”

Sara hurled the apple core into the forest. She tried to adjust the knot in her dress. The tree canopy had cleared at the river. The sun was brutal overhead. The problem with auburn hair was that it came with skin that lent itself to self-immolation. She could already feel her bare shoulder starting to burn.

She added sunscreen to the list of things she missed.

The temperature dropped slightly as she reached the riverbank. All of Dash’s children but Adriel were sitting in a circle. Gwen was on a wooden stool in the center. She was reading aloud from the Bible in her lap.

“‘From there, Elisha went up to Bethel. As he was walking up the path, some small boys came out of the city and jeered at him, chanting—’”

Gwen looked up, frowning at Sara.

Sara frowned back. She wasn’t sure why this woman would choose this particular moment to tell her daughters a story about bad little children being mauled to death by bears. They had already lost two of their friends. Their sister lay seriously ill in the bunkhouse.

Dash said, "I don't think we've all been properly introduced. Girls, this is Dr. Earnshaw. Dr. Earnshaw, meet"—he pointed as he went around the circle—"Esther, Charity, Edna, Grace, Hannah and Joy."

Joy was the oldest, her wary-eyed stare a stark contrast to her name.

"Hello." Sara had to wad up the back of the sheet so she could sit on the ground. She smiled, reminding herself that she couldn't punish these children for having awful parents. "It's very nice to meet you."

Grace, who was around nine or ten years old, said, "Mama told us you were married."

"I was." Sara looked at Gwen, but her head was down as she silently studied her Bible.

Another child asked, "Did you have a big wedding?"

Sara had married Jeffrey in the backyard of her parents' house. Her mother had stood in stony silence, furious that they weren't in a church. "We went downtown to the courthouse. A judge married us."

Even Joy seemed disappointed. Sara didn't know if this was because they had been taught that marriage was the only thing that gave them validation as women or because they were girls and weddings were romantic, dreamy affairs.

"I'll tell you another story." Sara shifted, trying to get a lump of material out from under her ass. "There's something called a White Coat Ceremony in medical school. That's the first time you wear your lab coat. You take an oath promising to always help people." Sara chose not to dwell on that fact. "It's a very big deal. My entire family was there. We had a party afterward at my aunt's house. My mother made a toast, then my father, then my aunt. I was tipsy by the end. It was the first time I drank real champagne."

Grace asked, "Was your husband there?"

Sara smiled. "I hadn't met him yet. But your mother did this, too. Right, Gwen? Nurses have their ceremony at the start of their clinical work?"

Gwen inhaled deeply. She closed the Bible. She stood up. "I have work to do."

Dash didn't seem bothered by her departure. He took Gwen's place on the stool. He held out his arm and Joy sat in his lap. She leaned her head on his shoulder. He rested his hand on her hip.

Sara watched the water spilling over the river rocks. She wasn't comfortable seeing a fifteen-year-old girl sit in a grown man's lap, even if that man was her father.

Dash told Sara, "Gwen doesn't like to talk about her time before."

"She should be proud. Graduating from nursing school is quite an accomplishment."

Dash patted his leg. Grace carefully crawled up to his knee. She tucked her fingers into his sling. He stroked her hair.

Sara had to look away again. Maybe she was reading into it, but there was something unsettling about the way Dash touched his children.

He said, "I think my daughters would tell you that working at home, taking care of your family, is quite an accomplishment, too."

"My mother would agree. She was very happy that she could choose that life for herself. Just like I was happy to choose something different."

Joy's eyes were on Sara. The wariness had turned into curiosity. She didn't seem embarrassed to be sitting in her father's lap. Given their isolation on the compound and the infantilizing way they dressed, her maturity level could lag behind that of a typical fifteen-year-old.

Still, something about the situation made Sara uneasy.

Dash said, "Dr. Earnshaw, we live a simple life here with traditional roles. This is how the early Americans not only lived but thrived. Everyone is happier when they know what's expected of them. Men do the work of men and women do the work of women. We don't allow the modern world to interfere with our values."

Sara asked, "Did those solar panels on the bunkhouse come over on the *Niña*, the *Pinta* or the *Santa María*?"

Dash gave a surprised laugh. He likely wasn't used to being challenged, especially by a woman. He told the children, "Girls, those are the names of the ocean ships that brought the Pilgrims to the New World."

Sara chewed at the tip of her tongue. He had to know that the ships had been part of Christopher Columbus's expedition from Spain. The Pilgrims arrived over one hundred years later. These were basic facts that almost every American child knew by the time they graduated elementary school. They were taught songs about it, forced to act it out in Thanksgiving plays.

Dash said, "Some believe the Mayflower Compact was a covenant with God to advance Christianity in the New World."

Sara couldn't wait to see where he was going with this.

"In fact, the Compact was a social contract that bound the settlers to a standard set of laws and regulations." Dash continued to absently stroke Grace's hair. "That's what we've set up here, Dr. Earnshaw. We are some of us Puritans, some of us settlers, others of us adventurers and tradesmen, but we are bound together by the belief in the same laws and regulations. That is the hallmark of a civil society."

At least he'd gotten his Wikipedia right. "The Pilgrims were on the King's land, just like the land we're on right now belongs to the federal government."

Dash smiled. "Are you trying to get me to confirm our location, Dr. Earnshaw?"

Sara wanted to kick herself for being so clumsy. "The laws and regulations of the United States supersede whatever you've got going on inside your Camp. That's the privilege and price you pay for citizenship. As my grandfather used to say: Don't mess with the US Government. They won two wars and can print their own money."

Dash laughed. "Your grandfather sounds like my kind of man. But you should understand that we adhere to the original words in the Constitution. We do not interpret or amend. We follow the laws exactly as they were set down by the Framers."

"Then I assume you know that of the three criminal offenses listed in the Constitution, treason comes first. The Framers called for the death penalty against anyone who levies war against the United States."

"Thomas Jefferson told us that 'a little rebellion now and then is a good thing and as necessary in the political world as storms in the physical,'" Dash said. "The vast majority of the country agrees with what we're doing here. We're all patriots, Dr. Earnshaw. That's what we call ourselves. The Invisible Patriot Army."

Army.

Sara asked, "IPA? I've heard that abbreviation before."

"I like beer." His smile didn't falter. "Benjamin Franklin, another great patriot, wrote that beer is proof that God loves us and wants us to be happy."

Franklin had actually been talking about French wine, but Sara didn't correct him. She smoothed out the folds in her dress. She was sweating. Bugs were swarming around her face. Her skin was burning in the sun. It was still better than being confined in the cabin.

She asked, "You ever notice how George Clooney never goes around telling people how handsome he is?"

Dash raised his eyebrows, expectant.

"It makes me curious—if you're really a patriot, do you have to put it in your name?"

Dash chuckled, shaking his head. "I wonder, Dr. Earnshaw, if I was a writer, how would I describe you in a book?"

Sara had read books by men like Dash. He would list the color of her hair, the size of her breasts and the shape of her ass. "Are you writing a book? A manifesto?"

"I should." His jocularity was gone. "What we are doing up here, what I have created, must be replicated if our people are to survive. The world will need a blueprint to follow after the pillars fall."

"What pillars?"

"Dash!" Lance's panicked scream broke the moment.

Instinctively, Sara was on her feet. The man looked as if he was on the verge of hysteria. He was running toward them, rifle gripped between his hands, mouth wide open.

He screamed, "Tommy fell! It's really bad. His leg is all—" He stopped a few feet away, bending at the waist to catch his breath. "It was during the drill. His leg—" Lance shook his head, unable to put words to the image. "Gwen says bring the doctor right now."

Dash studied Lance. He had not moved. Neither had his girls. Joy waited until he patted her on the leg like a dog, then got down from his lap.

He told Sara, "I hope you don't mind joining me?"

For the first time since she'd met this sadist, Sara was actually willing to go with him. She wanted to see this place where Tommy was doing drills.

Dash kept to his usual pace as they walked through the forest. Lance rushed ahead, almost frenzied. He stumbled over a fallen log. His rifle flew out of his hands. He tried to stand up, but fell again.

"Steady, brother." Dash picked up the rifle. He wiped off the dirt. He handed it back to Lance. "Deep breath."

Lance's inhalation was shallow. His breath smelled sour when he exhaled.

"Good man." Dash patted his shoulder, then continued up the path.

He was clever. Sara had to give him that. She used the same technique in the emergency room. Trauma tended to heighten emotions. When everyone was freaking out, being calm instantly put you in a place of authority.

"This way, please." Dash was leading them away from the greenhouse, over the hill to what Sara had assumed was the main compound.

She could hear a siren wailing in the distance. Then she realized it wasn't a siren. Someone was screaming at that blood-curdling pitch that could only be achieved by being in excruciating, life-threatening pain.

Sara started to run toward the sound. The path opened up onto another clearing. It was twice the size of the other one.

More cabins, more women cooking on open fires, but she didn't stop to count the number of people or take in her surroundings. She lifted her dress and ran as hard as she could toward the wailing man.

There was an open structure at the crest of the hill. It was massive, but incomplete. Only the framing existed. Wood studs for walls, plywood on the floors, open stairs, safety railings. Two stories high. The second level was no more than a balcony that ringed the open floor below. There was no roof, no Sheetrock or siding. Two layered tarps served as a ceiling. The material on the bottom one was in the familiar, thermal-blocking silver. The top was dark green to help the structure blend into the forest.

A group of men stood in a circle at the base of the stairs. They were dressed in black tactical gear with padded vests. Sara looked up as she entered the building, because that's what it was—they had mocked up an actual building. The span of one tarp wasn't enough to cover the space. There were eight large pieces patched together. The surface area was roughly fifty yards square, half of a football field. The walls and floor were spattered with various colors of paint, probably from paintball guns. There were paper targets representing security guards. Muddy footprints showed where men had run in and out of the building.

Sara could think of only one reason to mock up a structure in this manner, and that was to practice taking over the building, possibly killing or kidnapping the people inside.

Drills.

The men broke their circle to allow Sara inside. Gwen was wringing her hands into her apron. She looked startled. They were all startled, as if it had never occurred to them while they were playing toy soldiers that one of their own could get hurt.

The injured man had clearly fallen from the upper floor. He was on his back, but not flat. He'd managed to land on the only furniture in sight, a metal desk with a rolling chair. His body curved backward over the pieces. His head had broken the plastic arm off of the chair. His tailbone wrapped around the edge of the desk. His legs dangled to the floor. A white shard of bone stuck out of his thigh like the dorsal fin of a shark. His left foot had twisted around the ankle. The toe of his boot pointed back toward the desk.

Sara took his hand. His skin was ice-cold. His fingers were straight and lifeless. "Hi," she said, because no one had acknowledged him or tried to comfort him.

He stared at her. He was around eighteen years old with pale blond hair. Blood seeped from his eyes like tears. He had stopped screaming. His lips were purple. His quick, panicked breaths reminded Sara of Vale.

"I'm Sara." She put her hand to his face. He obviously could not feel anything below his neck. "Tommy, can you look at me?"

His eyes started to roll back in his head. The lids fluttered.

Sara didn't have to examine him to know that his back was broken. His ribs had crushed into his chest. His pelvis would be shattered. The open fracture in his leg was the most visibly disturbing injury, but it was also the least of his problems. Even with immediate surgical intervention, his foot would likely be amputated. And that was assuming he could be stabilized for transport.

There was no way Dash was going to life-flight this man off the mountain.

Gwen said, "I've sent for a splint so you can set the fracture."

Sara felt her jaw tighten. She stroked Tommy's hair. "And then?"

Dash said, "We'll take him to the hospital, of course. We don't leave men behind. We're soldiers, not animals."

Sara was so sick of hearing him spout these empty phrases. Tommy clearly believed him. The boy was visibly relieved. He was watching Dash with the devotion of a child.

"All right, brothers." Dash turned to the assembled group, trying to calm them, "This is a terrible thing that's happened to one of our best soldiers, but it doesn't change our plans. We'll continue drills later. We're too close to compromise on preparation. But right now, brothers, I think you've earned some time away. Gerald, take the van. Let's get these boys some red meat."

"Yes, sir." Gerald was the oldest in the group, early forties with a military bearing. The rest were around the same age as the broken boy on the desk. Their necks were scrawny, their limbs like sticks. Sara would've said they were boys playing dress-up, but this was not a game.

They had built this Structure to practice an infiltration, a siege, a terrorist attack. She looked up at the second-floor balcony. There were no distinguishing features. It could be a mock-up of a lobby to a hotel or office building, a movie theater—anything. All Sara knew for certain was that whatever they were planning was happening soon.

We're too close to compromise on preparation.

"Let's move, soldiers." Gerald herded the young men out of the Structure. Their boots were heavy across the plywood floor. They disappeared down the slope of the hill.

Only Gwen, Dash and Sara were left with Tommy. Sara pressed her fingers to the side of his neck, searching for a pulse. It was like touching the wings of a butterfly.

"Well." Dash adjusted his sling. He had yet to acknowledge Tommy. That fact alone told Sara exactly what kind of leader this man was. "I wonder what that desk was doing there."

Gwen was staring at him. No words were exchanged, but something passed between them. Dash nodded before walking away.

Sara tasted blood in her mouth as he disappeared down the hill. Instead of sitting with a dying, terrified kid who clearly wanted nothing more than to please him, Dash was returning to his daughters so they would boost his ego.

Sara did not have the luxury of his cowardice. She kept her hand pressed to the side of Tommy's face. She asked, "Tommy, can you open your eyes for me?"

Slowly, his eyelids opened. He focused on Sara. The white of his left eye was filled with dark blood. His mouth moved, but he couldn't bring forth more than a murmur. Terror was his single, overriding emotion. He could not feel his limbs. Pain signals were misfiring up and down his brain stem. He was cognizant enough to understand he was not going to walk down from this mountain. He knew just as well as Sara that Dash had washed his hands of one of his *best soldiers*.

"Puh . . ." Tommy's desperation was heartbreaking. "Please . . ."

Sara felt her eyes sting, but she would not let this boy see her cry. She kept herself outwardly composed. Her hand stayed pressed to his cheek. A drop of blood dribbled out of his ear.

She told Gwen, "We have to—"

Sara couldn't say the words.

Tommy was going to die. It was only a matter of how and when. His brainstem could eventually swell enough to stop his breath. His lungs could collapse before that. It could take as long as three minutes for him to lose consciousness, another five minutes for him to suffocate to death. Or his organs could start shutting down, beginning the slow process of a grueling, fully cognizant decline. Tommy was young and strong. His body would not easily give up life. Absent outside help, the only way Sara could ease his terror was to hasten the inevitable.

Eighteen years old.

Sara asked Gwen, "Do you have potassium chloride, or morphine—"

Gwen shoved Sara so hard that she fell backward onto the ground.

At first, Sara was too stunned to get up. Then she scrambled to stop what she knew was coming.

Gwen's hand clamped down over Tommy's mouth. She pinched his nose closed with the other, cutting off his breath.

"Don't!" Sara clawed at the woman's hands, tried to pry up her fingers, but Gwen's grip was too strong. "Please!" Sara cried, but she didn't know why. It was pointless. All of this was pointless.

"We can't—" Gwen's voice caught from exertion, not emotion. Her arms shook as she pressed her full weight into her hands. "We can't waste our supplies."

Sara was struck dumb by her cold calculation. This was why Dash had sent the other men away. This was what Dash could not abide to witness.

Murder.

Tommy's eyes were wide open. Adrenaline had brought him into full consciousness. His vocal cords vibrated with a reedy, sucking sound. He stared at Gwen, unblinking, terrified. His throat clenched for air. His useless arms and legs trembled as the nerves urgently tried to fire. He broke his gaze away from Gwen and looked for Sara.

"I'm here." She knelt down beside him. She pressed the back of her hand against his cheek. His tears rolled over her fingers. Sara denied herself the luxury of looking away. She silently counted off the seconds, the minutes, that slowly stretched out between his life and death.

12

Monday, August 5, 2:30 p.m.

Faith scrolled through her emails as she waited in an empty conference room inside the CDC's sprawling headquarters. The place was like Fort Knox. She'd had to check her gun at the gate. They'd made her pop open the trunk and hood of her car. A guy with a mirror on the end of a stick had swept underneath for bombs. Then a very disciplined Belgian Shepherd had ignored the Cheerios under the seats as he'd sniffed for explosive residue.

Considering all the nasty things percolating in their labs, it made sense that access into the facility was tightly controlled. Faith's only question at this point was why her mysterious meeting was taking place at the CDC. Amanda had given her the usual prep—or lack thereof—texting Faith to be there at exactly two-thirty, but offering no additional details. Faith didn't even have a contact name. By process of elimination, or just by plain *duh*, she could assume she was here to receive a confidential briefing on Michelle Spivey. The same group who had abducted Michelle had taken Sara. So maybe, possibly, hopefully, please God, Faith would be able to take a piece of information she learned here and spool it down a path that led straight to the asshole who was still holding them both hostage: Dash.

Dash.

Faith hated the man just for his stupid nickname. What was

it short for, anyway? Or was he called Dash because he was a really fast runner, or worked as a delivery guy, or was he always in a hurry, or prone to diarrhea?

She had absolutely no idea.

Her entire evening had been wasted trying to find the leader of the IPA. And speaking of the Invisible Patriot Army, good luck scrolling through the approximately 3,347,000 results that search generated. It was like looking for a needle in a haystack without knowing what, exactly, a needle looked like. Will had been useless. The FBI had been useless. Faith needed an age range. An identifying scar or tattoo. A vehicle. A known hangout. A last known residence. Even a possible regional accent would've been something.

Usually, the one thing criminals reliably did was spend time with other criminals. All you had to do was find somebody who knew somebody who was in a jam and wanted to make a deal. That TV stuff about not snitching was a load of crap. Everybody talked when talking would save their ass from prison. Faith had concentrated all of her searches on Carter, Vale, Monroe and Hurley, looking for a credit card charge or an ATM withdrawal or a phone number or a parking ticket or a GPS location that connected them to a Dashiell or Dasher or Dashy or any fucking body whose first or last name started with a D.

Nothing.

Faith stood up and looked out the window.

All that she knew right now was that Michelle Spivey had worked in this building. Or one of these buildings. There were several on the compound, with a rock garden and bridges and a daycare center for the children of employees. It was a stark contrast to the giant white box the GBI worked out of, but then the CDC had been a dump up until the 2001 Anthrax Attacks. Congress had suddenly realized that maybe it was a good idea to fund the organization that responded to anthrax attacks. It helped that two of the people who had been mailed the deadly bacteria were United States Senators. Crime was never more egregious than when it victimized a lowly politician.

Her phone vibrated with a new email. She'd forwarded Sara's

list of medications to two pediatricians and a GP. None of them had spotted anything abnormal. None of them could infer what the drugs were meant to treat. The new email was from Emma's pediatrician, who'd sent a last-minute guess: *Could be miliary tuberculosis?*

Faith had heard of tuberculosis, but not that particular type. She pasted the words into her browser. *Miliary* referred to the millet-seed-like spots that showed up in lung X-rays. The symptoms were pretty horrific, especially if you were talking about a child.

Coughing, fever, diarrhea, enlarged spleen, liver and lymph nodes . . . multiple organ dysfunction, adrenal insufficiency, pneumothorax . . . 1.3 million deaths worldwide . . .

She opened her medical app and found Emma's vaccination list.

Varicella—chickenpox; MMR—measles / mumps / rubella; DTaP—diphtheria / tetanus / whooping cough; BCG—tuberculosis.

Faith hissed out a relieved sigh. She went back to Google. Yesterday, Kate Murphy had said that Michelle Spivey's recent work was in the area of pertussis, or whooping cough.

Runny nose, fever, coughing that induces vomiting and can break ribs . . . high-pitched whoop as they gasp for air . . . can last for ten or more weeks . . . pneumonia, seizures, brain damage . . . 58,700 deaths in 2015 . . .

Faith closed the browser. She could walk around the gutted remains of a murdered drug dealer but thinking about a child suffering from this was too much.

She sank down into her chair and let out a long, heavy sigh. Exhaustion was not new to Faith, but this was next-level fatigue. She could not believe that only yesterday she had been sweating her way through the Martin Novak transport meeting. The *high-value prisoner* had been an abstract, a briefing book filled with data, diagrams of cars and roads. And then the bombs had started going off and the only person who seemed convinced there was a connection between Martin Novak, Dash and the IPA was planted at the CDC sweating her balls off as she waited for a stranger to come find her.

Faith looked at the time.

2:44 p.m.

She wondered if she'd been forgotten about. Faith had dozens of things she could be doing right now, mainly working on trying to find Sara. She was close enough to Emory to go back at Lydia Ortiz, the surgical recovery nurse, see if she'd remembered anything new about Michelle Spivey or Robert Hurley. Ortiz had spent time with both of them while Michelle was coming out of anesthesia. There had to be a detail, a stray comment, that could pry open a clue.

Failing that, Faith could be providing backup to Will. Beau Ragnersen was taking him to meet Dash's flunky at 4:00 p.m. The whole thing gave Faith a bad feeling, and not just because the Alberta-Banks Park in Flowery Branch was located off a city-owned street that was still called Jim Crow Road. She was worried the surveillance team wasn't covering all the access points. She was worried that Will's concussion was getting worse. What she was mostly worried about was Beau Ragnersen. Faith didn't trust confidential informants. They were criminals. They always had their own agendas. Beau was also a serious drug addict. Black tar heroin was no joke. His role in this ruse was not a minor one. He was supposed to convincingly introduce Will as a former Army buddy who had fallen on hard times.

Hard times was not a stretch. Faith had barely recognized Will this morning. Without Sara, he had started to revert to his feral state. His scruffy beard, along with the scars on his face, made him look like a thug. If Faith had seen him in the street, her first impulse would've been to make sure her gun was visible.

She should be in that park right now, giving him support.

The door opened. Faith was surprised, but then she realized she shouldn't be surprised, because of course Aiden Van Zandt was here.

He held open the door with his foot as he looked down the hallway. His glasses were no longer being held together by a white strip of tape. He was back in a suit and tie. Still not a Westley. His FBI credentials were on a lanyard around his neck.

He said, "Sorry I'm late. Murphy couldn't make it, but she sends her best."

Faith gave a genuine laugh.

"Seriously, she likes you. You remind her of your mother." Van leaned out into the hall. He had his hand in the air, as if he was signaling for a taxi. "Can you let her know we're ready?" He turned to Faith. "Bring your stuff."

Faith grabbed her bag and followed him down a long hallway, because her life lately was either stairwells or hallways. "How does Murphy know my mother?"

"How does anybody know anybody?" He changed the subject: "Any news on your missing agent?"

Faith could change the subject, too. "Is the FBI still denying there's a connection between Martin Novak, the bombing at Emory, and the IPA?"

"Reply hazy. Try again later."

Faith didn't like this game. "All right, Magic Eight Ball. I googled the IPA. It's not on the internet. Not anywhere. Which I know doesn't mean that it's not real, and there's the dark web and blah-blah-blah, but why isn't it on the internet?"

"Ask again later."

Faith wanted to punch him. "I need you to cross-reference Michelle's files to see if she's ever interacted with a man named Beau Ragnersen."

He stopped, his hand on a closed door. "What makes you think I can do that?"

"Because you're the FBI's liaison with the CDC." She assumed when he did not correct her that she had guessed correctly. "Ragnersen with an -en."

"That's Danish," he said. "The s-e-n means—"

Faith reached past him and opened the door. A nervous energy filled her body. The room felt like the kind of place a civilian shouldn't be allowed to see. The large space reminded her of a NASA control room. There were rows of empty open-plan cubicles with computer monitors and signs—South America, Latin America, Europe, Eurasia. Digital clocks gave ALFA, OSCAR and ZULU time. Giant monitors spanned the rear wall. A map of the world showed flashing red, green and yellow dots in various locations. The words "Red Sky" were in the corner alongside different tabs.

Faith assumed the red dot on Atlanta was because of yesterday's attack, but asked, "Why is there a flashing yellow dot on the Georgia coast?"

"Hurricane Charlaine," Van said. The late-July storm had slammed into Tybee Island and raged into the port of Savannah. The damage was so bad that the governor was calling a special session to fund the clean-up.

Van explained, "It's yellow because the disaster is still in progress. Red Sky is part of Situational Awareness. Different branches have different levels of access. This room is the hub of the Incident Management System. If a big storm is being tracked, or there's a critical health crisis or a terrorist attack, every desk is filled. Like, yesterday, this room was packed to the walls. We're talking north of one hundred people. Scientists, specialists, doctors, military liaisons, Watch Staff. There's a direct link to the White House, Pentagon, NORAD, Alice Station, Menwith Hill, Misawa, Buckley—all your SIGNIT from ECHELON goes into the portal. The Global Incident Team sends data directly into these monitors so real-time assessments can send people and resources where they're needed."

Faith gave a solemn nod, pretending like this Jason Bourne shit didn't thrill the hell out of her. She was dying to take out her phone and grab some photos.

Van said, "It's some cool shit, right?"

She shrugged. "Unless you're on the coast and still boiling your water."

Van held open another door for her. A row of small lockers lined the wall. At the end of the hall was a closed door with a red light overhead. "You ever been in a SCIF?"

Situational Compartmented Information Facility.

"Yes," Faith lied. She had seen one of the ultra-secure rooms on *The Americans*, so that had to count for something.

Van took his cell phone out of his pocket and placed it inside one of the lockers.

Faith opened her messenger bag. She had more than a cell

phone. Her laptop and iPad had to be stored, because no electronic devices or anything that could record any information was allowed inside of a SCIF.

"I always forget my watch," Van said, taking off his Garmin.

Faith unbuckled her Apple Watch. She felt nervous, because it was starting to sink in that she was inside one of the most secure facilities in the country and now Van was taking her into an even more secure location.

Michelle Spivey had top-secret clearance. Faith had to think that somehow, Amanda had managed to get Faith a read-in on whatever project the scientist had been working on before she was abducted.

The IPA didn't snatch Michelle out of a parking lot because she studied whooping cough.

"Ready?" Van pressed a green button on the wall.

There was a loud buzz, then the door opened. They went inside. The *thunk* from the door closing was like a vault sealing shut. Another buzz cracked the air. A red light over the door started to roll like the light on top of a police cruiser.

Faith took a deep breath. The air felt weirdly muffled. The room was bare bones, just six chairs around a conference table and a clock on the wall.

A young woman sat at the head of the table. She was wearing a Navy Service Khaki uniform with no name tag and colorful bars that Faith could not identify. Her glasses were thick. Her dark hair was cut short. She was the worst kind of young—the type of young that made Faith feel old. She was clearly so damn happy to be here, as eager and wide-eyed as Baby Jack-Jack. She had several folders stacked in front of her. She grinned at Van. Lipstick was smeared on her teeth.

Van rubbed his own teeth to let her know, which was incredibly decent of him.

He told Faith, "This is Miranda. Miranda, this is the agent I told you about."

Faith assumed that was it for introductions. She sat down at the table.

Van took the chair beside her.

Miranda said, "Okay, so what factor or factors have historically led to upticks in membership in white supremacist groups?"

Faith was immediately lost. She tried to make a connection to Michelle. The woman was married to an Asian-American doctor. They had chosen to have a child that reflected their heritage. "She was targeted because of her family?"

Miranda gave Van a confused look. "I'm sorry, who was targeted?"

Van shook his head. "Different topic for a different day. Keep going."

"Okay." Miranda took a moment to adjust. "Okay. So, the popular wisdom is that more people join white supremacist groups in response to a sudden influx of immigration, or economic downturns, right? The harsh monetary reparations in the Treaty of Versailles. The Greater East Asia Co-Prosperity Sphere. Operation—excuse me—Wetback."

"Hold on." Faith needed a moment, too. She was having a hard time following the shift in direction. This meeting wasn't about Michelle Spivey. It was about the Invisible Patriot Army.

A white supremacist group.

"Let's back up." Faith had to talk it out so her brain could understand. "You're saying that membership in these racist groups surges because the economy goes into the toilet, jobs are scarce, people look around for someone to blame and—"

"Not so fast." Miranda opened one of her folders. She placed a black-and-white photograph in front of Faith. A guy in a dark suit was leaning on a desk with a Sherlock Holmes pipe in his mouth. His hair was bouffanted into a classic Clark Kent. The photo was clearly from the 1950s.

Miranda said, "George Lincoln Rockwell. Founder of the American Nazi Party." She put down another photo of another white guy "Richard Girnt Butler, founder of the Aryan Nations." She kept dealing out photos. "Thomas Metzger, leader of the White Aryan Resistance. Frazier Glenn Miller, White Patriot Party leader. Eric Rudolph, linked to the Army of God and Christian Identity Movement."

Faith was still lost, but at least she knew enough to say, "Rudolph is the Centennial Olympic Park Bomber."

"Right. He also targeted abortion clinics and a lesbian nightclub." Miranda added a photo of Timothy McVeigh. "Oklahoma City Bomber." The next photo came down. "Terry Nichols, McVeigh's accomplice. What do all of these men have in common?"

Faith was too confused for the Socratic Method, so she narrowed it down to one man. "I know about Eric Rudolph because most of his attacks were in Georgia. He confessed to four bombings. He pled guilty to murdering a police officer. He worked as a carpenter. He was anti-government, anti-gay, anti-woman, anti-abortion. He denies any association with the Christian Identity Movement, though he lived on a compound with his mother when he was a teenager. After Rudolph was put on the FBI's 10 Most Wanted list, his brother videotaped himself cutting off his own hand with a radial saw to send a message to the FBI."

"Seriously?" Miranda was thrown by the last piece of information. "What happened to his hand?"

Van said, "Went to voicemail. FBI didn't get the message."

Faith realized something. "Rudolph was in the Army, right? He went through Fort Benning. They discharged him for smoking weed. And—" Faith pointed to McVeigh. "He was in the Army. He was awarded the Bronze Star during the Gulf War. He washed out of Special Forces." She tapped Terry Nichols' photo. "The Army gave him a hardship discharge after a few months. He couldn't hack it."

"Yep-yep-yep." Miranda excitedly slid the images around. "Rockwell was a naval commander in World War Two and Korea. Butler was in the Army Air Corps. Miller was in Vietnam." She had more photos—men in white hoods, men with swastika armbands, men with their hands raised in a Nazi salute. "Helicopter gunner in Vietnam. Retired Army lieutenant colonel. Air Force staff sergeant. Coast Guard Reserves."

"Wait a minute." Faith had to stop this. "My brother's been in the Air Force for the last twenty years. He can be an asshole, but he's not a fucking Nazi."

"I don't doubt it," Miranda said. "Look, I'm not bashing the military. My family has been at the tip of the spear since the Spanish American War. I'm Navy, but I'm also a statistician, and I can assure you that mathematically, these men are outliers. You have to consider the numbers. In any large group, there are going to be a certain number of bad actors. Teachers, doctors, scientists, police officers, dog catchers. There are always bad seeds. So, extrapolate that to the military. Between active and Reserve, there are almost two million service members. If you take even half a percent, that's—"

"Ten thousand people." Faith gripped the edge of the table. She wanted to stand up and leave the room. "You need to draw some hard lines between these dots for me. I don't like any of these implications."

"Neither did Congress," Van said. "A team at the Department of Homeland Security generated a paper on the white supremacist movement inside the military and they not only lost their funding, they were forced to retract their findings."

Faith had to stand up, but not to leave. She needed to push oxygen into her lungs. The room felt like a prison. She leaned against the wall. She crossed her arms over her chest. She waited.

Miranda said, "Let's go back to the beginning. I asked you what causes historical upticks in membership in white supremacist groups. You said immigration and the economy, but actually, it's war. War is the common thread for all of these men. They went off to fight, they came home, and nothing felt the same. To their thinking, the government abandoned them. Their women had moved on or grown more independent. Their kids were strangers. They didn't know how to make sense of the world going on without them, and they needed someone to blame."

Van said, "I blame the Jews myself."

Faith wasn't up for his weird humor right now. "Two of Hurley's men—Sebastian James Monroe and Oliver Reginald Vale. They were discharged out of the Army."

Van said, "Robert Jacob Hurley was an Air Force munitions officer."

Faith asked, "What does this have to do with the Invisible Patriot Army?"

"Ah." Miranda shuffled through her folders. "So, these guys are what we're calling New Nazis. They're not skinheads. They don't shave their heads and get tattoos and dress the part. Their point is to blend in. Dockers and polos. Nice, clean-cut guys."

Faith remembered the protesters carrying tiki torches in Charlottesville. The young men had all looked so normal until they'd started chanting about blood and soil and screaming *Jews will not replace us*.

Faith said, "The Unite the Right Rally—"

"That's why they're careful online," Van said. "After Charlottesville, the internet turned against them. People identified them from the videos. 'Hey, that's my delivery guy. What's he doing kicking a black woman in the face?' They got fired from their jobs, cast out from their families, lost their security clearances, got dishonorably discharged. So, they learned to be careful. When the camera starts rolling, they cover their faces or wear masks."

Miranda took over. "Charlottesville was a watershed moment. Groups came from thirty-five different states. This wasn't a spontaneous get-together. They'd been staging smaller rallies all over the country, mostly in California, but usually twenty people showed up, maybe a handful of Antifa looking to bust heads and some hippie-wannabes looking to throw around flowers, but the media pretty much ignored them. After Charlottesville, their entire world changed. They got validation from the top down. Those guys went home energized, organized, ready to take action. Their membership soared."

She showed Faith another photo. This one was a color mugshot of a young man. "Brandon Russell, Florida National Guard. Also a member of Atomwaffen Division. Atomwaffen is German for *atomic weapons*. They had a big presence in Charlottesville. May of 2017, the month before the rally, Russell was found with a bomb-making lab in his garage, swastikas all over his apartment and a photograph of Timothy McVeigh in his bedroom."

Van said, "They found HMTD in Russell's garage. It's a highly explosive organic compound. It's also the same material that was used in the two bombs that were set off in the Emory parking deck yesterday."

Faith's mind brought up the image of the smoking crater she had seen from the helicopter yesterday afternoon. They were still combing through the debris this morning. Another body had been found in the last hour.

She nodded for Miranda to continue.

"As far as the big groups, there's Atomwaffen, RAM, which stands for the Rise Above Movement, Hammerskins, Totenkampf. The list goes on. Sometimes it's ten guys, sometimes it's fifty. What we're seeing take place is the incarnation of the leaderless resistance. An attack on the level of 9/11 or 7/7 takes coordination, discipline and money. None of these groups really have those resources. What happens is one guy says to himself, 'Hey, I'm sick of talking about this. I'm going to do something about it.' Dylann Roof, Robert Gregory Bowers, Nicholas Giampa, Brandon Russell—they were heavily involved in white nationalism, but there was no master plan. They acted on their own."

Faith said, "Like suicide bombers."

"Not even that sophisticated. It can literally be a twenty-year-old with a lot of guns lying around who decides one morning to grab them all up and go to a synagogue."

Van said, "These guys are big-time into hero-worship. It's not just McVeigh they revere. Lone-wolf shooters are turned into gods. Check online the next time one of these attacks takes place. Within minutes, there's fan pages, fan-fiction, contact info. If the fucker lives, they post his inmate number so people can fill his commissary, and the jail address for fan mail."

Faith didn't bother asking what the hell was wrong with people. "The shooter's motivation is fame?"

"In some ways, yes," Miranda said. "They're incredibly disaffected. They feel marginalized, powerless, misunderstood. We've heard a lot of chatter lately about the Great Replacement."

Van explained, "I'm sure you've heard it all before. White women aren't giving birth at the same rate as minorities. Feminism is ruining the Western world. White men are being turned into cuckolds."

Miranda said, "Which brings us back to the military. The men in these groups crave the discipline, the masculine affirmation of a military structure. We've noticed a concerted effort to recruit veterans, active duty and reserve. Primarily, they want these men for their combat skills and the validation of their military service. From the other side, it's very attractive for a soldier whose fighting days are behind him to relive those moments. There are Hate Camps all over the country where ex-soldiers run kids through drills and exercises. Clearing rooms, target practice, ordnance training. One of the larger camps is in Devil's Hole in Death Valley."

Faith remembered the photographs in Kate Murphy's IPA files. They showed young men running around in camouflage. "Devil's Hole is where Charles Manson was going to hide after Helter Skelter brought on a race war."

"Exactly." Miranda seemed impressed. "While Manson was in prison, he corresponded with a man named James Mason. Big white supremacist. He also wrote a book called *Siege*, where he advocated strongly for the leaderless resistance. You could call it the bible for the modern white supremacy movement."

Faith asked, "So what does this bible tell them to do?"

"The same things that the Taliban and Al-Qaeda do. They produce highly sophisticated recruitment videos. They create online forums where hate is not only accepted, it's encouraged. They target angry young men and tell them that they're part of a greater cause, that they need to fight to regain their white power and that women will flock around them when they do."

Van said, "A lot of those guys like Hurley, Vale and Monroe served over in Iraq and Afghanistan. They paid attention to what the other side was doing. They saw the damage that an improvised explosive device can do. How one guy infiltrating the police force or a battalion could kill dozens of people. They learned from the insurgency, and they brought it back to America."

"The insurgency." Faith nodded to the stack of unopened folders. She still needed to know how Dash fit into all of this. "Tell me about the IPA."

Miranda took a breath. "Okay, so they're smart, which is what makes us nervous. They don't talk about themselves online. There's stray chatter where other groups say things—mostly about how the IPA is planning something big, how they're going to bring on a second American Revolution. That's how these guys talk so it's hard to separate the boasting from what could actually be the truth." She paused for another breath. "We think the IPA are survivalist. The reason I gave you this long preamble about how these groups operate is because that's how we *think* the IPA operates. A small cell, advocating the leaderless resistance, possibly training so-called soldiers to embed in law enforcement or military and bring about holy war."

Faith's mouth had gone dry. "If they're so quiet, how did you find out about them?"

"That was me," Van said. "It's kind of my field to monitor these groups. There are hundreds of them, and just as many lone wolves sitting in their trailers spewing crap about killing all the blacks and raping feminazis. I started to pick up stray mentions of the IPA a few years ago. It felt different the way they were talked about. I sent out a bulletin asking for information. I got back a memo from Valdosta State Prison that they had an inmate whose recorded phone calls contained heavy mentions of the IPA."

"Adam Humphrey Carter." Faith finally felt like some of her questions were being answered. "You got him early release off his rape charge so he could serve as your informant."

Van nodded. "You've got to understand there's a pattern to these groups. They usually burn themselves out. There are constant power struggles. One guy isn't racist enough. Another guy gets caught looking at gay porn. The internal squabbling leads to disbandment, splintering. They're basically fuck-ups and losers. There's a reason the only thing they're holding on to is the color of their skin." He leaned across the table. "The IPA felt highly organized. Very focused. The way Carter talked about Dash was the same way these guys talk about McVeigh. And we had nothing on him. No photos. No files. No nothing."

Faith had hit the same dead ends last night, and Van had spent a hell of a lot more time on it.

Miranda said, "You might think it's good that Dash and the IPA are not in the system, but it's really, really bad. In our experience, the more these guys talk, the more full of shit they are. It's the quiet ones who do the most damage."

Van added, "It's only through Carter that we found out what little we know about the IPA. Dash didn't start the group, but he's the one who gave it direction. He has them radio silent. They keep their names and affiliation out of the chat groups. There's an aura of mystery about them that the other white power guys really key into. We're one day out from the bombing and the online groups are already saying the IPA is responsible. Half of Totenkampf is already on their way to Atlanta to take advantage of the chaos. We've got a Polish white nationalist we were able to turn back at the Canadian border. A group from Arizona tried to hire a private plane so they could transport their weapons."

"Arizona." Faith had read about a citizens border patrol from the state just a few short hours ago. "Who started the IPA? Was it Martin Novak?"

Van shrugged. "It doesn't matter who placed the fuse. Dash is the match that's about to light it up."

"He's right." Miranda's demeanor had turned deadly serious. "If you asked me what keeps me up at night, it's knowing that Dash is out there planning something, and we have no idea what it is."

Faith asked the obvious question. "If you're so worried about him, why isn't there a task force or—"

"The FBI can't fund hunches," Van said. "There are plenty more bad guys out in the open they can go after. I had to get on my knees and beg my bosses to let me turn Carter into an informant. Like I said, he gave us a lot of high-value information on other groups. We were able to crack open a lot of cases. But as far as the IPA, Carter was always very tight-lipped. What I got from him is that they're planning something big and there's one guy at the top calling the shots."

Faith asked, "Why did they take Michelle Spivey?"

Van said, "Carter took Michelle Spivey. We don't know that Dash ordered it."

Faith wasn't going to swim in that bullshit again. She nodded to the stack of folders in front of Miranda. She'd only opened one so far. "What else does Pandora have in her box."

Van nodded.

Miranda opened one of the folders. "This is the only photo we have of Dash."

Faith walked across the room. Her stomach had turned queasy. She didn't know why the thought of looking at Dash made her nervous. She was expecting a mugshot, but what she saw was a glossy snapshot of a college-age kid standing on the beach in shorts and a T-shirt.

Miranda said, "This was taken on the western coast of Mexico in the summer of 1999."

Faith wasn't buying it. "Mexico doesn't seem like the right vacation spot for a future white supremacist."

Van supplied, "Hate the sinner, love the sin."

Faith studied the kid's face—angular and goofy with a patchy goatee and mustache. He could've been one of her son's annoying fraternity brothers.

Or he could've been one of the innocuous-looking young men in Charlottesville.

Miranda showed Faith another image, this one with the patchwork quality of an Identikit. "Here's what the FBI came up with when we asked for an age progression of what Dash would look like today."

Faith was not impressed. "How old is Dash now?"

Miranda shrugged. "Mid-forties? But we've done a hell of a lot with very little. Our Naval analysts believe, based on the landmarks in the distance, that the beach Dash is standing on is on Isla Mujeres. There's technical stuff about erosion and the angle of the sun that I won't bore you with, but they're damn good at their jobs."

Faith returned to the beach photo. "This isn't a surveillance shot. It looks like it's from a vacation album."

Van pulled out her chair. He waited for Faith to sit down.

He said, "In June of 1999, a guy named Norge Garcia was staying at the Mujeres La Familia Resort with his wife and kids. He noticed a preponderance of single, young, white, male

Americans hanging around the beach. As the name implies, this is a family resort. Real kid-friendly. The frat boys are usually at the adults-only places because that's where the girls are. So, Garcia starts asking around—Where are these guys staying? What are they up to? Why are they here?" Van paused to ask Faith, "Are you following me?"

"Not really," she said. "Why was this Garcia poking around? And how do you know so much about him?"

Van gave her an appreciative nod. "I know about him because I flew down to Mexico to interview him. And he was poking around the resort because, in 1999, Garcia was an inspector with the Federales. That's Mexico's version of the FBI with a dose of the Army."

Faith knew about the Federales from a heavy addiction to Netflix narco-porn. "How does Dash fit into this?"

Instead of answering, Van nodded toward Miranda.

She slid another beach snapshot across the table. The lens had focused on a bunch of kids building a sandcastle. About ten yards behind them, the blurred image of a man was circled in red Magic Marker. Dark hair. Sunglasses. Stocky build. He was waving to someone behind the camera. Both arms in the air. More like a semaphore. His face was shadowed by a baseball hat, but it was crystal-clear that two fingers on his left hand were missing.

Faith leaned back in her chair.

Martin Elias Novak was missing two fingers on his left hand. He had blown them off while he was serving as an explosives expert in the United States Army. In 1999, he would've been forty-one years old.

She looked up at Van, searching his face for confirmation.

He shrugged. "Who's to say?"

Faith motioned for him to continue.

Van said, "This mysterious, older white guy with the missing fingers—Inspector Garcia gets a bad vibe off of him. What's he up to? He's always got this revolving group of frat boys around him. He's not a guest at the resort, but he's on the beach right in front of it every day. He rents a chair and watches the kids playing in the water. Single guy. No wife. No kids. Garcia's Spidey senses tell him something ain't right. He starts asking questions, and the locals working at the resort tell him 'Oh, don't mind him. That's just Pedo'."

"Pedro?" Faith clarified.

"No, *Pedo*, like *pedófilo*."

Faith's stomach dropped. She could see the beach. The laughing children. The creepy middle-aged man intently watching the kids jumping over the waves outside of a family resort.

She felt herself starting to shake her head. Nothing in the Martin Novak briefing had even hinted at pedophilia. The man had a daughter he'd raised on his own. He'd served in the military. Yes, he was a bank robber and a murderer, but that made him a criminal. This new information, if it was true, made him a monster.

Van said, "They called him Pedo because of the way he looked at the children. Sometimes he gave them candy—no kidding. Sometimes he would offer to watch the kids while the parents went for a walk."

Faith nearly gasped. "They let him?"

"It was the late nineties. Nobody knew that clean-cut, all-American men could be pedophiles. Priests were still saints. Hell, we still thought Columbine was a one-off."

Miranda had another snapshot. "This is the only other image we have of Pedo."

The man who had to be Martin Novak was turned away from the camera, but Faith recognized the same T-shirt and build from the earlier image. His three-fingered left hand was at his side. He was talking to a kid whose face was angular and goofy with a patchy goatee and mustache.

Dash.

Van said, "Pedo was renting a villa about three hundred yards from the resort. He paid cash, signed the rental agreement with the name *Willie Nelson*."

He gave her a second to let that sink in. At the car accident, Carter and the rest of the men had given Will fake names taken from country music singers.

You didn't get more country than Willie Nelson.

Van continued, "Inspector Garcia was told that Mr. Nelson was holding retreats for *like-minded* individuals. Every week, six Yankee frat boys would show up with their suitcases. At the end of the week, they'd go back across the border, then six new frat boys would show up in their place. It went on like that all through the summer."

Faith had questions, but she quickly answered them herself. Before the 9/11 terrorist attacks, Americans only had to show their driver's license to go through the border crossing into Tijuana, and no one was keeping records. There was no facial-identification software. No license-plate readers. No digitized passports.

"This is the villa that Pedo was renting." Miranda showed another photo, this one of a two-story ramshackle house with a large porch. Red Swastika flags were draped over the railings like drying beach towels.

Van said, "Garcia couldn't go undercover for obvious reasons, but he called in reinforcements. They started tailing the frat boys from the villa. What they saw was, most of them were hanging out with Pedo on the beach. One guy was sitting in the bar outside the bathrooms. A girl, nine years old, went into the toilet. The guy at the bar waved to his buddies on the beach. They waved back. Then the guy at the bar got up and went into the toilet."

Faith's hand went to her throat. "Did he hurt her?"

"The Federales stopped him before anything physical could happen. He had his hand over her mouth, but that was it." Van said, "They dragged him down to the station. They put him in an interview room and he started talking."

"Wait—" Faith had to know. "Was it Dash?"

"Bingo," Van said. "Garcia put him in a room to sweat it out. When they got to him, Dash was ready to talk. He said his name was Charley Pride."

Another country music singer. Also an African American, which had to be a racist, inside joke.

Van continued, "Dash apologized profusely for being in the wrong toilet. Said he'd had too much tequila, didn't speak Spanish, it was an honest mistake, he put his hand over her mouth because she was going to start screaming and he panicked. He was a real polite kid—yes, sir and no, sir and I'm sorry, sir. He told Garcia that he was a senior at UC-San Diego. Got a late start because he was in the Army. He came down to Mexico with a friend who wanted to attend the retreat. He claimed he didn't know his friend was a Nazi until he got down there."

"Garcia believed him?" Faith asked.

"Not at all, but even Federales need evidence, especially when they're jamming up an American. The murder of Kiki Camarena casts a long shadow. So, Garcia had to kick Dash loose and close the investigation, but—"

Van held up his hand, telling her to wait.

"Two weeks later, Garcia starts to get annoyed about the situation. On his own, he goes to the resort. He dresses like a tourist. He sits at the bar and watches. This is what happens. Same set-up as before: Pedo on the beach with the frat boys. One guy at the bar. A girl goes into the toilet—eight years old. Bar guy exchanges a signal, but this time, another girl, maybe eleven or twelve, goes into the toilet. She comes out with the first kid. She takes her down to a shed where surfboards are stored, and she leaves the kid inside. The frat guys from the beach show up a minute later. One goes inside. The others stay outside and wait their turn."

Faith pressed her lips together so she wouldn't beg him to stop.

"Garcia was on his own. The guys outside the shed ran off the second he showed up. He grabbed up the frat boy inside before he could do anything." Van stopped. "I mean, other than psychologically damage this poor little girl for the rest of her life."

Faith asked, "What name did the frat boy give? Tim McGraw?"

"Garth Brooks," Van said. "Which was pretty stupid. He was the biggest act on the planet at the time. It took about five seconds of pushback from Garcia before the guy says his *real* name is Gerald Smith, aged twenty-one, resident of San Diego. He tries the same story Dash gave him—'Sorry, sir, I was a little drunk, sir, I didn't know the girl was in there, sir, I thought it was a men's toilet, so that's why my jalapeño was hanging out, sir.'" Van shook his head. "Garcia brings in his bosses. He sends Gerald to holding. Next thing he knows, Gerald is gone."

"Did the inmates kill him?"

"Unfortunately, no. Garcia thinks he was allowed to slip back into the US. Pedo disappeared at the same time. The frat boys ghosted. Garcia was vague on the details, but I got the feeling his superiors saw Gerald and Pedo as American problems, and figured America could deal with them."

Miranda said, "As a coda, there's not a significant overlap between the white supremacist movement and pedophilia or child molestation. At least not one larger than the population as a whole."

"What a relief." Faith wanted to go home and take a scalding hot shower to wash the stink of these men off of her. She hoped like hell that Dash wasn't around any children right now.

Something occurred to her.

She asked Van, "How did you connect the Dash from the IPA to the 1999 Dash from Mexico?"

Van said, "I got Carter shitfaced. He was always tight-lipped about Dash, but something was different about him. This was around the same time Carter started pulling at his leash. We were halfway into a second bottle of Johnny Walker Red and he started telling me about Dash's war service in these real hushed, reverent tones—how Dash was a Navy SEAL who did Black Ops until he knew too much and the government sent an assassin out to kill him and—" Van made a jerking off motion with his hand. "Anyway, I pried it out of him that Dash had a really old tattoo on his calf. It's in script, yellow ink with a blue outline: *Freedom Is Not Free*."

"That's a military tattoo," Faith said.

Miranda provided, "It's predominantly Army. SEALs go for the frogman, bone frog, Seal Tridents, anchors, *toughest of the tough*. Back in '99, regulations forbade a sailor from having a tattoo on his lower leg. And no Navy man would highlight the color of cowardice."

Van took over again. "I ran the tattoo through the FBI's biometric database, and *nada*. Then I ran it through INTERPOL. Usually, when you get a hit, you click on a link and you can read the arrest warrant or sometimes the case file. All I got was a name and phone number. Norge Garcia, Inspector Jefe with the Policía Federal." He shrugged. "So I jumped on a plane and went down for a conversation."

"He remembered quite a lot of detail," Faith said.

"He still had the files, photographs, notes, statements. It stuck with him. That's why he put the tattoo on INTERPOL. They didn't have computers in '99. As soon as he figured out what a computer was, he told one of his guys to enter in the information. Garcia felt like he'd missed something with Dash. Spidey senses. Even twenty years later, he still had a bad feeling."

Faith sat back in her chair. Her brain was so full that she could barely hold it all in.

She told Van, "Novak has a daughter. She would've been ten or eleven years old around the time he was being Pedo on the beach." She waited, but Van said nothing. "The girl who took the kid into the surfboard shed was around that age. Novak had his own daughter trick out little kids for him and his buddies, right? That's what you're saying."

Miranda had one more photo. "This is the most recent picture we have of Gwendolyn Novak. Taken when she was nineteen."

Faith looked at a photocopy of an ID card from Georgia Baptist Hospital. Gwen Novak was plain-looking, with mousy hair and sad eyes. Faith wanted to read something into the sadness. Gwen had been her father's pimp. She had lived in a house full of pedophiles. There was no way she hadn't been abused. But then she had become an instrument in the abuse of other children.

Miranda said, "Gwen was an orderly with dreams of going to nursing school, but at this point, she didn't even have her GED. She already had two children, a ten-month-old boy and a five-year-old girl."

"At nineteen?" Faith felt ashamed of her judgmental tone. She had been fifteen when Jeremy was born. And she hadn't been raised by a racist pedophile. "What about the father of her children?"

Miranda shook her head. "Both birth certificates leave that area blank. The girl was eventually enrolled in an elementary school on the westside, but she was pulled out after a few months. The department of family and children's services was sniffing around the baby. One of the neighbors suspected abuse. But Gwen followed in her father's footsteps and dropped off the grid. No credit cards, bank accounts—not even school records on the girl. Joy, the daughter, would be fifteen now."

"Joy," Faith wanted to hold on to the name, to believe that Gwen had protected her daughter from her rapist father and his friends. "What about the baby?"

"We've got a death certificate. The cause is listed as SIDS." She handed Faith the form. "Poor thing suffocated in his sleep."

Faith didn't take the form. It felt like bad luck to even look at it. She wanted to feel sorry for Gwen because of what she had gone through as a child, but the woman was grown now. She was no longer a victim. If she had given a pedophile access to her child, she was an abuser. Worse than an abuser, because Gwen knew intimately what it felt like to be a helpless kid who lived under the constant threat of rape.

Van said, "Thank you, Miranda. I know you've got another meeting."

Faith told the woman, "Thanks. I mean, this is all awful, but thank you."

"I hope I've been helpful."

"You have." Faith went to collect her bag, but Van stopped her.

"Could you hang back for a minute?"

Faith sat down again. She looked at the clock.

3:52 p.m.

Beau Ragnersen and Will were probably at the park. Dash's flunky was supposed to meet them at four. Faith wanted to hit pause and tell Will everything she had learned. The military stuff was important. The fact that Dash was a pedophile. He could use both to angle his way into the group.

Or Will could finally snap and just beat the shit out of the flunky until he agreed to take him to Sara.

The door buzzed as Miranda left. Van waited for the click, the red light to roll indicating that the room was secure again.

He said, "All right, Mitchell. Give me your best shot."

She was already locked and loaded. "You had Naval Intelligence analyze Garcia's beach photos to verify the place and date on his story. You're telling me you can't find experts to look at the stumps on Pedo's left hand where his fingers used to be and match him to Martin Novak?"

"All of our stump experts are trying to break up the Dam Mafia."

Faith stared at him. "We're a quarter of a mile from a graveyard where a parking deck used to be."

He could not be chastened. "Carter and Vale are dead. Hurley is in custody."

"Thanks to my partner," Faith reminded him. "I get the leaderless resistance and the lone-wolf stuff, okay? But Martin Novak's bank robberies netted half a million bucks. Miranda said that 9/11 took coordination, discipline and money. From where I'm sitting, the IPA has all of that, which means they're not lone wolves, they're a full-on domestic terrorist operation. And I'm just going to say it: it's fucking negligent that your boss is so busy covering her ass that she won't let the FBI do its job."

"Oh, hey, did you see this?" He held up the ID card on his lanyard. "I actually work for the FBI. This whole thing today, all the cloak and dagger, that's the FBI helping local law enforcement. Because I work for the FBI. And I ran an FBI informant who gave me intel on Dash. And I flew to Mexico looking for Dash. And I'm talking to you right now because I, me, the FBI agent, want to find Dash."

Faith probably owed him an apology.

She couldn't be chastened, either.

Van said, "I know you've got a two-year-old at home. These guys, they're a lot like two-year-olds. They want attention, and they're willing to destroy things to get it."

That was a dirty trick. "How do you know about my kid?"

Van ignored the question. "McVeigh inspired dozens of copycats. *The Unabomber's Manifesto* has four and a half stars on Amazon. If we tell the press that the Invisible Patriot Army bombed Emory, then we're going to be dealing with dozens of copycats, and Dash is going to go even farther underground than he is now."

Faith was already shaking her head. "Dash was early twenties, sweating it out with a Federale, looking at time in a Mexican prison. There's no way he wasn't making up shit as he went along. Maybe he really was a student at UC-SD. The name he gave Garcia—Charley Pride. Based on the pattern, you could assume Dash's real last name starts with a *P*."

"Terrific. You get the stack of mattresses. I'll find a princess." He took off his glasses and tossed them onto the table. "Look, it's been one day, Mitchell. I get that you're scared for your agent. We all want Sara Linton back. We want Michelle Spivey back. We've been working that case for a month with nothing to show for it but a shit-ton of brick walls. But don't for a minute think that the FBI isn't taking the IPA seriously. I don't hold meetings in SCIFs because I've got a thing for bossy, opinionated women."

She raised her eyebrows, because that had come out of nowhere.

He said, "Sorry, I meant that as a compliment."

"Still weird."

Van bought himself some time by cleaning his glasses with the end of his tie. "Proof. That's what we need. All we've got now is conjecture and gut feeling. We *think* that's Novak in the beach photo. We *think* that's Dash talking to him. We *think* Dash took over the reins of the IPA when Martin was captured. We *think* Dash was the fourth man at Emory yesterday. We *think* that the IPA abducted Michelle. We *think* that they're planning something bigger." He looked up at Faith. "Since we're tossing around unproven theories here, I'll tell you one of mine: my gut tells me that Gwen Novak is married to Dash."

"Shit."

"Shit is right, because there's no marriage certificate, no financial ties, no overlaps, but I'm doing the math here and I know how these groups value bloodlines. You want to take over from the king, you marry the king's daughter."

"Do you think Gwen had more children?" Faith's queasiness made her head start to ache. "That's Gwen's job, right? She entraps kids for her dad and his frat buddies? Maybe Gwen found an easier way with Dash—she makes her own supply."

Van rubbed his tie into his glasses so hard that the lens flexed.

She said, "Martin Novak is in custody. Go back at him and—"

"Novak hasn't talked for over a year and he's not likely to start now." Van put his glasses on. "Novak *wants* whatever is about to happen to happen. He rejoiced when he heard about the explosion yesterday. He wants people to die. He wants to disrupt society and take down the government. He understands that his arrest left a leadership void. If there's a grand plan, Novak isn't a part of it. And he's happy about that. He's happy to see what comes next."

Faith knew he was right. She'd spent hours studying Novak as part of the special transport team. The man lived for chaos. "So, what do we do? What's the plan?"

"I'm working my informants. Carter's not the only white supremacist I do business with."

"Carter was such a huge success for you."

Van acknowledged the dig with a smile. "Finding these guys is the hard part. Once I locate them, it's basic RASCLS framework."

Faith tried to hide her excitement over learning a new acronym. "Are you trying to impress me with shop talk?"

"Of course I am," Van said. "How do you flip a bad guy into a confidential informant? Reciprocation. Authority. Scarcity. Commitment. Consistency. Liking. Social proof. RASCLS. Fortunately, I'm an expert at empathy, sympathy, and handing out cash."

Faith had to ask, "They don't know you're Jewish?"

"Yeah, but it's funny—you slip them a little money, you keep them out of jail, you listen to their problems without judgment, and they're all, like, 'Hitler? I hardly knew him.'"

Faith forced a laugh, but only to cut him some slack over the recent weirdness.

Van said, "I've got informants in all the major groups, but what we really need is someone inside the IPA. That's what I'm working toward; a guy who knows somebody who knows somebody. The IPA is four men down now. Not just regular men, but soldiers. We don't know what Dash's medical condition is after the car accident. Whatever he's planning next will take a certain level of expertise. According to Carter, Dash's group is comprised of old men and boys. Soldiers like Carter, Hurley, Monroe and Vale were the real leaders. Dash is going to have to recruit some qualified men, pronto."

Faith looked at the clock.

3:58 p.m.

Beau and Will would be waiting to meet Dash's flunky.

She asked Van, "Why am I here?"

"Is that an existential question?" He saw that he wasn't going to get another laugh out of her. "My boss wants you guys to know exactly what kind of people you're dealing with. The IPA has Sara Linton. We know she's family. Your family is our family." He got to the point. "I've got a file waiting for you downstairs with everything we have on Michelle Spivey's abduction. I had to redact the top-secret stuff, but as far as locating her, there's not a lot of *there* there. Maybe a second set of eyes can break something apart that twenty of our analysts couldn't."

"Okay." Faith offered, "I can send you the forensic reports from the motel, the autopsy reports. Everything we have is yours."

He asked, "Everything?"

Faith couldn't figure out his tone. He either thought she was lying or he was making another lame attempt at flirtation.

She flipped the Magic Eight Ball back in his direction. "My sources say no."

13

Monday, August 5, 3:58 p.m.

Will groaned as he climbed out of Beau Ragnersen's truck. The aspirin had definitely worn off. His muscles were locking up. He glanced around, noting a few cars, some dog walkers, but the Albert-Banks Park was experiencing an afternoon lull. Will nodded for Beau to lead the way. The man kept his head straight, hands in his pockets. Will did the same, following him across a strip of neatly cut grass.

There were no tracking devices on either of them. Amanda hadn't suggested it and Will would not have let her anyway. His bigger concern was that he might not be able to bluff his way through his backstory. Will's bona fides had him as an ex-soldier with an ax to grind. Will had used the identity before and learned the hard way that he wasn't up on any military lingo. He hadn't taken the time since then to study for the part. All he could do now was go for the quiet, menacing type. The quiet came naturally. The menacing had fallen into place the second Sara had been taken.

Will's face was still unshaven. His hands were cut up. He was wearing a baseball hat and dark sunglasses. His wrinkled gray suit was in his work locker. Will had changed into jeans and a black, long-sleeved shirt that he normally wore to the gym. His biceps strained against the material. His running shoes were splattered with rusty red stripes that looked like dried blood.

Paint.

Two months ago, he had remodeled his bathroom to surprise Sara. Will hadn't realized until she'd pointed it out that the chocolate-colored walls made the small room feel even smaller. He'd put in a new vanity so she had a place to store her lady things. He'd painted the walls red to brighten the space, then he'd painted over the red with three coats of light gray because Sara was surrounded by bloody crime scenes almost every day. She probably did not want to shower in one.

Beau's hands were out of his pockets. He gave an audible sigh as he stepped off the paved path. He was pouting, which was irritating. He'd made it clear he didn't want to be here. Amanda had made it clear that he would end up dying in prison if he didn't help Will get into the IPA.

How that was going to happen exactly was still up in the air.

Beau sighed again as he turned toward the baseball diamond. Will shifted the duffel bag full of medications to his other hand. He clenched his fist. He told himself it would be a bad idea to punch Beau in the back of the neck if he sighed again.

This was for Sara. That alone was enough to unclench Will's fist. He had to convince Dash's Flunky to make an introduction. Beau had mentioned a guy in a van who served as backup during the pill trades. Will assumed that the van driver was higher up the food chain. That was the guy he needed to meet. Dash was four men down. He was planning something big. He seemed to like to work with ex-law enforcement and military, and he would be actively recruiting. Will's first obstacle was convincing Dash's Flunky to make a call to the Driver. The second obstacle was making sure that the Driver didn't shoot Will in the head.

He looked around. No sign of a van.

Beau took another turn, gave another sigh.

Sweat dripped into Will's eyes. He was glad to have the dark glasses. The sun was pounding onto the top of his head. He wished that Faith was here. Her meeting was probably important, but he knew if shit went down, Faith would always have his back.

He spotted the first undercover GBI agent sitting on a bench by the playground. A baby stroller was in front of her. She had her head down, her nose in a phone. Another agent was jogging on a paved path between the tennis courts and one of the baseball diamonds. A green station wagon was in the far parking lot with a male and female agent who were playing the roles of married people who were not married to each other. There was a second chase car parked at a tavern down the street and another parked at the water treatment plant but to Will's thinking, none of this was going to work because his gut was telling him that Beau was going to fuck him over.

Was his gut right?

He wasn't getting the bad feeling off the pitiful sighs or the Charlie Brown drag of Beau's feet across the grass. It was because the man was a junkie, and all junkies cared about was getting high. Amanda had let Beau keep a handful of pills in his pocket, but Beau had started tossing them back like Chiclets before they'd left the building. The special ops soldier could do the math as well as Will. Eventually, the pills would run out, and by the time that happened, Beau could be on the wrong side of a jail cell.

Will tried to think like Beau was thinking. There were three ways the man could get out of this situation: He could send a signal to Dash's Flunky that Will was a cop. The Flunky would shoot Will, end of story. Door number two, Beau could make a run for it. He wouldn't get far, but he didn't know that. The third option was the most troubling. Beau was a highly trained combat soldier. His brain didn't have to be fully functioning for his muscles to remember how to kill a man. Will's folding knife was in his pocket, but he still wasn't good with it. His Sig Sauer was held to the small of his back by an inside-the-waistband holster. He was a very fast draw, but not with a broken neck.

"This way." Beau walked along the pie-shaped fence lining the ballfield. He looked at his watch, so Will looked at his watch.

3:58 p.m.

They were supposed to meet the Flunky at four. There was no going back now. Whatever Beau was planning, it wouldn't be improvised. He had clearly already made up his mind. He seemed thoughtful, almost contemplative, as he let his hand brush against the chain-link fence.

Will's gut sent up another warning flare.

When faced with danger some guys hyped themselves up, pounding their chests, screaming for blood, blinding themselves with so much adrenaline that they ran straight into the bullets. Then there was the other kind of guy, the one who knew the only way to survive the hell that was about to rain down was to lull himself into a trance.

Beau was that second kind of guy. The transformation was obvious. This wasn't the pills. His training had taken over. His breathing had slowed. He'd stopped fidgeting and sighing. He oozed Zen like a Buddhist monk.

Will recognized the signs, because he was experiencing them, too.

"This is the spot." Beau climbed the bleachers to the third row and sat down. He looked at his watch. "Might as well park it, bro. He's not always on time."

"Where's the van?"

"Fuck if I know." Beau stretched out his legs. "These guys aren't stupid. He's not gonna drive up and show you his face. That's what the Flunky is for."

Will tossed the duffel bag onto the seat between them. He sat down. He looked out at the baseball diamond. The fence was nice, covered in black vinyl. The park felt foreign to Will, who'd always lived in the city. No needles or junkies or homeless people. Just women wearing Gucci as they walked their well-groomed dogs.

Will had already studied an aerial map of the twenty-three-acre green space. The entire undercover team had spent hours strategizing, proposing alternate routes and scenarios, discussing the best places to park the cars and station the female agents. Twelve lighted tennis courts. Three baseball fields. A rubberized ballfield. A tennis center. A large picnic pavilion.

Will worked to get his bearings. He had never been good with left and right, but he knew that they were sitting beside home plate on the diamond that was farthest from the main road. The clay tennis courts were behind him, which meant that the elementary school's football field was on the other side of the woods.

The school was a no-go zone for obvious reasons. The last bell had rung an hour ago, but there were after-school activities that put at least one hundred kids and a handful of teachers and administrators in the building. Technically, Dash's Flunky could approach from that direction. Beau had told them the man would park in the nearby lot, but Beau was a junkie liar.

Here was the problem: If push came to shove, Will couldn't chase the Flunky into the schoolyard with his gun. The cover agents couldn't risk parking a chase car in the lot without alerting school security, and school security would not be happy to hear that the GBI was conducting a covert operation on their premises. They would be especially pissed off if they found out it was taking place in a public park.

Will was desperate to find Sara, but neither one of them could forgive him if he accidentally hurt a child.

Beau said, "Dude, you look like you're in some pain."

Will shrugged as if his joints were not lined with concrete.

"Bro, say the word. I can Perc you up no problem." Beau reached into his pocket. He offered Will a round, white tablet.

Will considered accepting the pill. He wouldn't take it, but it would be a good idea to try to get Beau on his side. It was hard to kill a man if you knew him. Rejecting the offer could be seen as yet another reminder that Will was a cop, and the cops were the ones who had him by the short hairs.

"Your loss." Beau popped the pill into his mouth. He swallowed. He grinned.

Will stared at the field. He could hear the *thonk* of a heated tennis game on the courts behind him. His head turned when he heard the flicker of a lighter.

A cigarette dangled from Beau's mouth.

Will told him, "Put that out."

Beau squinted past the smoke. "Relax, bro."

Will punched him in the ear.

Beau's arms shot out as he struggled to stay upright. The

cigarette dropped from his lips. He cursed, touching his fingers to his ear, checking for blood. "Jesus, bro. You need to chill."

"I'm not your bro," Will said, another fantastic reminder that they were not on the same side. "Don't do another God damn thing that makes me think you're trying to signal Dash's man."

"Just chill, all right? It wasn't a sign." Beau used the toe of his boot to stamp out the cigarette. He leaned back against the bleachers. The long sigh he gave could've come out of a fog horn.

Will looked down at his hand. Beau's ear had re-opened the skin. He rolled his wrist, making the blood slide across his palm the same way he used to play with caterpillars when he was a boy.

One of the first times Will was inside of Sara's apartment, his hands were bleeding. Will had gone off on a really terrible human being, which was understandable, but also not the kind of cop Will wanted to be. Sara had guided him to the couch. She'd brought over a bowl of warm water. She had cleaned his wounds, bandaged the cuts, and told him that doing bad things was a habit that you could either give in to or try to break.

Will wiped his hand on his jeans. He no longer cared what kind of cop he was going to be. He was the man who was going to bring Sara home to her family.

"That's him," Beau said.

Dash's Flunky was in the parking lot, exactly where Beau had said he would be. He was getting out of a blue four-door sedan. Still no sign of the van. The Flunky traversed the lot with a rolling gait. He rounded the fence at the back of the field. Short dark hair, white polo shirt, khaki cargo shorts and white sneakers. He was early twenties, probably a former high school baseball player, judging by his keen interest in the ballfield. He wore a backward baseball cap. His sunglasses wrapped around his face. A blue canvas backpack was slung over his shoulder. He looked like a frat boy in search of a kegger.

Will asked, "You recognize him from before?"

"Nah, man, they all look like that." Beau stood up. He walked down to the fence. He shoved his hands into his pockets. He waited.

Will left the duffel on the bleachers and joined Beau by the fence. He looked at the scuffed home plate. He counted down a few seconds. He looked up at the kid.

The Flunky was playing it cool. Taking his time. Beau had already told Will what usually happened: the Flunky walked behind him and traded out the contents of the duffel bag for the contents of his backpack, then he kept on walking around the field and got into his car.

Real James Bond spycraft.

This time, Beau was supposed to stop the Flunky for a conversation. He was going to introduce Will as an old Army buddy. He was going to say they needed to talk to Dash. The Flunky was going to call the guy in the van instead. Will was going to work some as-yet-to-be-determined magic and wrangle an invitation to meet the leader.

Only the Flunky didn't seem interested in playing his part.

He had stopped twenty yards away from them.

Will could almost hear the gears clicking in the kid's head. He had been told there would be one man near the bleachers. There were two men near the bleachers. Should he still make the exchange?

The Flunky looked back at his car. Checked the parking lot. Checked the woods. He looked at the tennis courts. He looked up at the sky for—*drones*? Finally, the Flunky returned his attention to Beau and Will. His hand went into his pocket. He tapped the screen on his phone and put it to his ear.

Will asked Beau, "What's he doing?"

"Ordering a pizza." Beau had his hands out of his pockets, hanging loose at his sides. Ready to fight? Ready to run? Ready to signal?

Will looked again for the van. He saw nothing, just the agents who were waiting to spring into action. Unless they were time travelers, none of them could reach him soon enough to do anything but call the coroner.

Will tried to appear casual as he reached behind him. His fingers wrapped around the Sig Sauer P365. The gun was a micro-compact, designed for concealed carry, but held ten in the magazine and one in the chamber. Most cops trained on their service weapon. Will had spent hours at the firing range with the Sig. He was just as accurate with one as the other. The stock was short, but the purchase was like a glove. He could draw the weapon and fire in under one second.

The Flunky ended his call. Will guessed he was still debating. Go or stay? Follow orders or take the consequences? He was skinny, this kid, with gangly arms and legs that were accustomed to lifting dumbbells and swinging bats, not fighting off two grown men or running for his life.

He resumed his long walk toward the bleachers. He was trying to act normal, but his hand had gone into his pocket and he might as well have dangled a sign down from his balls that said GUN.

"'Sup?" He lifted his chin at Will, because he assumed that Will was in charge.

Beau said, "Tell Dash we need to talk."

The Flunky clearly didn't want to work with another flunky. He asked Will, "Everything good, bro?"

"He's not your contact, dickslap." Beau thumped the Flunky's chest. "Tell Dash I want more money."

"For what?"

"For fucking your mother."

Will was two seconds ahead of what happened next.

The Flunky started to pull his gun out of his shorts. Beau's hands were already up, because he was in the prediction business, too. He was prepared to take the gun and turn it on the Flunky.

Except the Flunky's shorts were too baggy. What was it with these guys stashing their guns in their pockets? He should've holstered the weapon, or stuck it inside the backpack or maybe the idiot should've just paid attention to his surroundings because he had no idea what was coming until Will kicked the ever-loving shit out of his knee.

The crack was like a bat hitting a baseball.

The kid dropped to the ground.

"Fuck!" he screamed. He was rolling on his side, clutching his knee. He was clearly more concerned about the blood than the damaged cartilage. Understandable, because he wouldn't really get that the cartilage was important until he heard it from an orthopedic surgeon in twenty years.

"Good one, bro." Beau was nodding his approval. He had the gun in his hand, a Glock 19, but not Will's Glock 19. He wasn't pointing it at Will, so Will let him keep it.

Will told the Flunky, "Call your boss."

"I don't—" The pain caught his breath. "Fuck, man, is my kneecap supposed to move around like this?"

"Like you popped it off a can of Dinty Moore?" Beau was laughing. "No, bro, that's some bad shit."

"Fuck!"

Will dug around in the kid's pocket until he found the phone. He pulled up the last dialed number. There was an initial beside it—the letter *G*.

Will tapped the call button.

There was no *hello*, just—

"Kevin, what the hell? I told you to get it done. We need those pills. This is an infantry-level operation."

Will had to swallow before he could speak. Did the voice on the end of the line belong to Dash? He sounded irritated, the way you'd be if your kid dinged your car.

Will said, "It's not Kevin. Beau told me you were down a few men. I served with him in the sandpit, worked CSR."

Combat Search and Rescue.

Will asked, "You interested or not?"

The man was quiet, thinking. Then he let out a long stream of air. Not a sigh, but an indication of deepening frustration. A *this is the last shit I need today* kind of sigh.

He said, "Put Beau on the horn."

Will gave Beau a hard look of warning before passing over the phone.

Beau shoved the Glock into his waistband. He was still smiling. Will couldn't tell if he was high from the pills or relishing the sudden violence. "It's me," he said into the phone. "Yeah, I'm an asshole. Yeah, I get that." He looked at Will, eyebrows up like he was getting ragged by the teacher. "Yeah, I know, but—"

He shook his head. "Listen, Gerald, I didn't—" He stopped again. "Motherfucker, will you shut up a minute so I can tell you?"

Gerald.

Will's lips parted. He let out his own frustrated breath. Then he told himself that Kevin was a flunky and Gerald was his boss, which meant the guy above Gerald could be Dash.

Beau laughed into the phone. He told Gerald, "Dash said he'd take care of me if I could find him a couple of solid guys." He smirked at Will, acknowledging that this wasn't information he'd shared with Amanda. "His name is Jack Wolfe. Airborne, tough as shit. My word should be enough to vouch for him, and if it's not, you can suck my fat dick."

Beau was grinning when he handed Will the phone.

Will wanted to beat him with it. Instead, he got back on the line, telling Gerald, "It's me."

"Wolfe." Gerald paused, then asked, "How long you been out, son?"

He didn't sound old enough to be calling Will *son.* "Long enough to know it was all a bunch of bullshit."

Beau laughed.

Gerald had gone quiet again. He was thinking. Again.

Will did his own thinking. Beau was not acting right. He was too amped up, bouncing on his toes. There was nothing Will could do about him. Beau was going to do what Beau was going to do. Kevin was another matter. If Gerald said no deal, Will still had the Flunky. He would shove his Sig into the kid's mouth and put his finger on the trigger if he had to.

Gerald said, "I'll call you back."

Will heard the line go dead. He clocked the time.

4:03 p.m.

If Gerald took more than two minutes, then he was making his way up the chain of command. If he took less than two minutes, he was calling Dash directly.

The latter scenario would put Gerald as Dash's right-hand man.

Will pocketed the phone. He reached down to Kevin and grabbed the backpack.

"What the fuck?" Kevin complained.

Will motioned for Beau to walk with him to the bleachers. His hands were sweating. Every part of him wanted to stare at the phone until it rang and he found out whether or not he was one step closer to finding Sara or one step toward pounding Kevin into the ground.

"Dude," Kevin said, "come on, gimme that."

"Shut up." Will unzipped the backpack. He pretended to examine the bricks of cash while he mumbled to Beau, "Dash told you to bring him a couple of guys, huh?"

Beau's mouth smirked up another notch.

Will said, "I'm thinking a guy like Dash doesn't trust many people, but he trusts you. Which means you lied about how well you know him."

Beau tucked his hands into his pockets. He wasn't looking for a fight. He just wanted to fuck with Will. He said, "Gotta keep some cards hidden up my sleeve, right, bro?"

Will told him, "Start thinking about where to hide things when the guards tell you to grab your ankles and cough."

Beau laughed.

"Do I look like I'm joking?" Will counted the money. There was at least thirty grand in the backpack. "You pull that shit again—"

Will's threat was cut off by the phone ringing.

4:04 p.m.

He felt like he was going to throw up, but he let two more rings go by before answering, "Yeah?"

Gerald said, "All right, Wolfe, you can thank your buddy for vouching for you. Captain Ragnersen's word goes a long way with the boss."

Will opened his mouth and pulled in some air. "How much?"

"I can give you ten grand for a small job I got going tonight. Little try-out to see if you're the real deal."

Will made himself silently count to five. "How small?"

"Not a lot of risk. In and out. We've done it before. There's a guy on the inside."

"There's always a risk," Will said. In the silence, he counted off to five again. Ten grand was killing money. Or these guys had no idea what the street value was for a hired thug. He pressed, "Fifteen thousand."

"Deal," Gerald said, which meant that Will should've asked for twenty. "Hand the phone to Kevin."

Will worked to hide his elation as he gave Kevin the phone. He was in. He was on the very edge, but he was in.

"Yes, sir," Kevin told Gerald. The whininess had drained from his voice. "Yeah, I know where that is. I can meet him there in fifteen or twenty—okay, but—"

The call was ended.

Kevin slid the phone into his pocket. He told Will, "Help me up, Slenderman."

Will grabbed his arm and lifted him up like a rag doll.

"Damn, that hurts." Kevin limped to the bleachers. Blood had pooled into his shoe. White showed at the tip of his kneecap. He fell onto the seat. He unzipped the duffle. There had been no way to hide a GPS tracker inside the medications. Beau had been very specific about how everything was supposed to be prepared. The pills had been transferred to labeled Ziploc bags. The ointments and creams were out of the boxes, wrapped together with rubber bands, and still sealed.

Kevin exchanged the stacks of money from his backpack for the contents of the duffel. He said, "I need your phones and your IDs."

"Fuck you," Beau said.

Kevin shrugged. "You vouched for him. Gerald said either you and Wolfe go together or nobody goes."

"We'll both go." Will tossed his wallet onto the bleachers. "I don't carry a phone. I'm not gonna let the government track me."

"No prob," Kevin said. "I feel you, bro."

Will's wallet had opened on the seat. The driver's license and credit card were in his fake name, Jack Phineas Wolfe. Unless the IPA had access to the Pentagon's servers, Wolfe's military service, a restraining order and two DUIs would clear any background check.

Will told Beau, "Come on, bro. Let's do this."

"This is fucked up." Beau started shaking his head, but he added his wallet and phone to the stash. Will studied his face. Nothing about Beau felt right. He had capitulated too easily. Even high as a kite, he had managed to arm himself with the Glock. Will hadn't heard Gerald's side of the conversation with Beau. For that matter, he didn't know what Gerald had told Kevin.

Will's gut started screaming like a banshee.

He told Kevin, "We'll follow you in the truck."

"You're not going with me. Gerald is in charge of the missions. Either one of you got outstanding warrants in North Carolina?"

North Carolina?

Will asked, "Who's taking us to Gerald?"

"Hold your horses." Kevin transferred the wallets and Beau's phone into his backpack. "He'll send us a location."

Will fought the urge to look anywhere but the parking lot. Beau had told them that Dash sent a new flunky for every meet-up, but Beau hadn't described the guy in the van. He obviously knew Gerald. He had lied about his relationship with Dash. Will had to think that both Beau and Gerald knew every single way out of this park. And neither of them would be worried about the kids at the school next door.

Beau asked Kevin, "What about my money?"

"Give me the keys to your truck. I'll put it under the seat."

Beau capitulated again. He tossed Kevin the keys. His hands were loose at his sides. He was Zen again, ready to jump this thing off.

Kevin's phone chirped. Will could see a pin on a map. Gerald had sent him a location.

"Thattaway." Kevin pointed in exactly the direction Will thought he would, toward the woods. "When you get to the center of the field, take a right into the woods again. Go past the nursing home. A black van will meet you at the end of the driveway."

Beau asked, "What field?"

He hadn't studied the aerial map. He hadn't worked for hours with a team of highly trained undercover agents who were searching for the best positions to monitor every single route in and out of the park.

All of the routes but one.

"The football field," Kevin said. "It runs along the back of the elementary school."

Will sat in the back of the packed van sweating so hard that he felt like he was boiling in a pot of water. The windows were painted black. A partition separated the cab from the rear. The dome light was on, but the bulb was so weak that Will could only see outlines of his fellow passengers. One measly vent in the ceiling shot out a cool stream of air conditioning, but it was over one hundred degrees outside and they were in an aluminum box, so no amount of air was going to keep them from baking.

They'd gone through the Gatorade in the cooler within the first two hours.

Will looked at his watch.

7:42 p.m.

Over three hours of transit time. They could be deep into North Carolina by now. Or Kevin could be a more convincing liar than Will had guessed and they could be in Alabama or Tennessee.

Beau grunted in his sleep. His shoulder was jammed into Will's. His head had dropped down. He was snoring. Four young men were crammed together on the other side of the van. Their sweat smelled like raccoon musk if raccoons wore Axe Body Spray.

No introductions had been made when Gerald told them to climb into the van. Will found the kids so similar that he thought of them as One, Two, Three and Four. Each young man had a sidearm on his hip. They were all no more than eighteen, all dressed in black, and their expressions kept ricocheting between boredom and terror. They must've been exhausted from keeping their knees tucked up to their chins. They were clearly scared that their feet or legs would accidentally brush the wrong person in the wrong way.

Beau was that wrong person. Will was that wrong person. The two of them together took up as much space as One through Four.

There was a kind of electricity coming off the kids. The quick glances they kept giving across the van, the nods they exchanged between themselves. Will could only describe it as a kind of awe. These kids were looking at genuine war heroes. They were going to do a mission alongside real soldiers. They had guns on their belts. They had dressed for the part. They were clearly eager to start the mission.

Which made Will very worried. He assumed the fanboys would probably know more about the Army than he did. Every branch had its own lingo. All it took was one wrong phrase and Will would find himself on his knees with a gun pressed to his head.

Gerald was clearly not convinced of Jack Wolfe's usefulness, but Will had to think that being four men down had made Dash desperate for qualified fighters. Still, Gerald had appraised Will like he was a side of beef. He'd clocked the Sig Sauer at Will's back. He'd taken Beau aside and rapid-fired some questions. If Beau was going to rat out Will, he was waiting for the right moment. Gerald had seemed satisfied with the answers he'd been given. He'd nodded once, and the young man Will thought of as Four had scanned Will with a wand. He was searching for a signal from a GPS tracker. Beau hadn't been wanded. Which meant that Will still had a lot to prove.

And that Beau was a fucking liar because these people clearly thought of him as part of the team.

Will's time in the van had given him ample opportunity to consider all the ways that Beau could fuck him over. But Beau was only part of the problem. Gaining Gerald's trust was Will's only path to finding Sara, but there were too many unknowns about their destination to generate a meaningful strategy.

North Carolina.

Were they going to rob a bank? It was too late in the day for that. Were they going to knock-off a quickie mart or a check-cashing place? Why go out of state when there were thousands of stores closer? Were they being driven into the mountains where Gerald would throw open the doors and shoot them all with his AR-15?

Always possible, especially once they had finished the mission.

Will assumed that Amanda was looking for him. She was probably spitting nails at the team. Faith was probably spitting just as many. She wasn't much of a rule-follower. Will had seen her exploit the baby seat in the back of her car on more than one occasion. She would have set herself up somewhere in that school parking lot just in case.

But she hadn't, so the fake jogger, the pretend mother with the stroller, the couple in the parking lot, the chase cars—none of them would've seen Will disappear into the woods. Even if they had, there was no way they could predict where he would come out. The nursing home on the other side of the football field had not come up in the briefing.

Faith would have figured it out in two seconds.

Will leaned his head against the side of the van. The vibrations from the road drilled into his skull and tailbone. His headache had returned. He closed his eyes. He breathed in the thick, putrid air. He thought about getting Sara back. What he would say to her. How their lives would look after this.

Here was the problem: Sara's family was the most important thing in her life.

Cathy clearly hated Will. There was no sugar-coating it. Eddie was making more of an effort, but Will wasn't sure that would last for much longer. The truth was that he had never expected to fit in with Sara's family. His only hope had been that eventually, possibly, he would end up like that stray piece of a jigsaw puzzle that no one could find a place for, but no one could bring themselves to throw away.

The last time Will had seen Cathy Linton, she couldn't even say his name.

The van hit a rut in the road. Beau sniffed himself awake. He scratched his balls, used his sleeve to wipe the drool off his mouth. He opened the cooler. He slammed it closed. "Which one of you pencil dicks drank the last Gatorade?"

"There's one by the door," Three said. "It's a little warm."

Beau saw through the trick. He kicked Three in the shin. "You think I've never had to drink piss, boy?"

No one laughed. They were contemplating how desperate a man had to be in order to drink his own urine.

Four asked the question Will had been dreading. "What was it like over there?"

Beau nodded toward Will. "He's the one who saw the real action."

Will kept his body still so that he wouldn't punch Beau in the neck.

Three said, "Come on, dude. What was it like?"

Will looked up at the dome light. He cleared his throat. These kids were armed. They were heading into a possibly dangerous situation. Their biggest fear was making a mistake because their buddies would laugh at them. Death was not a concept they could hold in their little minds. They hadn't been hurt enough by life to understand that it was precious.

He told them, "I didn't watch my buddies die so I could entertain a bunch of pissants with stories."

Beau chuckled. "True dat."

Their disappointment was palpable. Four groaned. Three tapped his head against the metal wall. Two started biting his fingernails. One shifted, trying to stretch out a cramp in his leg without making physical contact with anyone else.

The back of the van was tight, but One through Four had left inches of space between them. At that age, you didn't touch another guy unless you were hurting him. You talked about screwing girls who had never even heard your name. You bragged about flipping your skateboard or crashing your bike like you hadn't almost shit yourself when it happened. You were still trying to figure out what to do with all the rage and lust and anger that sparked up like a forest fire for no reason.

Will had been exactly like them at that age—so damn desperate for someone to show him how to be a man. He'd see a cool guy strolling down the street and try to match his gait. He'd hear another man flirt with a woman and try out the line on an unsuspecting girl. Or at least Will would tell his friends that he'd tried out the line. And that it had worked. And that she had been amazing.

"It sucks," Will said. "Killing somebody. It sucks, and you hate yourself."

Beau didn't crack a stupid joke. He was listening. They were all listening.

Will considered his words. He was supposed to be Jack Wolfe right now, ex-Army soldier, disillusioned with life. On paper, the man's experiences were not his own, but they shared some qualities. Will had no remorse for shooting Sebastian James Monroe, but Monroe was not the first man he had killed.

He told the boys, "There's no glory in taking another human being's life."

The air was tense. The only sound was the tires droning against asphalt.

"People say you're strong, or that you're a hero, but you're not." Will wiped his mouth with his shirt sleeve. "Even if the guy deserved it. Even if what it came down to was that you had to kill him before he killed you, you feel like shit."

Beside him, Beau started flexing his hands.

Will said, "People ask you about it all the time, but you can't tell them the truth, because that's not what heroes do."

"Damn straight," Beau mumbled.

Will leaned forward, because he wanted these stupid kids to hear him. "It's not cool when it happens. The blood sprays. It gets into your eyes. You can see bone and cartilage. You think you're ready for that shit because you've played *Call of Duty* ten billion times, but it's not the same in person. The blood smells like copper. It gets into your teeth. You taste it in your throat. Sniff it into your lungs."

"Damn," Three whispered.

Beau was looking down at his hands. He shook his head.

Will said, "The man you shot, he had a family, just like you have a family. He had a life. You have a life. Maybe he had kids. Maybe he had a fiancée or a girlfriend or his mother was sick or he ached in his balls to go home the same way you ached to every second of every day." He looked at each of them, One through Four. Their eyes were wide. They were hanging on every word. "That's why it sucks. Because—"

Will shook his head. He had told them the because. He hoped to God they would never find out for themselves.

Beau sniffed again. He wiped his nose.

Two was the first to break. "Because what, dude?"

Will stared at the blacked-out window. He could hear Beau's raspy breathing.

Two repeated, "Because what?"

Beau said, "Because when you kill somebody, you kill a part of yourself."

The tires droned in the silence. There were no more questions. Will marked the passage of time on his watch. Ten more minutes. Fifteen. He felt the van take a soft turn. They were leaving the highway, merging onto an exit.

He stared at his watch.

7:49 p.m.

The van slowed for another turn. Sharper, probably onto a side street. The turn sent Will's shoulder into Beau's. Across from them, the kids struggled to maintain the space between them.

The van's speed stayed around thirty for a few minutes. Will listened for the sound of other vehicles. He heard the occasional hum of traffic. They were still close to the highway. Or maybe it was an interstate. Or maybe he'd been in this van so long that he'd lost his sense of hearing.

The floor felt like it was dipping. The van was going up a ramp. Will heard the rumble of an idling diesel engine. Close by, probably parked next to the van. There was a whirring sound. A motor, chains hitting metal. The *click-click-click-click* of a brake preventing a gear from rolling back.

Will recognized the sound. He had worked at a shipping company to help pay his way through college. He knew what a receiving dock door sounded like when it was rolled up for a delivery.

The van shifted as Gerald got out of the front. He was talking to someone. Will couldn't make out the words. He assumed money was being exchanged.

Not a lot of risk. We've done it before. There's a guy on the inside.

The doors to the van finally opened. Will had expected a blinding light, but all he got was more darkness. Gerald had backed directly into the receiving bay. The thick black seal around the open door blocked Will's chances of seeing the outside. A man who looked like he'd just come from the gym was walking toward the exit. His back was to Will. He had an envelope in his hand that was so stuffed with cash that the flap wouldn't close. Red ball cap, baggy shorts, black Nike T-shirt, thick in the waist.

"Let's go." Gerald kept his voice low as he waved for them to hurry.

One through Four quickly scrambled, pairing off in different directions. They kept their hands on their firearms as if any second, this could turn into the O.K. Corral.

Will's eyes darted around the warehouse as he climbed down from the van. Most of the lights were off, but there were spots to see by. The warehouse was around the size of a football field. Rows of metal racks contained stacked, sealed cardboard boxes. They were all the same dimensions, around thirty inches square. Each was stamped with numbers that corresponded to the different signs on the racks below. Every single box had a plastic sleeve with a shipping label inside.

Will had to get one of those labels. The contents, shipping and receiving addresses, company names and contacts would be on the forms.

"Beau." Gerald nodded him toward the rear of the warehouse.

The Glock was already in Beau's hands. He walked in a low crouch, weapon pointed down, looking for security guards or anyone who might cause trouble.

"Wolfe." Gerald's hand was on Will's shoulder. He spoke quietly. "That way."

Will saw the bathrooms, an employee breakroom, the shipping office, a door that probably led to the administration side of the warehouse. He drew his Sig, pointed it down at the ground, and crouched his way toward the bathroom.

Before he went inside, he glanced behind him. A second bay door was open onto the back of a box truck. Cardboard boxes that looked identical to the ones on the racks were packed to the ceiling. Two and Three started unloading them. Whatever was inside was heavy enough to require two men per box. Gerald went to the racks. He had a piece of paper in his hands. He was looking for a corresponding number. He pointed to a row in the middle. One and Four got to work taking them down.

Why break into a warehouse to replace a bunch of boxes?

Gerald caught his eye.

Will went into the women's bathroom. He checked the stalls. He needed something—a name tag, a newspaper, that could help pinpoint his location. There were lockers, but they were all unlocked and all empty. He cleared the men's room with the same bad luck. He went back into the warehouse. More boxes coming out of the truck. More boxes being taken down from the racks.

The door to the shipping office was locked. Will looked through the glass. Papers were everywhere. It was too dark to make out any logos or addresses.

Behind him, the kids were working quickly. The boxes were out of the truck. Half of the new boxes had been loaded in. They were working by rote. They had all done this before. They were afraid, but not terrified. Their nervous energy came more from the excitement of being criminals.

Will entered the breakroom. Vending machines, kitchenette, sink, two refrigerators, tables and chairs for around thirty people.

One person sitting at the table by the Coke machine.

Security guard.

At first glance, he could've been dead, but Will realized that the man was asleep. His head had dropped back against the chair. His mouth gaped open. His hat covered his eyes and nose. His hands rested on his large belly. The uniform was black cotton. No logos or name tag. Black work boots. White gym socks.

Will started to edge out of the room, but then he clocked the ID badge on a lanyard around the man's neck.

The card was turned around. The back was white. The other

side of the card would show the man's name, the company, the address.

Will debated.

He could hear a bay door rolling closed in the warehouse. They had loaded up the semi. They were probably looking for him.

Will tucked the Sig into his holster. He flicked open his knife.

He took a step toward the sleeping guard. He was snoring hard, had probably been out for at least an hour.

Will took another step. He clicked his tongue, testing the amount of noise he could make before the guard woke up. The rolling door hadn't stirred him. The smell of hard liquor was pungent as Will got closer. He clicked his tongue again. The man did not stir.

Will took another step. He reached out with his blade to cut the ID card off the lanyard.

"Ssst!"

The noise had come from behind Will.

Gerald was in the doorway. He furiously shook his head, motioning for Will to leave the guy alone. There was something like fear in his eyes.

He'd thought that Will was going to stab the guard.

"Wolfe." Gerald waved for him to leave.

Will looked down at the ID card. He was so fucking close.

But Gerald had told him no. Will's mission was not to locate the address to a warehouse. He was here to work his way into the IPA.

He kept the knife in his hand as he backed out of the room. He stared at the ID card with the same kind of longing he felt for Sara. He scanned the room for identifying features. The usual signs about choking and chemical burns on the walls. An eye-washing station. A first-aid kit. There was nothing that would differentiate this breakroom from every other breakroom inside the hundreds of thousands of warehouses in the country.

Will jogged behind Gerald to the van. His eyes found the boxes on the metal rack. They all had the same number: 4935-876.

"Wolfe." Gerald's hand went to Will's shoulder. His voice was low. "Next time, check with me before you do something like that."

Will nodded. He climbed into the van. One through Four were already inside. Beau had taken his place behind the driver's seat. He was silent, looking down at his hands. They were all quiet. They had all expected, maybe even hoped, for the worst to happen, and they didn't know what to do with the letdown.

The drive back to the nursing home passed in silence. Four hours, by Will's watch. One through Four had fallen asleep. Beau stayed tensed beside him. He was thinking, probably planning how he was going to get out of this once the van stopped. Run. Fight. Kill.

Will was thinking, too, but not about that.

4935-876.

The numbers on the sides of the boxes.

He kept chanting them in his head like a mantra. The tires kept rolling. The kids kept sleeping. Will's tailbone started to ache from the metal floor. The display on his watch had flipped to midnight by the time the van finally slowed to a stop.

The kids did not wake up. Beau grunted as he edged along the floor. The shrapnel in his back was probably killing him. He'd stopped reaching into his pocket about an hour ago. Either his pills were gone or he wanted to be clear-headed for what was about to come next.

Gerald opened the van doors. They were at the mouth of the driveway to the nursing home. He had their wallets, Beau's phone and keys.

He said, "Thank you very much for your service. Money's under the seat of your truck. Good doing business with you fellas."

Beau took his belongings, started shoving them into his pockets.

Gerald headed toward the front of the van. The driver's door was open. The engine was idling.

He was going to leave. He couldn't leave.

Will asked, "That's it?"

Gerald slowly turned around. He studied Will. He couldn't

quite make up his mind. After too many seconds had passed, he said, "You want more, Major Wolfe?"

Major.

They had gone through Will's wallet, run a background check on Jack Phineas Wolfe, honorably discharged, former Airborne.

Beau cleared his throat. "Come on. Let him go."

Will couldn't tell who he was talking to.

Gerald asked Beau, "What's this pussy shit, Ragnersen? You taking away your endorsement?"

Will held his breath, waiting for Beau to rat him out.

Beau took his time offering an answer, but in the end, he shook his head. Once. Not emphatic. The equivalent of a shoulder shrug.

Will thought about the Sig Sauer at his back. He was sweating so hard the leather holster was glued to the tail of his shirt.

"Come on, Ragnersen." Gerald clearly wasn't satisfied. "You think he's got what it takes or not?"

Will looked down at the ground. He gauged the distance between him and Gerald, thought about One through Four sleeping in the van, the old folks in the nursing home, the cars that might drive by on the road.

"Fuck yes." Beau let his face split open with a grin. "Wolfe had my back over in the sandpit more times than you've scratched your balls."

Will worked on keeping the anger and relief off his face. He grabbed Beau by the shoulder the way a buddy would, but his fingers dug in hard enough to let him know he was going to pay for this bullshit later.

Gerald crossed his arms. He asked Will, "How bad is your life?"

Will shrugged.

Gerald asked, "Are you willing to give everything up? Leave town? Don't look back?"

Will's heart started thumping so hard that he could feel his pulse in his fingers. This was it. His last chance to find Dash. His only chance to save Sara.

He asked Gerald, "What does it pay?"

"$250,000."

"Shit," Beau hissed.

Will asked, "What do I have to do?"

"You'll know when it's time to know," Gerald said. "You show up, be ready to leave your old life behind. Don't pack any bags. Don't tell anyone what you're doing. The payday is crazy for a reason. You do this job with us, you've got to disappear when it's over. You can't return to your old life. And if you try to, then we'll have to deal with you, your family, your woman—anybody who might say the wrong word. You understand?"

Will pretended to think about it. The money wasn't just crazy, it was stupid crazy. There were hundreds of bad guys who would strangle their own mothers for a quarter of that. It was the kind of money you offered when you knew you weren't going to have to pay it.

Will asked, "When?"

Beau kicked the ground.

"Tomorrow," Gerald said. "Fifteen hundred hours, sharp. Exit 129 off of I-85. There's a Citgo. I'll give you a little ride to meet the boss. He'll test you out, make sure you're a good fit."

Dash.

Gerald said, "If he gives the thumbs up, you're in."

Beau asked, "And if he doesn't?"

Gerald shrugged. He told Will, "Some wars are worth the sacrifice. The boss will fill you in. Believe me, you won't take much convincing. Maybe you'll want to go with us when we bug out. The mission you'll be a part of, the war we're fighting, it means something."

Will clenched his jaw. He had a siren going off in his head, not a warning, but—

Sara-Sara-Sara-Sara.

Beau stepped into it. "What's this mission?"

Gerald looked surprised. "You want a piece?"

"Fuck no, man. Not for twice that."

Gerald told Will, "Think about it, soldier. No pressure. If you want in, you've got to be all in. Show up tomorrow, exit 129, fifteen hundred. You'll find out what you're doing when it's time to find out what you're doing. That work for you?"

Will counted silently in his head. To five, to ten. He nodded once.

Gerald nodded back.

That was it.

Will started walking down the driveway to the nursing home. He heard the van door slam shut behind him. He skirted the building, looking up in the camera so his face was completely visible. His head was filled with numbers:

4935-876; 129 off I-85 at 15:00.

Beau's footsteps were behind him doing the Charlie Brown shuffle.

Will said, "You're a motherfucker."

"Hell yeah I am." Beau didn't seem worried about how angry Will was or where they were going.

"You should run," Will said. "You know they'll be waiting for you at your truck."

"You should run, too, Robocop." Beau jogged to catch up. "Don't be stupid. You know they dangled that money because they're gonna end up paying you with a bullet to the back of your brain. Don't risk your life to bring down these weasels."

"What are they planning?"

"You think they run that shit past me?"

Will kept walking. Beau thought that Will was dedicated to his job. He had no idea that this was about Sara.

"Bro, hey, hold up." He trailed Will through the woods. "Listen to me, okay? Dash is a fucking stone-cold killer. No joke. I've fought with dudes like that. You don't mean shit to him. You're collateral damage. The bullets start raining down, he'll turn you into his umbrella."

Will felt a sting on his forehead. He slapped away a mosquito.

Beau said, "That shit you were talking about in the van? I get it, bro. I'm spinning the same damn wheel every morning I get out of bed. You're either homicidal or you're suicidal."

"I'm not the one shooting black tar heroin." Will trudged across the football field. The grass was wet. The sprinklers had soaked the ground. He didn't need a lecture from a junkie looking at twenty years. He told Beau, "You want to help somebody? Help yourself, *bro*."

"I'm only trying—" Beau didn't get a chance to explain what he was trying.

Flashlights bounced around them like fireflies. Agents swarmed in. Guns drawn. Kevlar vests wrapped tight. Will didn't recognize them from work because they weren't GBI. They were all yelling the words they had been trained to yell at Quantico.

"FBI! FBI! Get on the ground! Get on the ground!"

Will had his hands in the air, but they pushed him out of the way.

Beau was slammed to the grass. He barely had time to *oof* out a breath. His hands were wrenched behind him. The Glock 19 was unloaded. His phone and wallet were tossed onto the ground.

An agent wearing glasses knelt down beside Beau. "Captain Ragnersen, I'm arresting you for possession of an illegal firearm inside a nature area."

"Fuck," Beau spat out the word. He looked for Will. "We had a deal."

Will walked away. His tennis shoes filled with water from the wet grass. He kept up his mantra—

4935-876, 29 off of I-85 at 15:00.

The moon shifted behind a cloud. Will concentrated on picking his way through the dark woods. Exhaustion pressed on every joint in his body. He let himself consider what he'd just signed up for. These men were terrorists. It was not news that Dash was a psychopath. He had bombed a hospital. He had orchestrated the abduction of a scientist from the CDC. His men had taken Sara right in front of Will's eyes. Dash had shot a man with Will's Glock. He'd had his right-hand man switch cardboard boxes out of a warehouse that was packed with—what?

Explosives made the most sense. Those boxes could be going anywhere. Schools. Office buildings. Hotels. Will hadn't managed to steal a packing slip. He hadn't been able to cut the ID card off the guard's lanyard. The warehouse could be anywhere. If

Will didn't infiltrate this group, there was no other way to stop whatever horrible thing they were planning.

But stopping them was not what he really cared about most.

How bad is your life?

Will didn't have a life without Sara.

His hand brushed the chain-link fence as he walked along the baseball diamond. He passed the tennis courts. He saw Beau's truck still parked in the lot. A silver Acura idled beside it. The headlights were on low beam. Exhaust curled from the back. The engine was pushing heat out through the wheel wells.

4935-876, 129 off of I-85 at 15:00.

Will opened the door. He angled his body into the seat, wincing from the pain. He closed his eyes. The air conditioning was on high. The sweat on his face started to chill.

Amanda asked, "Well?"

He nodded. "I'm in."

Tuesday, August 6, 2019

14

Tuesday, August 6, 7:00 a.m.

Faith sat at the kitchen table, yelling, "Oh my goodness gracious, I can't believe how delicious these blueberries are!"

She was not rewarded by the pounding of Emma's footsteps across the upstairs hall.

Ten minutes had passed since her daughter had broken into a crying jag about the injustice of string cheese. Before Faith could talk her down, Emma had flung herself up the stairs and locked her bedroom door. There was a paperclip on the ledge to unlock the door for this very reason, but then Faith had heard Emma singing to her stuffed animals and thought—*win/win.*

Faith got up from the table. She started loading the dishwasher. She checked the time, because her mother was going to pick up Emma soon. If Faith's precious baby was up in her bedroom right now taking off her clothes, Evelyn was going to walk into the scene of a murder/suicide. At the very least, Emma would be barefoot. Faith did not have the requisite hour to make her daughter put her left foot into her left shoe and right foot into her right.

She took a deep, calming breath and tried to summon memories of the sweet angel she had come home to last night. Emma had always been a sponge for Faith's moods. News of Will's disappearance had left Faith shaky. Dash was a monster. The IPA was filled with monsters. They were all planning to do monstrous things. What if Will wasn't able to fool them? He'd had two hours to prep for his undercover identity. What if he messed up? What if Beau flipped for his own self-interest? What if her partner, her friend, was lying dead in a shallow grave?

Emma had absorbed Faith's pensiveness. She'd been cuddly and accommodating and said so many precious things that Faith almost took her baby book out of the wrapper. Even bath time, which normally ended with one or both of them in tears, had been relatively easy. Emma had only made Faith read two stories. The only stuffed animal she'd had to sing "You're Welcome" to was Mr. Turtelle. Faith had done her best Maui yet.

Then she had switched on the nightlight. She'd turned off the lamps. She'd left the door open to the requisite six-inch gap. And Emma had unzipped her skin and a demon had jumped out.

Faith closed the dishwasher. She strained her ears, listening for breakage, crying or a Satanic voice saying, *What a lovely day for an exorcism.*

No sounds set off an alarm bell, which could be an alarm bell on its own, but now would be the only time that Faith had to straighten up. She crammed the blueberries into her mouth as she transferred the bowl to the dishwasher. She wiped down the sticky counter and table. She got on her knees and cleaned the sticky floor. She smelled the trash and decided it could wait. She washed her hands at the sink.

There was one more thing Faith needed to do before going upstairs.

She went to her desk and stacked together the documents from the Michelle Spivey investigation. Emma didn't need another coloring book. There were over two hundred pages, photographs, witness statements, and background checks. If the key to finding Sara was contained within this file, they were screwed. Van's redactions had turned the pages into Mad Libs, thick black lines covering the important words.

*Spivey was seen at*_________*with* __________*at the* _________.

There was plenty of *there* there, but Van was holding out on her.

So was Amanda.

Last night, she had refused to explain why she had let the FBI take Beau Ragnersen into custody. Faith had slammed down the phone so hard that she'd bruised her hand. Her fury had a double edge. Faith was the idiot who'd passed on Beau Ragnersen's name to Aiden Van Zandt. Yesterday, she had asked him to cross-check the name against Michelle's work files. Obviously, Van had found something. Obviously, he wasn't going to tell her what he'd found. Her livid reaction had been another classic line for the baby book—

You were two years old the first time you heard Mommy scream "cocksucker!" into a pillow.

"Oh . . . no . . ." Faith realized there was a cap from a Magic Marker on her desk.

Only the cap. No marker in sight.

She swung herself up the stairs. Emma's door was open. She was sitting on the floor, surrounded by colored pencils. She was trying to put them in the box. The bottom was open, so they kept falling onto her lap, where she would scoop them up again. By her delighted expression, Faith assumed her daughter believed she'd discovered an endless supply of colored pencils.

Faith asked, "Where are your shoes?"

Emma grinned at the cascading pencils. "Snack holes?"

"They're not in your pockets." Faith looked in the closet, under the bed, the dresser, the nightstands and the changing table. No shoes, but she had finally found the approximately eleven thousand mittens that Emma had lost last winter. "Get your shoes on before Nana comes."

"Nana's here!" Evelyn was making her way up the stairs.

Faith felt like a basketball player who'd been tapped out of a rough game.

"Already a scorcher outside." Her mother was smartly dressed in linen trousers and a matching sleeveless shirt. She kissed Faith on the cheek, telling Emma, "Put your shoes on, sweetie."

Faith asked her mother, "Do you know a woman named Kate Murphy?"

Evelyn didn't have to think about it. She knew everyone. "Kate was Maggie's partner back when we still carved our DD-5s into stone tablets. I believe she was part of the EEOC lawsuit that forced the FBI to put women in the field. That's a good girl. Where's your backpack?"

Faith did a double-take. Emma was wearing her shoes. On the correct feet.

What was this dark magic?

Evelyn suggested, "Mandy knows Kate better than I do. Hurry up, Emmybear."

Faith watched Emma spin in a circle as she tried to put on her backpack. "What about her boy, Aiden Van Zandt?"

She wrinkled her nose. "I don't trust men who wear glasses. Why can't they just see?"

Faith hissed out a long breath of air.

Her mother misinterpreted her exasperation. "Oh, sweetie, he's not your type. And, besides, his father was a sleazy womanizer."

"Do you have the father's number?"

"Ha. Ha." Evelyn scooped up Emma and rested her on her hip. They each gave Faith a kiss on the cheek, then they were down the stairs and gone.

Faith held on to the image of her daughter's face. Dark, almost black hair. Light brown eyes. Lovely brown skin. She had inherited none of the Mitchell genes, which came in a shade slightly more pale than a glob of Elmer's glue.

Emma's father was third generation Mexican American. Victor wasn't much into his heritage unless it helped him make a point. Faith's high school Spanish was ten times better than his. He could barely order a good margarita and forget whispering *palabras sucias* while *echando un polvo*. She should've known it wasn't going to work out the first time she'd seen Victor walking around the bedroom with his undershirt tucked into his boxer shorts.

Faith made Emma's bed, tucking the sheets in tight. Mr. Turtelle was returned to his proper place. Socks were paired. By a miracle from God, the uncapped Magic Marker was located. Faith found herself feeling melancholy as she tidied the room. The house always felt different with Emma gone. Cleaner, certainly quieter, but also lonelier. She straightened up a pile of clothes. She scooped up the colored pencils and carried them downstairs.

She stopped in the foyer. Will's head was showing in the glass at the top of the door. He was just standing there. He hadn't knocked. He seldom came over unless she needed an emergency repair. She saw his head turn toward the driveway.

"Don't go!" Faith juggled the handful of pencils so she could open the door.

Will was dressed in the same clothes from the day before. Relaxed jeans, black long-sleeved shirt. He looked at her. Through her. His eyes were bloodshot. He looked awful. She had never in her life wanted to hug someone as much as she wanted to hug Will right now. But they didn't do hugs. If he was sitting down, she squeezed his shoulder. Sometimes, she punched him in the arm the way she did with her brother. Right now, she worried that even a tap would knock him over.

He didn't speak, so she said, "Come in."

Will followed her through to the kitchen. She had no idea why he was here. It was obvious he hadn't slept. His eyes were rimmed with dark circles. His whiskers had grown into a legitimate beard. He should've been at headquarters by now. The team had worked through the night pulling maps and topographical information around the Citgo off exit 129.

Will was supposed to meet Gerald in eight hours.

What was he doing here?

"Sit down." Faith dumped Emma's colored pencils onto the kitchen table. "Do you want breakfast?"

"No, thank you." Will grimaced as he maneuvered into the chair. She had never known him to pass up breakfast. He started straightening the colored pencils, arranging them by color.

She said, "That kid from the baseball field, Kevin Jones. He went from the park to a shopping center. By the time our people were on foot, he'd already handed off the bag of pills. They followed him to a doc-in-the-box where he got his knee stitched up, then back to his parents' house. We've got eyes on him 24/7, but we can't pick him up until this is over."

Will nodded like he already knew. He said, "They lost the black van when it left the nursing home."

Faith gave him the same nod in return. Amanda had briefed Faith as it was happening. The van had quickly left the residential area near the nursing home. The driver had cut the lights. He'd headed into a more rural area where a helicopter would've shown like a beacon. The four chase cars could only get so close on the straight, narrow country roads. The drivers had dropped back, then farther back, then suddenly the van had disappeared.

Will said, "They found it burned out in a field an hour ago. No plate, no VIN. Too hot for the arson investigators. I don't remember anything about it. I didn't look for the plate when I got in or out of the van. I didn't get a shipping label or—"

He broke one of the pencils between his fingers. He looked at the jagged edges. The color was an orangey-white called *Flesh Tone* that Faith hated on principle.

He asked, "How long did it take you to figure out what happened?"

He meant his disappearance out of the park. Two seconds on Google Earth had told Faith exactly what had happened. "I would've been at the school."

Will sat stiffly in the chair, his palm tight to his ribs as if he needed to hold the bones in place.

There was only one way that Faith knew to help him. She pressed her hand to his shoulder as she walked over to her desk. She found the Michelle Spivey file. She dropped it onto the table and sat down. "Michelle's pre-op bloodwork from the hospital showed an unknown substance. Not a narcotic. It was probably toxic. They think that's what made her appendix burst."

Will paged through the photographs from Michelle's abduction. The parking lot. Michelle's car. Her purse that she dropped when Carter pulled her into the van. He pointed to the reports. "Why is everything blacked out?"

"Our friends at the FBI." Faith showed him one of the more heavily redacted pages. "Two things jumped out at me. This one says MH JACK SERV." She tapped to the line. "That has to stand for Maynard H. Jackson Service Road."

"The airport."

"Right." Faith flipped to the next page. "If you pick it up here, it says *Hurley* on this line, then it talks about *doubled over* and *in pain and vomiting*. I looked that up, and those are all the symptoms of—"

"Appendicitis."

"Right again." She sat back in the chair. "Michelle and Hurley must have been at the airport when she started getting sick. I kept wondering why they took her to Emory. She would've been in a hell of a lot of pain. They needed to get her to a hospital, but they couldn't risk taking her to one close to the airport."

"You're thinking whatever the IPA is planning will happen at the airport." Will scratched his beard. "They wouldn't need Michelle for reconnaissance if they were scoping out a possible attack. There are maps and videos of the concourses and terminals online. You can watch a video of the Plane Train. Michelle's face has been all over the news. They were taking a huge risk having her out in the open. There must be a specialized something that only she could do."

Faith said, "Over a quarter of a million people fly in and out of that place every day. That's more than one hundred million a year."

"Cargo flights," Will said. "UPS, DHL, FedEx. They move boxes night and day. The boxes from the warehouse had numbers stamped on them: 4935-876."

"Amanda's already got six different agencies on it. The number's not coming up on anything. The size of the boxes, thirty-by-thirty, is standard. Based on the fact that two guys needed to lift each one, we're assuming it's reinforced, but that doesn't narrow it down as much as you'd think."

He kept scratching his beard. The sound was like nails on a blackboard.

Will wasn't thinking straight, or he'd also be pointing out that the airport was a major port of entry into the United States. The CDC had facilities within the complex to screen international travelers who were exhibiting symptoms of disease like SARS or

Ebola. But the operation was focused on keeping bad things from getting into the country.

What if Dash was planning on shipping something really terrible out?

"There's more." Faith's bag was hanging on the chair. She found her notebook. She hadn't been allowed to write down anything inside the SCIF, but she ducked into the bathroom before she'd left the CDC and recorded as much as she could remember.

Without preamble, Faith started reading, giving Will the same crash course into Nazi 101 she had received the day before. She highlighted the most active groups, the leaderless resistance doctrine. Will nodded occasionally, as if what she was telling him made sense. He stopped nodding when she arrived at the part about Dash and Martin Novak's time in Mexico.

"Dash is a pedophile?" Will said the words without the disgust she'd expected. He looked out the window. His eyes glistened in the morning light. He was as close to crying as she had ever witnessed.

Faith was overcome by an angry helplessness. She had to stop this. To fix this.

"I thought—" Will's voice had an unfamiliar rattle. "I guess I was worried. Because of the rape. The possibility of rape."

She put her hand to her mouth in—surprise? Shock? Relief?

Her mind had not made that leap. Adam Humphrey Carter was dead. Vale and Monroe were dead. Hurley was in custody. As terrible as it was to learn that Sara was being held hostage by a pedophile, the fact of his mental illness meant that Dash was less likely to rape her.

Will wiped his nose with the back of his hand. He looked up, but not at Faith. There was something so broken about him. If someone had told Faith that he'd fallen off the side of a cliff, she would've believed them.

Faith got up from the table. She went to the sink. She turned on the water. She had nothing to clean. She took a plate out of the dishwasher.

He said, "Gerald Smith."

Faith nodded, encouraging him to steer the conversation toward the case again.

Will said, "The twenty-one-year-old who walked out of a Mexican holding cell twenty years ago could be the same Gerald I met last night. The age range lines up. Did you get a description?"

"No." Faith wiped her nose with her arm while she scrubbed the plate. "It would make sense they still know each other. These guys hang together."

Will said, "I need a favor."

Faith turned off the faucet. She kept her back to him as she dried the plate. "Sure."

"I think that—I, mean, I know—" He stopped, took a breath. "Sara's mother really hates me."

Faith put the plate in the dishwasher. She closed the door. She wiped down the counter again.

He said, "I know that she would want me to—to take care of them. Don't you think?"

Faith shook her head, because she didn't.

"It's a family thing, I guess, that you would do with families. I guess?"

Faith had to look at him, if only because his expression might help her understand.

He said, "Like, to let them know. Not that there's a lot to know. Or that I can tell them. We can tell—would be easiest. But, progress, right? Or just maybe to feel like—I was thinking it would be better if it was us. But maybe—"

"Yes." Faith almost started crying again, this time from relief. "I will go with you to talk to Sara's parents."

Faith stood beside Will, her eyes on the numbers above the elevator door. She had been to Sara's apartment more times than she could count. There were only five people on earth she would leave her daughter with. The person below Evelyn on the list was not Emma's father or her *abuela* or even her older brother. Faith was not going to pass up the chance to leave her baby with a board-certified pediatrician.

Tears flooded into Faith's eyes. She had thrown herself into the case because that was the best way to help find Sara. That drive had kept Faith from thinking too long about what was really happening. That Sara could be hurt. That she could be raped. Beaten. Wounded. Killed.

What would Faith tell Emma?

The elevator doors opened. Faith wiped her tears. She only allowed herself to cry at home in the kitchen pantry. The only way through this was to get it over with as quickly as possible. She walked into the hall. She knocked on the door.

There was talking inside the apartment—two women, both speaking at the same register. Faith's stomach flipped. One of them sounded exactly like Sara.

"Will?" A surprised-looking woman had opened the door. She was dressed in sweatpants and a white T-shirt. No shoes. No bra. No inhibitions. She threw her arms around Will. Her face pressed into his neck. "I'm so sorry we're meeting like this."

Faith could not tell if Will knew the woman or not. He clearly didn't know what to do with his hands. He settled on touching his fingers to her shoulder blades. He said, "We don't have any news."

"That's good, right? Nothing is better than something? You're Faith?" The woman reached for Faith's hand. "I'm Tessa, Sara's sister."

Faith felt stupid for not putting it together herself. Tessa had probably gotten on a plane the minute she'd heard about her sister. The trip from South Africa would have been grueling, but Tessa showed no signs of wear. While Sara was attractive, her little sister was a knockout. Perfect, porcelain skin. Lustrous strawberry blonde hair. She was Faith's age, but more successful at it. No woman's breasts had a right to be that high after childbirth.

"Come in, please." Tessa's words were tinged with a soft, southern accent. "I'm sorry I didn't introduce myself properly. I'm jetlagged and—Will, close the door. Mama, look who's here."

Cathy Linton was washing dishes at the kitchen sink. She offered Faith a slight nod of her head.

"Sara told me all about you. My goodness, you're a tall drink of water. But this—" She reached up and stroked his cheek. "Sara's not gonna like this."

Will's face reddened under the beard. He offered his previous line. "We don't have any news."

Faith explained, "We wanted to update you on what we're doing."

Tessa said, "We had to turn off the TV because it was all just blabbering nonsense. We should wait for Daddy. Right, Mama?"

Cathy gave a begrudging, "Yes."

"He's walking the dogs," Tessa explained. "The little one is so adorable. Mama, don't you like Betty?"

Cathy did not answer. She was like a skunk who could not stop spraying in Will's direction.

He cleared his throat. "I need to pack some clothes."

Tessa watched him disappear down the hall. She gave him a few seconds to reach the bedroom, then turned on her mother. "What the hell is wrong with you?"

Cathy asked Faith, "Would you like some coffee?"

"I—" Faith was caught between them. "No thank—"

Cathy was already filling the cup. She took down another one from the cabinet. She said, "I suppose he takes cream?"

"He drinks—" Faith and Tessa said the words at exactly the same time.

Tessa said, "Will drinks hot chocolate in the morning."

Cathy scowled. "He's not six. He can't have chocolate for breakfast."

Tessa said, "He usually gets a biscuit on the way to work, and then he buys a breakfast burrito from the machine at the office."

"That makes it better?"

Faith prayed for invisibility.

"Tell me." Cathy stabbed her finger in Tessa's direction. "How is it that you know so much about that man's dietary regimen?"

"Do you really want to do this?"

Faith feigned interest in Sara's spacious living room.

Cathy said, "We need to come together as a family right now, and that man is *not* our family."

"Good Lord God, Mama, listen to your blind self. You can't even say Will's name."

"I don't recall your five-year liberal arts degree coming with a psychiatric license."

Faith slumped into the couch. She opened the pediatric journal on the coffee table.

Tessa said, "The way you're acting right now is exactly why Sara doesn't talk to you about him."

"That's not—"

"I'm not finished," Tessa said. "For the last year and a half, you've done your level damn best to push Will away from Sara because—"

"Because he was still married," Cathy insisted. "If a man cheats on his wife, he'll—"

"Will is a good man," Tessa said. "He's a mighty good man."

"If that was true, if he really loved her, he would ask her to marry him. Living together is not a commitment. It's a sleep-over with sex."

"Oh for fucksake."

"Exactly."

Faith studied an article on mycoplasma pneumoniae-induced redness of the fingers.

"Mama, you can't protect Sara from life happening again," Tessa said. "You're pushing Will out because you're so worried that he'll leave her, or break her heart, or cheat on her, or walk down to the mailbox one day and—"

"Stop."

Tessa paused for a moment. "Sara has decided on Will. That makes him our family. You taught us that rule. You need to start following it."

Faith prayed that the ensuing silence meant this nightmare had come to an end.

"All right." Cathy's tone did not indicate surrender. "You're the expert, smartass. What do you want me to do? What would make Sara happy? Throw him a party? Adopt him?"

Tessa's sigh indicated that she'd given up. "Just make him some damn hot chocolate."

Faith heard a saucepan hit the stovetop. The gas whooshed. Cabinets opened and closed. The fridge was slammed so hard that the bottles inside rattled.

Faith chanced a look at the two women. Cathy was pouring milk into the pan. Tessa had her arms crossed as she stared at the front door. The only thing that could make this more awkward was if they had the entire argument all over again.

What was taking Will so long?

Faith reached into her bag for her phone. She sent him a text message—

TF R U??

The delivered receipt came back, but Will did not respond. Faith was certain he'd heard the argument. The women had not kept their voices down. He was probably crawling out the window. The only thing Will hated more than talking about his feelings was hearing other people talk about theirs.

A cabinet door slammed. The milk was returned to the fridge.

Faith rested her elbows on her knees. She opened her emails. There were the usual things; requests for paperwork, a question from the state attorney's office. Amanda had not sent her a list of things to do, which was some kind of miracle. She would be supervising the planning for Will's rendezvous at the Citgo. Studying maps. Pulling up tax records and property lines. What happened at the park yesterday was not going to happen again. Amanda would be driving one of the chase cars. Faith planned to be right there with her.

The front door opened. Betty barked twice. She spun in a circle in the middle of the room. Sara's two greyhounds trotted into the kitchen and drank from the water bowls.

Faith had never met Sara's father before, but Eddie Linton looked nothing like she had expected. The first thing she noticed was his eyebrows, which shot off in every direction. He'd cut his jeans into a pair of shorts. The white pockets hung past the frayed ends. His legs were hairy. His T-shirt was more yellow than white. Holes were in the collar. His tennis shoes were falling apart.

Tessa said, "Daddy, this is Faith, Sara's friend."

Faith stood up to shake his hand. "I'm sorry to meet you under these circumstances."

He nodded. "I've heard a lot about you. Your girl, her name is Emma?"

"Sara's her favorite babysitter." Before he could ask, Faith told him, "There's no news, but we wanted to update you on what we're doing."

He asked, "We?"

Betty barked again. Will was standing in the hallway, his pained expression confirming that he had heard every single word of the argument. He was dressed in a black shirt and black jeans. His tactical boots were laced tight. His gym bag was over his shoulder. He looked like an actual burglar. The kind who would murder you for your grandmother's jewelry.

"Okay." Faith was so ready to get this over with. "Maybe we should all sit down over here?"

There were two couches. The Lintons took the one opposite Faith. Tessa curled into the corner. Cathy placed a steaming mug of hot chocolate on the coffee table before perching on the other end. Eddie stood in the middle, waiting, because he would not sit down until Faith did.

She took a deep breath, ready to start.

"Hold on." Eddie waved Will over. "Come sit down, son."

The soles of Will's boots squeaked across the hardwood floors. He sat beside Faith. She saw him wince as he leaned back. Betty scurried into his lap. She stretched herself along the length of his leg so that her head rested on his knee.

Cathy pushed the mug in Will's direction. He looked confused.

"It's hot chocolate," Tessa said. "I bet you've never had the real thing. Sara minored in organic chemistry, but she doesn't know how to boil milk."

Eddie put a hand on her foot to silence her. He told Faith, "Please, go ahead."

She took another deep breath and dove in. "Thank you, Mr. Linton. I want to start by saying that you've all been very good about not talking to the media. Your continued silence is vital to our investigation."

Their stoic expressions told her that they didn't need this part.

Faith took a third deep breath. She couldn't get into the details of the code Sara had left in the list of medications, but she was able to say, "We got confirmation that as of yesterday morning, Sara was still alive."

Eddie pressed his palm to his heart. His wife and daughter moved closer to his side. They each took one of his hands.

Tessa asked, "What kind of confirmation?"

"All I can share is that we believe Sara is doing everything she can to get back to you."

Eddie nodded, as if this was to be expected. "She's a smart girl. She knows how to take care of herself."

Cathy pressed together her lips. She looked down at the coffee table.

Tessa was a step ahead of her parents, "You said that you got the confirmation yesterday morning. There's been nothing since then?"

"No, but we didn't expect to hear anything else." Faith said, "We believe we know the name of the group that took her."

"Group?" Tessa asked. She had the same look in her eyes that Sara got when she was putting together a case. "Did they reach out with a ransom demand? Did they show a proof of life? If they want money, we'll find it. Why aren't you—"

"Tessie," Eddie said. "Let her answer your questions."

Faith said, "They're not that kind of group. She's not being held for ransom."

"Then what do they want?" Tessa asked. "What you're saying doesn't make sense to me. A group took her, but why? Is it connected to the bombing? What about that other missing doctor? She worked at the CDC. The Emory campus is right down the street from there."

"I want to acknowledge your questions, but I can't answer them." Faith tried to get on top of this. Tessa was just as clever as her sister. "None of this information I'm giving you is public knowledge. It's very important that it stays that way. You don't want to hear the questions you're asking on the news."

Eddie said, "They'll dig a grave with all of their useless speculation."

"Please," Cathy said, her voice low. "Let's not talk of graves."

Tessa looked out the window. Tears fell from her eyes.

Faith tried again. "All that I'm authorized to tell you is that we're developing a plan to locate her."

"A plan." Tessa rolled the words around in her mouth. She was looking at Will now. The way he was dressed. The beard. Sara didn't seem to hold back much from her sister. She would've told Tessa that Will often went undercover. That he risked his life to save other people. That he came home with cuts and bruises and the next morning, he went out and did it all over again.

Tessa asked. "Is it dangerous, the plan?"

Faith said, "Everything we do—"

"No," Tessa interrupted. "I'm asking Will. Is it dangerous?"

Will said, "No. It's not dangerous."

Tessa was not fooled. "I don't think Sara would want anyone risking—risking anything. Do you understand what I'm saying? It wouldn't be worth it to her."

Will ignored the observation. He scratched Betty's ears, taking himself out of the equation.

Eddie asked, "When do we find out if the plan worked?"

"I can't tell you that." Faith had already said too much. "I don't want to mislead you. None of this is guaranteed. I just want you to understand that we're doing everything we can. Sara means a lot to us. As a colleague. As a friend." She ended the list there. "We all want her back."

"We do," Tessa said. "But we don't want anyone else to get hurt."

Faith nodded, but not in agreement. Sara's involvement made this deeply personal, but this was the job that they had signed up for. Faith was keenly aware of the risks she took every time she put on her badge.

"Okay. Thank you." Cathy held on to her husband's hand.

She told Faith, "If you don't mind, I'd like to pray with my family."

"Of course." Faith stood up. She lifted her bag onto her shoulder.

Will couldn't move as quickly. He hugged Betty to his chest. He slid to the edge of the couch. He gave an uncomfortable laugh to acknowledge his slow pace.

"Will?" Cathy was reaching out for his hand. "Stay."

15

Tuesday, August 6, 12:40 p.m.

Sara kept her toga dress hiked up, doing lunges across the cabin while "Baby Got Back" endlessly pounded away inside her skull. *Back* was the one thing she had never had, but she thought Will appreciated it, so she had started adding an extra ten minutes of glutes to her gym routine in a vain attempt to turn water into wine.

His ex-wife was full of back. And hips. And everything else. Angie was J. Lo "Ain't Your Mama" curvy, though she had never worked out a day in her life. Her genes were those blessed kind that thrived on potato chips and cheap wine. Collagen would eventually be her downfall. Literally. That kind of skin looked great until it started slipping. Objectively, Sara could say that she had better breasts than Angie, but that was like saying that two Hershey's Kisses looked better on an ironing board.

"Crap." Sara gave up on self-improvement.

Her hamstrings buzzed like a swarm of bees. She had no sense of time. Her growling stomach was no indication of lunchtime. Her vegetarian breakfast had consisted of a hard roll and an even harder piece of cheese. Dysentery was not going to be a problem in the foreseeable future. She could feel the temperature rising outside. Inside, the cabin was shrinking to the circumference of the sun's asshole. Sara was sweating on top of sweat.

Worst of all, the children inside the bunkhouse needed her.

The antibiotics and ointments had arrived yesterday evening. The pills were in Ziploc bags instead of sealed bottles, but Gwen had assured Sara that they were the real thing.

Sara was not convinced.

This morning, she had expected to find that some if not most of the children had either stabilized or at least started to turn a corner. Her rounds had revealed otherwise. Benjamin was getting sicker. The oldest patient, a twelve-year-old girl, was showing new symptoms. The two four-year-olds were about the same. Only the two ten-year-olds and the one eleven-year-old were stabilized.

Was Gwen behind this?

At the Structure yesterday, the woman had proven that she would not waste her medical supplies if she felt the patient had no chance of recovery. Sara had stood helplessly by while Gwen had murdered a young man with her bare hands. The memory of the woman's shoulders shaking as she pressed her weight into Tommy's nose and mouth was etched into Sara's brain. Her own hands could recall the coldness of his fingers when the life had finally, brutally, been pushed from his body.

But Adriel, Gwen's youngest, was one of the sicker children. The infection in her left retina had spread to her right. The sound of her double pneumonia had taken on the quality of dried leaves. Sara could not think that Gwen would let her own daughter, no more than a baby, suffocate.

Then again, she had borne seven children with Dash. She knew everything that went on inside the Camp, seemed to be directing the cooking ladies and controlling the children and she certainly had made her disapproval of Sara well known.

Which meant that Sara should probably be more careful around her. Dash was a horrible person, but men tended to be horrible in predictable ways. A furious woman was capable of inflicting immense psychological damage, the kind that stuck around long after the wounds healed.

There was a loud *click* outside the door.

Not the key turning in the padlock. The greenhouse generator had cycled back on. Sara listened to muffled exhaust huffing out of the engine. The noise had lasted throughout the night. The amount of heat that thing gave off would not be easy to hide from a helicopter. Sara had to think that whatever was going on inside the greenhouse was reaching its conclusion.

She had to get inside that greenhouse.

Her thoughts fell into a familiar track as she considered all of the possible bad things that were taking place inside. This high up in the mountains, there were sure to be marijuana farms. The river provided enough water for hydroponic farming, but the generator would have been running non-stop for the grow lights, fans and humidity controllers. Besides, the greenhouse was on the small side. Given the amount of risk involved, there was not enough reward at that scale.

The more obvious explanation for the cloak and dagger was some kind of bomb-making factory. The Structure Tommy had fallen from was clearly meant to represent a building. What type of building was unknown. Two stories, at least. A balcony with a set of stairs running up the middle and splitting off to the left and right. Sara knew the men were running *drills* inside the Structure, that they were training for a *mission* and that they thought they were at *war*. So maybe Dash was planning a covert operation where they would sneak into this unknown building, plant several bombs, then sneak out and wait for the moment of destruction.

Which could possibly explain the Structure, but not the greenhouse and thermal tent, because you didn't need a secluded, shielded glass house to process explosives. You hardly needed more than ten square feet. There were probably handfuls of people all over the world right now assembling suicide vests and building IEDs inside garages and apartments.

Michelle was the outlier. She was an infectious disease specialist. Dash had not kidnapped her at random. At the CDC, they studied the worst bugs known to man. And probably some bugs that were known only to a few men.

Or known to Michelle Spivey.

Plenty of nasty biological agents could be synthesized by an amateur chemist, but using them was a different matter. Storage, transportation, delivery—these were all logistical problems that made biological terrorism arduous if not impossible for non-governmental groups to successfully pull off. It was much cheaper to build a bomb or store up a supply of ammunition.

Dash had already proven that he knew how to build and detonate bombs. He had killed people at the hospital. Sara had seen his pleased reaction when the numbers came rolling in on the news.

Pleased, but not ecstatic.

Which meant she had made a giant circle back to the same question as yesterday: What was he planning?

Sara considered the characteristics she had gleaned about Dash. Primary among them was that Dash was a highly organized leader. The Camp had not appeared overnight. There was the feeling of a planned community about the place. The two separated areas. The greenhouse. The Structure. The readily available food. The way the women and men were dressed. The compliant obedience of the followers. The sense that rules were being followed.

Rules made by Dash.

He was clearly capable of strategizing and long-term planning, which was harder for most criminals to pull off than the average non-criminal would believe. Dash had also passed one of the biggest deterrents to male criminal behavior: turning thirty. Sara guessed he was in his mid-forties. He did not come across as well-educated, but he exhibited a type of intelligence that served a very specific purpose. You couldn't persuade a group of people to give up modern life if you didn't have a certain amount of emotional intelligence. All of which pointed to a very high level of arrogance. People didn't believe in you unless you convinced them that you believed in yourself.

Sara tried to slot Gwen into the equation. She was loath to assign Lady Macbeth qualities to another woman, but there was something sinister about Gwen from the very beginning. Her complicity in the measles outbreak. The way she used Bible verses to scare her children. The callous disregard for life. Sara wasn't even sure that Gwen was qualified to be a nurse. She was clearly willing to do Dash's dirty work. All she had needed was a nod from her husband and as soon as his back was turned, Gwen was suffocating Tommy to death.

Sara could easily see someone like Gwen coaxing and cajoling Dash, pushing him toward even greater acts of terrorism. Whatever Dash was planning, Sara had no doubt that Gwen had approved every detail. Maybe even added some sadistic details of her own.

But, what?

Sara started pacing the cabin again, this time to work her brain instead of her glutes.

Post-9/11, explosions and bombs had not become ordinary in American life, but neither were they wholly unexpected. The shock value had diminished with each attack. Mass killings, shooting sprees, school shootings—all of these attacks still horrified Americans, but by the following week or month, they would resume their regular lives until news came of the next attack.

Sara could imagine that Dash was aware of the diminishing returns of these sudden acts of violence. Every time she tried to put herself inside his head, she came out thinking that what Dash really wanted to do more than anything else was to make a name for himself.

Which brought her back to Michelle.

Which brought her back to a biological attack.

If you wanted an agent that scared the shit out of people, anthrax, with its 90 percent mortality rate, was highly effective. The 2001 Amerithrax attack had paralyzed the postal service and parts of government. The spores could be aerosolized, but person-to-person transmittal was not going to happen. Also, because of the earlier attacks, finding a source bacterial strain was nearly impossible.

Botox was another option, but you'd need to raid every single plastic surgeon's office in America, and then you'd still end up only having enough to kill a handful of people. And you would have to inject them individually, so—

Sara paced in a circle.

She mentally flipped through her basic *how nature can murder you* knowledge from medical school. Rickettsiaceae, Bunyaviridae, Marburg, Chlamydophila psittaci—all incredibly dangerous and all almost impossible to weaponize. Vaccines, antibiotics and quarantine procedures deprived most of these viruses and bacteria from infecting multitudes.

Dash would want multitudes.

There were so-called select agents such as ricin, staphylococcal enterotoxin B, botulinim toxin, saxitoxin and myriad mycotoxins. But the possession, transfer and use of these organisms was heavily regulated by the Select Agent Program. Not that a regulatory body was necessary. Most of the toxins could be whipped up in the average kitchen. You didn't need a secret greenhouse to cover your tracks. And you didn't really need a sophisticated toxin to make a huge impact.

In 1984, a rogue faction of the Rajneeshee had easily synthesized enough *Salmonella enterica* Typhimurium to sicken over 750 people in the state of Oregon. In Chicago, in 1982, a still-unidentified poisoner had laced Tylenol capsules with potassium cyanide and forever altered the way medications were packaged.

Sara considered the Structure where Tommy had died. At least two stories tall. An open main floor, a balcony ringing the second floor. Stairs up the middle.

Could anthrax be inserted into an air conditioning unit?

If that was possible, someone would've tried it by now.

Legionellosis occurred naturally in fresh water.

Exposure was hit-or-miss, not person-to-person and the bacterium *only* had a 10 percent mortality rate.

"Crap," Sara repeated.

Right back at the beginning again.

She had to stop pacing before her muscles cramped. She couldn't do another lunge. She was out of lyrics except the one she couldn't recall about the waitress working at the bar. Only Will could tell her the name of the song. She would hum it, and he would tell her that she couldn't hum, and in the end, he would guess the song anyway.

Sara pressed her fingers into her eyes.

She could not let herself fall into another crying jag. She had passed the stage of longing for Will and had returned to worrying about him. Had he seen the heart she had left for him at the motel? Did he know about the code inside the medication list?

Tessa should be in Atlanta by now. Sara wanted her sister to hold Will. No one ever really held him. Sara wanted Tessa to tell him that everything was going to be okay. She wanted—needed—her mother to wrap Will into the family to protect him because with every passing hour, Sara found herself closer to accepting the fact that she was not going to make it home to any of them.

"Sir." Lance was outside the cabin door. Sara heard him shuffle to his feet. She hadn't known him to take a break in the last two days.

As usual, whatever Dash told him was too low for Sara to hear. His soft murmurs made her miss Will's deep, masculine tone even more.

Lance said, "Understood, sir."

Sara's ears strained as she listened for the key sliding into the padlock. She was as anxious to go for a walk outside as her dogs were when Sara got home from work.

Finally, the padlock clicked. The door opened. Dash stood on the log that served as a step. His sling was crooked. His hand was too low. "Dr. Earnshaw, I'm about to take lunch with my family. My little girls have specifically requested your presence."

Sara wanted to kiss each and every one of his daughters.

She pulled up her toga and stepped down into the sunlight. The sweat on her skin turned to steam in the heat. She had given up longing for fresh clothes. Right now, she'd settle on any part of her body being immersed in clean water.

Dash adjusted the sling. The strap had worn a spot on his neck. He said, "I've heard our children are not responding to your ministrations."

"They're not responding to the medications," Sara told him. "Are you sure they're legitimate? The black market isn't always—"

"I appreciate your concern, Dr. Earnshaw. Our source wouldn't sell us bogus goods."

Our source.

Sara wondered if the source was Beau. If Beau was in custody. If Will knew that Sara was doing her damnedest to reach out to him.

"Whoa there," Dash said.

Lance had stumbled. Sara did a double-take as he righted himself. Her sentry looked like he should be on his back. Pale complexion, heavy eyelids, shortened breaths. She had heard him running down to his makeshift toilet most of the night.

Sara continued her walk toward the clearing. Lance should really see a doctor. Dysentery killed around one hundred thousand people a year.

Dash said, "Gwen tells me that Adriel had a fitful night."

"I'm worried that the children are developing a secondary issue. Some kind of virus or bacterial infection." She ducked as Dash reached past her, but he was only pushing away a branch. "I'd like to check on them again."

"I'll make sure you have as much time in the bunkhouse as you need."

"Thank you." Sara heard her voice crack with gratitude. She cared about the children, but the thought of being freed from her cabin cell was elating. "Benjamin, especially, is not doing well."

"Gwen would say *suffer the children.*"

Sara had seen proof that Gwen didn't care who suffered, so long as it served Dash's purpose.

He said, "If God does exist, and He knows about the suffering of our precious lambs, then He is no God that I would seek to know."

Sara's mother would've found it hilarious that Sara was on the other side of this argument. "God has given us the tools to help all of them, but they're being denied access."

He laughed. "Your feistiness is one of the reasons I like having you around, Dr. Earnshaw."

Sara looked at the ground so that he would not see her eyes roll. She'd known he'd eventually get around to calling her feisty.

They had reached the clearing. She could feel the sun baking her bare shoulder. Women were tending pots over open fires because they were always cooking or boiling sheets and clothes and the endless number of cloth napkins. Gwen stood with her hands on her hips, barking orders to frightened-looking minions. Sara felt her stomach clench at the sight of her. If the woman really was a nurse, she would have known exactly what she was doing when she deprived Tommy of a peaceful end to his short life.

Dash said, "Dr. Earnshaw. You remember my lovely little ladies."

The girls were already seated at one of the long, communal picnic tables. Sara ran through their names—Esther, Charity, Edna, Grace, Hannah and Joy of the Wary Eye.

Their manners were impeccable as they simultaneously offered, "Good afternoon, Dr. Earnshaw."

Grace, the talkative one, excitedly scooted down the bench so that Sara could sit beside her. She practically trilled when her wish was granted. Sara stroked the girl's wispy hair. She saw two small indentations in the skin of her forehead. Old chicken pox scars.

Dash said, "Thank you, sisters."

The women from the fires had approached with the meal. Steak for Dash, bowls of stew for the girls, and a plate of cheese, crackers and fruit for Sara. Her stomach growled, but the thought of eating more cheese made her tongue feel thick in her mouth.

Grace asked, "Dr. Earnshaw, where did you meet your husband?"

"At the hospital where I worked." Sara felt her lips part in surprise. She had answered the question without thinking, and she had answered it incorrectly. She had met Jeffrey at a high school football game.

She had met Will at the hospital.

"What were you wearing?" Grace asked.

"Uhm," Sara felt weepy again. She chewed a cracker to give herself time to recover. "At hospitals, doctors wear scrubs. Green pants and a matching shirt."

"And a white coat," Esther said. She'd remembered Sara's

description of the white coat ceremony from the day before.

"Yes," Sara said. "And a white coat. And a stethoscope. And black rubber shoes because doctors stand around all day and our feet hurt."

Grace steered the conversation back to her favorite topic. "Did you wear a wedding dress when you went to get married at the core house?"

"Courthouse," Joy said, using the *you stupid idiot* tone that Sara had often adopted with own little sister. "It's where the judge is. He can marry people."

"Papa Martin's going to the courthouse," Edna said. She had a serious look on her face. "The judge is going to make it so that he won't ever come back."

Dash cleared his throat. He shook his head at Edna.

Sara made a mental note to drive herself crazy with that new factoid when she was locked up later. Martin Novak was the obvious proxy for *Papa Martin*. The bank robber was going to be sentenced at the courthouse in a few weeks. Sara knew from Faith's grumblings that Novak had spent time with an anti-government group on the southern border. If Martin Novak was Gwen's father, then her marriage to Dash would've conferred upon him an enormous amount of legitimacy. It also meant that Gwen would have been steeped in the racist ideology of the IPA for most of her life.

Grace sniffed to let everyone know her feelings were hurt. Her bottom lip rolled out. "I was only asking about her dress."

Sara smoothed down Grace's hair. She thought about Will's favorite black dress. His pleased look every time she went to the effort of grooming and shaving and plucking and wearing heels for him.

Actually, anytime Sara made an effort especially for Will, he was happy.

She told Grace, "I wore a regular dress, but it had pretty little flowers stitched here," she indicated the neckline. "He likes—liked—me to wear my hair down, so I left it on my shoulders even though it was very hot outside. And I wore high heels that pinched my toes."

"How high?" the question had rushed out of Joy's mouth. She blushed. "I mean, because you're tall. Men don't like that. Is what I hear."

"The right men do," Sara told her, a lesson that had been hard-learned during her teen years as she'd waited for the boys to catch up to her height. "And the right man isn't intimidated by a woman who's comfortable with who she is."

"Amen." Dash had freed his hand from the sling so he could cut his steak. The knife was long with a serrated blade.

Sara wondered if they counted the silverware when the table was cleared.

Grace said, "I want to wear a white dress to my wedding, with flowers and horses."

Joy rolled her eyes.

"And ice cream." Grace giggled.

Dash said, "You'll get ice cream tonight."

There was a chorus of cheers.

He told Sara, "We're having a celebration to mark the completion of our greatest achievement."

His sly smile said he knew that he had her attention.

He said, "Tomorrow is a very important day for us."

Sara did not give him the satisfaction of asking the obvious question.

"Little ones, listen to Daddy." Dash jabbed his fork into the potato. "You must put us all in your thoughts tonight. Enjoy the celebration and the ice cream, but understand that what we are about to embark on is a serious mission. Everything we've been working toward for the last three years comes down to tomorrow."

Three years?

He said, "Daddy and his men are going to go out into the wicked world, and we're going to remind them what the Framers of the Constitution had in mind when they sat down and wrote that glorious document."

Grace said, "One nation under God."

"Exactly," Dash confirmed, though the line was from the Pledge of Allegiance, not the Constitution. "The country needs to be shocked back into its senses. It is time to send the message. We have gotten so far off track that the white man doesn't know his place anymore."

He forked a mound of potato into his mouth. Obviously, he wasn't finished with his speech, but he wasn't content to play the game without Sara.

She cleared her throat. "What kind of message?"

He took his time drinking from the glass of water. "The Message will make it clear that the white man will not be conquered. Not by any other race. Not by a certain type of woman. Not by anyone or anything."

Sara waited for the real Dash to make his appearance. She saw the early indications in his cheekbones, which got sharper, and his skin, which blanched with zeal.

He told Sara, "Those people, those mongrels, are trying to breed us out of existence. They're infiltrating our culture with their music and their easy morals. They're taking advantage of our women. Selling them a false bill of goods about who they are, where their place is in society."

"Like Michelle," Edna said.

"Yes!" Dash slammed his fist into the table. The mask had fully dropped. "Michelle is a living example of the kind of woman whose selfish and hedonistic choices are destroying the natural order. They have to be made an example of. Witches used to be burned in this country."

Wrong again. No witches were burned during the Salem trials. They were either hanged or pressed to death.

"It's a man's job to decide what's best for his family." Dash banged the table again. "Just look at what got us here. White men wielding white power have protected white society for thousands of years."

Sara bit her lip so that she would not antagonize him.

Dash seemed to take note of her reticence. He wiped his mouth with one of the cloth napkins. He slipped back into character, smiling at Sara. "I'm not racist. I'm for *my* race. I'm not sexist. I'm for *my* gender." He shrugged, as if the logic held up. "The white man is being pushed aside. Our benevolence, our generosity, is leading us to the brink of extinction. We ceded too many rights to women, to the negro and the brown man. We dangled the hope of opportunity, and they took too much for their own advantage."

The girls were all looking up at their father as if he was delivering the Sermon on the Mount. To Sara, it sounded more like Neo-Nazi pop-psychology. Dash had stumbled upon one of the many vulnerabilities in *the contact hypothesis*. Levels of prejudice were generally reduced when reasonable people shared interpersonal contact. It was hard to hold on to a stereotype about an entire race when you were face to face with an individual who disproved your prejudice. One of the biggest obstacles to success was the denial of the opposing group's equal status to your own.

"Dr. Earnshaw." Dash put down his fork. He rested his elbows on the table. "You are a woman of science. You understand from your history books that every major leap in history, from the Industrial Revolution to the Digital Age to the Internet Age to whatever comes next, was made possible by white men."

Sara could think of multiple facts to contradict him, but there was no use arguing with a person who would not accept basic truths—another hindrance to the contact hypothesis.

"Even our mastery of technology is a double-edged sword. Jobs that men do are becoming obsolete." Dash pointed his finger at Sara. "The number one occupation for men without college degrees is driving vehicles. What's going to happen when self-driving cars and trucks take over the roads? Technology, innovation, education. White men are being deprived of the dignity of a paycheck. When women control the purse strings, men are demoralized. They turn to alcohol and pills. They leave their families, abandon their children. We cannot let that happen."

Sara guessed respecting and appreciating your wife was not an option.

Dash wasn't finished. "American politicians have spent the last two hundred years trying to accommodate and appease the black and brown man. Republican, Democrat, Libertarian, Independent—they all do it. We give the mongrels schools and they want white schools. We let them ride the bus and they want to sit in the front. We pay them to entertain us and they try to shove their opinions down our damn throats."

"Daddy," Grace whispered, as if swearing was the worst of his crimes.

"Accommodate, accommodate, accommodate." Dash had started banging the table again. "There's not enough clean water and air and food to go around. Not everybody can live in a nice house with a big TV. Letting the mongrels wrongly believe that they are entitled to what the white man has is exactly why we are at this inflection point. We cannot let them take our power."

Another loophole in the contact hypothesis—the fear of competition.

He said, "This is why the Framers of the Constitution specified the right to bear arms in the Second Amendment. So we can take up arms and tell the government that they are wrong. White men were the only men endowed with those rights. Our lives are the only lives that matter."

Sara bit her lip. The Framers had not written the Second Amendment. They had devised the process by which the Constitution could be amended.

He said, "The focus of our government has at its own peril turned away from nurturing the white family. It's basic economics. If you take care of us, then everything else will fall into place. There are enough scraps for the rest of them. You're a doctor. You know the scientific facts. Superior genetics preordained the white man to lead the tribes of the world. We cannot allow ourselves to become relegated to second- or even third-class citizens."

Sara could not let that one go. Medical history was riddled with this crackpot nonsense. The study of humors, blood-letting, phrenology, female hysteria. None of it was harmless. The so-called *science* of the American eugenics movement had inspired the atrocities of Nazi Germany. Will's severe dyslexia was the type of disability that would have qualified him for forced sterilization or outright murder.

She told Dash, "It would really suck to be treated like a minority, wouldn't it?"

"You're making fun, but you're hitting my point exactly. White women with their abortion and their birth control and their careers are choosing their own selfish desires over the propagation of the race. Miscegenation, inter-breeding mongrels, whatever you want to call it. Every problem this country faces can be boiled down to the coming doom of the Great Replacement."

His eyes glowed as he said the words. Sara could see where a person as angry as Dash, as isolated and alienated, would think of his philosophy of hatred as the solution to their problems.

It's not your fault, brother. It's everybody else.

"My ladies." Dash made sure his girls were paying attention. "Listen carefully, because this is the most important lesson that Daddy will ever teach you. The races fall into a pyramid. The white man is always at the top, then as his subordinate you will find the white woman, who need only serve one master. Below, you have your various races. Not every person on this earth is equal."

"That truth isn't self-evident?" Sara invoked the opening lines of the Declaration of Independence. "I thought all men were created equal?"

He wagged his finger in her direction. "You don't want to argue the Constitution with me, Dr. Earnshaw."

Sara held back a pained sigh. Dash was a stupid man's idea of how a smart man sounded. And his philosophy didn't matter. His noxious racism and sexism and xenophobia did not matter. What mattered was the greenhouse, the Structure, the Message he was planning to send.

Everything we've been working toward for the last three years comes down to tomorrow.

Sara asked, "What are you going to do about it?"

"The Message, that's what we're doing about it. There will be great sacrifices, and I always mourn the loss of life, but we have got to accept losses if we are going to make true and meaningful change. The enablers, the mongrels, they grow like weeds and periodically, we have to cut them down." Dash shook his head. "It's terribly sad, but it's the natural order of things. Sometimes you have to cut back a rosebush to make a beautiful flower."

Sara felt the threat behind his flowery language. "How many lives will be lost?"

"Multitudes. So many will be dead that I doubt historians will be able to tally a final number." Dash retrieved his fork and knife. He cut into the steak. "I'll tell you what, Dr. Earnshaw. I am a man of my word. I said you'll be freed and I meant it. We'll need a witness to the Message. I think an articulate, thoughtful lady such as yourself will make a persuasive argument on our behalf."

Sara tried not to fixate on the fact that the defining trait of a witness was survival.

Was he giving her false hope?

Joy asked, "Daddy, when will we know if the Message worked?"

"You'll know when you know." This came from Gwen. She was standing behind Edna, her fingers digging into the girl's shoulders. Her dour demeanor put a look of trepidation on her children's faces. "I want these plates cleaned or no one will get ice cream tonight."

The girls obediently picked up their spoons and started to eat.

Gwen wrung her hands in her apron as she sat down. She was eating the same food as the girls, but on a plate instead of in a bowl. Sara noticed a rash on her hands. She had managed to rub the skin raw with her apron.

Sara hated the thought of talking to Gwen, but she asked, "Is Benjamin any better?"

Gwen's lips snapped into a straight line. She was no longer trying to hide the hostility she clearly felt toward Sara. "The Lord will decide his fate."

"I might need to adjust his medications." Sara offered, "I can re-examine all of the children. I'd be happy to help wash them down, change sheets, anything to make them more comfortable. I'm sure you're tired."

"I'm not tired." Gwen picked up her spoon. "You will return to your cabin where you belong."

Dash said, "I've told Dr. Earnshaw that she can spend as much time as she likes inside the bunkhouse."

Gwen's fist tightened around the spoon. Her eyes locked with Dash's.

Was she jealous?

Dash said, "Gwendolyn, let's remember that Dr. Earnshaw is a guest here. We should make use of any help she offers."

His tone was enough to send Gwen into an angry silence. She shoveled food into her mouth so quickly that the sauce dripped down her chin. Her children absorbed her mood. Some of them looked like they wanted to cry. Grace's bottom lip started to tremble.

Sara gave in to a desire to punish Gwen for the misery she brought. "Girls, you know how I met my husband. Do you know how your mother met your father? I bet it's a very romantic story."

Gwen's spoon hovered between the plate and her mouth.

Sara felt regret warm her face. The question was meant to be shitty, but the math made it cruel. Joy was fifteen. Gwen was in her early thirties. Dash had passed forty a few years ago.

"Well." Dash adjusted his sling, though judging by the way he'd moved his arms, he no longer needed it. "That's a funny question, isn't it, my little ladies?"

The girls silently waited. They had clearly never heard the answer before.

Dash said, "We were high school sweethearts. What do you think of that?"

Grace gave a dramatically long sigh. To a young girl, the idea was romantic, but she wasn't considering the age difference. The only way Dash would've been in high school at the same time as Gwen was if he was working on the staff. There was nothing romantic about statutory rape.

Dash said, "Papa Martin introduced us. Isn't that right, my darling?"

Martin Novak.

The bank robber was in his sixties. Dash would've been like a son to him. And then Novak's son had married his underage daughter.

"We were on a beach," Dash told the girls, contradicting his high school story. "Your mother was walking along the water. The waves were lapping at her feet. The sun was behind her, and I thought it made her look like she was wearing a halo." He winked at Sara. "She hasn't taken it off since."

Sara swallowed what felt like a mouthful of glass. She asked Dash, "I'd like to go to the bunkhouse, if that's okay?"

Gwen's spoon dropped onto her plate with a loud clatter.

"That's fine, Dr. Earnshaw." Dash looked at Gwen as he spoke. "Joy, escort Dr. Earnshaw, please. Your mother and I have to talk through the plans for tonight's celebration."

"Yes, Daddy." Joy led the way to the bunkhouse, her head down, her eyes on her feet. Sara kept a few paces behind her. She felt disgusted by her own behavior. Gwen was fair game, but her daughters were innocent. Sara was not normally the type of person who deliberately hurt other people. Then again, she was not the sort of doctor who wished her patients dead.

Which was no excuse for what had just happened. Sara thought about how to apologize to Joy. Of all the children, she would've been hyper aware of the implications.

Before Sara could get a word out, Joy mumbled, "She's worried."

Sara guessed she was referring to Gwen. "About Adriel?"

Joy shook her head, but didn't explain further.

"You know," Sara said. "I just realized that Benjamin is the only little boy I've seen on this side of the Camp. Are there more on the other side?"

"Some little ones." Joy was still keeping her voice low, though no one was close by. "Daddy sends them away when they turn twelve."

Sara nodded, her heart pounding, because she could think of only one reason why a grown man would send away all of the boys before they reached the age of puberty.

He didn't want the competition.

Sara asked, "Do you know where they go?"

"Arizona, so they can train for the war."

Arizona. All the pieces that put Martin Novak into the frame were falling into place. Sara prayed that Will and Faith were finding the same clues. The bank robber was in custody, looking at spending the rest of his life in prison. If there was a deal to be made, now was the time.

Joy stopped at the sink outside the bunkhouse. She turned on the water for Sara. "Are they going to die?"

Sara understood she was talking about the eleven children in the bunkhouse. "I haven't figured out what's wrong, but I'm working on it."

Joy started to speak, but her face contorted in pain. She pressed her hand to her stomach. She leaned back against the shower stall. "My tummy hurts."

"Is it your period?"

She blushed the shade of a tomato.

"Sweetie, it's nothing to be ashamed of. It's natural. It's terrible, but it's natural." She rubbed Joy's arm, trying to get a response. "I can give you some Advil for the pain."

"It's not—" The sentence was interrupted by a torrent of vomit flooding out of her mouth.

Sara jumped away, but not quickly enough to save her shoes. She looked toward the picnic table for Gwen, but the girl's mother was angrily dressing down one of the cooking women. The younger girls sat at the table with their heads bowed, trying to disappear into the scenery.

"Let's go inside." Sara helped Joy up the stairs. The bunkhouse was empty but for the sick children. Sara wondered where the three women had gone. She supposed they had taken their lunch breaks. The timing could work out for Sara. Joy was old enough to notice what was going on inside of the Camp.

"Here." Sara helped Joy climb onto an empty cot. She asked, "Can you tell me what's hurting?"

Joy clutched her stomach in response.

Sara took the girl's blood pressure, which was low, and her temperature, which was normal. She listened to Joy's chest and bowels. She checked her pupils. The girl could barely keep her eyes open. Her throat clicked as she tried to swallow.

Sara asked, "Did you have the measles before?"

She nodded.

"I'll be right back." Sara found a pitcher of water and filled a glass. She glanced around the room. Most of the children were sleeping. The ones who were awake watched her carefully.

Joy tried to sit up, but dizziness immediately pulled her down to the bed. Sara helped her drink from the glass. Her jaw kept clenching in pain. Her hand was still clutching her stomach.

There were several tests that Sara could order in any hospital that would likely tell her what was wrong with Joy, but none of them were currently at her disposal.

"Joy." Sara sat down on the cot beside her. "I need you to talk to me."

"I don't—" Her tears started to fall in earnest. She was clearly scared. "I'm sorry I got sick on you."

"I'm just glad it wasn't spinach. That's the worst."

Joy didn't smile.

"How long have you been feeling bad?"

"Since . . ." She closed her eyes as another wave of pain shot through her belly. "Since last night."

"You're sure it's not your period?"

She shook her head.

"Are you sexually active?"

Joy became a study in mortification. "I haven't—I mean, I wouldn't. No, ma'am. The boys aren't allowed around us and Daddy—" She vehemently shook her head.

Sara had been lied to about sexual experience almost as many times as she'd been puked on. "I'm going to press down here, okay? Tell me if anything hurts."

Joy watched Sara's hands move around. She blushed furiously when the exam moved below her bikini line. There was no speculum to do a pelvic, and as much as Sara despised Gwen, she wasn't going to perform one without the mother's permission.

At least not for another half hour.

Ectopic pregnancy was always Sara's first concern with a girl Joy's age. Having experienced the same disastrous complication herself, she knew the consequences of not acting quickly. Appendicitis was a close second. Ovarian cyst. Bowel obstruction. Kidney stone. Twisted fallopian tube. Tumor. All would require diagnostic tools that Sara did not have, and surgery that she was in no position to perform. "I need to talk to your mother."

"No!" Joy sat up, panicked. She grabbed onto Sara, light-headed from the drop in her blood pressure. "Please, let me stay here for a minute. Please."

She was scared of her mother, which made Sara scared for all of Gwen's children.

"It's all right." Sara gently helped Joy lie down. "Has your mother hurt you, Joy?"

The girl's eyes watered with tears. "She gets mad, is all. We don't—sometimes we don't do what we're supposed to do, and that makes it harder for her. She has a lot of—a lot of responsibilities."

Sara stroked the girl's hair. "Has your father ever—"

"Am I—will I be all right?" Joy kept clutching her stomach. "Please, tell me. Why does it hurt so bad?"

Sara felt her pediatrician's instincts ringing like an alarm. In any other setting, she would be on the phone to children's services, making sure that Joy did not go back to her parents until there was a thorough investigation.

Unfortunately, Sara was not in a normal setting, and she had no ability to control anything but how she responded to this scared child.

She told Joy, "You probably ate something that didn't agree with you."

This was unlikely, as the girls all seemed to eat the same thing at every meal and only Joy was showing symptoms.

"Are you—" Joy was still terrified. "Are you sure?"

"I think what you need is some rest, and then you'll feel better. Okay?"

Joy relaxed into the cot, eyes closed.

Guilt weighed on Sara. Normally, she would've been honest with a patient of Joy's age. Sara would have told her that she wasn't sure what was going on, but she was going to find out what was causing the problem and do everything she could to make it better. But this was not a normal situation and there was no way to find out what was wrong other than to wait for the bug to resolve or for more symptoms to appear.

Sara could at least make herself useful to the other children. She told Joy, "I'll be over here, okay?"

"Michelle—" Joy looked like she wanted to grab the word and shove it back into her mouth.

Sara sat down on the cot. She tried to keep the desperation out of her tone. "Did you see her?"

"I—" Joy tried again. Her eyes closed. She turned her head away from Sara. "I'm sorry."

Sara had crossed a lot of lines since being kidnapped, but this one felt different. The girl was scared. She knew something important, and she knew that telling Sara would get her into a great deal of trouble.

Sara said, "It's okay, sweetheart. Try to sleep."

"She's—" Joy stopped to swallow. "Behind the—behind here."

Sara tried to measure her response. "In the glass house?"

Joy shook her head. "In the woods. Mama left her in the woods."

At first, Sara did not understand what she was being told. Her body reacted before her mind could. There was a shaking sensation that traveled from her heart and out to her limbs. The words "left her in the woods" echoed alongside it.

Chained to a post? Left to scorch in a metal box? None of these scenarios seemed beneath a woman who would suffocate a young man to death.

"Try to sleep." Sara pressed her lips to Joy's head. "I'm going to get some air."

Joy let out a heavy breath.

Sara walked through the bunkhouse. There were two doors; one at the front, one at the rear. She opened the back door. No stairs, just a four-foot drop. She jumped down to the ground. Her spattered sneakers disappeared into the thick prairie grass. She lifted her toga and walked into the forest.

Birds chirped. Sara looked around. No guards in deer stands. No young men with rifles, knives, pistols. The steady hum of the generator told her that the greenhouse was to the right. Sara went to the left.

Her nose picked up on the unmistakable odor of rotting meat.

The body of Michelle Spivey was about thirty yards behind the bunkhouse. She was lying on her left side, snarled in an overgrowth of brambles. Her spine was curved. Her left knee was bent. Her right leg jutted out behind her. She looked as if someone had tossed her into the woods. Thrown her out as if she was trash. Her right arm was draped over her head, hand clawing at the air. She was fixed in place, the muscles slowly depleting of oxygen as rigor mortis paralyzed her body. First in the eyelids, then the jaw and neck. Given her age and muscle mass, along with the extremely high temperature, Michelle had likely been dead anywhere from two to four hours.

Sara looked back toward the bunkhouse.

The door had closed. No one was coming. No one had even noticed that she was gone.

Running was an option, but Sara was not going to run right now. Michelle Spivey had been broken by the time the car accident brought Sara into her world. The woman had barely spoken more than a few sentences. She had stabbed a man to death. She had served as Dash's compliant accomplice. But she had also been a mother, a wife, a doctor, a human being. This was a time for some sort of meditation, a kind word that acknowledged Michelle's life.

Sara was not going to do that, either.

She got down on her knees. She grabbed the collar of Michelle's dress and ripped open the back. The woman's ribs protruded like whalebone. Red welts had rubbed into the thin layer of skin covering her vertebrae. She had been carved into with a knife, punched repeatedly in the kidneys. The yellowing bruises indicated that at least a week had passed since she had been beaten. The wounds had scabbed. The burns were more recent.

Sara knew what a cigarette burn looked like.

She ripped the dress the rest of the way down. Michelle's underwear was stained. She had started to leak. The intense heat was boiling the fat from her skin and oiling the ground beneath her.

The entire left side of Michelle's body was such a dark, reddish purple that she looked as if she had been dipped halfway into a vat of ink. When the heart stops beating, blood always settles to the lowest point. *Livor mortis* was the Latin phrase used to describe the color of the skin as heavy blood cells sank through the serum. The process sped up with heat. The stain that went down Michelle's hip and leg, up to the arm that she'd laid her head on, indicated that the woman had died exactly where she'd been lying in the woods.

Tossed here like trash.

Michelle was bloated from the bacteria swirling inside of her body. The heat hadn't done the worst of the damage. Gwen had lied about giving Michelle antibiotics. Or maybe the antibiotics hadn't worked. Either way, Gwen was responsible. Sara knew exactly who had left Michelle to die out here.

Her passing would have been agonizing. Falling in and out of consciousness, disoriented, perhaps hallucinating, burning with fever. Sepsis had swollen her abdomen so much that the skin had cracked. Alongside the fissures, Sara could make out the faint stretch marks where twelve years ago, Michelle's belly had expanded to accommodate the baby she was carrying inside her womb.

Ashley.

Sara remembered the child's name from the newspaper article.

She closed her eyes and turned her face up to the sun. The heat drilled open her pores. Sara tried to feel something, anything, but found herself numbed by the relentless brutality. There was no way for Sara to accurately gauge how long it had taken Michelle to die out here. The place seemed to have been chosen to maximize her suffering. Far from the Camp. Tossed onto the thorns of a bramble bush. Beaten and battered. Pain literally slicing open her body.

Behind Sara, the bunkhouse door banged open.

She ducked down her head. Sara was hidden by the overgrowth, but she didn't know for how long. She worked quickly, examining Michelle as closely as she could, checking for chemical discolorations or some indication of what the scientist was doing inside the greenhouse. She smelled her hair. Looked at her fingernails. Rigor had sealed shut her jaw, but Sara checked inside her gums, her nose and ears.

"Dr. Earnshaw?" Dash had cupped his hands to his eyes. The sunlight narrowed his field of vision. "Are you back here?"

Sara dug into the pockets of Michelle's dress, slipped her fingers around her bra, the band of her underwear. She was about to give up when she noticed the positioning of Michelle's left hand. The fingers were folded in, but the thumb was straight out in a hitchhiker's pose.

Death grips were extremely rare. They came when a chemical reaction inside the body was triggered by abject terror. Michelle had been given ample time to contemplate her death. She had placed her hand under her bent knee, forcing the fingers to stay closed, of her own volition.

There was something written on her palm.

"Dr. Earnshaw?" Dash was turning his head slowly, scrutinizing the forest in sections.

Sara leaned over Michelle's body to get a better look at her hand. Vomit slid up her throat. The smell of rotting tissue was noxious. Sara held her breath. Up close, she thought maybe Michelle had written two words, or one really long one. Black marker. Only the bottom edges of the letters were exposed. Michelle's fingers covered the rest.

"Where are you, Dr. Earnshaw?" Dash's voice was calm, but she did not trust it to stay that way.

Sara picked at Michelle's fingers, trying to pry them open. She was sweating too much. The fingers were too swollen. Sara couldn't find purchase. Her only option was to break the rigor mortis in the wrist. The muscles had hardened like plastic. Sara gripped Michelle's fist and forearm and twisted each of her hands in opposite directions.

She was rewarded with a loud *snap*.

"Lance?" Dash had heard the noise. "Hey, brother. Do you mind coming out here with me?"

Sara clawed at Michelle's fingers. The nails folded back, but they would not budge. She tried pressing upward with her thumbs.

Dash jumped down from the bunkhouse door. A second set of feet hit the ground. Thirty yards away. Tall grass. Thick trees. He was talking to Lance. Sara was too panicked to understand him. Her heart was pounding. Her eyes felt shaky. She had to get Michelle's hand open. She had to read the words. She looked around for a stick or something that she could use to force them up. There was nothing.

Sara would have to use her mouth.

She bit at Michelle's clenched fingers, trying not to break open the skin.

"Dr. Earnshaw?" Dash called. Lance coughed. They were getting closer.

Sara caught the ball of Michelle's first knuckle between her front teeth.

She pulled back.

Snap.

Middle finger.

Snap.

Ring finger.

Snap.

"Dr. Earnshaw?"

Dash was standing several feet behind her. His voice sounded nasal. He had pinched together his nostrils to ward off the stench. Lance was behind him. He belched once, then vomited against a tree.

Dash's crushed nose turned his sigh into a honk. He said her name again, "Dr. Earnshaw?"

"She's dead." Sara had already folded herself over Michelle's body. She forced out a cry, feigning grief. "You let her die. She was all alone."

Dash told her, "I'm sorry you're upset. She was a flawed woman, but she redeemed herself in the end."

Sara tried to close Michelle's hand. The fingers would no longer hold their shape.

He said, "Let's not drag this out, okay? The smell is terrible and I—I said you could stay in the bunkhouse. Let's take you back now. It's cool in there and you can—"

Sara got to her feet.

"Doctor—" Dash called, but Sara was already jogging through the overgrowth toward the bunkhouse. She pulled herself up through the door. Gwen was standing inside. She looked anxious but she was always anxious.

Sara walked directly to the medicine cabinet. She found the rubbing alcohol. She stuffed a folded bed sheet under her arm and walked toward the front door.

"Dr. Earnshaw." Dash had taken off his sling so he could climb up to the floor. "If you could—"

Sara slammed the door closed behind her. She stepped over Joy's mess and headed straight for the outdoor shower. The latch wouldn't cooperate. She cursed until her shaking fingers managed to close it. She draped the clean sheet over the stall. She wrenched the cap off the rubbing alcohol and poured it straight into her mouth.

The bunkhouse door opened. Dash stood at the top of the stairs.

"Oh, sorry." He turned away from her, covering his eyes. "I was hoping—"

The rest of his sentence was lost to Sara swishing the alcohol between her teeth, trying to kill whatever bacteria she had picked up from Michelle's decaying flesh. She splashed the cool liquid onto her face, neck and hands.

"Dr. Earnshaw?" Dash tried for the hundredth time. "If we could just discuss—"

"Leave me alone." Sara struggled with her toga, cursing at the knot, the wadded-up material, the pain of getting out of the damn stupid thing.

Dash tried again. "I really must—"

"I said *leave me the fuck alone!*"

Sara turned on the water. She grabbed the soap.

Dash scampered down the stairs. So much for his white male pride when a woman was ready to rip his fucking head off.

Gwen opened the bunkhouse door. She glanced at Sara, then rushed after her husband.

Sara got the water as hot as she could stand it. She tried to generate lather with the lye soap. The grit felt like a million pieces of sand.

She waited for Lance to make an appearance, but he chose to stay inside with the children. Or with the air conditioning. Sara had caught sight of him as she'd jogged toward the bunkhouse. Lance had stared at her through heavy eyelids. His skin was pale. He had probably caught Joy's stomach bug. Unless there was something else going around the Camp.

Something that Michelle had been working on in the greenhouse.

Sara spat onto the floor of the shower. The rubbing alcohol still burned her gums. She opened her mouth and let the water hit the back of her throat. Her skin felt scalded. She was literally sweating underneath the spray of the shower.

Michelle Spivey had survived unspeakable horrors. She had been raped and beaten. She had been pressed into labor inside of the greenhouse. She had been left to rot to death in the heat. The infectious disease expert would have been intimately familiar with sepsis, the most common cause of death in people who have been hospitalized. Sara imagined the doctor had monitored her qSOFA score up until the end. The quick Sequential Organ Failure Assessment was a point system that rated blood pressure, respiration and mentation. The higher the score, the higher the risk of mortality. While Michelle probably hadn't had access to a blood pressure cuff, she could've monitored her own respiration and neurological symptoms. She would have known not only that death was coming, but what it would look like.

One of her last acts had been to find a black marker and write a message on the inside of her hand.

Two words.

Several possible meanings.

A coffin? A device to defeat telephone toll charges? A TV show or film? A type of experimental theater? An FDA warning? The briefcase that carried the nuclear codes?

Sara turned around, letting the sharp spray of water needle her scalp.

In computing, the term could be used to describe the transfer characteristics of a device whose inner workings are unknown. Or a type of software. Or a type of software engineer.

She ran her fingers through her hair, trying to break the knots.

In aviation, it referred to the recorder that was used to document the flight path data and the pilot's voices. The device was painted bright orange, but the common name was exactly the same two words that Michelle had written on her hand.

BLACK BOX.

Sara rubbed her face with her hands. What did Michelle mean? Why had she chosen those specific words? Sara had blown her chance to run, had risked her life, her safety, and for what? She was plagued by the same maddening question from before. Except now, there was a clock winding down on her search for the answer. Dash had told her as much himself.

The Message would be delivered tomorrow.

16

Tuesday, August 6, 2:50 p.m.

Will leaned his head against the car door as Interstate 85 rolled by. The hour-long taxi ride to exit 129 had brought on a wave of exhaustion. With every passing mile, he'd slumped farther down in the seat. His knees pressed into the partition between the front and rear seats of the car. His skull vibrated against the glass in the door. Before Sara, Will had never been in the back of a taxi. She had wanted to leave a party early. Their ride wasn't ready to go. She had called a cab. Will had climbed inside and nearly had a heart attack when he saw that the meter already had five dollars on it.

Which was why he had never been in a taxi before Sara.

Will made himself sit up straight. He scratched his jaw. The Brillo pad of his beard pricked at his fingertips. The unfamiliar roughness was a reminder that he had to slice himself off. The man who loved Sara could not save her. Jack Phineas Wolfe, disillusioned ex-soldier, pissed off at the world, was the man he would have to be for that job.

Will looked down at his hands. He pressed his thumb into his knuckle until a trickle of fresh blood came out.

Gerald would be Wolfe's first obstacle. If he could not persuade Dash's second-in-command that Wolfe was all in, then Gerald would probably point a gun at his face and pull the trigger.

Will didn't think it would go down like that. He'd banked some credit with Gerald during the warehouse mission. The fact that Wolfe had been willing to stab a security guard to death for fifteen grand was enough proof of concept.

Dash was going to be the real challenge. This close to pulling off whatever he was planning, the leader of the IPA would be highly paranoid, especially about a new recruit. Dash was a racist pedophile and a mass murderer. He had also inspired men as different as Robert Hurley and Adam Humphrey Carter. Will assumed that Dash was a classic con man, always looking for a weakness to exploit.

Will puzzled out Wolfe's vulnerabilities.

Pedophilia seemed like the most obvious way in, but the language of pedophiles was as intricate and arcane as Army lingo. The people who raped children were constantly evolving. They coordinated on the dark web. They were extremely careful in public. It wasn't as easy as saying that a child looked mature for her age.

Will gladly discarded the approach.

He thought about Faith's information on the IPA. They revered the military. Wolfe was a trained fighter with no more battles to wage. Maybe he felt beaten down by the system. He was desperate for money. Couldn't find a job, couldn't keep a woman. He was angry that his life had fallen into shit. Eager for a fight. Maybe he was a gambler who'd lost his life savings. He would be blaming everybody but himself.

Will silently shook his head.

A money-motivation was too easy. Dash would never trust a hired gun. He would want a warrior for the cause.

Beau Ragnersen was a man in search of a cause. That was why he had capitulated to Amanda, to Will, to Kevin, to anyone who shoved him in a direction. Beau hadn't really relaxed until Gerald had locked them inside the van. His shoulder pressed against Will's, four armed, anxious kids across from him. Everyone else had been wired, but Beau had fallen soundly asleep. His fidgeting and his sighing and his Charlie Brown shuffle were gone. Will had interpreted Beau's erratic behavior as a sign that the man was going to betray him. The truth was that Beau Ragnersen only felt whole when he was part of a unit. Like a lot of ex-soldiers, he was desperately looking for something to fill the hole that war had punched into his chest.

That was the same kind of desperation that would be key to Jack Wolfe infiltrating the IPA. Dash would want to fill the hole in Wolfe's chest. He would use racism or religion or whatever it took to bring Wolfe around to his side. With guys like that, it was never about *what* you believed. It was about *who* you believed.

Will looked down at his hands again. He rubbed his thumb along his bare ring finger. The pieces of Jack Wolfe that he had so carefully stitched together started to pull apart.

Will would do whatever it took to get Sara back. If that meant shooting more people, killing more people, then he was going to do it. He wasn't just fighting for himself. Sara's whole family was waiting for Will to bring her home. They were counting on him. Asking God to help him. Praying that Sara was unharmed.

Will had never prayed before. When he was a boy, the local church had sent a bus to the children's home every Sunday morning. Most of the kids jumped at the chance to get out of the house. Will had always stayed behind. The opportunity to be alone, even for a few hours, was more important to him than getting to drink purple Kool-Aid from tiny glasses and eat thin wafers.

Now, he tried to remember Cathy's prayer. She had spoken like she was writing a letter—

Dear Heavenly Father, we ask for your blessing in this time of need.

Will had known to bow his head, but he had looked to Tessa for further guidance. Her eyes had been closed, so Will had closed his eyes. She had kept silent, so Will had kept silent. The ritual of the prayer had been comforting. The soft cadence of Cathy's voice. The closeness of other people who cared about what he cared about.

This was what Will worried about as he held on to Cathy's small hand:

That he would not find Sara. That it would be his fault that her family would never see her again. That Gerald would kill him at the Citgo. That Dash would shoot him before he got to see Sara. That Michelle Spivey would recognize Will and wig out on him the same way she had with Carter. That Dash wouldn't kill Will right away because he wanted to make Sara watch him die.

Then there was the worst-case scenario:

Will would beat all of the odds, making it past Gerald, talking Dash into welcoming him into the fold. He would finally find Sara, but he wouldn't be able to help her because he was too afraid.

Will felt tortured by the fear that had gripped him at the scene of the car accident. He had been reaching into Sara's BMW, inserting the key into the glove box, when he'd seen Hurley holding a gun to Sara's head. Instead of reacting, instead of turning the key, grabbing his Glock and killing them all, Will had frozen.

Because he was afraid.

Will clenched his teeth. Major Jack Wolfe. Airborne. Two deployments to Iraq. Two DUIs. One restraining order from his last place of employment. Over $36,000 in credit card debt.

The taxi coasted onto the exit. Will recognized the logos for gas stations and fast-food restaurants. Exit 129 would take him into Braselton. 12.5 square miles spread across four counties, all of them within Atlanta's Metropolitan Statistical Area. Less than 10,000 inhabitants, 83 percent of them white, 4 percent living below the poverty line. One police station. Four cops. One hospital. One upscale winery. The terrain was lush and hilly. Most of it was still thickly forested, like every other Georgia town this far into the Appalachian Mountain chain. The Chattahoochee National Forest hovered at the top of the state like an upside-down umbrella.

The Citgo sign was two red lights away. Will listened to the taxi's engine idle at the stop. It was only now that it was too late that he let his mind wander into the worst worst-case scenario:

Dash could've been pretending to be knocked out at the car accident. He could've seen Will's face. He could know exactly what was coming at him and already be planning a way to neutralize the threat.

Will's thoughts spiraled down even lower:

Sara could already be dead.

The taxi driver pulled into the Citgo. There were four cars at the twelve pumps. Will recognized one of the men as a GBI agent from the southern region of the state. Faith's red Mini was parked in front of the Dumpster. She had a blanket over her shoulder. She was pretending to nurse a baby. Amanda would be inside the store using a cane, bent like an old woman to render herself virtually invisible. There were unmarked cars at each end of the road that ran in front of the gas station. Two agents were hidden in the woods behind the building.

Amanda hadn't been content to leave it at that.

Will had a GPS tracker inside the leather holster at his back. The slim chip of plastic was sewn inside the liner. The power was off in case he was searched for a signal again. Will had spent half an hour blindly reaching behind him and pressing the power button so that the motion was locked into his muscle memory.

He wasn't going to touch the damn thing unless he was looking directly at Sara. There was no guarantee that Dash was keeping her close by. For all Will knew, Sara could be stashed two hundred miles away. If he brought in backup too soon, she could be lost forever.

"This good?" the driver asked.

Will paid the man $120, which hurt like hell, even though it wasn't his own money. His legs were stiff when he climbed out of the car. He stretched out his spine, arms in the air. He adjusted his holster. He looked around, trying to spot Gerald. He looked at his watch.

3:02 p.m.

Another car pulled in to the station to fill up. Someone else went into the store. Will walked over to the air pump. He stuck his hands in his pockets. He kicked at the curb. He was wearing the same outfit that the kids from the warehouse seemed to favor. Black pants and long-sleeved shirt. Black combat boots. The idea had seemed like a good one until he stood out in the open. Given his height, muscle mass and complexion, he looked less like a ninja and more like a guy who was probably going to start shooting people.

"Wolfe?"

Will recognized Three from the day before. The kid had changed into shorts and an Usher concert T-shirt. His ride was a bright red Kia Soul. Not the best car to blend in, but it worked with the Usher vibe. If a cop pulled him over, Three would look like any other spoiled punk from town.

The kid told him, "Go inside the store. Wait by the back door."

Before Will could respond, Three peeled away.

The GBI agent at the gas pump got into his car and followed the red Kia toward the interstate.

Will walked toward the store. He could feel Faith's eyes following his progress. The building was a typical interstate convenience store, wide but not deep, with a low ceiling and glass along the front. Will smelled hot dogs roasting on rollers as soon as he opened the door. Amanda was beside the self-serve coffee machines. Her usual helmet of hair was messed up. Her reading glasses were low on her nose. She leaned heavily into her cane, pretending like she didn't know which button to press.

The kid behind the counter glanced up from his phone as Will walked by. Two was wearing a blue polo shirt with a red-and-orange Citgo triangle on the chest. He tilted his head, indicating the back of the store.

Will found the rear exit by the refrigerated drinks. He tried the handle. Locked. One of Will's many college jobs had been at a convenience store. He assumed there would be a long hall, a small office, and a cramped storage area. The emergency exit door would be alarmed, but you could trick the system with a magnet and a piece of gum.

He leaned against the cooler. Cold air wafted from the glass doors. He looked at his watch.

3:05 p.m.

"Young man?" Amanda called Two over to the coffee machine. She started lecturing him on how computers were ruining the world. She would have no way of knowing that Two was IPA. She was trying to justify her lingering presence in the store. Will knew Amanda kept a loaded Smith and Wesson five-shot inside a Crown Royal bag in her purse. She could draw the weapon almost as quickly as most agents could pull their Glocks from their side holsters.

Will heard two knocks on the door.

He knocked twice in return. He waited. The lock clicked open.

Will opened the door. Long hall. Small office. Cramped storage. Magnet on the exit door alarm sensor, but held in place with Scotch tape instead of gum. Probably smarter. Gum was never as sticky as you thought it was.

One was waiting for him outside. He was the youngest and shortest of the four, probably more dangerous because he had something to prove. They did not exchange words. He was holding out the wand, the one that checked for transmissions from trackers. Will held up his arms. He let the kid have his fun.

And it was clear that One was having fun. All of this Mission: Impossible drama was probably busting these kids' nuts. If adult Will didn't know what racist, criminal pieces of shit they were, kid Will would've been jealous.

One finished with the wand. He left the machine by the back door. He nodded for Will to follow him into the woods. Will stuck his hands into his pockets, the signal to the two agents hiding behind the trees that everything was good so far. Faith had gamed out the possible escape zones to within two miles. With the Citgo behind him, Will knew that the woods would lead into an L-shaped residential area. Two more chase cars were parked on the streets. That seemed like the most obvious place for Gerald to pick them up.

Sweat was dripping down Will's face by the time they reached Chardonnay Trace. He kept his hands in his pockets as he followed One across the road. The houses were big, with deep yards. The roar of traffic from the interstate had dampened. One picked up the pace, following the line of a fenced-in backyard, heading into another forest behind the neighborhood.

Still within the escape zone.

Will oriented himself by the beeping car horns on the main road. The aerial maps had shown a lot of clear-cutting for shopping centers and outlet malls. If they kept heading straight, they would find themselves in farmland.

Beyond that, Will was clueless.

One stopped beside a tree, took out his phone. He was looking at the longitude and latitude on a map. A pin showed that they were close to the right coordinates. He nodded for Will to follow him. Will looked up into the trees. The canopy was thick. A helicopter team wouldn't be able to see down into the forest. If the pilot dropped low enough to use the thermal imaging camera, One would take off, Will would have to chase him and Sara would be lost forever.

One dropped his phone into his pocket. A dirt bike was flat to the ground. Tao Tao DB20 110. Air-cooled, single cylinder four-stroke, street-legal, but no license plate. The plastic seat raked back like a fin over the rear wheel.

One had done a piss-poor job of covering the bike with leaves and broken limbs. He started clearing them off. Will didn't help him. He thought about taking his hands out of his pockets. The two agents behind the store would've followed them from a distance. They were on foot, but to Will's thinking, that was not the biggest problem.

Two helmets. One bike.

Will knew how to handle a bike. What worried him was the thought of One's arms gripping his waist while they rode through the forest. Whatever thing that was torn inside of Will's ribcage was not getting any better. He had four emergency aspirin in his pocket that Amanda had sealed in a plastic pouch. Will knew from experience that it would take at least half an hour for the medication to kick in.

One was a foot shorter than Will and at least fifty pounds lighter, most of it baby fat. If Will rode on the back of the bike, either the plastic fin would break off or the front wheel wouldn't touch the ground.

Pulling a Patrick Swayze helping Demi Moore at the pottery wheel would not be ideal for either of them. Will was mindful of the several inches that One through Four had kept between them in the van. They clearly had firm ideas about what gay looked like, and none of them were going to cross that line. At least not in front of their friends.

One's problem was Will's solution.

He scooped up a helmet. He asked One, "You gonna go butts to nuts with me on this thing, little Princess?"

One's mouth went slack. "No, man. Shit no. I'll hold on to the seat." He added another, "shit" to prove he was serious.

Will buckled the helmet strap tight under his chin. There was no guarantee he wouldn't hit a rut or spin out over a rise. If that happened, One would instinctively grab on to Will and Will would probably end up driving them into a tree.

One struggled to lift the one-hundred-pound bike. Will didn't help him, and not just because Jack Wolfe was a dick. If he was going to pop one of his ribs, it would not be to help this junior Nazi idiot save face.

The kid finally managed to lever the bike up onto two wheels. Will got on. He waited for One to get settled behind him. The muffler was directly under the seat, so it was going to be interesting to see what happened first: either One was going to fall off the bike or the flesh was going to melt off of his fingers.

Again, this was a One problem.

Will put the gear in neutral. He engaged the electric starter, glad he wasn't going to have to deal with a kick start. He revved the engine, letting it screech like a cat. If the agents in the woods had lost him, they would know where he was now. He was glad he wasn't the one who was going to have to tell Amanda that they had lost Will again.

One pointed into the woods. Will twisted the throttle about an eighth of an inch and slowly let out the clutch. The rear tire slid out. One's hands went to Will's shoulders, which was an option that had not occurred to either of them until now.

Will drove into the woods, leaning into the roller-coaster turns around the trees. He gave the throttle a little more throat. He used his fingers to coax out the clutch's sweet spot. The bike picked up speed as he ran through the gears. He wondered if the bike belonged to One. They would get to the end of this ride eventually. Faith would locate the dirt bike if she had to walk every inch of the forest. Amanda would crack the kid open like a walnut.

And Will would find Sara.

The bike caught air as they crested a hill. The forest peeled away. They were traveling through farmland, which gave way to more forest, then One pointed again and they were following the clear-cut strip for high-voltage power lines. Will gave up on worrying about the pain in his body. He let out the clutch, figuring the best way to endure the ride was to get it over with as quickly as possible. One's fingers dug into his shoulders. The kid's ass kept popping off the fin. Will was so intent on moving forward that he didn't register One furiously tapping his shoulder to slow down.

The road came up quickly. The bike lurched against the rear brake. One's face popped against the back of Will's helmet. He slid to a stop, used his heel to drop the kickstand, peeled his aching fingers off the grips.

One stumbled from the bike. His lip was bleeding. His face had gone white. He looked like he couldn't decide whether to throw up or piss himself.

Will took off his helmet. He counted three houses. The lots were at least five acres each. Will looked at his watch.

3:58 p.m.

Faith would be panicked. Amanda would be furious. Especially when she realized that he wasn't going to turn on his tracker.

"There he is." One wiped his mouth. Blood smeared across his chin.

Will looked up the road. Four was the only kid he hadn't seen today, but it wasn't Four who pulled up in a white van.

Gerald rolled down the window. He told Will, "In the back, Wolfe."

Will opened the rear doors. No seats, just a bunch of racks with painter's supplies. At least the air conditioning was on. Will climbed inside. One shut the doors. The big boy got to ride up in the front this time.

As with the other van, the windows were blacked out. There was a cooler with ice and water. Will drank two bottles in quick succession. He rubbed the ice along the back of his neck. He dug into his pocket and found the pouch of aspirin. The plastic bag was wet from his sweat. The tablets had turned mushy in the heat. He considered for a moment what all this moisture was doing to the battery in the tracker. He bit off a chunk with his teeth and washed it down with cold water.

Will closed his eyes. He leaned back his head. He gamed out what would happen when those doors opened again. Gerald was going to shoot him. Gerald was going to take him to Dash. Dash was going to shoot him. Dash was going to welcome him to the IPA. Sara was being held somewhere else. Sara was being held wherever they were taking him.

Dear Heavenly Father, we ask for your blessing in this time of need.

Will felt the temperature slowly drop to a bearable number. The rural feel of the terrain did not change. Gerald was using backroads, some paved, some gravel. Gravity told Will they were heading up. Or maybe Will had no idea and Gerald was driving around in circles.

Almost an hour had passed when the van finally stopped. The gear went into reverse. The van swung around, then the engine was cut. Will had heard dirt kicking into the side panels. They had left any semblance of a cleared road a few miles back.

5:03 p.m.

One opened the doors. Will felt like the sun was reaching into his brain. He squeezed his eyes closed. He scooted along the floor of the van until his feet found the edge of the bumper. Will could only look down at the ground as he waited for his eyes to adjust. The van wasn't the only vehicle that had driven in this area. Deep tire tracks indicated a box truck had recently backed into the grass.

A box truck had backed up to the motel where Sara had left him the message.

One said, "Cool, right?"

Will rubbed his jaw. He looked around.

Beside him, One did the same. He was something between a sponge and a shadow.

Will walked, so One walked. He had to double-step to keep up with Will's longer stride.

Will had to stop caring about One. They were clearly in a staging area. Five black vans were parked in a row. Two dozen AR-15s were in a rack. Three men were loading magazines, 55 grain, full metal jacket with a lead core and a gray, polymer-coated steel case. The FMJ didn't expand on impact like a hollow point, so you could hit your target, then accidentally hit another target downrange.

For unknown reasons, the cartridges were laid out in rows on top of terrycloth towels. The men handling them were wearing black nitrile gloves. The loaded magazines were handed off to more gloved men who packed them into plastic containers about the size of a file box. Eight boxes had been filled so far, about a thousand rounds each. Two men holding clipboards monitored the progress. Two more guys were carrying coolers filled with bottles of Gatorade up the hill. Another group was taking a break at a picnic table. They were all dressed in tactical black, all wearing gloves. Will counted sixteen men total, most of them in their mid-twenties with a couple of gray-haired older men ordering them around.

The air felt different. No one was joking around. They were doing serious work here. Will got the feeling they were ready to leave this place at a moment's notice.

But where, exactly, was this place?

They were definitely in the mountains. Trees were everywhere. Birds were chirping. A stream or a river was nearby. What caught Will's eye was a metal storage building just beyond the vans. The doors hung open. Sealed cardboard boxes were stacked inside. All the same size, about thirty inches square. All with packing slips in clear plastic pockets. All with the same number stamped onto the side.

4935-876

"Wolfe." Gerald had finished talking to a man with a clipboard. He waved Will over. "We're gonna put you straight to work, soldier. That good with you?"

Will grunted, lifting his chin.

Gerald said, "Dobie, you, too."

"Cool!" The kid Will had named One ran ahead of them.

Dobie.

Gerald kept a slower pace going up the hill. Will's fists were clenched. Everyone was armed. His Sig Sauer had ten in the magazine and one in the chamber, but Will would be dead before he could reach for his holster. He was getting that same shaky feeling he'd had at the car accident. What if Sara was at the top of the hill? What if he found her tied up? What if he found her dead? What if he didn't find her at all?

Will's hand went up to his cheek. The beard had turned into a talisman. All he had to do was rub it, and he changed into Jack Wolfe. "What's the kid's story?"

"Dobie?" Gerald watched him trying to navigate the hill. The kid's feet slipped in the grass. He jumped up and disappeared over the top. "He's like all of 'em. Young, dumb and full of come."

Will felt his teeth grit. He couldn't square the idiot kid with what he knew about groups like the IPA. Was Dobie a violent racist who wanted to kill all the Jews or was he just a rudderless young man who'd met the wrong people at the wrong time?

At this point, it was a distinction without a difference.

Gerald told Will, "We'll let you watch a few times before we put you in."

Will didn't ask what the *in* was, because he saw it for himself at the top of the hill.

Only the framing existed in the two-story wooden structure. Will could tell by the gray color that the fake building had been left to the elements for at least six months. Plywood served as the floor. There were openings to indicate doors, but no windows.

Safety railings marked the upstairs balcony. The stairs were open-backed, too skinny to be practical. They split into a T in the middle, feeding into either side of the balcony. There were cardboard bad guys with targets on them. A patchwork of tarps served as a ceiling. Two layers, one camouflage, the other thermal blocking to defeat heat-sensing cameras. A lot of work had gone into building and hiding the fake building. Will guessed the space was slightly larger than two regulation basketball courts.

He counted eight men standing watch, all suited up for a raid, only their eyes showing behind clear, plastic goggles. Five more men were already inside the fake building. Two were on the ground floor. Three were running up the stairs to the balcony. Their AR-15s were at their shoulders. Their knees were bent. At the landing, they swiveled in perfect synchronicity and T'd up the next flight of stairs toward the balcony. Another few paces, then the lead man held up his fist to stop. He walked in a crouch. Three steps, then he was at the wall. He pretended to open a door and everyone started firing.

Will saw Dobie jump at the *tap-tap-tap* sound.

The kid said, "So fucking cool, bro."

He wasn't afraid. He was excited.

Will could tell that this wasn't the first time the fake building had been raided. The wood was spattered with pinpricks of orange, red and blue paint. They were using Simunition, a type of non-lethal ammunition. Will had fired the marking rounds during training exercises. The GBI required all agents to complete active shooter simulations inside of school buildings, abandoned houses, warehouses. They hired actors to play bad guys and civilians. Music was usually blaring. The lights flickered constantly, or sometimes they were off.

You couldn't do this with real bullets. Your adrenaline ran too high. You couldn't do it with fake guns, either. The feel had to be the same, so they used blue conversion kits to replace the bolt carriers in rifles and the slides and chamber blocks on nine-mils. The magazines were clear plastic. The dummy rounds had colored paint inside the points so you could tell whether you'd hit a target or killed your partner. Even though the marking rounds weren't lethal, they hurt like hell. Agents were always made to suit up in black hoods that covered everything but their eyes. Helmets, plastic goggles, padded vests, gloves and padded jocks. There was no better way to train for a real-world force-on-force environment.

Which was exactly what the men inside of the fake building were doing.

Hotel lobby? Office building? Synagogue? Mosque? The men were entering on the ground floor, not through a basement or loading dock. There would be security, but thirteen guys against two retired cops who were supplementing their pensions was not a fair contest. And that didn't even include the number of civilians who would be inside.

They were planning for a massacre.

Gerald asked Will, "You ready to suit up?"

Will was ready to turn on the tracker inside his holster. These men were planning a full scale infiltration. They had to be stopped.

But what about Sara?

Will found the tactical equipment piled up on the ground. Guns had been tossed onto the grass. Typical law enforcement-issue Glock 19s, but Will's Glock 19 was not among them. Nothing looked right. Magazines were half-filled. Some of the AR-15s were caked with dirt. Conversion kits laid around in pieces. Someone had known enough to order the gear, but had not taken the time to instruct them in the proper handling.

Dobie was already strapping down his helmet.

"Hood first," Will told him.

Dobie turned red. He took off the helmet. His eyes followed Will as he put on the gear, the same way Will had looked to Tessa for cues during Cathy's prayer.

The kid was so amped up he couldn't stand still. Was this why Dobie had joined the IPA? Running around playing soldier was a hell of a kick. But the point of drilling was to prepare you for the real thing. Will knew for a fact that Dobie wasn't ready for the real thing. Watching the guys in the fake building, he wasn't confident they would do any better. But it didn't take skill or even luck to kill a lot of people. Only the element of surprise and a willingness to pull the trigger.

Will tightened down his belt. He checked his weapons. He made sure the magazines and chambers were filled with blanks because he didn't trust these people. Technically, he should take the Sig Sauer out of his holster and clear the chamber. During simulated drills, no live rounds were allowed on the premises.

But nothing about this was a simulation to Will.

"Wolfe, you're C-Team." Gerald pointed up the stairs. "To the left."

Will had wondered why the three men had peeled off in the same direction, leaving their rear open to attack. Another mistake. You didn't drill one team at a time. It was all or none.

"Dude, it's cool, right?" Dobie was still bouncing like a meth head. All that Will could see of his face was his bugged-out eyes behind the goggles. His vest had been hit at least six times with Simunition. His jock looked like a multi-colored Rorschach. He should've been anxious. This wasn't a game of paintball. They were going to take this building in real life one day. Probably soon, if Faith's contact at the FBI was right about the recent chatter.

Will pulled the hood up over his nose. He adjusted his goggles. He told Dobie, "There's a difference between shooting a piece of cardboard and killing a human being."

"Yeah-yeah-yeah." Dobie's breath flexed against the hood over his mouth. "I got it, bro."

Will wanted to punch some sense into the little shit. Instead, he showed Dobie how to hold the rifle. "Put your finger here, along the trigger guard. Never, ever touch the trigger unless you're ready to kill somebody."

"He's right, brother." Another suited up man had joined them, bringing the team to sixteen. He started firing off orders. "Alpha, take the breach. Secure the first floor. Bravo and Charlie, you're second wave. Up the stairs. Bravo, go right. Charlie will take the left." For Will's benefit, he explained, "You're Charlie. We'll go to the rear. We'll wait for the cue. Dobie will open the door. Let's go."

They didn't run up the stairs. They all stood outside the fake building. Will looked down. The grass had been worn away from dozens of men standing right here and waiting to go in. The framing was open to the width of a set of double doors.

They should've used real doors. You couldn't see through walls in a real building. You couldn't look through doors and spot the bad guys. The paper targets in the middle of the room were covered in paint. They probably hadn't moved them during a single drill. You had to know a basic set of facts before you stormed a public space. Where was the furniture? What were the obstacles? Roughly how many people were inside? Which direction would they run in when the bullets started flying? Where were your exits? Who was your target? How were you going to keep yourself and your team safe?

"All right, brothers." Gerald had a stopwatch in his hand. He shouted, "Go."

Eight men rushed inside. Rifles pointed, knees bent. The two targets were double-tapped. The men split off into teams of two, covering all four walls. They moved silently, stealthily, using hand signals, tapping each other on the leg to stop or go. Fake doors were opened. Triggers were pulled. Paint hit the trees outside the building. Magazines were reloaded.

"Go!" Gerald repeated.

The three men in front of Will moved forward. Dobie followed. Will kept his rifle pointed down. Adrenaline shot through his body like fire. His vision narrowed. His heart started pounding. He forced himself to breathe in and out.

This was why you practiced. This was why you wore the gear and you hid behind walls and you opened real doors because your body was dumb and it didn't know the difference.

Bravo team pounded up the stairs and swiveled up the T. Charlie was close behind. Will saw two letters spray-painted on the floor.

LG.

Will followed Dobie up the opposite side. They ran down the balcony. They stopped in front of a fake door. There was another letter painted on the plywood.

G.

Dobie looked at Bravo. He got the signal. He pretended to open the door.

Will kept his rifle down. Dobie unloaded into the opening. He kept pulling on the trigger until his magazine was empty.

Gerald called, "All right, that's it. Twenty-eight seconds."

The whole thing had felt like ten minutes. Will's heart was pushing its way up into his throat. The heat was getting to him. He took off the helmet, pushed back the hood and goggles.

"Tell me, brother." Will felt a hand on his shoulder. "Why didn't you shoot?"

Will looked at the man. He'd taken off his gear, too.

Average weight and height. Brown hair and eyes.

His thumb was hooked over his belt buckle, but his arm was bent at a strange angle. He wasn't resting his hand. He was trying to take the weight off of his shoulder because he'd been shot two days ago.

And then his men had kidnapped Sara.

Dash tightened his grip on Will's shoulder. "Major Wolfe?"

Will had to say something. He couldn't grunt and nod his way through this. He rubbed his beard, summoning up Jack Wolfe. "Don't touch the trigger unless you're ready to kill." He shrugged. "There was nothing to kill."

"Ah," Dash said. "Following your own advice."

"Training," Will managed. Every ounce of his energy was being used to study Dash's face for any sign of recognition. "If you shoot, shoot to kill."

Dash said, "Why don't you walk with me? We're planning a little celebration. I bet a big fella like you enjoys a rare steak."

Will's stomach rolled itself into a fist. He should turn on the tracker. Dash was right here. The entire plan would fall apart without him.

But what about Sara?

"Let's go." Dash made his way down the stairs. The men opened up a path around him. He told Gerald, "Drill Team One again. I want them under ten seconds before we breach."

"Yes, sir." Gerald gave him a crisp salute. The men from the staging area were pulling on hoods and helmets. Sixteen more men. Glocks and rifles at the ready.

Will said, "I've never been on the second team before."

Dash laughed. "It's good news for you, brother. The first wave always has the highest number of casualties. The generals call them cannon fodder."

He said this right in front of his men. They didn't seem to mind the casual disregard for their lives. In fact, they looked energized by it.

Dash told Will, "We'll take another turn after the celebration."

"Celebration?"

"We go in tomorrow. We have a Message to deliver. It can't wait another day."

Will felt like thumb tacks were rolling around in his gut.

"Don't sweat it, Wolfe. I can tell from one run-through that you know what you're doing." Dash tossed his gear onto the pile. He didn't bother to change out his Simunition. The blue plastic frame was like a beacon inside the holster.

Will recognized the grip of his own Glock 19. Dash had taken his gun out of Sara's car. He had used it to kill two people and probably to threaten Sara. No matter what happened next, Will was going to take back his gun and jam it down Dash's throat.

Dash said, "We've trained over one thousand hours for this mission."

Will nodded as if the number wasn't idiotic. SEAL Team Six had only a few days of training before they'd raided Bin Laden's compound.

"We've built something here," Dash said. "Our community is young, but we're driven. There will be some sacrifices, some casualties, but the Message is more important than any one man. You'll see that when you meet the rest of the group. I want you to sit with my family. Get to know us. You'll understand what we're fighting for."

Will doubted Dash was going to sacrifice himself. Megalomaniacs talked a big game, but they always came out without a scratch. The highest casualties would be all the *brothers* who thought running around in black tactical gear made them ready for war.

Will said, "Lot of young guys here."

"They are indeed. That's why we need tough, battle-hardened soldiers to train them up. Maybe you could be one of those soldiers, Major Wolfe."

Will gave a noncommittal shrug. They were heading into the woods. He noticed two older guys with rifles. There was a platform built into one of the trees. A gray-haired man was leaning on the railing. His AR-15 was slung over his shoulder.

The Sig Sauer could take out one of them before Will was shot down. If they were using the same FMJs from the staging area, the bullet would run through Will's chest like water and go straight into Dobie's head.

"This way, Major." Dash led Will toward a cleared trail. Dobie was tagging behind them like a puppy. The B and C Team straggled a few yards behind.

"I think you'll like it here." Dash walked beside Will, though the trail was narrow. "Gerald tells me you're a friend of Beau's."

"Yeah, but I'm not—" Will feigned injecting a needle into his arm. "That's not my thing."

"What *is* your thing, brother?"

Will shrugged. He couldn't make this easy.

Dash said, "Quarter of a million dollars is a lot of money."

Will could feel Dash studying his face. "It is."

"What are you going to do with it, Major Wolfe?"

The question wasn't as simple as Dash had made it sound. Will took his time thinking through an answer. Now wasn't the time for Jack Wolfe to go into some racist tirade or rail against the government for failing him. "I guess I'll go somewhere like this. Just me and nobody else."

"You wouldn't take a woman with you?"

He shook his head. He glanced at Dobie, who was listening intently. "I don't like complicated."

Dash nodded, but Will couldn't tell if he'd given the right answer. It didn't matter. There was no taking it back. They'd reached a clearing. Small cabins were tucked into the tree line. Women were cooking over open fires, filling up bowls and plates. Eight in all. Three old guys on platforms in the trees. Three more on the ground. Twelve younger women at the picnic tables putting down silverware and plates. Children were running around, spinning in circles, screaming, laughing. There were too many for Will to count.

"You like kids?" Dash asked.

Will felt like his breath was trapped in his chest. If there were kids here, then Sara might be close by. But there were so many of them. Will couldn't start shooting if there were children. Some of them were barely old enough to walk.

"Major Wolfe?"

Will realized that he was staring at the girls. And then he realized that a man like Dash wouldn't find that creepy. "They're pretty. The little blonde ones."

Dash chuckled. "My girls love their Daddy."

Will swallowed down his disgust. "How many are yours?"

Dash looked Will in the eye and said, "Every single one of them belongs to me."

He meant it as a warning. Will forced his fingers not to curl up into fists. He turned around slowly, looking at Dobie. The kid had stuck a piece of grass in his mouth. He swatted away a fly.

Will asked Dash, "He got anybody coaching him up?"

Dash smiled, as if he finally understood Major Wolfe. "You can have him if you want him."

Will nodded. "Sure."

Dobie grabbed at the fly, trying to catch it in his hand.

Dash called to him, "Dobie, brother, keep an eye on Major Wolfe for me." He patted Will on the shoulder. "I'll find you after the celebration, my friend. That's when the real work starts."

Will nodded. He shoved his hands deep into his pockets as Dash walked toward the children. They ran toward him, yelling *Daddy! Daddy! Daddy!*

Will spit out the bile that had filled his mouth. Dash wasn't really training these toy soldiers. He didn't have a plan other than to murder a hell of a lot of people. If Will had to guess, he would say that the only *brother* who had practiced making it out of that building alive was the racist pedophile who was leading them into it. This was a suicide mission, plain and simple.

He thought about the GPS tracker. He was running out of time to find Sara. Will would give himself fifteen more minutes. More than that, and he wouldn't be the kind of man that Sara would want to come back to.

"Didja see those bullets, man?" Dobie hovered at Will's elbow. "They sprayed them with pork brine in case we hit any Muslims."

Will couldn't think of a more asinine idea. Salt corroded metal. Guns were made of metal. These people sure liked jamming their weapons.

Dobie asked, "Did Dash say anything, bro? Did he tell you what we're gonna do? Nobody knows. He's always talking about the Message, and we've been training, but—"

"Shut up." Will let his eyes travel across the clearing. He'd counted forty men so far, forty-one if he included Dobie. The eight cooking women were older, but the twelve women at the tables were all in their early twenties. Even in the weird wedding dresses, Will could tell they were attractive. That explained what kept Dobie and his Three Amigos here.

"Come on, bro," Dobie begged. "We're a team now. Tell me what Dash said."

Will saw a long, low building across the clearing. There was a sink and shower stall by the steps. The windows were covered in white paper.

Will watched the door open. "Go find us some Gatorade."

Dobie said, "Dash told me to keep an eye on you."

A woman came outside. Tall, willowy. White dress. White scarf around her head.

Dobie started to speak, but Will palmed his face and shoved him backward onto the ground.

The woman sat down on the stairs. She was putting on her shoes.

Will held his breath.

Dobie whined, "Fuck, man. What'd you do that for?"

The woman looked up at the sky. Her pale skin was already burned from the sun.

Will couldn't remember how to exhale. His lungs started to fold in.

"Dude, what the fuck is wrong with you?"

The woman wiped her face with the hem of her dress. She pulled off her scarf. Her long, auburn hair fell around her shoulders.

Sara.

17

Tuesday, August 6, 5:32 p.m.

Sara folded her impromptu scarf into a neat square. She had wrapped one of the cloth napkins around her head in hopes that it would keep her hair from curling up as it dried. She wanted to press her face into the material and cry—about Michelle and Tommy and every other appalling thing she had witnessed—but she lacked the will to summon any emotion but hopelessness.

None of the children were improving. Joy could not stay awake. Three more adults had showed up at the bunkhouse reporting nausea, fatigue and breathing issues. Benjamin was in a stupor. Lance's dysentery had resolved, but he was slurring his words and complaining of double vision. The varied symptoms could point to anything from a tick-borne illness to Guillain-Barré to glaucoma to mass psychosis.

Nothing Sara had tried was working. The medications had to be bad. The various antibiotics and prophylactics were either mislabeled, placebos, or poison.

Poison.

Was Gwen some kind of Dark Angel?

In the course of her medical career, Sara had heard plenty of talk about hastening the death of a terminally ill patient. Wanting to end a person's suffering was a natural desire. Sara had never seen anyone act on the impulse, no matter how dire the situation. The children in the bunkhouse were ill, but there were treatments, medications, that could help them rally. Two days ago, Sara had assumed that Adriel would be protected by her mother. Now, Sara knew that Gwen was not above murder if the calculus was in her or Dash's favor. The woman shared her bed with a mass murderer. She parented her children by fear and intimidation. God only knew what else she was capable of.

Sara looked around the clearing. Women were rushing back and forth, making preparations for the party, staying well out of Gwen's way in case they invited her rage. Tonight's celebration was all about gearing up to deliver the *Message*. If Dash got his way, everything would change tomorrow. Sara was supposed to be his *Witness*. She shuddered to think what that would entail. He had predicted more deaths than could be counted. She was yards away from the greenhouse, but getting inside would not stop what was going to happen. It would only burden Sara with the horrific knowledge of what was to come.

She had never felt so alone on this god-forsaken mountain.

Sara made herself stand up. She walked down the stairs, across the grassy clearing. She lost count of the new faces, the young ladies setting the tables, the little boys who had joined Dash's brood of little girls. The armed men were still on guard. The hum of the generator had died down a few hours ago. She kept hearing loud *pops* from over the hill. She assumed the preponderance of gunfire meant that Dash had stepped up the drills.

Sara's brain had given up on song lyrics and replaced them with a mantra:

Black box, the greenhouse, the Message, tomorrow.

She was rethinking her biological agent theory. Sara had been too focused on the infectious disease part of Michelle's job title. The CDCs Clinical Chemistry Branch serves as the world reference laboratory for certain infectious disease. Their National Biomonitoring Program measures levels of exposure to toxins such as anthrax, botulinum, pertussis and aflatoxins. In order to translate that data into practical treatments, Michelle would have to have a deep understanding of chemistry.

Sara had minored in chemistry as part of her pre-med. She knew that thermite was made from aluminum and ferric oxide. Naphthenic and palmitic acids combined to make napalm. Phosphate rock heated in the presence of carbon and silica creates white phosphorous, a waxy solid so volatile that it has to be stored underwater to keep it from self-igniting.

Any one of these substances could be synthesized in a commercial lab. Or a greenhouse with a commercial lab inside. With proper handling, you could insert an incendiary munition into anything from a hand grenade to a missile to a *black box*. The resulting explosion would be catastrophic, especially in a heavily populated area. Phosphorous could burn a hole through skin and organs. Pouring water on thermite created a steam explosion, spraying hot fragments in every direction. Napalm could cause an array of maladies, from subdermal burns to death by asphyxiation.

If Dash was planning to detonate the black box inside a building like the Structure, hundreds if not thousands of people could be murdered.

"How is she?" Gwen's raw hands were in her apron. She was standing beside a table with several ice-cream churners. She had been cranking them by hand. "Adriel? Is she any better?"

Sara shrugged and shook her head, conveying her exact feelings. "Why? You're not going to do anything to help her."

Gwen started cranking one of the churns. Chunks of rock salt hit the table. The scent of fresh vanilla was in the air. All that Sara could think was that cyanide had a similar odor when it was processed through the body.

"Good evening, ladies." Dash was grinning as he struggled to walk. A child was wrapped around each leg. Esther and Grace were giggling like monkeys.

He asked Sara, "Everything good, Dr. Earnshaw?"

Sara nodded. She had not spoken to him since she'd told him to fuck off. She supposed that, like most psychopaths, he couldn't handle confrontation.

He asked, "Tell me, how are your patients doing?"

She tried, "I'm not pleased with their progress. Are you sure the medications are—"

Grace gave a squeak. Her mother had filled two small paper cups with ice cream.

Gwen said, "Share with your sisters."

The girls ran off, squealing with delight.

Dash said, "I'm not a medical expert, Dr. Earnshaw, but am I correct that little children often get sick for no reason at all?"

Sara was annoyed by every part of the question. "As a medical expert, I can tell you that the symptoms are not sequela to a measles infection."

"Hm." He made a show of thinking while she enjoyed the fact that he had no idea what *sequela* meant.

Gwen said, "You should probably say something before we begin."

Dash smiled at his wife. He asked Sara, "If you don't mind, Dr. Earnshaw, I'd like it if you walked with me."

He didn't lead her toward the picnic area. Instead he indicated the direction back toward her cabin prison. If he thought confining her was a punishment, he was wrong.

Dash said, "It's a lovely evening. I think we're getting a break in this heat."

Sara did not respond. The gun in his holster looked different. She recognized the blue slide that retrofitted the gun for Simunition.

Dash said, "I'm sorry to have to bring this up, Doctor, but it appears that you've upset my wife."

Sara chewed her lip. He had never admonished her before.

He said, "I really can't have discord in the Camp. Especially not tonight. What we're doing tomorrow is too important."

Sara turned around to look at him.

She could tell he had no intention of backing down. One side of his smile was higher than the other. This wasn't the mask slipping. This was a joyful anticipation of cruelty.

He said, "I had hoped that, given Michelle's rapidly declining help, you would be able to take over her job as our Witness."

Sara looked away first, chiding herself for playing Russian Roulette. She was a hostage. He was a murderer. She had seen him shoot two men. She knew that he'd set off those bombs at

Emory. He was planning something even more spectacularly awful. Confronting him, pushing him, was the quickest way to her death.

Dash told her, "Gwen says I've given you too much freedom."

Sara watched him lift the gun from his holster. The blue slide stood out on the top of the frame. He had no idea that Sara knew the marking rounds were not lethal. He was enjoying the idea of toying with her.

"You're right." She tried to talk him down. Dash's gun wasn't a threat, but there were three dozen men in the clearing who carried the real thing. "I've been frustrated because of the children. I shouldn't have talked to Gwen that way. Or you."

"It's not for my sake I'm doing this." Dash didn't point the weapon at her. Instead, he tested the weight in his hand. "Between you and I, it's not often I meet my intellectual equal. Perhaps I've let myself enjoy parrying with you too much."

"I—"

He pointed the gun at her belly. "Let's finish this by the river."

"Wait." Sara's eyes desperately scanned over his shoulder, as if anyone would help. The girls were seated at the picnic table. They were surrounded by men dressed in black. Young faces, old. All clean-shaven but one.

Tears flooded into Sara's eyes. She gasped.

"Dr. Earnshaw?"

She covered her mouth with her hands.

Will?

Standing by the picnic table. Laughing with the girls.

Was it really him?

Dash said, "Doctor—"

"I'm sorry!" Sara blurted out the words. "Please, I'm so sorry." She clasped together her trembling hands, begging him. "Forgive me, please. I'm sorry. Please." She couldn't stop pleading. Had Will seen her? He wasn't even looking this way. "I'll be better. I promise. Please. Just let me—you said I'm your Witness. Let me—I'll tell them that you—that you are a community. A family."

Dash's eyes narrowed. Her reaction had been too delayed.

"Please." Sara's hands were shaking so hard that she couldn't hold them together. Will had turned away from her. She saw his back, his broad shoulders. "Dash, please. I'm so sorry. Please don't—don't hurt me. Please. I don't—I don't want to be hurt. Please."

"What is this?" he demanded. "You think I'm going to rape you?"

"No—" Sara was so desperate she almost screamed the word. "No, of course not. I was—"

"I assured you that you would remain unmolested."

"I know you did, but—" A sob rolled out of her mouth. She looked at Will, begging him to turn around. "Please. I saw the gun and I thought—"

"We adhere to the rules of the Geneva Convention." Dash waved the gun around as he spoke. "I told you. We are not animals. We are soldiers."

"I know. I know. I just—I'm sorry. I shouldn't have said—I'm upset about the children. They're so sick. And Michelle—"

Turn around-turn around-turn around . . .

"Dr. Earnshaw, I'm a married man."

"I know." Sara gave up trying to wipe her tears. "I'm sorry. I should know you better by now. I realize you would never—that you're an honest man. You always keep your word."

"I do."

"Dash, I'm so sorry. I just—I saw the gun, and I panicked, because my—my husband was shot with a gun like that." She had no idea where the lie had come from, but Dash seemed to like it.

He said, "Shot by a filthy mongrel, no doubt."

"I'm scared of guns. They terrify me. And they're all around. Everywhere. And I'm so scared. All of the time. I'm sorry I'm not—"

Dash gave a dramatically drawn out sigh. He slowly returned the weapon to its holster. He tightened the Velcro strap to make a point. "It is my ardent wish, Dr. Earnshaw, that what we're doing tomorrow will ensure that good white women such as yourself are no longer afraid." His hand went to her shoulder. "Once the world is wiped clean of the mongrels and their enablers, we will be free of the kind of crime that took your husband away from you. Police officers will be safe on the streets again. Law and order will be restored. You will be the last widow of your kind."

Sara nodded. She couldn't give him more than that. She was shaking uncontrollably. Her eyes went to the ground. Tears slid down her nose and pooled into the dirt.

Dash patted her shoulder. "Straighten yourself up, Doctor. We don't want the children seeing you like this."

Sara's teeth were chattering as she followed him back to the clearing. She could barely lift her feet. Every nerve was exposed. After feeling nothing for so long, she could not stop feeling everything. Sara kept staring at the ground because she was afraid that if she looked at Will, she would collapse.

At the picnic table, Gwen was hectoring the girls about manners. Sara allowed her gaze to skip over Will's face. His hair was stringy with sweat. Dark circles rimmed his eyes. The beard was patchy and disgusting.

She was suddenly light-headed. The sense memory of the man who had raped her flooded Sara's body. *The rough beard that smelled of cigarettes and fried food. The clamminess of his pale skin when he thrust against her.*

Bile surged into her mouth. She swallowed it down, her eyes burning.

"Have a seat, Dr. Earnshaw." Dash snapped out his cloth napkin and laid it across his lap. "Major Wolfe, this is our resident pediatrician. We've had some sick children up here. Thankfully, most of my girls have weathered the storm."

Will grunted. He was looking down at his steak.

Sara took her usual spot by Grace. Will was across the table at the opposite end. A teenage boy was beside him, arms crossed, spine straight, mimicking Will's posture.

She dug her fingernails into her palms. She struggled to pull herself back into reality. It was just an ugly beard. Sara was not chained to a bathroom stall. Will would never hurt her. She loved this man. He loved her. He was here because of Sara. To save her.

She looked around the clearing. The guards in the woods. The rifles and Glocks and hunting knives and the children.

How could he save her?

Dash told Sara, "Major Wolfe served in the Airborne forces alongside our friend Beau."

Sara's hands were still trembling. She concentrated on the food. She had cheese and crackers again. An apple was by her plate. The other women had bowls of stew. The men had steaks and potatoes, bottles of water and yellow Gatorade.

Dash told Sara, "We were down a few soldiers after our last incursion. I feel confident the major will be instrumental in helping us send the Message."

Sara couldn't keep ignoring Will. She made herself look at him—to really see him.

He was cutting into the steak. Blood seeped from the middle. Sara recognized his abject disgust. Will preferred his meat cooked into a rubber puck. She had treated him to one of the best steakhouses in Atlanta for his birthday and watched him pour ketchup onto a ninety-dollar Wagyu New York Strip.

Her breath suddenly came back. She felt dizzy from the sudden rush of oxygen.

This was the memory she needed to hold on to. The first time Sara had worn Will's favorite black dress was for that dinner. She had read the menu to him in a sexy voice. She hadn't let him see the prices because he would've mathematically quantified the volume of T-bones he could've consumed for the same amount at Waffle House.

"Dr. Earnshaw?" Dash was too keyed into her moods. She had to stop this emotional rollercoaster.

"Sorry." Sara broke off a corner of cheese. She pushed it into her mouth. She could do nothing to stop the tears that formed a river down her cheeks. She had made Will taste her Scotch at the restaurant. He had nearly coughed up a lung. They had held hands all night, made out like teenagers in the car.

Grace asked, "Daddy, can I ask Major Wolfe if he's married?"

Dash smiled. "I think you just did, sweetpea."

Grace bounced with excitement. "Major Wolfe, are you married?"

Will chewed the steak the same way Sara's greyhounds chewed the bitter medication she gave them for heartworms. He swallowed audibly. "No."

Grace deflated like a balloon.

"I, uh—" Will swallowed again. "I went to a wedding once."

Sara knew that Will had barely attended his own wedding. The entire shitshow was predicated on a double-dog dare.

Will said, "They served fresh muffins at the reception."

"Ohh." Grace was intrigued. "What kind of muffins?"

"Chocolate chip. Oreo. Cranberry. Blueberry. Snorkelberry." Will scratched his hideous beard. The girls could not tell if he was being serious or not. "Did you hear about the two muffins that were baking in the oven?"

Grace was so excited she could only shake her head.

"One muffin, he's looking around the oven, and he says, 'Wow, it is really, really hot in here.'" Will wiped his mouth, drawing out the suspense. "And the other muffin, he starts screaming, 'Help! A talking muffin!'"

The girls were not used to jokes. There was a slight pause before they erupted into laughter. Even Gwen smiled. Grace was so taken in that Sara had to keep her from falling backward off the bench.

Dash started tapping his fingers on the table. The laughter stopped abruptly. Sara thought about the pre-pubescent boys Dash had sent away.

He did not want the competition.

Dash said, "I didn't realize you were funny, Major Wolfe."

Sara tried to break the tension. "Grace, did I tell you about—"

"Dobie," Dash said. "Could you escort Dr. Earnshaw to her cabin? I'm afraid Lance is still under the weather. And Major Wolfe, you'll keep him company. You can drill with the team later. It's better in the dark anyway. I'll send someone to find you when we're ready for you."

Sara felt a rush of heat go through her body. Will taking her to the cabin. That silly kid hanging around. Will could easily knock him out. They could run, but where? Will had to have a plan. He always had a plan. She gripped her hands together under the table to keep them still.

Dobie stood up. He sat down again when he realized Will wasn't joining him.

Sara felt her teeth on edge. What was he doing? This was their chance. They could run into the woods and—

Get shot by the men in the deer stands. Or the guards in the forest. Or Will could return fire and end up killing one of the children.

Sara's tears began their endless flow again.

Will swirled the Gatorade in the bottle and gulped the rest of it down. Beside him, Dobie did the same. His throat worked like a stork's. Will finally stood. His little shadow followed him around the table.

Will grabbed Sara's arm.

She cried out, though he hadn't hurt her.

Dash said, "Gently, Major Wolfe. Dr. Earnshaw is a very important part of the Message." He nodded to Dobie. "Keep an eye peeled."

Sara stood up. She felt like her knees were going to give out. She walked ahead of them, through the clearing, down the path. The entire time, she thought about walking to her BMW two days ago, the fear that had welled up inside of her chest as she'd realized that she was going to be taken.

What now? What now?

Will's footsteps were solid behind her. Dobie was dragging at a slower pace. Sara wanted to turn around. To pause the world and let Will hold her for just a few seconds.

They were at the cabin. Sara stepped up onto the log. Will's hand was at her back. He barely touched her, but her body shivered from the idea of him.

The door shut behind her.

"Dude, I guess we're being punished." Dobie's voice was close by as he fumbled with the padlock.

Sara wanted to scream. Only Dash had the key.

Dobie said, "I wanted ice cream."

Will offered, "You can go and get some."

"Shit no, bro. Dash'll rip my hide." He howled out a tremendous yawn. "Damn, I'm tired."

"Adrenaline." Will was sitting on the log outside the door. His voice was different; deeper, rougher. "Go ahead and get comfortable. We're gonna be here for a while."

Sara laid flat to her belly. She looked under the door. She could see Will. The gap was wide enough for her to slip her hand underneath. She could touch him. Her heart fluttered with longing and fear and panic. The boy might see. Could she risk it? She could just brush her fingers along his back to anchor herself again.

Couldn't she?

Dobie yawned. "What I think is—" Another yawn broke his train of thought.

Will said, "It's a big day tomorrow."

"Yeah, the Message. Whatever that is." Dobie's head thumped repeatedly against the door. The padlock rattled. "Did Dash tell you what we're doing?"

Will must have shaken his head. "Do you know?"

Dobie must have shaken his head, too. The rattling had stopped.

Will said, "I've got to admit, I'm a little scared, man. It's not easy doing something like this. People are going to die. I counted around ten thousand rounds in the staging area. Three dozen AR-15s. Forty men. Five black vans. Two teams training to take over a hotel lobby or a mosque or a shopping center or—I don't know what."

Sara felt a switch flip on in her brain. He was telling her what he had seen.

Will said, "Bravo goes in one direction. Charlie goes in the other. We're Charlie, right? That's six of us, all in Team Two. But what about the thirty-two guys in Team One? What are they going to do before we get there? And I keep wondering, why go to the trouble to cover the bullets in pork brine? Dead is dead, am I right? And what about those boxes we replaced at the warehouse?"

Black boxes?

Will said, "Why replace a bunch of boxes with the exact same type of box? There were at least two dozen. Brown cardboard with shipping labels, about thirty-by-thirty inches. The ones we stole are stuck over in that metal storage building on the other side of the fake building. What happened to the ones we left in the warehouse?"

"Dunno." Dobie's voice was faint. He sounded like he was drifting off to sleep.

"We're running those drills," Will continued. "Up the stairs, T off at the top. There's an *LG* spray-painted on one side. A *G* on the other. What does that even stand for? The *LG* is close to the top of the stairs, but the G is at the other end of the balcony. Maybe it's not an *L* in the *LG*. Could be a capital *I*."

Dobie smacked his lips.

Will said, "It's crazy. Right, bro?"

Dobie offered no response. His breathing was deep. Sara looked under the door, but she could only see his narrow shoulders.

She heard Will snap his fingers. The sound was like a stick breaking.

"Dobie?" he asked. Then, "Hey, kiddo?"

Sara watched Will lift him up like a child. He turned away from her. He walked into the woods. She saw him disappear in pieces, his legs, then his shoulders, then the top of his head. Sara waited. And waited. She got up on her knees, pressed her palm to the door.

What was he doing? Was he leaving? Would he come back?

"Sara?" Will's hand reached under the crack in the door. He wriggled his fingers, searching for her. "Sara? Are you there?"

She was overcome. All she could do was lean over and press her lips to the palm of his beautiful hand.

"Sara," Will's voice was strained, "are you okay?"

She sobbed quietly, her face resting against his palm. His fingers held on to her. All of the longing from the last two days broke open inside of her.

I love you. I need you. I missed you so much. Please don't leave me.

"I'm here." Will cleared his throat. He sniffed. "I'm here."

Sara cried harder, because she knew he was trying not to.

"Babe." His voice raked up on the word. He cleared his throat again. "Is that—is that a new dress?"

Sara laughed through her tears.

He said, "It really brings out the red in your skin."

She laughed again. She held on to his hand with both of hers. "I made it myself."

"Really?" Relief filled his voice. "I couldn't tell. It's so—it's beautiful."

Sara leaned her forehead against the door. She closed her eyes, banishing the piece of wood that separated them. Her head on his shoulder. Her arms around his waist. "What happened to Dobie? Can he hear us?"

"Well, uh, there's a funny story behind that." Will paused. "I've been taking some pills Amanda gave me. I think it's Percocet."

"What?" Sara's shock overrode her concern. He never took anything for pain. He just winced and groaned until she wanted to strangle him.

"Amanda told me it was aspirin, but then I realized it was the same thing she gave Beau when we went to the park." Will skipped the details. "Anyway, it all got smooshed in the pouch, because I got too hot, but I guess I put about two and a half tablets in Dobie's Gatorade." He paused. "Did I kill him?"

"I don't—no." Sara shook her head in frustration. Why the hell was he drawing out a stupid story about Dobie?

Her heart sank.

Will was talking about Dobie because there was nothing else to talk about.

He didn't have a plan. At least, not a plan that would get Sara out of this living hell. He had seen the Structure. There was something new about cardboard boxes. Ten thousand rounds of ammunition covered in brine. Forty armed men. All for an attack that was going to take place somewhere—anywhere—tomorrow.

Will said, "I have a tracker in my holster. I tried to turn it on, but I think the battery shorted. Or maybe we're too high in the mountains. It doesn't have a satellite uplink. It works off cellular networks."

Sara leaned against the door. She laced her fingers through his.

He gripped her hand. "I could shoot a lot of people, but—"

"The children." Sara knew there was more to it than that. The only way for Will to stop Dash was to keep pretending to be Major Wolfe so that Dash took him on the Mission.

Every ounce of her being was yearning to be away from here, but Sara told Will, "Dash wants me to be his witness, whatever that means. He promised me that I would be freed tomorrow."

Will was silent, but she felt his skepticism permeate the door.

Sara took a deep breath. "I'm okay up here. He's not hurting me. No one is hurting me. And there are children—they're very sick, Will. I thought it was measles; well, it *was* measles, but now it's something else. I don't know what's wrong with them. People keep falling ill, and I need to stay here to take care of them. Michelle was working on something in a greenhouse. It's—"

"On the other side of the trail," Will finished. "I saw it. The thermal tent. There are two guards outside. One in the trees. I don't know who else is there. I can't get inside now. Maybe later, but I don't know."

Sara felt herself sinking into despair. "Michelle wrote a message on her hand. I found it when I—I found her body." She bit her lip so the pain would keep her from crying. "She wrote the words 'black box'."

"Black box," he repeated. "Like on an airplane?"

"I don't know. It could be a bomb. It could be a biological agent." She told him, "Will, you have to stop them. You can't worry about me. This is bigger than one person. You must've seen what they did at Emory. I know Dash. He's planning an even more spectacular display. That's what the Message is. He's going to murder hundreds, maybe thousands of people."

Will did not respond. She knew that he had already thought this through, tested the weak spots, looked for the angles. There was no way out of this but forward. He would not be worrying about the danger he was going to face tomorrow. He was agonizing over the thought of leaving Sara.

"It's okay." She couldn't be strong for herself, but she had to be strong for him. "Baby, I'll be okay."

Will took a stuttered breath.

"My love." Sara's throat tightened into a fist. "I'll be okay. We'll both be okay. We'll get through this. I know we'll get through this."

He cleared his throat again. She could feel him doing the same thing that she was doing, trying to hold himself together, to be strong for her.

He said, "Your family prayed for you. Your mom asked me to do it, too. We all bowed our heads. I think I did it right."

Sara closed her eyes. Her family. They had taken him in.

He said, "Your sister is a touchy kind of person. As in, she touches people. A lot."

Sara smiled as she imagined the look on Will's face when he got the full Tessa treatment. "You're going to have to get used to that."

"Yeah." Will sniffed again. "You know I, uh, I need to tell you something else. Confess something else." He paused, purposefully drawing it out. "I watched the *Buffy* episode where Giles gets fired for messing with the Cruciamentum."

Sara made herself play along. "You motherfucker."

His laugh sounded just as forced. "You've been gone for two days. What was I supposed to do?"

Sara let herself revel in the deep pitch of his voice. The roughness was gone. This was her Will.

She asked, "Hey, babe, do you know that song, the one where the guy is, like, *you were at a motel bar, but you got too big for your britches* and the girl is like, *yeah, I was at the bar and it was great, loser, but I'm outta here*?"

He cursed under his breath.

"And then he's like—"

"'Don't You Want Me'. Human League. And it was a cocktail bar."

"Dammit, I was so close." Sara didn't have to fake her relief. "Also—"

"Sara, if you fuck up another song, I swear to God I'll leave."

She grinned, because everything about this felt so normal. "It's not another song. It's that fungus growing on your face."

"Babe, it's my disguise."

"It's gross, and it has to go." Sara felt her smile start to falter. She was running out of things to talk about while they tried not to talk about the things that mattered. "Will?"

"What now? You don't like my outfit?"

She looked down at their hands.

His left. Her right.

She said, "Thank you."

"For what?"

"For letting me love you."

He went quiet. His fingers wrapped tightly around her hand.

Sara had railed against him so many times for his silence, but in this precious moment, words were unnecessary. Will's thumb traced along the inside of her palm. He gently caressed the lines and indentations, then pressed into the pulse at her wrist.

Sara closed her eyes. She leaned her head against the door. She listened to her heartbeat through the peaceful, easy silence until it was time for him to go.

PART THREE

Wednesday, August 7, 2019

ONE HOUR BEFORE THE MESSAGE

18

Wednesday, August 7, 8:58 a.m.

Will sat in the back of another van, his AR-15 gripped between his hands. Dobie was on one side of him. Dash was on the other. The three men from Bravo team were on the opposite side of the van. They were suited up in their training gear, including the padded vests that would stop a BB pellet but not a real bullet. Their black hoods were rolled back to fight the heat. Their rifles pointed up at the ceiling. Their holstered guns and sheathed, eight-inch hunting knives tapped the metal floor as the tires rumbled over asphalt.

They were in slow traffic, probably on the interstate. Rush hour stop-and-go. Possibly heading into Atlanta. Possibly not.

Will looked at his watch.

8:58 a.m.

The vans had left the compound two hours ago. Will hadn't had a chance to return to the clearing. They had practiced infiltrating the fake building until midnight. They had slept together. Pissed together. Eaten breakfast together. The world had closed in. The compound had gone eerily quiet. The sun wasn't even up when they were told that it was time to prepare for battle.

Gwen had been the only woman to preside over their leaving, feeding them a cold breakfast, blessing them with a prayer as she stood in her white wedding dress. She had read a short verse from her Bible, a warning about destruction being in their midst, oppression and deceit in the streets. Everyone had bowed their heads, clasped together their hands. Gwen's prayer was nothing like Cathy's humble request that Sara be returned to her family. Her voice had been filled with hatred and righteous indignation as she commanded God to rid the world of the mongrels and their enablers.

"Blood and soil!" she had screamed, her fist raised.

Every single man but Will had chanted along, "Blood and soil!"

Forty men in total. Armed to the teeth. Clad in black. Sitting in the back of five vans rolling down the interstate toward a scene that would soon erupt into unspeakable violence.

"Fuck." Dobie shifted on the floor beside Will. He was sullen and confused. He didn't understand why he had woken up in the woods. He was angry about missing the drills. He was mad at Will for teasing him about it. He was clearly hung over from the Percocet.

He was still a boy, but he was just as willing to commit murder as the rest of the men.

Will looked away from Dobie's miserable face.

He had seen the aftermath of a mass shooting before. For obvious reasons, the news reporters always fixated on the number of dead, but it was the survivors Will thought about now. The ones with traumatic brain injuries, lost limbs, deep scars, wounds that would not heal. Some of them would live in fear for the rest of their lives. Others would be paralyzed by guilt. They would live, but life as they knew it would be over.

Unless Will could stop it.

"Fuck," Dobie muttered again. He was looking for attention.

Will kept his voice low, telling the kid, "You don't have to do this."

"Shit," Dobie angrily crossed his arms. "What am I supposed to do, bro, sit behind a cash register at the Kwiki Mart like some raghead?"

Will couldn't stand to look at him again. He knew that the core thing he hated about Dobie was the same rotten core that had festered inside of Will's own eighteen-year-old self. Dobie had no real autonomy, no moral compass. He was nothing but a loaded gun waiting to be pointed in any direction.

The difference for Will had been Amanda. She had descended into his life six months after he'd been forced to leave the children's home. Will was sleeping on the street. Stealing food. Working for bad men who paid him to do bad things. Amanda had dragged Will away from a life of crime. She had pushed him into college. She had forced him to join the GBI. She had made it possible for Will to be the kind of man who could be with a woman like Sara.

He told Dobie now what Amanda had told Will all those years ago. "You do what's right, not what's easy."

Dash said, "Amen, brother."

Will gritted his teeth so hard his jaw throbbed.

He'd spent the last twelve hours looking for opportunities to kill Dash. The man was never alone. Gerald shadowed him. At least two *brothers* were always flanking his sides. The blue Simunition kit on his Glock 19—Will's Glock 19—had been changed out by the time Will had left Sara's cabin. Even now, Dash kept habitually checking the chamber to make sure the gun was loaded. Will was not against a suicide mission, but there had to be at least a 10 percent chance of success.

Dash said, "We do the Lord's work today, Major Wolfe."

Will grunted. He didn't need to be Jack Wolfe anymore. He slipped his fingers under the padded vest. Sara's headscarf was folded against his stomach. Will had found it where she'd left it at the top of the stairs. A single red hair was wrapped inside. Now, he rubbed the hem between his fingers. He could feel her lips pressing into the palm of his hand.

My love.

Dash tapped the butt of his rifle on the floor. Every time he felt the men start to lag, he made another speech. "Brothers, today, we reclaim our dignity. That is our Message. We won't be ignored. We are the leaders of this world!"

Feet started banging on the floor. Fists were raised as they cheered.

This was what Will was going to do when they arrived at their destination:

As soon as the van doors opened, Will would use his Glock and his Sig Sauer to kill as many of these men as possible. The rifle was too risky. Will didn't know how many civilians would be on scene. The fact that all of his targets were wearing black uniforms easily identified them as the enemy. They were overconfident from the endless drilling. They would panic the second bullets started firing back at them.

Will had sixteen rounds in the Glock, eleven in the Sig Sauer. Two more magazines on his belt increased the total by thirty.

Forty men. Fifty-seven bullets.

The first two shots were going to stop Dash's heart.

19

Wednesday, August 7, 8:58 a.m.

Faith looked at her watch.

8:58 a.m.

She was sitting on a bench inside Atlanta airport's international terminal. Her head was in her hand. Her cell phone was burning the tip of her ear. Amanda had been livid since they'd lost Will yesterday afternoon, and her temper had reached DEFCON levels when she'd been ordered to brief the governor at the Capitol this morning.

She told Faith, "Everything we've found out so far points to the airport. Michelle Spivey was there right before the bombing. Dash and his crew must have been with her. What were they planning? Why did they risk exposure? Did they succeed? Is there a second part to the plan?"

Faith didn't need to be reminded of the questions. She had worried them around in her head like an oyster making a pearl as she fought traffic to get to the airport this morning.

Amanda said, "The last thing that I should be doing right now is standing around watching a bunch of greedy politicians shove biscuits into their mouths."

In the background, Faith could hear footsteps and voices echoing around the Capitol's marble atrium. The governor had called a special session to vote on funding the latest hurricane clean-up. The building didn't have a cafeteria, but where there were politicians, there were always lobbyists willing to bribe them with free food.

Amanda said, "Lyle Davenport didn't pick his attorney out of the phonebook."

Faith got a bitter taste in her mouth. Davenport was the punk who'd driven the red Kia up to Will at the Citgo yesterday. Amanda had sent a highway patrolman to pull him over for speeding. The subsequent search had revealed an unlicensed weapon in his car. The kid was already holding his lawyer's card when he was told to lace his fingers behind his head.

Faith told Amanda, "Spending a night in jail hasn't persuaded Davenport to mention Dash or the IPA. His arraignment is in three hours. First-time offense, white kid from the suburbs, he might get bail."

"And if we tip off the prosecutor to who he is, then Will's cover will be blown." Amanda uttered a very rare, very nasty curse.

Faith silently ran through several of her own. Her anger was not restricted to the jackass kid who'd invoked his legal rights. Faith had spent two hours hanging out of a helicopter with a pair of binoculars looking for Will. It was only by sheer perseverance that she'd spotted the dirt bike outside of the two-mile radius. None of the residents in the area had recognized the bike. No one reported seeing a teenager and a man on the road, let alone another vehicle picking them up. The bike's VIN number had been scratched off with a grinder.

She told Amanda, "Forensics is going to try an acid treatment to raise the VIN. If that doesn't work, I have some other ideas."

There was a loud noise on Amanda's end, a bunch of men laughing. Faith heard Amanda walking away from them. There weren't a lot of areas in the Capitol for privacy. The Gold Dome was basically an echo chamber.

"Talk to the airport commander," Amanda ordered, as if Faith wasn't at the airport right now to do that very thing. "I don't care what you have to do or what lies you have to tell, but find out what Michelle Spivey was doing on that service road Sunday morning and report to me the second you hear. The very second."

The background noise abruptly stopped.

Faith looked at the time.

9:01 a.m.

The commander of the Atlanta Police Department's airport precinct was officially late for work. Faith had a feeling that he wasn't going to be much help anyway. Everybody had a piece of the airport. The man couldn't take a crap without coordinating with the FAA, the TSA, Homeland Security, and various law enforcement agencies representing Fulton and Clayton County as well as the cities of Atlanta, College Park and Hapeville.

Then there was the FBI.

Faith assumed that Van had confiscated any relevant security footage of Michelle Spivey. This entire morning already felt like the worst Groundhog Day ever. Will had disappeared again. Sara was still missing. So was Michelle Spivey. There were no more leads to follow. They had no idea what Dash was planning. Another night had dragged out with Faith pacing and cursing and fuming and looking up useless information online.

She had never for a minute trusted that stupid GPS tracker in Will's holster. The device was too thin. It wasn't waterproof. The signal relied on the old 3G network. Despite Amanda's orders, there was no way in hell that Will was going to turn it on unless he was actually physically in possession of Sara. God only knew what he was doing right now. He could be injured or lying dead in a ditch. Dash was a psychotic killer. Michelle was stone-cold crazy. Sara had no way of protecting herself. The IPA was so terrifying that the woman who was in charge of monitoring them was losing sleep.

Faith dropped her head back against the bench. She stared at the squiggly blue neon arcing across the high ceiling. Every agency in the state was on high alert, but no one knew what they were supposed to be looking for. They were in *Bin Laden Expected to Attack in US* territory. The presidential briefing had hit a month before 9/11, but in what intelligence agencies called a *Failure of Imagination*, no one had thought something so outrageously brazen would ever happen.

As Aiden Van Zandt had said, there wasn't a lot of *there* there.

The piercing wail of a toddler pulled Faith out of her misery. There was a certain amount of peace in knowing that she was not the mother on the other end of that wail.

Faith stared at the massive security screening area. The precinct commander would exit through the employee line. Passengers slowly funneled through the eight open lanes, unpacking their bags, taking off their shoes, standing with their hands up in the scanning machines. Faith couldn't believe the airport was so busy this early in the morning. The international terminal was huge, almost as big as a soccer field, with a balcony ringing the second story of the atrium. There were fast-food places and a fish restaurant and a bookstore and cafes and airplanes waiting to whisk you away from your life.

Faith had never been on an international flight. Her cop's salary, along with her propensity for having children out of wedlock, had put a major dent in her travel budget.

"We've *got* to keep meeting like this."

Faith didn't bother to turn around. The sound of Aiden Van Zandt's voice had drilled into her brain like an earwig.

He sat down beside her. He was cleaning his glasses with his tie. "Good morning, Agent Mitchell."

She got to the point. "Why are you here?"

"There's a lot of us here."

Faith took a closer look at the passengers inside of the terminal. Not all of these things were the same. Two businessmen stood with rolling suitcases at the top of the stairs. To the right, a woman leaned over the balcony railing reading her texts. To the left, another businessman paced down the corridor as he talked into his phone. On the ground floor, two women were having breakfast at the bookstore cafe. Another man stood in a TSA uniform by the exit for security.

The fact that Faith had only been here for fifteen minutes was no excuse for not noticing that they were all wearing the springy earbuds that FBI agents favored. Her brain quickly jumped to a conclusion. The chatter from the hate groups must have picked up. Michelle Spivey had been at the airport last Sunday, so the FBI was at the airport.

Just like Faith was at the airport.

She thought about calling Amanda at the Capitol, but she didn't want to get her head bitten off for telling her boss something that she likely already knew. Whatever information exchange Amanda had going on with the FBI was not something she was choosing to share.

Faith told Van, "You've got a lot of agents here."

"I like to think of them as my posse."

Faith knew better than to ask a direct question. She leaned back against the bench. She asked him, "When did the right to hate become conditional?"

"I'll need more context."

"I've been reading about these militias and anti government groups."

"Ah."

Faith said, "At the Bundy standoff, militiamen pointed guns at federal agents, and they were allowed to walk away. At Standing Rock, a bunch of Native American protesters were shouting and holding up signs, and they got attacked by dogs and shot with water cannons."

"Both of those things are true."

"It reminds me of my son when he was a little boy. All kids do this, really. They get to this point in their lives where they realize that things are unfair. It pisses them the hell off. They can't bend their little minds around it. They whine about it constantly—*it's not fair, it's not fair.*"

Van nodded. "That is a familiar whine."

Faith didn't ask how it was familiar. She was more concerned with her brown-skinned daughter and how armed groups like the IPA might get away with hurting her. "I've put up with a lot of shit in my life, but I've never gotten shit because of the color of my skin. I'm sick of things only being fair for some people. It's not right. It's not American."

Van seemed to think about what she'd said. "That's a fairly provocative statement for a law enforcement officer."

She shrugged. "Provocateur's gonna provocotate."

Faith watched a kid begging his mother for a pack of cookies. The two female agents in the bookstore were studiously avoiding the conflict.

She silently returned to her original question, the one that Van wasn't going to answer.

Why was he talking to her?

The FBI had taken Beau into custody two days ago. Faith assumed that because Beau had flipped for one agency, he would flip for the other. Which meant that Van knew about the plan for Will to infiltrate the IPA. Either Kate Murphy had sent him here for information or he was trying to hone his way in.

Faith tested her theories. "This is the part where you tell me how Michelle met Beau, and what you've gotten out of him since you snatched him out from under us."

"I thought this was the part where I asked if I could buy you a cup of coffee."

Faith had to nip this in the bud. "Listen, I've spent the last twenty years of my life raising children. There is not one item of clothing in my closet or in a drawer that isn't stained with some kind of fluid. I cheat at Chutes and Ladders. I have sacrificed my own son's life to win at Fortnite. I will destroy any stupid moron who claims that Jodie Whittaker isn't the best Doctor Who, and I will quote every single line from *Frozen* until your eyes start to bleed."

He asked, "Do you really expect me to believe that you hang up and fold your clothes?"

"Let it go."

Van laughed. "All right, Mitchell. Follow me."

Faith picked up her messenger bag and looped it over her shoulder. She looked up at the balcony as they walked toward the gates. The agent talking into the phone was tracking their progress. The businessmen had started rolling their bags.

Van took a right, leading her down a long, anonymous hallway. His badge worked on the door because his badge apparently worked on every door in every secure building. Faith heard a loud buzz, then they were inside a darkened room with dozens of large, color monitors and rows of tiered desks with people intently studying their screens.

She bit her lip. She was going to end up blowing this guy just for his access to secret government control rooms.

Van said, "This is the nerve center for F concourse. The ones for T and A through E are even more amazing than this. Then there's the north and south terminals, the Plane Train, the parking areas. Holy Moses, don't get me started on parking. It's like Frogger over there."

Faith was more interested in what was right in front of her. Every gate, every restaurant, every entrance to a toilet had at least two cameras pointing at it. Even the outside grounds were covered, down to the service roads.

Van stopped at an empty desk and tapped on a keyboard. The monitor showed a second-story view outside the international terminal. Van toggled out until the shot widened to the adjacent buildings. He pointed to a street.

Faith said, "The Maynard H. Jackson Service Road." She watched a silver Chevy Malibu drive slowly up the road. The windows were tinted, but she could make out two people up front, two in back. Faith looked at the time stamp. "This is from Sunday morning, five hours before the bombs went off."

The Malibu came to a slow stop. The camera was high resolution, but it wasn't a magnifying glass. Faith could only guess by the platinum blonde hair and slim build that the woman who got out of the car was Michelle Spivey.

Michelle took four steps, then started to fall forward onto the grass.

Van paused the image. "She got sick earlier. This is the second time he pulled over for her."

Faith nodded, but that wasn't exactly how she saw it. She'd been behind the wheel of a car when someone was about to blow. You didn't glide to a stop. You stood on the brakes and pushed the person out the door.

Van said, "We think Spivey's appendix must've been hurting for some time. She passes out from the pain, and then—"

He tapped another key and the driver was running to Michelle. Tall and wide, most likely Robert Hurley. He lifted up her unconscious body. He placed her in the front seat of the car. He ran to the other side and drove away.

Van said, "That's it."

"Hm," Faith said. That wasn't really it. The video had been edited.

This is what Faith had been shown: The car had stopped. Michelle had gotten out. Walked four paces. Collapsed. In the frame where she was dropping, Hurley was already climbing out of the car. He was holding something in his hands.

Then the image skipped ahead 1.13 seconds.

Michelle was already lying on the ground.

Hurley was twisting back toward the car, placing something on the seat that was heavy enough for him to have to use both of his hands.

That was the part that Van did not want Faith to see—that Hurley had started to get out of the car to join Michelle. That he was carrying something heavy or cumbersome, like bolt-cutters that could be used to cut a hole in the fence.

Faith asked Van, "Is that fence electrified?"

He shook his head.

She pointed at the building that Michelle had been walking toward. "What's this?"

"Air Chef, where they make all of the food for the planes. Alleged-food." He jabbed around the screen, identifying the white squares. "Cleaning and janitorial services for the planes. Concourse maintenance. Sign shop. Machine shop. Delta Operations."

He was a regular Mapquest. She pointed to the only square he'd left out. "What's this?"

"Government building."

Faith looked at him. "A CDC government building?"

He squinted at the monitor. "Is it?"

Faith reached down and tapped the keys to zoom in on the

door. There was no sign, no indication of what was inside, but there was a hell of a lot of security. She pointed it out for him. "That's a camera. That's a card reader. That's a handprint scanner."

"You don't say?"

"The day Michelle was abducted, she left work early, picked up her daughter from school, then went to the store. Her purse was never located at the scene. Her CDC badge would've been inside."

"Would it be?"

Faith leaned in for a closer look. There wasn't even a doorknob. A red light was mounted over the jamb. What did the IPA want that was stored inside of that building? They had risked exposure by bringing Michelle here. Then they had risked taking her to the hospital. Had they been planning to drive her back to the airport once she'd had surgery? The handprint scanner wouldn't work without her actual hand being attached to her body.

Faith stood up. She faced Van. The room was so dark and the monitor was so bright that her own reflection stared at her from his glasses. "You facilitated that briefing for me at the CDC. You gave me case files on Michelle that would lead me to the airport. You had this edited video cued up for me before we walked into this room."

"Edited?"

"Michelle and Hurley were supposed to get out of the car together. Hurley was going to use bolt-cutters to cut open a hole in the fence. Michelle was going to use her CDC ID card and her handprint on the biometric scanner to open that door, and then they were both going to go inside that building."

"You think?"

"Here's what I think: Your boss and my boss are friends, but they're quarterbacks playing in different conferences. So your boss told you to tell me *some* things, but not *everything*, but you think I can actually help you, which is why every God damn interaction I have with you gets turned into a teaching moment."

"I love that you know about football."

Faith hissed out air between her teeth. Amanda was waiting for her at the Capitol. Faith was supposed to be finding out what the hell had happened at the airport with Michelle. All she had right now was what she always had: supposition and gut instinct. The only tactic that had ever worked with this maddening FBI asshole was honesty, so she tried a version of it now. "This is what my boss doesn't want me to tell you. My partner is missing. He's undercover with the IPA. We haven't seen him since three yesterday afternoon, and I'm worried that whatever Dash is planning is going to happen today, as in right now, and I think that you feel the same way, too."

Van gave a curt nod, as if this was what he'd been waiting for. "Let me buy you that coffee."

20

Wednesday, August 7, 8:56 a.m.

Sara sat in the cabin with her back against the door. She had Will's pocket knife in her hands. He had slipped it under the gap before he'd left last night. She kept pressing the button and springing out the blade. The noise had a rhythmic comfort. After so many days, so many wasted hours of feeling helpless, the knife gave her a feeling of power. Dash didn't know that Sara was no longer defenseless. Gwen was clueless. The sentry outside had no idea that Sara was armed. She could hurt someone with this. Kill someone.

At the motel, Michelle had provided a roadmap with Carter.

The jugular. The windpipe. The axillary arteries. The heart. The lungs.

Sara folded the knife. She pressed the button again. The blade flicked open. Her distorted reflection showed in the stainless steel. She folded down the blade.

She could feel Will on the knife. On the other side of the door. Wrapped around her hand. His essence had infiltrated every part of the cabin. Sara was reminded of the first time she had walked through the house after Jeffrey had died. One of the most devastating parts of losing him was that she had not lost their things. The bedroom furniture they had picked out together. The massive TV he had hung over the fireplace. His tools in the garage. The smell of him that had lingered on the sheets and towels and in his closet and on her skin. Every item, every scent, had been a stark reminder of her loss.

Sara thought back to three days ago, a lifetime ago, when she'd watched her mother snap beans in Bella's kitchen. Cathy had been right. Or close to right. Sara's weepiness was not because she could not let go of Jeffrey. It was because she was terrified of holding on to Will.

She folded the knife closed again. She studied the lines across the floor, checking her crude sundial. The blue light filtering through cracks in the walls had long ago turned yellow. Eight-thirty? Nine o'clock?

Her head pressed against the rough boards. She was exhausted from doing nothing with her body. She tried to tune herself into the regular cadence of the Camp. The cooking women. The little girls spinning like tops. Gwen glowering over every perceived slight or misstep.

Sara was not one to believe in auras, but something felt different in the air around her. Was she missing the *pops* as the men trained inside of the Structure? The giggles and cheers of the children? The smoky scent of wood burning, laundry boiling, food cooking?

Were they gone? Was this part of Dash's *Message*, to send away his followers so that Sara could bear witness to their utopian mountain community?

She stood up. She stored the knife in her bra. The underwire was already stabbing her in the side, so the discomfort was added to a very long list.

Her desire to pace had left with Will. Sara's hands went to her hips. Dash had usually unlocked the door by now. She assumed he had left the Camp. Delivering the Message. Or trying to.

Sara had to think that Will would stop him. He hadn't put much trust in the GPS tracker, but Sara knew that he wouldn't stop until Dash was taken down.

She pressed her hand against the door, testing the padlock. She heard metal scrape against metal. The hinges groaned, but did not give. Gwen would have the key. It would be exactly like the heinous bitch to let Sara stew inside the cabin.

She listened for the sentry outside the door. The new man had not bothered to introduce himself when he'd replaced Will. Sara assumed Lance was still in the bunkhouse. Not-Lance had sat on the log all night. He was heavy-set and clearly suffered from sleep apnea. He kept gasping himself awake with panicked gurgles between deep snores.

Sara got down on her knees. She looked under the door. Not-Lance was broad through the back, blocking her view of anything but his black shirt.

"Hello?" Sara waited, but there was no response. "Can you open the door, please?"

Still nothing.

Sara thought about the knife in her bra. Will's hand had barely fit underneath the door, but she could wedge under most of her forearm. She could stab Not-Lance, below his left shoulder. The blade was long enough to pierce his heart.

"Hello?" She decided against murder. She pushed out her hand, her fingers stretching to jab at him. "Hell—"

He tumbled forward, slamming head-first into the ground.

Sara backed up in surprise. She listened. She waited. She put her eye to the gap under the door.

Not-Lance had fallen face-first onto the ground. The impact had pushed him over to his side. His body was still locked into a sitting position. The fall had been hard. The muzzle of his rifle had opened up a furrow of skin along the side of his neck.

Sara watched the wound, studying it the way she would a piece of art. She waited for a drop of blood, but there was no blood coming out of the deep gash because Not-Lance's heart had stopped beating hours ago. Rigor had already stiffened his muscles. His ankles were ringed with purple livor mortis. His pants were soaked where he'd defecated and urinated on himself.

He was dead.

Sara sat on her knees. She brushed the dirt off of her hands. Her heart banged inside of her chest. Had the apnea killed him? Was it something else?

A sudden, eerie sense of wrongness took hold of Sara. She shivered, though she was sweating. The fine hairs on her arms rose to attention. Her senses strained to pick out the usual activity from the Camp. The odors, the sounds, the feeling that she was not alone.

Was she alone?

Sara stood up. She walked to the back of the cabin. She tested the wall with her hands. She found the springy section where the nails had rusted. The boards flexed against her palms. Sara shifted her weight onto her heels. She braced her hands against the wood. She pushed until the muscles in her shoulders started to burn.

"Shit," she mumbled. Splinters had dug into her skin. The board had moved, but not enough. The space between the slats showed more sunlight.

Sara wiped her grimy hands on her dress. The splinters flicked like tiny needles. She did the same thing again, pushing with all of her strength until the boards started to bow. There was a small crack, like a twig breaking, then the board started to split.

But still not enough.

Sara looked down at her hands. The palms were bleeding. She stepped back. She kicked the boards as hard as she could.

The wood splintered. The crack was much louder this time, more like a bolt of lightning spiking through a tree.

Sara waited, listening for sounds outside the door. The men in the deer stands. The armed soldiers in the woods. Gwen, Grace, Esther, Charity, Edna, Hannah and Joy.

Nothing.

Sara kicked at the wall again. Then again. She was sweating when she finally managed to break off enough of a section to climb through.

Her feet gently touched the ground. The air felt crisper behind the cabin. She couldn't quite understand her emotions, but Sara realized what she was feeling was freedom.

No one had come running. No one was trying to stop her or threaten her or shoot her.

Her gaze took in the area behind the cabin. The forest floor was dense, thick with vines and poison oak.

The greenhouse.

Sara walked around the cabin. She found the path, tentatively making her way, eyes moving left and right to see if anyone was coming to stop her. There were no armed men blocking her progress. The deer stands were empty. She lifted her dress as she stepped over a fallen log. Humidity thickened the air. Her eyes kept darting back and forth, this time in search of the greenhouse. She had seen it twice, both times by happenstance. She made herself stop. She listened for the river. The waterfall made a shushing sound to her right, but to her left, she heard a kitten mewing.

Sara turned. She took a few steps down the path. She listened again.

She hadn't heard a kitten.

A child was crying.

Sara was running toward the clearing before she could make a rational decision. The path narrowed in front of her. The child's crying intensified. She felt like she was running on a treadmill. The harder she pushed, the farther away the clearing seemed.

"Help!" a small voice called.

Sara's heart was gripped inside of a vice. Her life's work had been answering the calls of children. She knew what they sounded like when they were afraid, when they were looking for sympathy, when they were terrified that they were going to die.

She raced into the clearing. She spun around the neatly tended grass the same way the girls had countless times before. What she saw was not the same. The eerie sense of wrongness tightened her skin. The cabin doors hung open. The fires smoldered in the cooking area. There were no women, no children, just pieces of white confetti scattered around the grass. The wind picked at the pieces. White material floated feather-like in the air before settling to the ground. She saw a bare foot, the glint of a white leg, a hand clutching the dirt, a face turned up toward the sun.

Sara stumbled. Her knees started to give out. Her heart gave a sharp, painful beat inside of her chest.

Not confetti.

White dresses. High collars. Long sleeves. Young and old faces bloating in the morning sun.

"Oh, no—" Sara fell to her knees. She pressed her forehead to the ground and let out a low moan. Her heart had frozen mid-beat. Her thoughts kept racing around, pushing away the truth until she forced herself to confirm it.

Sara crawled through the grass. Her fingers trembled as she checked for pulses, stroked silky blond hair away from unseeing eyes.

Esther. Edna. Charity. The cooking women. The young ladies who had set the picnic tables. The men in the trees. The guards hiding in the woods.

Dead.

"Help," Grace whispered. She was lying under one of the picnic tables. Her frail body was curled into a ball.

Sara crawled to her. She pulled the little girl into her arms. Grace's eyelids drooped. Her pupils were wide. She stared up at Sara. Her lips moved soundlessly.

"Sweetheart." Sara smoothed her hair, pressed her lips to the child's forehead. "What happened? Please tell me what happened."

Grace tried to speak. The words gurgled in her mouth. Her arms draped lifelessly to her side. Her legs were dead weight.

"Oh, my lamb, hold on." Sara lifted her up, carrying her toward the bunkhouse. "Hold on, sweetheart."

White dresses blurred in Sara's peripheral vision. Bloated bellies. Constricted muscles. Signs of agonizing, brutal death.

The bunkhouse door was already open. Sara could smell the bodies from the bottom step. She laid Grace down on the ground. "I'll be right back, baby. Stay here."

The request was unnecessary. The child could not move, could not speak. Sara ran into the bunkhouse. Benjamin. Joy. Lance. Adriel. She checked each one. Only Joy was still alive.

Sara grabbed her by the shoulders, shook her awake. "Joy! Joy! What did they do?"

Joy's eyes were unmoving. Her abdomen was as round as a ball. Her expression was slack, but she was clearly conscious. Drool slid from the corner of her mouth. The pillow was wet with it. Her arms were limp. Her legs were paralyzed. She could not move her head.

"No—" Sara whispered. "No."

She bolted through the door, down the stairs, over Grace. Her feet pounded across the clearing. She found the path, headed toward the river. The rush of the waterfall got closer.

Sara spun around, looking for the greenhouse, screaming, "Where are you!"

Sunlight mirrored off the glass.

Sara tripped through the undergrowth. Two men clad in black lay on the forest floor. Another man had fallen from a deer stand. His neck had been broken by the fall. His head was turned backward. His arms were splayed to the side.

Sara kept walking toward the greenhouse, the glass serving as a lighthouse to warn her away. The pungent odor of death cut into the back of her throat. Sara opened her mouth to breathe. She could taste the simmering fluids leaching out of bodies. The closer she got, the more her eyes watered. She was reaching the epicenter of death. Whatever Michelle had been concocting inside of the greenhouse had taken as its first victims the men and women working inside.

Sara gagged. The bodies outside the greenhouse had started to melt in the heat. Skin slipped from bone. Eyes bulged. Gaping mouths showed pools of blood and vomit that had caked into throats.

They were young and old, men and women, dressed not in black but in white lab coats. Their faces showed the horror of their deaths.

Fully conscious. Paralyzed. Slowly suffocating.

Sara knew what had killed them.

She shoved hard against the greenhouse door. A body was blocking the way. Sara pushed him with her foot. She walked into the thermal tent. The heat was almost blinding. The electricity was off. The air conditioners had gone dormant. The thermal tent and glass acted as a magnifier for the sunlight, boiling the contents inside.

She saw exactly what she had expected to see.

A commercial laboratory.

Beakers and flasks, ring stands, pipettes, tongs, burners, vacuum tubes, test tubes, droppers, thermometers.

Spray bottles filled with clear liquid were scattered along the table. A metal rack contained raw materials. Sara pushed aside bags of spoiled apples and rotting potatoes.

Black box.

In Sara's long list of possibilities, this was the last thing she had expected to find at the other end of Michelle's message. The small box of HBAT was actually white. The *black box* was literally a printed black rectangle around a warning mandated by the Food and Drug Administration:

> DANGER! USE EXTREME CAUTION! EQUINE SERUM REQUIRES ESCALATING DOSE CHALLENGES TO OBVIATE SENSITIVITY AND POSSIBLE MORTALITY

Sara opened the box. The vial inside was from the US Department of Health and Human Service's Strategic National Stockpile. The agency stored and controlled push packages of emergency antibiotics, vaccines and anti-toxins that were sent out under armed guard in case of a biological attack.

Biological attack seemed like a muted way to describe what Dash was planning. This was why he had predicted that historians would never be able to accurately calculate the number of people murdered today. The Message was excruciating, unforgiving death. Sara was holding in her hand the only thing that could stop it in its tracks.

HBAT was specifically designed to treat botulism, the most acutely poisonous toxin known to man.

21

Wednesday, August 7, 9:17 a.m.

Faith stirred a packet of blue stuff into her black coffee. Van was still at the counter adding approximately one pound of sugar to his mocha latte. Her phone had buzzed with three shotgun-style texts from Amanda demanding an update, which meant that Amanda hadn't been called in to see the governor yet, which meant that she was probably stomping around the Capitol like an angry lunatic, raving about how everyone was wasting her time.

Faith texted a simple response—*working on it.*

Amanda fired back immediately—*work harder.*

Faith turned the phone face down on the table. She watched Van add chocolate sprinkles to his latte. She had only given him the information he had probably already gleaned from Beau Ragnersen: Will was going undercover. They knew that the IPA was planning something big today. Faith had kept in her pocket the information about Will being whisked away from the Citgo on an untraceable dirt bike. And Lyle Davenport, the Kia driver who'd met him at the gas station, invoking his right to remain silent. And the GPS tracker in Will's holster that was apparently not tracking anything.

In Faith's experience, if you were going to successfully lie, you'd better have a few more truths to throw around in case you were called on your bullshit.

Van finally sat down at the table. He sipped his coffee. Faith waited for some roundabout story, but for once, he got straight to the point. "Last September, Beau was admitted to Emory Hospital with a case of wound botulism."

Faith understood the individual words, but they made no sense together. "Wound botulism?"

"*Clostridium botulinum* is a bacteria that naturally occurs in soil and water. Under certain circumstances, it turns into botulinum neurotoxin, or botulism."

All that Faith knew about botulism was that rich women used it to freeze their faces. "What circumstances?"

"With Beau, he was muscle-popping black tar heroin that was cut with dirt. Wound botulism occurs very rarely. Maybe twenty cases are reported in the US each year. Beau presented at the ER with droopy eyelids, facial paralysis, muscle weakness, breathing complications. With the needle tracks in his arms, they assumed he'd overdosed on opiates. They shot him up with Narcan, and he got worse."

Faith found herself in the rare position of being unable to form a question.

"Botulism is extremely difficult to diagnose. Unless the doctor is thinking *botulism*, it's going to be the last thing that comes up. And the symptoms mimic a lot of things. Could be more people die from it than what's reported."

She still had no questions. Her phone buzzed on the table. Amanda had probably been called into the governor's office. She wanted updates, but Faith needed more from Van before that could happen.

She said, "Keep talking."

"The CDC is the only agency that knows how to test for botulism and who can administer HBAT, the antitoxin that stops the progression of the poison." He rolled the coffee cup in his hands. "You can't just give them a shot to make it all better. The drug is derived from horse serum. Initially, from a horse named First Flight, if you're interested. The FDA black-boxed the serum. You have to cut it down with another drug, then slow infuse it through an IV in order to make sure the treatment isn't killing the patient. And whatever state the patient is in—if they're on a ventilator, if their limbs are paralyzed, that's probably not going to fully reverse. Once the neurotoxin bonds to the nerve terminals, that's it. Beau was lucky Michelle figured it out before he had lasting damage."

Faith didn't see any luck here. "So he paid Michelle back by putting her in Dash's crosshairs?"

"That's not how it happened," Van said. "Adam Humphrey Carter was Beau's only visitor in the ICU. We know from Michelle's chart notations the exact times she was at the hospital. When Carter showed up, he was being his usual dick self. He made Michelle very uncomfortable. She had the staff call security. Security gave him a warning and filed an internal report."

Now she had questions. "You didn't think to tell me this two days ago when I asked you to cross-reference Michelle's files with Beau Ragnersen?"

"I didn't know two days ago. Spivey had thousands of patient files and worked on hundreds of projects, a lot of them top secret. But Ragnersen was a name that stood out. I did some digging at Emory yesterday morning, talked to the ICU staff, checked in with security. The internal report was just that—internal. I had to manually search the filing cabinets to find the actual document."

Faith realized that Kate Murphy's reticence to call Michelle Spivey's abduction an IPA operation rather than a sex-trafficking case suddenly made sense. "So, did Carter kidnap and rape Michelle to pay her back for calling hospital security on him, or did he kidnap her for the IPA?"

"That was our question," Van said. "Carter hated women. He wanted to punish them for—well, for whatever. It's not like hating women is a crazy, new idea. If you accept that Carter took Michelle because he wanted to punish her for turning him into security, then it makes a kind of sense that he'd want to keep her alive so he could continue to torture her. Open and shut case of kidnap and rape."

"What changed your mind?"

"The bombing. The car accident where your partner put Carter with Dash and the others. The clincher was a RISC alert I got on Sunday night. That's—"

"The Repository for Individuals of Special Concern."

"Correct. Michelle's details were already in RISC. The network is tied to servers around the country. The updates aren't in real-time, but we get them faster than you'd think. The RISC alert made it to my phone around six o'clock Sunday night, nine hours after the airport's facial recognition software pinged Michelle on *that* service road, on *that* day, in *that* spot, in front of *that* building."

Faith's phone buzzed with another text. Amanda was probably climbing the Capitol's marble walls.

She prompted Van, "What's *that* building?"

He glanced around, then told her, "It's a CDC Quarantine Station, part of the National Strategic Stockpile. For our purposes, think of it as an armamentarium for biological attacks. The CDC assembles what they call *push packs* of emergency medication that can be sent out on a moment's notice. That includes anti-dotes, anti-toxins and antibiotics. All your favorite antis for the coming apocalypse."

She asked, "Is HBAT stored there?"

"Yes."

"Was Michelle there to steal the anti-toxin or to destroy it?" Faith put together the answer before Van could tell her. "Dash already had two pipe bombs wired up and ready to go when they broke Michelle out of Emory. You don't just drive around with explosives in your trunk. He had to be planning on using the bombs to blow up the quarantine station, but then Michelle got sick and shit hit the fan, so he decided to use them on the parking deck instead."

"I like that you think like a terrorist."

"Couldn't Dash stick the bombs to the outside of the building?" Again, she answered her own question. "The building is reinforced, right? All that security, the steel door. Michelle was their only way inside. They needed her biometrics to open the door."

Van shrugged. "Did they?"

"Aren't there other quarantine stations?"

"Yes, but—" He didn't provide the *but*.

Atlanta was within a two-hour flight time of 80 percent of the US population. It made sense that the bulk of the warehousing would take place at the busiest airport in the world.

Faith asked, "How long does it take for someone to die from botulism poisoning?"

"Depends on the level of toxin. In its purest form, we're talking seconds. Something less refined, like a naturally occurring food contaminant, could be a couple of days, maybe a couple of weeks. Without treatment, you're pretty much a goner." He explained, "The neurotoxin slowly paralyzes everything. Your eyelids, your facial muscles, even the eyeballs in your head. Usually, you're awake, but you can't speak, and your brain is desperately sending out signals to move your muscles, but your muscles aren't responding. Eventually, all the mechanisms that you need to breathe are paralyzed, and you suffocate."

Faith felt her lips part in horror.

"Animals can get it. Mostly fish or things that eat fish. There are five types of strains that infect humans. Botulism can be food-borne, inhaled through spores, injected, but thankfully not transmitted person-to-person. The toxicity has something to do with temperature and oxygen level. There's a type of infant botulism babies get in their guts."

Faith's own gut clenched.

Van said, "This is a nasty, nasty bug we're talking about, Mitchell. All it would take is one kilogram to kill the entire human population."

Faith remembered the cardboard boxes Will had traded out at the warehouse. Two dozen thirty-by-thirty containers, two strong young men to lift each box. One kilo was a little over two pounds.

"Okay," Faith had to talk this out. "Carter visited Beau in the hospital. He heard about the wound botulism. He knew how deadly it was. Did he know what Beau went through before he was finally diagnosed?"

"Yes."

"So, Carter probably told Dash about the botulism, right?

And instead of being freaked out, Dash got the idea to weaponize it."

"That's the assumption."

She dreaded hearing the answer, but she had to ask, "Could Michelle make enough botulism for a large-scale attack?"

"The short answer is yes."

"Give me the long answer."

"We are hoping, in that scenario, Michelle managed to fake the science."

"*Hoping?*"

"The IPA has been holding Michelle for over a month. She's been raped and abused. We assume by her appearance that she's being starved. She probably has sepsis from her appendix rupturing. She went berserk on Carter at the motel. We know that Carter was threatening her daughter." He leaned his elbows on the table. "Look, I'm gonna lay it out for you. Michelle Spivey is a strong, brilliant woman, but our profilers and our psychiatrist aren't sure that she'd be able to hold up under that kind of relentless physical and psychological torture."

Faith doubted anyone could. "Do you think Michelle is desperate enough to make the real thing?"

"I think that Dash would force her to keep trying until he was one hundred percent certain that every drop she produced was the real thing."

Faith spotted a problem. "You said that the CDC is the only agency that knows how to test for it. Michelle could fudge the test."

"There's another way to test for botulism." Van shrugged when she didn't try to guess. "Give it to a bunch of people and see if they die."

22

Wednesday, August 7, 9:23 a.m.

Sara opened the box of HBAT. She unfolded the dosing directions.

> *20 mL diluted with 0.9 percent sodium chloride in a 1:10 ratio infused in a volumetric pump for slow administration 0.5 mL/min for the initial 30 minutes . . .*

She looked up at the ceiling. Sara had thought it impossible to cry more tears after Will had left, but now, she was coming undone.

There was nothing she could do for Grace or Joy or anyone else.

She clutched the useless vial of serum as she walked out of the greenhouse. The white confetti in the clearing brought more tears to her eyes. She went to Grace. The girl had already stopped breathing. She found Joy in the bunkhouse. She was alive, but her raspy gasps told Sara that she had only a few minutes more.

Sara sat with her, silently crying, until she was gone.

Black box.

An FDA warning. A death sentence. A coffin.

She looked at the vial of antitoxin that she still gripped in her hand. The metal ring around the seal had been broken. A single needle hole was in the rubber stopper.

Had Sara been infected, too? Her first day at the Camp, she was too upset to eat. Then Dash had changed Sara to vegetarian meals. Was Dash planning all along to make Sara his Witness?

Death was her testimony. Death was the Message.

So many will be dead that I doubt historians will be able to tally a final number.

Not all of the people in the Camp had been poisoned last night. Their deteriorating bodies told the story. They had been infected in groups of five or ten. That was the horrible beauty of botulism: every person reacted differently to the toxin. Even in a hospital setting, it was difficult to make a diagnosis. The symptoms were diverse, mimicking other ailments. One person might die in a few hours, another person might die in a few weeks, another person might walk away. Dash had experimented on his own people. He had known that he was slowly murdering his followers even as he had eaten with them, preached at them, railed against mongrels, and watched them all slowly succumb to the literal poison he was feeding them.

If Sara had to guess, she would say that Benjamin had been patient zero. Lance's droopy eyelids and slurred speech indicated that he'd been given a slower-acting version. Joy's early abdominal pain pointed to her poisoning coming in a third or fourth wave. Michelle would have had the knowledge to control the potency. The other children had been fine last night, so they must have been injected with a faster-acting form of the toxin before they went to bed.

Sara put her head in her hands. She could not understand how Dash could murder his own children. Acting the part of the good father came too naturally to him.

She felt her head start to shake. Dash would not have dirtied his hands with the job. Gwen would've injected the girls. Or maybe she had hidden the poison inside of the ice cream. She was in charge of the Camp. She was Dash's partner in everything.

His Dark Angel.

His Lady Macbeth.

Sara compelled herself to move. Murdering the people inside the Camp was only part one of the plan. Part two was spreading the toxin to the unsuspecting people Dash called *the enablers and the mongrels*. Sara wanted to believe that Will would be able to stop him, but he was surrounded by armed men who were ready to lay down their lives for the IPA.

She had to find a way to warn Faith and Amanda. Dash had been communicating with the world somehow. Sara's first morning at the Camp, she had asked him a question about the number of victims at Emory. He had readily provided the answer. There had to be a phone or a tablet or a computer somewhere.

Sara left the bunkhouse. She walked up the hill. She wanted to run, but she was in a daze, her body shocked by all of the senseless, devastating violence. The sweet little girls. The spinning tops in their white wedding dresses. The way Grace had laughed so hard at Will's joke that she had almost toppled over.

Sara wiped her eyes with the back of her hand. The skin was raw from the salt in her tears.

The Structure loomed into view. Sara thought about the men training for so many hours. Two teams infiltrating in two different waves. The bullets Will had told her about were not coated with pork brine. They had been coated with botulism. Dash wasn't content to just kill. He wanted to make sure any survivors suffered the same agonizing death as his brothers and sisters at the Camp.

Sara started to cry again as she thought about the sweet, innocent children. Was she mis-remembering the smile on Gwen's face when she'd handed Esther and Grace each a cup of ice cream? Sara could clearly remember Gwen offering her a serving. There had definitely been a smirk on her lips, but it was hard to tell whether Gwen was smiling because she was offering Sara poison or because she had known what Sara would find when she left her cabin this morning.

Sara heard a car engine revving.

Her heart jumped into her throat.

She ran to the crest of the hill. Below her, a green sedan was parked by the metal storage building. Exhaust plumed from the tailpipe. The car shook as the engine roared.

"Wait!" Sara yelled, darting down the hill, hands out. "Wait!"

The car was not moving. The driver's door hung open. Gwen

was behind the wheel. Her foot was stuck on the gas. The gear was in neutral. Her body sagged against the seat belt. Her eyelids were half-closed. She was reaching out, her fingertips brushing the handle as she tried in vain to pull the door closed.

Sara kicked the door out of the woman's reach. A suitcase was on the back seat. Gwen was dressed in jeans and a white blouse. Her hair was styled. She was wearing eyeshadow, blush, lipstick.

She had stopped to put on make-up while her children were dying.

"You knew." Sara's throat closed around the accusation.

The cooking women. The bunkhouse. The children—her own children. Gwen knew what Michelle was doing in the greenhouse. She knew the men were running drills inside the Structure, that they were training for a *mission* and that they were at *war*.

"You knew!" Sara grabbed Gwen's arm and wrenched her out of the car. She fumbled for the knife in her bra. "You killed them!"

"Dah . . ." Gwen looked at Sara through heavy eyelids. Her jaw was slack. Her belly was swollen, the same as Joy's, the same as Grace's, the same as the people she had murdered at the Camp.

Sara sat back on her heels. The knife rested in her lap. She had expected to see fear on Gwen's face, but there was nothing but the same cold look she had given Sara while she was suffocating Tommy.

"Dahh . . ." Drool slid from the corner of Gwen's mouth. "Did he poh . . . poison . . . me . . . t-too?"

Sara felt an incredulous laugh slip out of her mouth. "Of course Dash poisoned you, too, you stupid bitch."

"Buh . . ." Her throat worked. "Buhh . . . he . . ."

Sara leaned over Gwen, their faces inches apart. "Where is Dash going? What is he planning?"

Gwen's eyes slowly moved to the left.

Sara had dropped the vial of antitoxin.

"You want this?" Sara held up the HBAT so that Gwen could

read the label. “Tell me where they’re going, and I’ll save you.”

“The ch-children . . .”

“Don’t pretend you’re worried about your children.” Sara pressed open the woman’s eyelids to make her see. “They’re all dead, Gwen. I know that you murdered them.”

“He . . . p-promised . . .” Gwen’s jaw was going slack. Her eyes were fixed.

“What did he promise?” Sara demanded. “Tell me!”

“W-we . . .” Her chest pumped desperately for air. “We would . . . make . . . m-more.”

The last word disappeared inside of her throat. Her vocal cords had frozen. All she could do was gurgle the same way Grace had done before she’d choked to death on her own saliva.

Sara hoped she was conscious until the very last moment.

She checked Gwen’s pockets. She looked inside the car. The phone was in the console between the seats.

Sara flipped open the phone. She saw the time—

9:49 a.m.

Her fingers trembled as she dialed the number. Gwen’s gurgling persisted. Sara was still gripping Will’s folding knife. She wanted to drive the blade into Gwen’s neck, but the woman did not deserve mercy.

Sara walked toward the metal storage building. She listened to the phone ring.

Faith said, “Mitchell.”

Sara’s throat closed at the sound of her friend’s voice. She had to cough out the words. “Faith, it’s me.”

“Sara?”

“I—” Sara looked at her hands. She was plagued by an uncontrollable shaking. “I’m in the mountains. On a compound. Everyone is dead. Dash had Michelle synthesize botulism. He killed them all.”

“Okay, hold on.” Faith’s hand covered the phone. She was relaying the information to someone else.

“I don’t know where Will is,” Sara told her. “He left with Dash and the other men. I think this morning. There were—” She tried to remember what he’d told her. “Forty men with

AR-15s. Over ten thousand rounds of ammunition. Dash had them sprayed with botulism."

"Jesus Christ," Faith hissed. "I'm putting you on speakerphone. I've got the FBI with me. We're tracing your call."

"The boxes from the warehouse are here." Sara peeled open one of the shipping packets. "The shipper is called the Whisting Company in North Carolina. The recipient is ACS, Inc. 1642 Airport Parkway. There's a part number, a quantity of two thousand."

"We're looking up the address," Faith said. "Can you open the box?"

Sara was already cutting the tape with Will's knife. The contents were knotted into a plastic bag. At first, she did not understand what she was looking at. "They're aluminum tins, like the kind that frozen foods come in."

"Oh, God." Faith sounded astonished. "Air Chef Services. They make airplane meals. Dash contaminated the containers with botulism. He's going to poison hundreds of thousands of people."

"Wait—" Sara started running up the hill. "There's something else. Dash mocked up a two-story building. It's at least half a football field. He had teams practicing infiltrations in full riot gear. Two teams, two waves of attacks."

"What does it look like?"

Sara ran into the Structure. She circled around, looking for clues that would help identify the target. "There's a second-floor balcony. The stairs go up the middle of the room, then there's a landing, then two more sets of stairs branch off to the left and right."

"Can you see anything else?"

Sara had reached the landing. She looked to the right.

"The letters *LG* or *IG* are painted on the floor at the top of the right-hand branch of stairs." She ran up the other side. "If you go left, then to the end of the hall, there's a capital *G* spray-painted in front of what looks like a door."

"Door?" Faith asked. "No windows?"

"Only doors. Five on the right side, three on the left. Then there's four more opposite the stairs, three in the hall behind the landing where the stairs T off." Sara looked down from the railing. "I don't know what it's supposed to represent. A hotel lobby? Will thought maybe a synagogue or—"

"Wait," Faith said. "I know what you're describing. It's an atrium."

23

Wednesday, August 7, 9:58 a.m.

"Two minutes out, brothers." Dash pulled back the slide on his Glock to make sure a bullet was in the chamber. "Remember our cause, my friends. Remember the sacrifices our families have made to bring us here today."

There were murmurs of agreement all around. They were all clearly scared, but just as clearly, they were eager to do harm.

"What we do today is the first step in cleansing the country of the enablers and mongrels," Dash said. "We must destroy this corrupt society in order to remake ourselves as the Framers intended. This country will be reborn. *We* will be reborn. That is our Message. We will bathe ourselves in the blood of the lambs and spread our seed into the wilderness."

The chanting started again. "Blood and soil! Blood and soil!"

Will looked at his watch.

9:58 a.m.

Five black vans. Forty armed men.

Will mentally walked through what was supposed to happen once they reached their destination.

Team One, the bulk of their number, would go first. Cannon fodder, Dash had called them. Will assumed this meant that security at the incursion was high. Maybe half of the men would make it into the building. The other half would be pared down on the first floor.

That was when Team Two was supposed to charge in.

Bravo toward the *LG*. Charlie toward the *G*.

Will could not let it get that far. He would have to take out as many men as he could before they walked through the entrance.

Take out.

He couldn't let himself reduce these men to collateral damage. Will was going to have to shoot them in their chests, their backs, their heads. They weren't paper targets with circles over their bodies. Will had spent the last sixteen hours with them. He knew some of their names, what they liked and didn't like, their bad jokes and origin stories.

They had no idea that Will was going to kill them.

"Damn." Dobie's hands were sweating so much that he couldn't pull the slide on his gun. "What's wrong with this thing?"

Will stared at the closed back doors. He had purposefully placed Dobie behind him. Will would be the second-to-last out. He was going to shoot Dash, then take out the rest of Bravo and Charlie as they started to run.

The van lurched to a stop. The tires burned rubber as it swerved into reverse.

Will looked at his watch.

9:59 a.m.

Dash said, "Steady, brothers."

Everyone rolled down their black hoods, clipped on their helmets. Will unbuttoned his shirt. He pulled out Sara's white headscarf. His only hope of not getting shot by one of the good guys was to tie it around his neck.

The van squealed to a stop.

Dash said, "Not yet, brothers!"

Another van stopped beside them. Then another. Four in all. The time for pep speeches and prayers had come and gone. Doors banged open. Feet started pounding concrete. Instantly, guns began to fire—rifles, Glocks, the *pop-pop-pop* overlaid by men and women screaming for their lives. The sound of their panic reverberated into Will's ears.

Gerald banged on the side of the van.

Will tied the scarf around his neck. His heartbeat turned into a stopwatch.

Tick-tick-tick.

The doors broke open.

Sunlight blinded him. Will narrowed his eyes. He saw a sidewalk, some concrete stairs. Neatly trimmed grass and tall trees. Tall, white pillars holding up limestone.

Bravo and Charlie team were already on the move.

Will cracked his elbow into Dobie's face. The kid's head gonged against the van before he dropped to the floor.

"Go! Go! Go!" Dash yelled, firing his AR-15 from his hip.

Will felt suspended in the air as he jumped from the van. He took his first look at the target. The sparkling gold dome. The four-story portico. The neoclassical architecture. The east and west wings that housed the legislative chambers.

They were at the Georgia State Capitol.

"Let's go!" Gerald sounded exhilarated by a happy rage. He shot one of the Capitol police officers. A mist of red exploded from the man's head. He shot another officer in the stomach. The bullet chunked into the limestone. Civilians were screaming, running out the door, ducking across the grass. Gerald opened fire on them. Tens, maybe hundreds of people, were all running blindly into a wall of bullets.

Will shot Gerald in the face.

The woman behind him screamed.

"Get out of here!" Will pushed her away. He searched for Dash, checking faces, shooting any man he saw in a black hood. A bullet whizzed past his head. Will grabbed the dead cop's hat and put it on. He dropped his rifle. He drew the Sig Sauer out of his holster. With his Glock, he shot another hooded man. A guy in a suit slammed into Will.

"Move!" Will shoved him aside.

So many people were streaming out of the doors that Will was washed back toward the sidewalk. He spun around, trying to find a target. He shot another hooded man, then another. He aimed at a third. The guy's eyes went wide.

Daryl.

The man liked to fish. His wife had left him two years ago. His kids wouldn't answer their phones when he called.

Will shot Daryl in the chest. He pivoted to the next hooded man, then the next.

Oliver, who hated chocolate. *Rick*, who loved French bulldogs. *Jenner*, who all night long had kept nervously asking what time it was.

Chest. Chest. Head.

"Please!" a woman screamed.

Will's Glock was almost touching her face. The slide was back. The gun was empty.

"Run," Will growled, dropping the magazine, snapping a new one into place.

Where the fuck was Dash?

Will scanned the area around the entrance. Blue dresses and black suits and red power ties and blood and bone and gray matter dripping along the sidewalks, staining the grass. He saw bodies splayed across flower beds, leaning against the trees, propped up against the monuments to Confederate generals and segregationists.

No Dash.

Will hurdled over the broken glass door and ran inside the Capitol building.

Bodies, debris, chaos. The four-story atrium was filled with light from the clerestory windows ringing the ceiling. Gunfire hailed down around him. Will hugged himself to the wall. The marble was cool against his back. The floor was riddled with bodies, mostly civilian. Six men in black hoods had been cut down at the foot of the stairs. That meant a dozen, maybe two dozen, had made it to the second floor. Or the third, where the legislators met in a large, oak-paneled room. Or the fourth floor, which had a viewing gallery.

Cleansing the country of the enablers and mongrels.

Will heard the crunch of a shoe behind him. He spun around.

Black man. Blue suit. Hands in the air.

Will pushed him toward the exit, then swung around. Three

more men were cowering against a closed door. Politicians with American flags on their lapels. Their hands silently scratched at the wood, begging to be let in. One of them was stiffly holding his arm. Blood sponged out between his fingers.

Will waved them toward the exit. He listened, his ears straining for sound over their hurried footsteps.

There was a lull in the firing.

Will scanned the large room, which was the exact same dimensions as the fake building at the Camp. He looked up at the three levels of balconies, searching for signs of Dash. He ducked down when the sudden *snap-snap-snap* of gunfire echoed around the atrium. Team One had reached the House of Representatives. The Senate chambers were on the other side of the rotunda. The distant *pop* of gunfire told Will that both sides had been breached.

He jogged across the open floor at a crouch, stepping over broken glass and fallen bodies. The grand staircase split the middle of the room. Carved marble, red carpet, wood paneling. Papers, shoes, broken eyeglasses, pools of blood, pieces of teeth and bone. Throats had been slit. Bodies were piled one on top of the other where a single bullet had killed two, three, sometimes four people.

Two injured women were sobbing on the stairs. They cringed, hunkering their shoulders at the sight of Will. A sheriff's deputy had tied his belt around his leg to stop the bleeding. His gun was raised at Will, but the chamber was empty. His finger would not stop pulling on the trigger. The rapid *click-click* of the hammer matched Will's pounding heartbeat.

He ran up to the landing with the same quick steps he'd practiced at the Camp.

The spray-painted *LG* was for the Lieutenant Governor's office.

The *G* was for the Governor.

Bravo team had been taken out before they could reach the door. Their chests had been ripped open by shotgun blasts. Tufts of white lining stuck out from their foam vests. One man was missing part of his jaw. Another was missing an arm. Will stepped over a disembodied hand that was still gripping one of the eight-inch hunting knives that all of the *brothers* wore on their belts.

Charlie team was nowhere in sight. Will crouched his way to the top of the stairs, hiding behind the thick, marble railing. He was about to peer around the corner when the sound of gunfire made him pull back.

The noise was coming from the floor directly above him. Bullets snapped like burning embers. The remnants of Team One. They were either finishing off the stragglers inside the House of Representatives or someone had managed to find a weapon to return fire.

Dash would be in the governor's office by now. He would have a gun to the man's head. He would be making demands.

White power. Kill the enablers. Blood and soil.

Will tried a second time to look around the railing.

He found himself staring into the muzzle of a Smith and Wesson five-shot revolver.

Amanda.

Her finger was in the process of moving to the trigger. Then she recognized Will. Slowly, she rested her finger along the trigger guard. He saw her mouth open as she took in a breath.

Will holstered the Glock. He kept the Sig Sauer in his hand. The balcony was empty. No black-hooded men. No civilians ducking and covering. No cops but Will and Amanda.

The gunfire had stopped. The silence inside the atrium felt like a tomb. Flickers of passing bodies strobed the sunlight in the high windows. SWAT was on the roof. Will heard sirens in the distance.

Amanda asked, "Where is Dash?"

Will's eyes found the closed door of the governor's office. Two highway patrolmen stood guard with pump-action shotguns. One of them had been wounded. Blood trickled from a hole in his bicep.

"Will?"

He shook his head, trying to put it together. The last time he had seen Dash was outside the van. Civilians were streaming out of the building. Gerald was murdering as many of them as he could. Dash's rifle was blazing. He was shooting from the hip, not his shoulder. He was screaming for his men to keep moving.

The wave of people running out the doors had engulfed Will, forcing him to give them cover instead of killing Dash.

By the time Will had been able to look for Dash again, the man had disappeared.

The hard facts punched Will in the chest. "He's a coward, not a fighter. He was never going to go inside."

Will ran down the stairs three at a time. He sprinted across the marble floor, around the bodies, then hurdled through the broken glass door and into the daylight.

Will jumped down the concrete stairs. He spiraled around, desperately searching for Dash. What he saw made him ill.

The park-like setting of the Capitol grounds had turned into a hellscape. People were moaning, crying, screaming. Bullets had torn through flesh, eyes were missing, chests were oozing.

Will saw Dash across the east lawn.

A large dogwood kept him in shadow. He was on his knees, but he hadn't been shot. He was frantically searching the pockets of the dead.

The psychopath had planned everything so carefully, drilling his *brothers* into a trance, sending them out to be slaughtered, but Dash hadn't once considered how he was going to make his escape without a set of keys.

Will raised the Sig Sauer, lining up the sights on Dash's heart, yelling, "Stop!"

Dash's head snapped up.

"Police!" Will said. "Hands in the air."

Dash dove to the ground. Will fired two rounds before he realized what Dash was doing. He had surrounded himself with wounded. He grabbed a woman by the arm, yanking her up to her knees so that her body shielded his. She had already been shot in the leg. Dash's hunting knife was pressed so hard into her neck that blood sagged into the collar of her white blouse.

Terror cut into every line of her face. She had passed the moment of fear and was paralyzed by the threat of darkness.

"Let her go." Will started walking toward Dash, both the Glock and Sig Sauer out in front of him. "Now."

"Two weapons," Dash said, his face ducking below the woman's shoulder. "You think you can make the shot, Wolfie?"

Will needed four more steps and he'd have this man dead on the ground. "I think I can kill you before you draw your next breath."

"Hey, asshole!" Dobie yelled.

Chunks of concrete spit up at Will's feet.

Dobie was shooting at him. The second bullet went wide. The third took out a window. The only reason Will wasn't dead where he stood was that the kick from the rifle had slammed Dobie back into the van.

Will ducked behind a metal garbage can while Dobie scrambled.

The kid yelled, "Come out, you fucking coward!"

Will kept his Glock on Dash. He trained the Sig on Dobie. His arms formed a triangle between the three of them.

He yelled, "Dobie, put down the rifle! Right now!"

"Fuck you, asshole." Dobie was out in the open, the weapon high on his shoulder.

SWAT was on the roof. Amanda was armed with her five-shot in the doorway. Sirens were roaring down the street. Bodies were everywhere. Someone was going to kill this kid.

"Hold your fire!" Will heard his voice scratch up like a needle on a record. "I'm GBI! Hold your fire!"

Dash was grinning, reveling in the horror. He had seen the armed men moving down the street, the snipers on the roof. He was shaded by a tree, on his knees, holding a hostage in front of him like a shield.

The only gun that had a possible shot on him was Will's.

"Dobie," Will kept his Glock pointed at Dash, but he begged the kid, "please, Dobie, put down the rifle."

"I'm gonna murder you, you fucking pig!" Dobie was furious, burning from the betrayal. "You were my friend!"

"Dobie, I'm still your friend." Will stood up from the trashcan. He waited for a bullet from either Dobie or SWAT. When nothing came, he took a step toward the kid, then another. His eyes stayed focused on Dash even as he got farther away from him. "Dobie, put the rifle on the ground. Please."

"Fuck you!"

Dash's grin was so smug that Will longed to put a bullet between his teeth. The knife was still tight against the woman's throat. Tears mixed with blood on her face. She was trying not to breathe, to keep her body as still as possible.

This was Will's calculation: There was a Glock on Dash's belt. The minute Will looked away, Dash would cut her throat, then draw the weapon and shoot Will.

Dash was clearly doing the same math. His smirk did not falter. He told Will, "Tricky situation, brother."

Will nodded once, as if he agreed, but Dash didn't know about Amanda standing just inside of the shattered doorway. He didn't know that she had a better angle at his head, that she was a better shot than Will.

"Fucking look at me!" Dobie demanded.

Will kept his eyes on Dash even as he moved closer to Dobie. He saw what Amanda was probably seeing: that the hostage wasn't the only concern. There were scores of people behind Dash, innocent civilians, broken bodies scattered like driftwood on the Capitol lawn.

The enablers and mongrels.

Secretaries. Politicians. Police officers. Janitors. Assistants.

"You lied to me!" Dobie raged at Will. "I trusted you, and you fucking lied to me!"

"Please." Will was only a few feet away. He turned to look the kid in the eye, knowing that he was giving Dash the open target of his chest. "Dobie, it's over. Please, put down—"

The sniper's bullet split open Dobie's head.

The kid's arms flew up. The rifle dropped.

Will turned away, but he could smell the coppery blood in the air, feel it draping his skin like a delicate piece of lace.

The sound of Dobie hitting the ground felt like a death blow to his own body.

Will looked down at the sidewalk. A string of blood wrapped around his boot. Dobie's blood. It was on Will's arm, stuck in his beard.

He looked up.

Dash had not moved. The woman was still acting as his shield. His head was low behind her shoulder. The Glock was still on his belt. The smug look was still on his face.

He hadn't killed the hostage, hadn't tried to kill Will, because he wanted something.

Will guessed the *what* before his eyes saw the answer. People were holding up their phones, recording everything that was happening. Even with their hands covered in blood and dead bodies all around them, they were still filming.

Will wiped Dobie's blood out of his eyes with the back of his arm. He told Dash, "Let the woman go."

"I don't think so, brother." Dash tightened his grip around his hostage. She let out a gasp, but remained still. "I found myself without my angels this morning. We'll need new sisters to replenish the flock."

Will felt his jaw tighten. The women at the Camp. Only Gwen had served them breakfast this morning. The food had been cold. Was that because the women who cooked the meals and cleaned the clothes and bore the children were dead?

Dash said, "The cause demands purity, brother. Untainted bloodlines. We lead by example. We wipe the world clean starting with ourselves. We march triumphantly for the last widows of the revolution."

"The women," Will said. "The children. Are they—"

"Cleansed." Dash's smirk had turned into a grin. "'The tree of liberty must be refreshed from time to time with the blood of patriots and tyrants. It is its natural manure.'"

Will couldn't breathe. The heat had punctured his skin. His brain was on fire.

Had he sacrificed Sara?

Dash said, "Those words were spoken by Thomas Jefferson, the father of the Declaration of Independence, one of the original Framers of our Constitution."

Will blinked blood out of his eyes. "Did you kill them? Just tell me if—"

"My name is Douglas Shinn. I am the rightful leader of the Invisible Patriot Army." Dash had turned his head away. He was talking directly into the cameras. "As the chosen prophet of Martin Elias Novak, I call on the white men of this country to look at our deeds and rejoice in the carnage brought on by the IPA. Join me, brothers. Join me in reclaiming your rightful place as men. You will be rewarded with riches beyond your imagination and the company of good white women."

Sara?

"We must turn away the disease-ridden, the desperate, the brown and black mongrels who will rape and murder our children."

Will looked at the woman's throat. Thin, like Sara's, with the same delicate indentation at the base.

"Join me in returning the world to its natural order, brothers. Pick up your arms. Raise your fists. Let the world know that we will not be cowed."

Will's finger slid down the side of the Glock to the trigger. All that mattered was the knife at the woman's throat. The polished lines of the blade reflected the blue of the sky. The blood weeping from the wound was dark red. Will's eyes tunneled onto the stainless-steel blade. Dash's hand was steady. There was no fear inside of him. He was exactly where he wanted to be: at the center of the world's attention.

Dash told the cameras, "Today, brothers, we sign our name on these Capitol grounds in our own blood. We sacrifice ourselves for the greater good. Let all the enablers and the mongrels take heed of our valor in battle. White blood! White power! White America! Forever!"

The tip of the blade started to move.

Will pulled the trigger.

The explosion of gunpowder filled his ears with a high-pitched whine. Will was temporarily blinded by the flash at the end of the muzzle. He felt the heat of the empty shell ejecting out of the side of the Glock.

The whine was replaced by a piercing scream. The hostage was frantically crawling away on her hands and knees. She gripped Dash's knife in her hands.

Dash lay on his side, eyes wide, mouth gaping open.

He was still alive.

Will's aim had been off by three inches. The bullet had ripped open Dash's scalp above his ear. The blood flowed like water into the ground.

Blood and soil.

Will stared down at the man between the sights of his Glock. The metal notches framed the crisp white of Dash's skull, the broken blood vessels and yellow fat and black follicles of hair.

Dash reached up to the wound. His fingers probed the deep gash. He touched the smooth bone. The glassy look left his eyes. He rolled onto his back, clutching his head.

"Fuck!" Dash screamed. "Fuck!"

Amanda took the Glock off his belt, cuffed together his wrists. Her jacket was off. She was down on her knees, wrapping it around Dash's head.

Will should help her. People were suffering all around him. The grounds had turned into a graveyard. But Will could not move. His body was made of granite.

The women at the Camp. The children. Dobie.

Sara?

Will's gun was still pointing at Dash's head. His finger had stayed on the trigger. His elbows were slightly bent to absorb the recoil. His feet were still in a shooting stance because his body wanted to shoot this man and get it right this time.

"Wilbur," Amanda called up to him.

Will sniffed. The taste of Dobie's blood came into his mouth, stuck between his teeth, settled into his lungs. He felt every single muscle between his brain and his finger working against each other as he tried to think of one reason not to murder Dash in cold blood.

"Sara's okay," Amanda told him. "Faith talked to her on the phone. Sara's all right."

Sara?

"Will," Amanda repeated. "Breathe."

An image teased at Will's rage like water lapping against the side of a boat.

He wasn't here anymore. The Capitol, the grass, the trees, were gone.

He was standing in Sara's apartment. She was about to kiss him for the first time.

This was bad.

Will should've kissed her first, a long time ago, but he wasn't sure that she wanted him to kiss her and he didn't know where to put his hands and he was so anxious and so scared and so fucking hard that just thinking about how soft her mouth would feel had sent a jolt into every fiber of his being.

Sara had put her mouth close to his ear and whispered—

Breathe.

"Wilbur?" Amanda snapped her fingers.

The sound was like a light switching on.

The Capitol. The grass. The trees. The monuments.

Will's mouth opened. Air filled his lungs. His finger moved off the trigger.

He returned the gun to his holster.

He nodded to Amanda.

She nodded back at him.

Will's senses continued to fill in the world around him. Rescue teams were everywhere. Fire trucks wailed. Sirens roared. First responders. Atlanta Police. Sheriff's deputies. Highway Patrol. Every law enforcement officer in the vicinity had heard the gunfire and started running toward the sound.

The good guys.

Amanda told Will, "We had a three-minute warning thanks to Faith and Sara. We got some people out or sheltered in place. The chambers were empty, but I'm not sure how many . . ." Her voice trailed off, but she didn't need to finish the sentence. There was no way to count the dead. There were scores of them around the lawn. More were inside of the building. Even the wounded looked like they were floating back and forth across the line between life and death.

"Miss?" Dash's voice trembled up an octave. "Miss, I need help. The bullet that struck me . . ."

"It's a flesh wound." Amanda stared down at him. "You'll live. At least long enough to be sentenced by a judge."

"Please, miss, you don't understand." Dash's teeth were chattering. Tears edged into the corners of his eyes. "Please. Call the CDC. I don't want to die the same way they did."

EPILOGUE

FOUR DAYS LATER
Sunday, August 11, 10:17 a.m.

Sara was pulled awake by the sound of a dog lapping water from the kitchen bowl. She squinted at her watch, but found only her bare wrist. She turned to see if Will was in bed, but there was no Will.

As usual, he had risen at the crack of dawn. Sara had listened to him stirring a packet of hot chocolate into a mug, talking to the dogs, doing his stretches, checking his email, because Will's bedroom door opened up next to the kitchen and Sara could never sleep late when she stayed here.

She pulled Will's pillow to her face. She could still smell him on the sheets. After wasting countless hours in her cabin prison cataloging the ways she was going to screw him, Sara had been unable to do anything for the last three nights but cry in his arms.

Will seemed content to just hold her. She knew that Dobie's death still weighed on him. The fact that he was even talking to Sara about it was evidence of his turmoil. He was plagued by *if*s. If Will had shot Dash before the van doors had opened. If he'd shot Dash outside instead of trying to get the people out of the way. If Will's two shots hadn't missed when he'd first seen Dash on the Capitol lawn.

If he'd managed to get Dobie to drop the rifle before the sniper's bullet had ended his short, hate-filled life.

Though Sara agreed with the choices Will had made, she hadn't tried to rationalize his actions or smooth away the blame. She knew that Will had to get there on his own. Sara was familiar with all the different ways your best, most educated decision could result in the worst outcome. Sara had always carried around inside of her the memory of every patient she had ever lost. Now, Benjamin, Grace, Joy, Adriel, all of those little pieces of white confetti, had joined the unforgotten souls that lived inside her heart.

She looked at the clock by the bed.

10:21 a.m.

They were supposed to meet her family for lunch in two hours. Sara had sequestered herself at Will's for too long. She had wanted to hide from the minute-by-minute deluge of information, that her father continuously watched on the news.

Eddie was obsessed with learning more about Dash. About Gwen and Martin Novak. About the surviving *brothers* who were still spreading their message of racist, misogynist hate to any reporter who would hold up a microphone to their ugly mouths.

Forty-six dead at the Capitol. Ninety-three wounded. All of the survivors had been infected with botulism by the coated bullets. All of them had been infused with HBAT.

Even Dash.

Fortunately, there had been no infections from the Air Chef meals. The aluminum food containers were being loaded onto the conveyor belts when the FBI had raided the facility. Testing had shown that botulism coated the bottoms of each tray. Had the food been processed and loaded onto planes, every passenger who ate a meal on any of the thousands of flights out of Hartsfield would've been infected with the toxin.

The assumption was that Michelle Spivey had been taken to the airport that day so that Dash could blow up the country's main strategic stockpile of HBAT. Without the anti-toxin, there would have been countless deaths. Botulism could be a slow-moving, unpredictable toxin. As Dash had said, even the historians would not be able to arrive at a final tally. Sara could only imagine how furious Dash had been when Michelle had collapsed just yards away from completing the mission.

Or maybe he hadn't been furious.

Maybe by the time they had driven Michelle to Emory Hospital, Dash had persuaded himself that the HBAT didn't matter. He had two bombs ready to go. He had a hospital deck with staff and visitors streaming in and out.

Brothers, let's go with plan B.

Sara's main question had been about how Dash had obtained a vial of HBAT in the first place. Gwen had recognized the anti-toxin, which meant that Dash had known about it, which meant that they were probably keeping an emergency supply in case they got infected. The substance was highly controlled, only available to civilians through Homeland Security or the CDC.

Beau Ragnersen had finally provided the answer. The HBAT had come from his personal cache.

Under Saddam Hussein, the Iraqi military had produced 19,000 liters of botulinum toxin. 10,000 liters of the toxin had gone into aerial bombs, artillery shells and warheads. They had tested the neurotoxin's effectiveness on Iranian prisoners of war. HBAT had been standard issue in US military push packs ever since. Beau Ragnersen had smuggled one home from Afghanistan as a souvenir. In addition to the anti-toxin, he had treatments for everything from chlorine poisoning to anthrax. Though Beau denied having any involvement with the IPA, the fact that he had handed over the anti-toxin was enough circumstantial evidence to tie him to multiple counts of murder in the first degree and conspiracy to commit two acts of domestic terrorism.

Amanda believed it was only a matter of time before he started telling the truth.

Will believed that Beau's nihilism would kick in and he'd ride out the death penalty.

Sara rolled onto her back. She stared up at the ceiling. The faces of the sick children from the bunkhouse swarmed into her vision. Benjamin, Adriel, Martha, Jenny, Sally. The infected eyes, the running noses, the hacking coughs. They would've likely all survived the measles outbreak, albeit with lasting scars.

Sara wondered when Gwen had decided that it wasn't worth trying to save them. As with Tommy, the woman wouldn't want to waste *supplies* on lost causes. The suitcase in her car was filled with medications she'd taken from the bunkhouse. There were more white dresses in the trunk, along with a list of hotels between North Georgia and Arizona, where Gwen had apparently been planning to meet Dash once the Message had been delivered. New Camp. New brothers and sisters. New children.

If Gwen had let herself think about it, she would've known that Dash was finished with her. The constant child-bearing, the lack of medical care and nutritional support, the relentless demands of either breastfeeding or carrying a new baby for so many years, had depleted her body of the ability to give Dash more children.

Sister, let's go with plan B.

Sara would not revel in Gwen's death, but neither could she mourn it. Finally, after a lifetime of abuse at the hands of Martin Novak and then Dash, after turning that abuse around on her own children, on the entire Camp, Gwen had run out of ways to supply the men in her life.

Esther. Charity. Edna. Grace. Hannah. Joy. Adriel.

All of the children at the Camp had been autopsied. All of them had shown signs of sexual and physical abuse.

Sara covered her eyes with her hands. She was plagued by her own *if*s. If she had realized sooner that the children were being abused. If she had connected the droopy eyelids, the paralysis, the slurred speech. If she had confronted Gwen. If she had stopped Dash. If she had managed to break into the greenhouse and destroy the botulism before anyone else could be infected.

If-if-if.

Sara had known about botulism since childhood, but only in an abstruse way. Cathy canned vegetables every summer. Tessa and Sara had been more interested in arguing over who got to read the thermometer than asking why the temperature mattered.

In medical school, Sara had been made aware that hypotonia,

colloquially called Floppy Baby Syndrome, could be a sign of infant botulism, but the symptoms—lethargy, difficulty feeding, an altered cry, a descending flaccid paralysis—were difficult to translate onto adults.

The only other time Sara could recall learning about the neurotoxin was when she'd read a paper in the *Journal of American Medical Examiners*. A prison inmate had died with no obvious cause. Guards had found a bag of pruno under his bunk. The prison wine had been fermented by combining a potato, a handful of hard candy, and a sock with a piece of bread inside. The sealed bag and the low temperature had created botulism.

Will's dog barked in the kitchen. The sound echoed down the two feet of hallway to the bedroom. Sara could hear Betty tapping her head against the flap in the dog door. This was normal morning behavior. The Chihuahua used the door to come into the house, but she refused to use it to go out. She would head-butt the flap until Will or Sara got up and opened the door.

Betty barked again.

Sara closed her eyes. Tiny pieces of white confetti floated across her eyelids.

She got out of bed. She opened the door for Betty. The kitchen TV was on, but muted.

Gwen and Martin Novak were being profiled again. Sara was glad that the sound was off so that she didn't have to hear Novak speaking by phone from his government safe house. The bank robber was taking full advantage of his First Amendment rights, granted to him by the legal system he claimed was irreparably corrupt.

On the television, the trip to Mexico was being documented with maps and photographs. MSNBC had located Inspector Jefe Norge Garcia, who was more than happy to discuss the racist American pedophiles he had kicked out of his country.

The image changed before Sara could look away.

Her hand went to her throat.

Dash.

The banner below had his real name—

Douglas Alejandro Shinn.

Sara turned off the television. She already knew that story.

All of Faith's guesses had been wrong. Dash's nickname was derived from his initials. The Douglas had come from his father. The Alejandro was courtesy of his mother. Shinn was from the medieval English for *skinner*.

Dash's formal way of speaking and his amateur understanding of United States history finally had an explanation. His father had been in his early sixties, working for an American oil company in Argentina's Neuquén Basin, when he'd met Dash's thirty-year-old mother. They were married in 1972. Dash had been born a year later. The family had lived in Latin America for twelve years before moving to Texas, where Dash had lived an unremarkable, upper-middle-class life.

All of which made his hatred of immigrants and minorities even more nonsensical. He embodied almost everything he claimed was wrong with America.

It's not you, brother. It's everybody else.

At the age of seventeen, Douglas Alejandro Shinn had been arrested in Uruguay for molesting a nine-year-old girl. At twenty-three, he had been accused by Colombian police of raping a twelve-year-old girl. There were more charges filed in other countries, but most of them had been dropped. Dash's money and his fluency in Spanish and English had worked to his benefit. He'd used his Argentine and US passport interchangeably, avoiding any possibility that his fingerprints or DNA would ever flag him for a crime committed in the United States.

Was Dash's pedophilia the source of his rage? Sara had nothing but disgust for anyone who raped a child, but she wanted to understand why Dash, the product of a wealthy American father and a successful immigrant, had become filled with so much hate.

Will's theory pointed to Martin Novak. Dash had been a teenager when his father had died. Novak would have filled those shoes, enticing Dash into the fold by offering up his own eleven-year-old daughter.

One of the most depressing parts of this whole tragedy was

that, in the end, Dash had gotten exactly what he craved: attention. The video of his speech outside the Capitol had over ten million views on YouTube. His manifesto had been found at the Camp and was already available online. Dash's screeds expounded on the highlights he had hammered Sara with during her captivity. Capitalism had ruined America. Access to birth control and abortion gave women too much power. White men were being marginalized. Minorities were taking over the country, changing our Judeo-Christian values. The only way to save the world was to destroy it.

Worse, if not wholly unexpected, all of the news outlets were bending over backward to show the *other side*, as if racism was something to be tolerated and understood rather than condemned and rejected. Martin Novak's scratchy voice could be heard over the phone line as he railed against mixing the races. Avowed Nazis in suits and ties were appearing alongside Holocaust scholars and hate crimes experts, as if they shared equal legitimacy. Apparently, their heated arguments were great for ratings and retweets. There were memes and Instagram stories and YouTube videos where everyone was shouting and no one was remembering that they were all Americans.

To Sara's thinking, the platforms were doing what they excelled at: commodifying hate.

Betty darted through the flap in the dog door. Her toenails scraped the hardwood as she made the sharp turn into the bedroom, then scooted back out to look for Sara's greyhounds in the living room. The walls were so thin that Sara could hear their collars jingle as Betty settled in between them.

Sara sat down at the table. She practiced some deep breathing, ridding her body of the earthquake that took hold every time she let herself think about Dash for too long.

She opened her laptop.

There were too many work emails to count. Sara scrolled down to one from Faith's Gmail account. She smiled as she watched a video of Emma giving a three-minute explanation on the difference between mozzarella and Swiss cheese.

Sara found her glasses so that she could read the body of the email message. Faith had pasted a few lines from Michelle Spivey's autopsy report:

Muscle tissue positive for botulinum toxin . . . concentrated levels of HBAT around needle tracks between toes of left and right feet as indicated.

Sara took off her glasses. She let the information settle. Michelle must have been micro-dosing the anti-toxin. That was why the metal seal on the vial of HBAT had been open. She had probably known from the beginning that Dash would poison her. Or maybe she had injected herself with botulism just to get it over with. The woman had a wife and child at home who were under constant threat from the IPA. In the beginning, Michelle must have thought that she could hold off. And then Dash had sent in Carter to work on her. The cigarette burns and open wounds on her body had told the story. Michelle had held out for twenty-nine days before she had finally given Dash what he wanted.

Another reason Sara could not watch the news. The reporters were obsessed with the question of Michelle's culpability. She had created the toxin. She had armed Dash with a biological weapon. Sara had felt ill watching pundits and commentators and the average American on the street claim that in Michelle's circumstances, they would've been stronger.

Stronger.

So many people thought they were invincible.

Until they were raped.

"Babe?" Will's keys clinked against the bowl by the front door. He was smiling when he walked into the kitchen. He kissed the top of her head. "Sorry, I had to go to the bank to get some cash for lunch. I didn't want to wake you."

She brushed her palm along his smooth face. "Betty woke me. Again."

He studiously avoided the topic, taking out peanut butter and jelly to make a sandwich because he couldn't last another hour and a half until lunch.

Sara watched the ropey muscles work along his shoulders. His shirt was stuck to his skin. The heat index had already reached one hundred, but God strike them all dead if the thermostat for the air conditioner went above the 78-degree mark.

She watched his fingers work the tie off the bread. She thought about holding his hand under the door at the cabin.

His left. Her right.

Their fingers intertwined. His thumb stroking her skin. Sara's eyes closed as she reveled in the thought of kissing him, holding him, being with him eventually, maybe, possibly for the rest of her life.

Another one of Cathy's edicts from Bella's kitchen came back to haunt her:

What the hell are you waiting for?

Sara asked, "Will?"

He grunted as he took a knife out of the drawer.

She asked, "Why do you pay for everything with cash?"

"Habit, I guess." He wiped the knife on a wet paper towel. The dishwasher was older than both of them. "I tried to get a credit card in college, but one of my foster parents stole my social security number and wrecked my credit. I could probably get one now, but the last time I checked, I don't even have a credit score."

Sara was both horrified and confused. "Why didn't you tell me about this before?"

He shrugged, a tacit acknowledgment that he didn't tell her a lot of things.

She asked, "How did you get a mortgage?"

"I didn't." He slathered peanut butter onto a slice of bread. "I bought the house for cash at a tax auction. I fixed it up when I had the money, but the land is worth way more than the house. Same thing with my car. It was burned out in a vacant lot. I paid some homeless guys to help me carry the frame down the street. It wasn't as heavy as you'd think."

"That's—" Sara couldn't articulate a proper response.

She had always thought of Will as frugal rather than cheap, but she had never put herself in his financial shoes before. Every hardship in Sara's life had sent her running to the safety of her family. Will had always been completely on his own, even when his noxious wife was around. He could never go home because the Home had told him to leave.

The chair that she was sitting in, the table, this room, this house—that was all that Will had.

And Sara.

"It's no big deal." He leaned down to make sure that the entire surface area of the bread was evenly covered before he moved to the next slice with the jelly. "I like my car."

She said, "There's a new jar of jelly in the fridge."

"This is plenty." Will used the knife to scrape out the .0001 ounces of jelly left in the very bottom of the jar. The clanging was like a Salvation Army bell.

She said, "Babe?"

Will grunted. He shook the jar over the bread. A drop fell out. He ate the sandwich in two bites. The bread and peanut butter went back into the cabinet. The jelly was returned to the fridge because there was still enough to cover one tenth of a piece of bread.

She asked, "Do you like working for the GBI?"

He nodded, wiping down the counter with the wet paper towel.

Sara waited for him to expound, or to at least ask her why she had asked the question, but then she remembered that he was Will.

She asked, "Why do you like your job?"

He hung the paper towel over the kitchen faucet to dry. He turned around. Sara could tell he wanted to say something, but that was hardly an indication that he would.

He finally shrugged. "I like the hunt."

"The hunt?"

"Chasing down the bad guys. Outsmarting them. I know I do stupid things and take risks." He was watching her carefully, trying to read her reaction. "I'm sorry."

"Why are you sorry?"

Another shrug.

"Did you think I hadn't noticed how competitive you are? You won't even let the jelly win." The serious look on his face was the only thing that kept her from laughing. "Will, this isn't shocking news. I know you get enormous satisfaction from your job. The fact that you're so good at it is one of the many things that I love about you."

He rested his hand on the counter. He was confused. He never understood when she didn't yell at him about the things that he thought she should yell about.

She asked, "How much money do you have?"

His wallet was in his hand. "How much do you need?"

"No, I mean how much money do you have in total."

He closed his wallet.

Sara tapped awake her laptop. She opened a file. She pointed to the number at the bottom of a spreadsheet. "This is my net worth."

His face turned pale.

She asked, "Does it bother you?"

"Uh . . ." He looked like he wanted to disappear into the floor. "It's not shocking news."

"But, does it make you feel—" Sara hated that Dash was back in her brain again. "Less?"

"Less?" He reached down and typed some numbers on the keyboard. "That's about what I have. Minus the house. It's—less."

Sara could see that.

"Does it bother you?" Will rubbed his jaw the way he always did when he was anxious. "Because, being an agent, making an agent's salary, that's probably not going to change. Like, I don't want Amanda's job. I don't want to be stuck behind a desk."

"You would be miserable behind a desk." Sara told him, "Baby, I'm really lucky that the job I love to do pays well, but a paycheck doesn't define success. Being fulfilled by your work, finding meaning in what you do, is my definition of success."

"Okay. Good." He nodded, as if that settled it. "I should take a shower before—"

"Wait." Sara felt a weird flitter in her heart. She pushed the words out of her mouth before she could stop herself. "I want us to talk to a real estate appraiser to find out how much your house is worth."

He stared at her, speechless.

Sara felt speechless, too. This wasn't how she had planned to have this conversation, but apparently, they were having this conversation. "Whatever number comes back, I'm going to spend the same amount of money remodeling your house."

Still no reaction.

She said, "I can't sleep late when you're banging around the kitchen."

"What?" Now he was irritated. "I can keep it down. There's no need to—"

"I want a second floor," Sara told him. "I want a big soaking tub, one that can hold more than two inches of water. And I need my own closet. And I'm not going to share a bathroom with you, so you can take the guest bathroom."

"Guest bathroom?" He laughed. "How big is this mansion?"

"I'm going to hire a contractor to do the work."

He looked appalled. "Is this a joke?"

"You can do the trim work. That's it. I'm paying other people to do the rest."

Will huffed out an incredulous laugh. "You're fucking with me, right?"

"There's one last thing, and I need you to hear me on this." Sara waited for his attention. "If we're going to live together, I have to control the thermostat."

Will started to protest, but then he seemed to realize what she had said.

If we're going to live together.

His mouth was already hanging open. He closed it.

Betty walked into the kitchen. She laid down in front of the refrigerator. Will watched the dog roll onto her back as if it required his complete and total attention.

This wasn't his usual kind of silence. Something was wrong. Sara was wrong. Embarrassment rushed heat into her face. She had hit him with way too much. He hated being pushed. They had just been to hell and back. She had told him she was going to destroy his little house with all of her mansion money. They had both been happy with their current arrangement. Why was she always trying to fix things that weren't broken?

"Will." Sara tried to find the right apology. "We don't have to—"

"Okay," he finally agreed. "But we'll have to get married in a church. I want your mother to be happy."

Acknowledgments

First thanks to the usual suspects: Kate Elton and Victoria Sanders. I'd like to add the fabulous ladies at the VSA team, led by the indomitable Bernadette Baker-Baughman, as well as Hilary Zaitz Michael and Sylvie Rabineau from WME. At HarperCollins: Liate Stehlik, Emily Krump, Kaitlin Hairi, Kathryn Gordon, Virginia Stanley, Heidi Richter-Ginger, Kathryn Cheshire, Elizabeth Dawson, Miranda Mettes, Annemieke Tetteroo, Chantal Hattink, Alice Krogh Scott and last but not least, Adam Humphrey, my dear friend of thirteen years, who has generously lent his name to humiliation and patheticness. And also to my fiction.

David Harper yet again helped me make Sara fairly legitimate as a doctor. Thank you, David, for almost two decades of free medical school. I'm sorry/notsorry I keep killing my patients. For insight into their workplace, my appreciation goes to Stacey Abrams and David Ralston. To my friends at the GBI, I am eternally grateful for your input, and as a Georgian, grateful for your professionalism and diligence. Special Agent Dona Roberts (ret), I always appreciate your take on LEO and the world at large. Thank you to the folks at the CDC for answering my questions. Thank you fellow author Carolina De Robertis, aka *Dr. Palabras Sucias,* for help with my Spanish. Michelle Spivey and Theresa Lee really wanted to be in this book (and support Save the Libraries) so I hope you are happy with your roles, as I know the Decatur

Library is happy to use your funds to help children learn to read.

A note on the plot: for obvious reasons, I've taken many liberties with layouts and design and methods. If you'd like to peruse my spoiler-filled research, you can visit: karinslaughter.com/tlwreferences. If you want to sing along with Sara: Joan Armatrading, Beastie Boys, Dolly Parton, Bronski Beat, Patti Smith, Edie Brickell, Red Hot Chili Peppers.

Last thanks as always goes to DA, *my love*, and my Daddy, who let me take care of him for five minutes this year and it almost drove both of us crazy. Let's not ever do that again.

Insights,
Interviews
& More . . .

About the author

Meet Karin Slaughter

Alison Rosa

Karin Slaughter is one of the world's most popular and acclaimed storytellers. Published in 120 countries with more than 35 million copies sold across the globe, her twenty novels include the Grant County and Will Trent books, as well as the Edgar-nominated *Cop Town* and the instant *New York Times* bestselling novels *Pretty Girls, The Good Daughter, Pieces of Her,* and *The Last Widow.* Slaughter is the founder of the Save the Libraries project—a nonprofit organization established to support libraries and library programming. A native of Georgia, Karin Slaughter lives in Atlanta. Her standalone novel *Pieces of Her* is in development with Netflix and the Grant County and Will Trent series are in development for television.

karinslaughter.com

/AuthorKarinSlaughter

karinslaughterauthor

@SlaughterKarin

An Interview with Karin Slaughter

Q: Did you start reading crime novels from a young age, or was it something you were drawn to later on?

A: I did love reading crime novels from a very young age. I particularly loved the puzzle-solving aspect, so series like Encyclopedia Brown, Nancy Drew and The Hardy Boys all really appealed to me.

Q: Who would you consider to be the crime writers who influenced you most growing up?

A: Growing up in the South, I was told there was something wrong with me because I was interested in the darker side of life. And then I started reading Flannery O'Connor, who is celebrated around the world for writing about dark subjects, and I realized there were other people like me out there. Flannery O'Connor isn't usually considered a crime writer, but the worldbuilding in my own novels owes a lot to her. Her books contain all the elements of a great crime novel—poverty, unusual characters, small towns, people who are up in your business. I was also told that women didn't write good books—in fact, even now some male readers tell me they don't read books written by women. So reading authors like Flannery O'Connor, Margaret Mitchell, Patricia Highsmith, Daphne du Maurier, Agatha Christie, and Anya Seton made me realize that there were all these really talented women who had come before me. They helped me realize that it's okay for women to talk about these dark, horrible things that are, more often than not, happening to women.

Q: How important do you think the characters are in creating a compelling crime story?

A: Characters are extremely important in crime stories, and they should be given as much attention as the plot. I've read lots of crime novels where there are fascinating characters but the plot doesn't make sense, and then I've read lots of crime novels where the plot is amazing but the characters are like ▸

wind through your ears. Each of those types of books appeal to a certain type of reader but I try to write books that I want to read, and because both characters and plot are equally important to me, I work very hard on both.

Q: What do you look for in an ending?

A: When I'm reading a crime story, I don't care if there's a twist or a shock or a regular resolution, but it has to make sense. If it doesn't, it makes everything else up until that point irrelevant, and I feel like I've been cheated. The ending of a story is just as important as the beginning, and as a writer you have to learn how to thread snippets through the whole story so that when the ending comes, readers can look back and see how it all came together. It takes a lot of discipline to write an ending like *The Last Widow,* where there's a big question that goes unanswered—I don't know that I could have done that with my earlier books because you really have to trust the reader and trust your ability to write, and that only comes with time.

Q: Do you have any pet peeves when reading crime novels?

A: Aside from a disappointing ending, my biggest pet peeve is when an author relies too much on the familiar—a character who is isolated, drinks, plays the sax, wears a fedora. . . . And I hate when the women are just there to be saved or screwed. Often female characters make really stupid decisions, which are intended to make the man look good. The more challenging—and rewarding—way to do it is to have smart female characters, because that means you have to find a way to make sure the men are smart, too. Will and Sara each have their own strengths and weaknesses, and they see things differently from each other. The aim is to have two vibrant characters who complement each other and who both make sense as three-dimensional, whole human beings. Otherwise it's just lazy. ▸

An Interview with Karin Slaughter
(continued)

Q: As well as writing your books following Will and Sara, you also write standalone psychological thrillers. What are the key differences in how you approach writing the two?

A: It's a very different process. You might think writing a series book is easier because you know the characters, but it can be a bit of a tightrope. For regular readers, you have to find something new and interesting to say, and for new readers, you need to find a way to fill them in on what's going on without getting bogged down and boring regular readers. It's not easy! When it comes to standalones, the stakes are much higher because you don't know who's going to live and who's going to die. Each character is a mystery, an unknown. Sometimes you get the answer to who they are by the end of the story and sometimes it's left up in the air, but good stories need to at least ask the question.

Q: For readers who enjoyed* The Last Widow, *what other books would you recommend?

A: I have a large backlist, so go back and read all of mine! Lisa Gardner and Lee Child are authors I'd really recommend. And *The Ex* and *The Better Sister* by Alafair Burke are great too.

Q: Can you tell us a little about what you have planned next?

A: My next book is going to be another Will and Sara story. And let's just say that people who think things are going to be easy for them don't know my books!

An Interview with Will Trent

Will Trent, thank you for taking the time to talk with us today. Fans around the world know you, but let me give a brief introduction for the uninitiated. Will Trent lives in Atlanta, Georgia and is a longtime investigator for the Georgia Bureau of Investigation (GBI). He is the leading man in nine novels written by Karin Slaughter. At 6'4", Trent is tall and lanky, though fit and muscular, with dirty brown hair and an angular face. Is he a heartthrob? Yes, according to his thirty-five million adoring fans and his longtime love interest, Sara Linton. Will Trent was nice enough to sit down and let me interview him. Herewith is our conversation.

**NOTE: This interview was transcribed from an audio interview with Will Trent and some of these questions were sourced from fans.*

Q: Let's start with some easy questions. What is your favorite food?

A: Peanut butter and jelly sandwiches. Pizza. Convenience-store burritos. The same kind of stuff everyone eats.

Q: What do you like to do with your free time?

A: I like to work on anything that has an engine or a motor. I have a Porsche 911 that I've fully restored from the ground up. I also like to work on my house, which is older and needs a lot of attention. I like spending time with my girlfriend. And I take care of my dog, Betty.

Q: Betty?

A: Yes. She is a normal dog that any man would have.

Q: OK, let's get a little more serious. You grew up in the Atlanta Children's Home, which was basically an orphanage. Tell us about what that was like?

A: I guess it was like any home that has a lot of kids—noisy, not clean but not filthy, either. We're not talking a Dickensian existence. We had food and a bed and we went to school like normal kids. I don't remember much about the early years. I was placed in some foster homes and some were good and some ▸

were bad. Around the time I hit my teenage years, I was pretty much in the home from then on because that's just how it goes. Mrs. Flannigan ran the place. She wasn't the warm, fuzzy type, but she was fair to the kids. If you messed up, you knew the consequences. I like knowing where I stand with people. I guess my first memory is from when I was about five years old. Mrs. Flannigan gave me a comb to keep in my pocket. It felt like it was something special because at the time I didn't own anything besides a Matchbox car that I got to pick out of the Secret Santa box at Christmas. On visiting days I would stand at the mirror trying to make my cowlick go down so I'd look like the kind of kid you'd want to take home with you. I kept that comb on me until I was eighteen. I aged out of the system, so I had to leave the home. It's hard to keep track of things when you're living on the street.

Q: Tell us about how you got your start at the GBI.

A: I was recruited by the GBI straight out of college, which was a good thing because I had absolutely no plan for the rest of my life. I might've made a good watchmaker, but how do you get into that line of work? You have to know people. Watch people. It's funny that I ended up a cop because, considering my juvenile record and the statistics about kids in state care, it was more likely I would continue to be in state care well into my adulthood. As in prison. But an understanding judge cleaned up my record after I did some community service and had a few college classes under my belt. I found out after I was hired that my boss, Amanda, was doing some string-pulling behind the scenes, which is weird because the only strings she likes to pull are the ones that are tied to short hairs. But at the time I was pretty sure that it was destiny and I was meant to be one of the good guys. My job comes with its own set of challenges. And it isn't that glamourous. And the pay is shit. And also, I could get killed at any time. But I love it. My partner, Faith, keeps me sane—when she's not driving me crazy. And my girlfriend understands. At least, I think she understands. She was married to a cop before, but we don't talk much about that. Which is okay. ▸

Q: You have a phenomenal success rate, and have solved nearly 90 percent of the cases you've investigated. What is your secret to success?

A: I like a good puzzle, which helps in my line of work. Most of an investigation is inside a cop's head. You think a lot about what's happened to the victim or victims, and what kind of person would do the terrible or stupid thing that happened. I'd say that usually stupidity is a big part of a criminal's downfall. Cops like to think that we're brilliant superheroes, but a lot of times you get a lead because someone slipped up or the bad guy made a mistake and then—enjoy prison, buddy. I do most of my best thinking when I'm doing stuff unrelated to the case, like running, which I try to do every morning, or watching TV or reading a book. My partner likes to write things down and do those crazy string-boards, but I like to shuffle the puzzle pieces inside of my head. It's like a real puzzle—once you get the corners, the rest fills in pretty quickly. If you're lucky.

Q: You and Sara Linton have been together for a while now. Not to pry, but how is that going?

A: It's going OK.

Q: Well, your fans want to know, is Angie going to continue to be a problem?

A: So, I look at it this way: Let's say you're allergic to cats and you go to a party where the host has a cat. The cat just knows, and somehow, even if there are two hundred people in the room, by the end of the night, that cat is going to end up sticking its ass in your face. That's Angie. History tells us that the minute my life is going great, I'll turn around and see her ass.

Q: If Sara were to say something about you, what would it be?

A: This reminds me of a recent heated discussion. For a smart man, I can make some pretty stupid mistakes. ▸

Q. What's next for Will Trent?

A: I hope good things. I'm kind of on probation with Sara right now. I screwed up some things (I told you I could've been a criminal), but I feel like she's forgiven me. But then I guess my gut isn't the greatest where these things are concerned. I know I can fuck up a lot, but Sara is a very forgiving person, right? I mean, you can just know her for ten minutes and you'll figure that out. She's just a kind, generous person. Loves kids and animals. Close to her family. And really smart, and not just because she's a doctor. Sorry, what was the question?

More Books by Karin Slaughter

Read on

PIECES OF HER

What if the person you thought you knew best turns out to be someone you never knew at all . . . ?

Andrea knows everything about her mother, Laura. She knows she's spent her whole life in the small beachside town of Belle Isle; she knows she's never wanted anything more than to live a quiet life as a pillar of the community; she knows she's never kept a secret in her life. Because we all know our mothers, don't we?

But all that changes when a trip to the mall explodes into violence and Andrea suddenly sees a completely different side to Laura. Because it turns out that before Laura was Laura, she was someone completely different. For nearly thirty years she's been hiding from her previous identity, lying low in the hope that no one would ever find her. But now she's been exposed, and nothing will ever be the same again.

The police want answers and Laura's innocence is on the line, but she won't speak to anyone, including her own daughter. Andrea is on a desperate ▸

journey following the breadcrumb trail of her mother's past. And if she can't uncover the secrets hidden there, there may be no future for either one of them. . . .

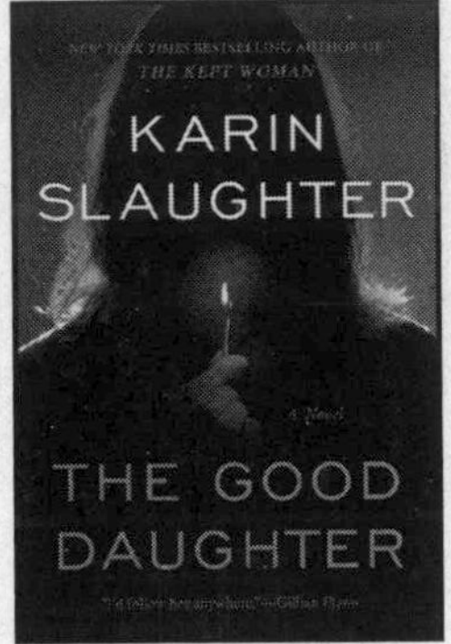

THE GOOD DAUGHTER

Two girls are forced into the woods at gunpoint. One runs for her life. One is left behind . . .

Twenty-eight years ago, Charlotte and Samantha Quinn's happy small-town family life was torn apart by a terrifying attack on their family home. It left their mother dead. It left their father—Pikeville's notorious defense attorney—devastated. And it left the family fractured beyond repair, consumed by secrets from that terrible night.

Twenty-eight years later, and Charlie has followed in her father's footsteps to become a lawyer herself—the ideal good daughter. But when violence comes to Pikeville again—and a shocking tragedy leaves the whole town traumatized—Charlie is plunged into a nightmare. Not only is she the first witness on the scene, but it's a case that unleashes the terrible memories she's spent so long trying to suppress. Because the shocking truth about the crime that destroyed her family nearly thirty years ago won't stay buried forever . . .

PRETTY GIRLS

Sisters. Strangers. Survivors.

More than twenty years ago, Claire and Lydia's teenage sister Julia vanished without a trace. The two women have not spoken since, and now their lives could not be more different. Claire is the glamorous trophy wife of an Atlanta millionaire. Lydia, a single mother, dates an ex-con and struggles to make ends meet. But neither has recovered from the horror and heartbreak of their shared loss—a devastating wound that's cruelly ripped open when Claire's husband is killed.

The disappearance of a teenage girl and the murder of a middle-aged man, almost a quarter-century apart: what could connect them? Forming a wary truce, the surviving sisters look to the past to find the truth, unearthing the secrets that destroyed their family all those years ago . . . and uncovering the possibility of redemption, and revenge, where they least expect it. ▸

More Books by Karin Slaughter *(continued)*

THE KEPT WOMAN

Husbands and wives. Mothers and daughters. The past and the future. Secrets bind them. And secrets can destroy them.

With the discovery of a murder at an abandoned construction site, Will Trent of the Georgia Bureau of Investigation is brought in on a case that becomes much more dangerous when the dead man is identified as an ex-cop. Studying the body, Sara Linton—the GBI's newest medical examiner and Will's lover—realizes that the extensive blood loss didn't belong to the corpse. Sure enough, bloody footprints leading away from the scene indicate there is another victim—a woman—who has vanished . . . and who will die soon if she isn't found.

Will is already compromised, because the site belongs to the city's most popular citizen: a wealthy, powerful, and politically connected athlete protected by the world's most expensive lawyers—a man who's already gotten away with rape, despite Will's exhaustive efforts to put him away.

But the worst is yet to come. Evidence soon links Will's troubled past to the case . . . and the consequences will tear through his life with the force of a tornado, wreaking havoc for Will and everyone around him, including his colleagues, family, friends—and even the suspects he pursues.